the Civilized

Sandi Tarreie

the Civilized

Decadence and Damnation in FRENCH INDOCHINA

By
Claude Farrère

Original illustrations by
Henri Le Riche

Foreword to the English edition by
Henri Copin & Kent Davis

Edited by
Kent Davis

Translated by
Pedro Rodríguez

DatASIA Press
MMXXV

About the cover

French illustrator Henri Le Riche (1868–1944), brought the deluxe 1926 limited edition of *Les Civilisés* to life with 53 original illustrations, including 17 full page plates. All of Le Riche's art appears fully restored in this first English-language edition.

In the cover scene, Le Riche captures our protagonists on one of their many Saigon soirées:

Elsewhere the city slept, but here every house glowed red from an open door, and peals of drunken laughter rang out generally… The big room was in turmoil on their return. Mévil, prey to baroque imaginings, was intent on coupling in illicit postures with poor Liseron, flabbergasted and sobbing…Fierce restored the peace, though he too could no longer walk straight…

Editor: **Kent Davis**
Translation: **Pedro Rodríguez**
Cover Design: **Becca Klein**
Text Design: **Pedro Rodríguez**
Photo Restoration: **Artsiom Yatsevich**

Note on the translation: Original French transliterations of the Vietnamese language and names have been updated to modern usage.

DatASIA Press — www.DatASIA.us

First English-Language Edition

ISBN 978-1-934431-75-7
Library of Congress Control Number: 2025936161
Printed simultaneously in the United States of America and Great Britain.

Claude Farrère

April 27, 1876 – June 21, 1957

A prominent French author and career naval officer, born Frédéric-Charles Bargone, who expertly blended his experiences at sea with literary creation. His extensive global travels, particularly in the Far East and the Ottoman Empire, provided authentic inspiration for his prolific output.

Writing as Claude Farrère, he first gained renown by winning the prestigious Prix Goncourt in 1905 for *Les Civilisés*, a novel exploring French colonial life in Saigon. Farrère's work is celebrated for its evocative descriptions of exotic places, naval adventures, and explorations of different cultures. His significant contributions to French literature, spanning dozens of novels, stories, and essays, earned him election to the Académie Française in 1935.

CARTE POPULAIRE

INDO-CHINE

CAMBODGE - COCHINCHINE - ANNAM - TONKIN

Dressée par *M. G. FAVRE,* chef de bataillon d'infanterie de la Marine

AUTEUR DU PANORAMA DE **SAÏGON**

Lauréat aux Congrès de Géographie de Nancy, Lyon et Bordeaux (Médailles d'Argent).

Exposition Nationale de Rochefort 1883 (Médaille de Vermeil), Section des Arts.

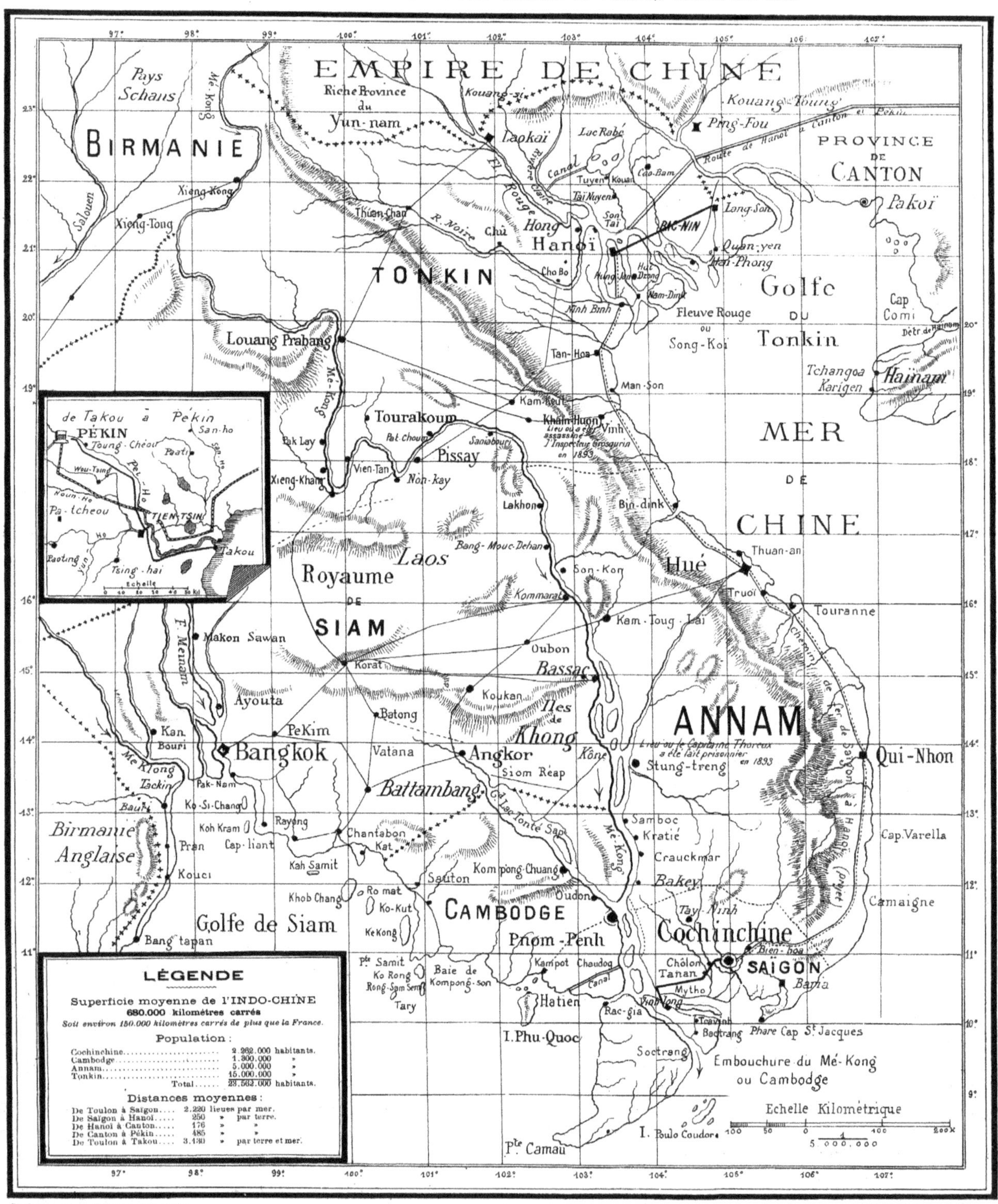

Bordeaux, 10 Octobre 1900.

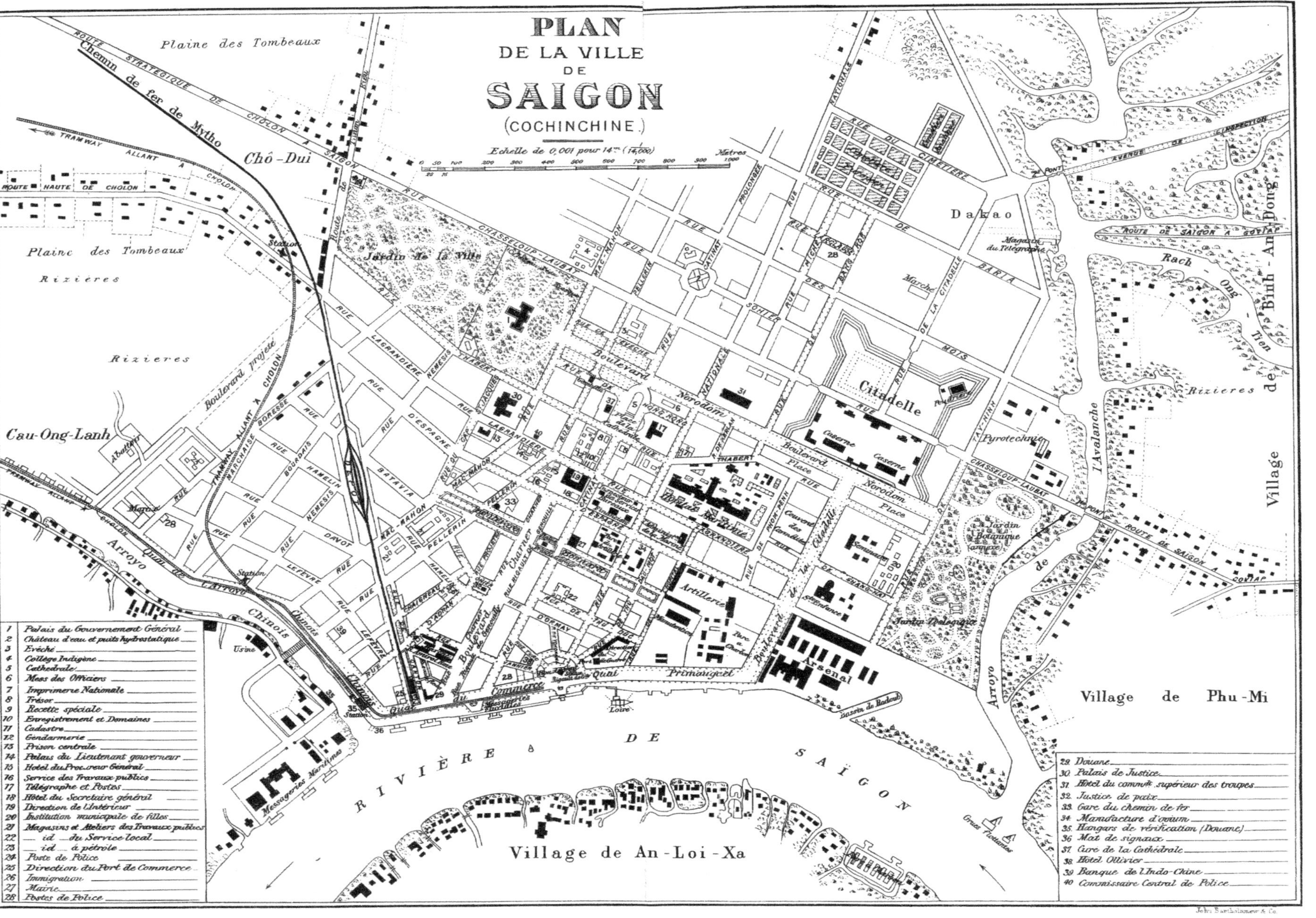
PLAN
DE LA VILLE
DE
SAIGON
(COCHINCHINE.)
Echelle de 0,001 pour 147m (14,000)

1 Palais du Gouvernement Général
2 Château d'eau et puits hydrostatique
3 Evêché
4 Collège Indigène
5 Cathédrale
6 Mess des Officiers
7 Imprimerie Nationale
8 Trésor
9 Recette spéciale
10 Enregistrement et Domaines
11 Cadastre
12 Gendarmerie
13 Prison centrale
14 Palais du Lieutenant gouverneur
15 Hôtel du Procureur Général
16 Service des Travaux publics
17 Télégraphe et Postes
18 Hôtel du Secrétaire général
19 Direction de l'Intérieur
20 Institution municipale de filles
21 Magasins et Ateliers des Travaux publics
22 id. du Service local
23 id. à pétrole
24 Poste de Police
25 Direction du Port de Commerce
26 Immigration
27 Mairie
28 Postes de Police

29 Douane
30 Palais de Justice
31 Hôtel du commdt supérieur des troupes
32 Justice de paix
33 Gare du chemin de fer
34 Manufacture d'opium
35 Hangars de vérification (Douane)
36 Mât de signaux
37 Gare de la Cathédrale
38 Hôtel Ollivier
39 Banque de l'Indo-Chine
40 Commissaire Central de Police

Plaine des Tombeaux
Chó-Dui
Cau-Ong-Lanh
Jardin de la Ville
Citadelle
Dakao
Arroyo
Village de Phu-Mi
Village de An-Loi-Xa
RIVIÈRE DE SAIGON
Rizières
Arsenal
Artillerie
John Bartholomew & Co.

Contents

Farrère only numbered his chapters. The editor has added chapter titles throughout, to produce a more useful table of contents. He has also divided certain chapters into two parts; hence the A and B.

Chapters

Appendices

The 'Civilized' Capital:
An Introduction to Farrère's Saigon

Henri Copin & Kent Davis

A Literary Scandal

**One of the most deplorable Goncourt prizes, in my opinion.
(Un des prix Goncourt les plus déplorables, selon moi.)**

Paul Léautaud, *Journal littéraire*, March 4, 1907.

In December 1905, the French literary world was abuzz with anticipation: the prestigious Prix Goncourt was about to be awarded for only the third time. Its founder, Edmond de Goncourt (1822–1896), was a prominent figure in nineteenth-century French literature. Indeed, Edmond, along with his brother, Jules, left a lasting impression on the literary and artistic landscape far beyond their time.

In his will, Edmond established the Goncourt Academy: a society of ten renowned writer/judges dedicated to supporting new literary talents by recognizing the author of "the best and most imaginative prose work of the year." The prize was a princely 5,000 gold francs; later reduced to a symbolic award, equivalent to only 10 euros. But, then as now, the prestige of winning guaranteed the author instant recognition and future wealth. Today, more than a hundred twenty years later, awarding the Prix Goncourt remains a pivotal event in the French literary world. The 1905 winner, however, proved quite controversial.

First, the Academy's members were split, five to five, over the decision; the president, whose vote counted for two, broke the tie.[1] And

---

1   See the appendix article, "Prix Goncourt Origins and the 1905 Farrère Judges."

so *Les Civilisés* — *The Civilized* — a novel by a relatively unknown French Navy officer, was selected. When the prize was announced, the public knew nothing about the book or its author. Claude Farrère, the pen name of Charles Bargone (1876–1957), was then a midshipman on the battleship Saint-Louis. As noted above, the award instantly changed the author's fame and his destiny.

Farrère set his novel in Saigon; the famed "Pearl of the Far East" in what was then French Indochina. But he did not spin a laudatory tale of France's mission civilisatrice ("civilizing mission"), the ideological term describing the nation's noble efforts to convert its foreign subjects into educated French citizens, thereby rationalizing and justifying colonialism.

Rather than a polite tale of rural idylls in the far-flung reaches of the empire, Farrère's novel focused on Saigon as a "mediocre capital" of debauchery, inhabited by lustful, opium-addicted, nihilist puppets dancing to the tune of their own desires. He thrust readers into the steamy heart of French Indochina, exposing the seedy underbelly of colonial life, and provoking one of those savory scandals that titillate the literary world.

Farrère's exposé apparently struck a nerve: *Les Civilisés* saw fifty-five printings in just the first six years, followed by over one hundred more to our present day! The next century saw translations into eight languages, including Russian (1909), Spanish (1912, 1916, 1926, 1938, 1962, 1964, 1969, 1994), Polish (1921), Czech (1921), German (1928), Portuguese (1938), Vietnamese (1999), and Chinese (2018). Despite its popularity, acclaim, and controversy, this title has never appeared in English…until now.

We are therefore delighted to introduce Claude Farrère's controversial novel, *The Civilized*, to English-language readers for the first time in this new edition. This foreword is a collaborative effort built upon Henri Copin's foundational scholarship, which Kent Davis has adapted and expanded for a broader audience; its goal is to provide essential context for appreciating the book's shocking reputation without revealing spoilers. Preparing the core components of this volume—the nuanced translation by Pedro Rodríguez, the extensive contextual footnotes, and the 1926 illustrations by Henri Le Riche,[2] expertly restored by Artsiom Yatsevich— was the work of editor Kent Davis and his collaborators over several years.

Now that we've sketched the background, let us meet the author of this exemplary work of French colonial literature.

---

2 A detailed profile of Henri Le Riche (1868–1944) is online at the Comité des travaux historiques et scientifiques (cths.fr).

The "Admiral of Letters"

Farrère's service in the French navy formed the foundation for his career and, well before he was thirty, the author had gained a wealth of global experience. After graduating from the Naval Academy in 1894, and training rigorously at French and Mediterranean ports, he departed on October 10, 1896, for his first overseas voyage aboard the wooden cruiser Iphigénie. The ship sailed to Portugal, the Canary Islands, Cape Verde, and Dakar before crossing the Atlantic to Martinique, Saint Thomas, and Jamaica, not to mention the American port of New Orleans, before a return to the Mediterranean by way of the Azores. But Farrère's globetrotting had only just begun.

In late 1897, he changed his initial plans for a Mediterranean posting to the Far East. In November of that year, his ports of call became more exotic: Port-Said, the Suez Canal, and Djibouti, crossing the Indian Ocean to Colombo, then on to Singapore and Hong Kong, followed by assignments in Ha Long Bay and the Gulf of Tonkin. He served aboard the Bayard, an early battleship with rotating gun turrets that was the flagship of Admiral Courbet, and on which author Pierre Loti, another luminary of the French Navy, had also served.[3]

Farrère would set his first major work of fiction in Ha Long Bay, a series of short stories collected in *Fumée d'opium* (later published in English as *Black Opium*); all infused with the essence of the divine drug. Like many French sailors who served in colonial Asia, Farrère became an opium devotee, and maintained the habit throughout his life, championing what he called *"la bonne drogue"* (the good drug). In one letter to his friend Pierre Louÿs, he confessed to having smoked one hundred and sixteen pipes in a single night.[4] This intimate knowledge of opium's pleasures and perils informed both his early stories and *The Civilized*, lending authenticity to his portrayal of colonial life's dark temptations.

The midshipman traveled through Haiphong, Hanoi, and, more extensively, Saigon, where he spent several weeks in 1899. He discovered that, thanks to French engineering, this city had emerged from the swamps in the

---

3 Admiral Courbet (1827–1885) and Pierre Loti (1850–1923) both served aboard the Bayard during their respective naval careers. Courbet, a renowned commander, achieved significant victories in the Sino-French War (1884–1885). Loti, pen name of Julien Viaud, was a celebrated author who influenced Farrère's career.

4 Quella-Villéger, Alain. *Le cas Farrère, du Goncourt à la disgrâce*, Presses de la Renaissance, 1989. Chapter IV "Istanbul forever."

1860s and 1870s and was still expanding as the century drew to a close. The town's rapid development and growing architectural sophistication inspired comparisons with the established grandeur of Paris: Saigon's Rue Catinat against the Rue Rivoli; the Quai du Commerce against the Quai d'Orsay; the Grand Opera House against the Folies-Marigny; and the Inspection Tower coach promenade against nothing less than the Champs-Elysées! Plus a government palace, neo-Romanesque cathedral, Grand Post Office, modern hospital, and racetrack: nothing was missing.

Residents traveled in tilburys, victorias, or more modestly in malabars[5] (449 were registered there in 1900), while the city council dreamed of a motorized tramway that would go as far as Go Vap and Hoc Mon. Meanwhile, one could always hail a rickshaw (there were 395 in 1900), with the first automobile appearing in 1903 (speed limit: 12 km/h, reduced to 10 in 1909). The wide city center streets were lined with "standardized" houses, but beautiful, lush vegetation gave them a singular allure. In the evenings, people met on the terraces, under the foliage of the boulevards.[6]

If Farrère succumbed to these charms, what he discovered above all in the Saigon of 1899 were the women, the pleasure houses, the opium dens, the joys of bachelorhood, and the company of a troupe of actors and actresses with whom he shared liberties and a hotel. The initiation marked him, and that same year he began the novel set in Saigon that later became *The Civilized*.

Through a brutal semantic reversal, Farrère's "civilized" protagonists were outcasts, sexual predators, and failures, challenging the very notion of European superiority that underpinned colonialism. In Farrère's view, Indochina was both very ancient and very new; a melting pot churned together of Aryan, Chinese, and Malay philosophies.[7] From it would emerge

---

5 All three carriages are "light" and suitable for personal use, but key differences exist. Tilburys are typically two-wheeled and open, and favored for their sporty appearance. Victorias, named for Queen Victoria, are four-wheeled with a collapsible hood, offering greater comfort, privacy, and weather protection. Malabars, less common, are also four-wheeled but characterized by their high perch and curved body, giving drivers a stylish and elevated view.

6 Meyer, Charles. *Les Français en Indochine, 1860–1910*, "La vie quotidienne" collection, Hachette, 1996.

7 Farrère viewed Indochina as a complex cultural crossroads where ancient philosophies converge. The "Aryan" reference points to both ancient Indian Hindu-Buddhist influences in Southeast Asia and contemporary European racial theories. Chinese philosophies, chiefly Confucianism and Taoism, profoundly shaped Vietnamese culture over centuries. Finally, the Malay reference acknowledges the wider Southeast Asian sphere, including animist and Islamic traditions. The French colonial presence actively transformed these established traditions, forcing East and West, old and new, into dynamic, new configurations.

a new civilization, born of all métissages,[8] blooming on the ruins of old, putrefied values.

By the time his book was published in 1905, this "Admiral of Letters" — as French novelist Roland Dorgelès later christened him — had known the Near and Far East quite intimately, and his radical visions of it provoked intense reactions. An appendix article by Kent Davis ("Civilized Reviews: The Good, the Bad, and the Ugly") presents a range of contemporary French reviews that greeted its publication. (Readers are cautioned to not consult these until they have finished enjoying the text, because they contain myriad spoilers.) Indeed, the book's reception ranged from high praise to savage condemnation, reflecting the deep divisions in French society over colonial identity, morality, and purpose in that era.

Predictably, the book aroused the fury of the colonial establishment: "a book of Indochinese defamation," thundered critic Ernest Rabut in 1906; while the *Courier saïgonnais* condemned it as "sumptuous rot…pornography… an atmosphere of amiable corruption…a silly, childish and pretentious novel." Yet, ironically, these very condemnations only propelled it to greater notoriety and success!

Dear reader, the controversy now passes to you. We invite you into the world of Farrère's award-winning novel — a landmark of French colonial literature, as controversial today as when it first scandalized readers over a century ago.

Take to the streets of old Saigon and meet the individuals Claude Farrère called "the civilized."

Henri Copin
Professor, Permanent University of Nantes

Kent Davis
Literary Archaeologist & Editor, DatAsia Press

April 27, 2025

---

8 The French term métissage holds complex meanings beyond simple "mixing" or "hybridity." While colonial discourse applied it to racial and cultural mixing, Farrère viewed it more philosophically, envisioning a fusion of civilizations and philosophies. The French term preserves this specific context and Farrère's radical vision, which challenged traditional colonial thinking about racial and cultural hierarchies.

Henri Copin

Born in Vietnam in 1945, Copin spent his childhood and adolescence in French
Indochina. After receiving his PhD in 1994 at the Sorbonne, Paris, he taught in
Senegal and France. In 1996, L'Harmattan published his thesis in 1996 under the title L'Indochine dans la littérature française des années vingt à 1954: exotisme et altérité. Presently he is a professor and lecturer at the Permanent University of Nantes, and an elected member of the Literary Academy of Brittany and the Pays de la Loire.

Photo: Laurence Copin

As an expert on the literature of French Indochina, Copin has contributed numerous forewords to DatAsia Press, including their translated works of George Groslier: *The Road of the Strong, Return to Clay,* and *Water and Light.*
henri.copin@orange.fr

Kent Davis

After working and traveling extensively in Southeast Asia since 1990, Davis and his
wife, Sophaphan, founded DatAsia Press in 2005. Since then, Davis has worked as a chief editor, translator, and independent scholar pursuing his passion as a literary archaeologist, discovering extraordinary books that have slipped into obscurity and become lost over time.

Photo: Vilai Baume

As a publisher, Davis restores the reputations and classic works of forgotten authors who made noteworthy literary contributions — both fiction and non-fiction — by reviving out-of-print books as expanded modern editions with added academic analysis, supplemental materials, illustrations, and original modern translations. *The Civilized* is a perfect example of Davis's craft.
kentdavis@gmail.com

To Mr. Pierre Louÿs

My dear Friend,

Last year I ventured to publish a first book, and that book — that fledgling — you insisted on presenting to the public yourself, shielding it with your name as under an aegis. You wrote an exquisite preface, and I know that a great many uncharitable souls pardoned the author out of admiration for the preface writer.

More than just lovely, your preface was deft, almost insidious. It piqued the reader's curiosity. A reader loves nothing more than to find the author himself beneath his written matter. The discovery has all the allure of sneaking into the literary theater's backstage. Your preface, my friend, led the reader in among us. You faithfully relate the singular happenstance that brought us together, and how I paid my first visit to Pierre Louÿs on the fifteenth of June, day of the Grand Prix. — My turn now to relate an anecdote. My friend, we are older acquaintances than you think. Our first meeting, the true one, occurred six years before the aforementioned fifteenth of June. But you cannot have retained any memory of it — for good reason.

I had just turned twenty years of age, and was about to embark on a very long journey: to Senegal, the Antilles, and New Orleans. I was spending my last week in France in Marseille, at a friend's house. A night of stubborn insomnia. On my table lay the three or four latest novels to reach print. I reached for one at random, the one that caught my eye with its pale-lemon cover and blue title. It was called *Aphrodite*. I opened to the middle, as one always opens a novel, and tried with its aid to conquer sleep.

But sleep was not to be had. I read in vain to the last page, then flipped back to the first and started again. And then started again. All for naught. Dawn found me wide awake. Six times that night I read a chapter that I reread even today — I'll pitch this at a whisper, lest I offend your modesty — the way I reread the impeccable classics of my treasured seventeenth century…

I've since looked back upon that night's reading, and it is categorical: no book has ever conquered me like *Aphrodite*. And I was probably more severe a reader then than I am now. I was fresh out of school. Sophocles, Racine, La Bruyère had taught me to disdain the moderns and their procedures: romanticism and naturalism I found equally irritating. I disdained the tumultuous, the agape, and the excessive as so many categories of impotent character. I despised all manner of brutality, violence, and emphasis. I hated line-deforming movement. Oh yes, I was a ferocious, sectarian reader, altogether intransigent in my religion…

In fact, my dear friend, let me tell you why your *Aphrodite* drew me in so fast, why it took me whole. It was quite simply of my religion, the religion of lovely lines harmonious and still, the religion of pure, naked Beauty. To put matters exactly, you gave me the very goddess I worship in my temple, and gave her to me alive, warm all over, instead of the cold statues that were all I knew back then. At the distance of centuries a literary work appears to us as fixed and dead. Beautiful as it might yet be, it pulses no more. Its flesh has turned to marble, and we can yield our love only to pulsing flesh. — *Aphrodite* was my first mistress — yes, the first materialization of my desire.

My dear friend, in reading *Aphrodite* I understood that it was possible in our age to write books at once modern and ancient — classical and alive. Your example blazed the path. If I have now in turn taken up a pen, you bear a bit of responsibility: you, whose disciple I profoundly feel myself to be. And so today, master, I ask you to accept the dedication of this book. It was written for you. Will you like it? I do not know. Welcome it nonetheless, as a token of my fervent admiration for your work, and of my friendship.

C.F.

the CiViLiZed

I

Into the poinciana-shaded courtyard, between a house and its gate, two Tonkinese errand boys led the rickshaw: an elegant specimen of its kind, lacquered and silvered. They harnessed themselves between the shafts, in single file, and froze in place, like yellow idols dressed in silk, to await their master. Rickshaw and errand boys made for a tidy ensemble, picturesque even in Saigon, where only nonentities still go about in man-drawn conveyances. But Dr. Raymond Mévil was an original, and in any case owned a victoria and some lovely trotters. And so people overlooked this fancy of his for rickshaws, and for the violation — the luxurious violation — of fashion.

It was four o'clock, time to rise from the afternoon nap. The doctor would receive no one any later — discreet procedure in a country where the streets are deserted until sundown. — Today Raymond Mévil was stepping out early, not for the traditional stroll before dinner but to pay a few semi-professional visits. These he was careful to space out thoroughly, as it was his tactic was to keep himself scarce.

A smooth-bunned *congaï*[1] opened the door and jeered at the errand boys before snapping to attention, now sweetness itself: the master was passing. Down the front steps he went, youthful but early to drag his feet. He ran a finger along the woman's breast, through the black silk of her *ke-hao*,[2] and climbed into the little vehicle, which set off full tilt, the Tonkinese legging it, so that the wind would cool the Westerner's face. At the windows, through the slits of shutters closed to the sun, womanly gazes admired the pretty white liveries with purple trim — admired the grace of the man on his drive, more seductive than the luxury with which he surrounded himself. Dr. Mévil was loved by women — first because he loved them, and loved only them, and then because his beauty was of the perturbing variety, so sensual and soft as to be indecent. He was white and blond, with dark-blue, overly long eyes and a small, red mouth. Though more than thirty years old he seemed an adolescent; though robust he seemed delicate. His long, pale mustache gave him the look of a decadent Gaul, whom the centuries had made a game of refining and smoothing over.

A coincidental resemblance. So civilized was Mévil, by his own boast, that blood of all origins commingled equally in his veins.

The rickshaw trotted along the streets between sheltering trees, the sunlight oblique but still hammering like a sledge. The master steered the errand boys with the end of his cane. "*Toï*," he said, with a tap to the shoulder, bringing them to a halt. They entered a garden in front of a villa. Along the gate were several waiting carriages, with Annamite grooms, barely taller than their boots, clinging to horse bits.

"Well, look at this," said Mévil. "It's *this* dear girl's turn today. I hadn't thought."

He hesitated, shrugged, drew from his pocket a card-wallet, and reviewed its contents: several notes from the Banque Indo-Chinoise. Raymond Mévil then tossed his cane to one of the boys, who had run on ahead of him, and entered.

The house, old and vast, was colonial through and through. Two antechambers led to a parlor, relegated to the darker wing, and extended

---

1   After the Vietnamese term *con gái*, young woman. In French colonial times the term became synonymous with *female companion* or *mistress*. See also the novel's own definition, in Chapter XIV.

2   Another term for the áo-dài, the traditional Annamite garment, worn by both men and women.

by a veranda shut in with thick awnings. The whole was big enough to
get lost in, and as tall as a church. The partitions fell short of the ceiling,
and the lukewarm air flowed beneath the joists. It was cool down below,
and the furniture, all of ebony inlaid with mother-of-pearl, gave off an
indigenous odor.

In the vestibule Raymond Mévil ran into someone on his way out — a
grave and glabrous person, with a lemon hue and measured gestures — the
master of the house, Ariette, attorney at court. The two men exchanged a
cordial handshake. The attorney's glum face even managed a welcoming
smile that, probably, not every visitor had the honor to receive.

"My wife is here, my dear friend," he said. "Most kind of you to come
see her. It's been quite a while since I've had the pleasure of your company
at home."

"Nothing but my own idleness has kept me away, my friend, I assure
you," averred Mévil. "Yours is always the friendliest house to me in Saigon."

The attorney seemed delighted, as if relieved of a concern.

"I'll leave you, then, my dear doctor. The Palace calls, as usual."

"Worthy suits?"

"Divorces, naturally. We live in a most scandalous time…"

Off he went, briefcase clapped under his arm, his step sharp and
automatic, his air austere and prim. Raymond Mévil smiled behind his
back, with a grimace.

In the parlor were eight or ten prattling women, elegant and unkempt
in Saigonese robes with the look of luxury peignoirs. Mévil took them in
at a glance from the threshold and strode easily across their circle to greet,
first, the hostess, a charming brunette with a chaste regard, who raised a
hand for him to kiss.

"Ah, the Faculty of Medicine," she said. "And what fair wind today?"

"The Faculty of Medicine," the doctor replied, "drops by merely to
pay its respects to the Bar."

He bowed to the visitors in turn, with a gallant and impertinent word
for each, and took a seat. All eyes fell on him. He was to the women's liking,
and his reputation as a Don Juan preceded him.

Not in the least unsettled, he engaged in the chat. He was not without
wit, and could play the part of a women's man. He was frivolous by nature
but had learned to seem more so than in fact he was, and used his frivolity
as a weapon in amorous pursuits. Women were grateful for his futile and
feminine nature. They could set aside self-esteem and confide in him.

"Now that you mention it," Mrs. Ariette broke in, "I was going to send for you, doctor."

"Feeling ill?"

"No, but I'm too hot. A nice December, is it not? Yet we can't go out to the country. It's the height of the season for criminals. You must help me somehow, by whatever means."

"Child's play."

"Your pills, correct? I don't have a prescription."

He rose and produced his card-wallet.

"I'll write you one."

"How, doctor?" someone said. "Do you hold sway over the thermometer?"

"Certainly. I give it written orders, like this, on the flipside of one of my cards…"

He was now writing at a pedestal table, in the corner. When finished he left the card there and returned.

"There you go. You'll have a fortnight's supply: a fortnight to believe yourself at the pole whenever you like."

"Oh, doctor," said a young woman, "give us the recipe, for the love of God!"

"The love of God is not enough," Raymond teased. "But come by the office, my little lady, and we shall figure something out regardless."

He had not retaken his seat, and now he departed, leaving a smile on all lips.

The next minute a curious woman walked to the table and read the prescription.

"Ah," she said. "Monsieur Mévil has forgotten his wallet."

"Monsieur Mévil is always forgetting something," said Madame Ariette, with a placid smile.

Raymond Mévil too was smiling as he climbed back into the rickshaw. "Cap'taine Malais," he said to the boys, and reclined on the leather cushions. The rickshaw trotted off.

Cap'taine Malais lived at the corner of Boulevard Norodom and Rue Mac-Mahon — across from the governor's mansion — the most sumptuous house in Saigon. — He was a financier — in Annamite jargon the word *cap'taine* means gentleman, rather than anything martial — a financier notable for his millions and for the use he made of them. Director of three banks, member of all boards, farmer of several taxes, he was a power for everyone to contend with. Also, he was not born to wealth but self-made, on the American model. And he was husband to a pretty, non-colonial wife.

Raymond Mévil found her to his taste, and was looking to make his approach.

Mrs. Malais, husband at her side, was reading on the veranda, an exquisite Louis XV boudoir, with balustrades of openwork white marble. The young woman's fine beauty was that of an endearingly blond and pensive marquise: resplendent in a setting made for her.

A European footman — rare luxury in Saigon — brought in Mévil's card.

"You've sent for the doctor?" the financier asked.

Mrs. Malais set down her book and signaled no.

"Well, then," said the husband, "he has come a-courting. Let him have his say, my dear, but do not accept his drugs…"

She blushed to excess. Transparent, too thin, her skin would turn purplish with the slightest emotion.

"Henri," she said, "what ever are you imagining!"

He laid a trusting kiss on her forehead.

"I'm imagining … that you are a darling girl … I leave you. — My taxes call. Stay with your gentleman, and snub him if he grows tiresome. After all, it's not the wretch's fault if he's come to the wrong address. A woman like you in Saigon, my sweet, is positively paradoxical."

He met Mévil on the stairs.

"Doctor, good evening," he said in his usual curt tone, far from the tender, caressing voice he had just employed with his wife. "Go on up. You're expected. Only no kidding around, all right? I don't want a single pill of your blasted cocaine in my house. All right?"

Mévil waved in protest.

"All right, understood. — Not a milligram. — My wife has not yet gone astray, and we'll leave her be, if you please. — Goodbye. Very happy to have seen you."

He set out in firm stride, an imperial tapping on the marble steps, and left without turning back.

II

"Cap'taine Torral," grunted Mévil at his errand boys as he came back down.

It had been a short visit. He had been faced with a defensive, almost monosyllabic woman.

Sullen for a moment — cares ran over his surface faster than ripples on the sea — he reclined in his rickshaw and lowered the visor of his pith helmet. But a victoria happened to pass, and he sprang up to salute the two women within. Disappointment already behind him, he murmured: "People are stepping out. I'll miss Torral if I don't hurry."

Torral was the only man in Saigon whose company he sought without hidden motive or calculation. Torral was unmarried and fit: two reasons not to attract a physician who loved women.

Still, despite their contrasting predilections and lives, the two men maintained a sort of friendship.

To general surprise. Georges Torral seemed ill suited to friendship.

He was an engineer, a mathematician steeped in logic and precision: a man through and through, brutal and rigid, and a professed egotist. Women despised the bulk of his head, his knotty chest, the malevolent irony of his eyes, like two hot coals. Men envied his lucid intelligence and the bruising superiority of his knowledge and talent. He in turn beheld both sexes indistinctly with contempt and hatred, and hid neither. Independent in his profession, because indispensable wherever he went, he lived in haughty separation from all others of his kind, far from the European district, in the southern quarter of Saigon, with the indigenous coolies and the prostitutes. — Dr. Mévil's errand boys, elegant people who did not mix with the populace, manifested a discreet disgust in trotting through those disreputable streets. These streets were nonetheless clean, and lined with trees, like all the streets of Saigon. There was nothing there to shock the eye.

The day's heat was on the decline, and Torral, eyelids heavy from too long a nap, was racing through sums at the blackboard. He worked in his opium den — for he smoked a bit, in moderation, as he partook of all things, boasting of his balance and temperance.

The back wall was a slate, with equations chalked there by the horde and deployed for battle. The engineer was on his feet, a short man reaching high, and scribbling at mad speed, integrating, differentiating, simplifying, running to the end of the board to jot his results between braces. When done he wiped the calculation away with great sweeps of a sponge, tossed aside his chalk, sat on a campstool four paces from the wall, and reflected on his solution while rolling a cigarette.

Mévil walked in, preceded by a twelve-year-old Annamite boy who walked with the swinging hips of a woman.

"Working?"

"I've finished," said Torral.

They would never exchange hellos or shake hands; such displays formed no part of their friendship.

"What's new?" asked the engineer, pivoting on his stool.

The campstool was the only seat in the den, but the floor was strewn with Cambodian mats and rice-straw cushions. Mévil had stretched out near the opium lamp.

"Fierce arrives tonight," he said. "He's telegraphed from Cap Saint-Jacques."[3]

---

3 Significant south Vietnamese port city, situated on a cape at the river delta outside Saigon. indeed, it is the last spit of land on the delta of the city's river, looking out to the China Sea. So

"Very good," replied the engineer. "We'll receive him. Have you arranged anything?"

"Yes," said Mévil. "We'll be dining at the club. I came by to invite you along. Just the three of us, of course."

"Perfect… Smoke a pipe?"

"*There is no way*," declared the doctor, parodying the native jargon. "It hasn't been agreeing with me for some time."

"That so?" scoffed Torral. "Your lovely friends find reason for complaint afterwards?"

Opium is known to produce a regrettable cooling of the amorous ardor.

"They complain," the handsome doctor muttered philosophically. "Sad part is, they're not wrong. I am, alas, thirty years old, my friend."

"As am I," said Torral.

The doctor looked him over, then shrugged.

"It shows less in the skin than in the marrow," he concluded. "To each his decrepitude. It's too bad, anyway. Life's value is in the living."

"Besides," observed the engineer, "our mothers didn't consult us before giving birth…. Why is Fierce coming? It's not that time of year."

"His cruiser's arriving from Japan. No one knows why. In any case, there's no penetrating the philosophy of maritime maneuvers. More than probable Fierce knows no more than we do, and his old fool of an admiral a bit less."

"It's very civilized," said Torral, "not to know where you're going and not to care. As long as I didn't have to fight — which would be too grotesque — I wouldn't mind being a naval officer… silly as *officer* sounds."

"Fierce is a sailor like he'd be anything else."

"No," said the engineer. "He's a sailor out of atavism. There've been lots of saber and spyglass bearers among his forebears, and it's rubbed off on him. It's to his credit not to be a barbarian, to engage in thought every now and then, and not to have donned a scapular."[4]

"What you're saying there, that would please his late mother," said Mévil. "The family chronicle affirms that she never figured out who sired her son."

---

named by the French government of Indochina, which laid out the old town on the shores of what was then called the Baie des Cococtiers (Bay of Coconut Palms) and for a while considered moving Saigon's port there. Vũng Tàu in Vietnamese. In the age of exploration the Portuguese called it Oporto Cinco Chagas.

4   A sleeveless monastic garment. Here not to don a scapular means not to become a priest.

"She had several friends at once?"

"She slept with all of mankind."

"A woman in your line."

"It amused her — and it amuses me."

They separated. Torral turned back to his slate wall and contemplated his algebraic equation like a painter stepping back to consider a wet canvas.

The sun was falling, swift and vertical in trajectory, toward the horizon; there is no dusk in Saigon. Reckoning himself short of time for a drive, Mévil guided his rickshaw to the river, so as to meet on the wharves the victorias returning from the "Inspection." Runners trotted along the banks of the Chinese arroyo, clogged with sampans and junks, before gaining the banks of the Donnai and slowing to a walk. Moored ships were unloading their merchandise, and coolies were throwing tarpaulins over piled crates and casks. There was an odor of maritime ports, dust, grains, and tar; yet the city's fragrance, of flowers and damp earth, laid such tight siege to this counterfeit odor that Saigon, even in this bustling quarter, retained the indelible mark of a voluptuous city. A low sun set the river ablaze. The evening was languid and beautiful.

Looking at the uncovered coaches, full of pretty, smiling women, Mévil did not see the big naval ship enter the port behind him — a hull long and straight as a sword — and four towering smokestacks belching ink. With hardly a ripple it glided on the water, blotting out the rays of the setting sun as if drawing a black curtain over the purple horizon. The scintillation of blossoming trees, stamping horses, and radiant ensembles along the wharf was instantly snuffed.

III

Dinner was coming to an end at the club.

Their table was set at the far end of the veranda, between two columns. The awnings had been raised, to let the night waft in. Bunches of pretty crystal-work made rainbows beneath the electric corollas, and there was a flower-path of orchids and hibiscus. Punkahs stirred the air above the diners; it was almost cool. Though the open doors gave onto a dining room full of noisy people, this bit of terrace produced a charming impression of semi-solitude, almost a sense of contemplation.

Dinner was coming to an end. Annamite boys, soundless in gesture, brought over rattan baskets of Asian fruits unknown to Europe: bananas speckled like panthers, mangoes ruddy like Venetian women, litchis of diaphanous silver, whipped and honeyed mangosteens, blood-red persimmons, or *kakis*, whose name drew giggles from the Japanese women.

They had dined in near silence, none of the three being of the talkative sort. Now, however, the wine was loosening tongues, and Fierce told of his voyage. His companions listened and watched, with the curiosity one has for people who have come from far and been away a long time.

He spoke in brief phrases and paused often to reflect. Reverie seemed his ordinary pastime. He was a stripling — twenty-five or twenty-six years of age — but seemed more serious and bitter than many an old man. He nonetheless had beautiful black eyes, passably regular features, a fine head of hair, a matte complexion, healthy teeth, a high and tight waist, long hands, a domed forehead, narrow joints: all that a man requires to harbor no hatred for life. And yet he harbored some. He was a singular companion, rife with contradictions. — In the same instant he could appear solemn, frivolous, mocking, sullen, obstinate, sad, indolent, willful, and fickle — yet sincere in every word out of his mouth, and never to have stooped to lie. His two friends forgave him his motley humor, more often black than grey, because, stray though he might, Fierce had a fairly steady head on his shoulders. Reason enjoyed a comfortable dwelling in his brain, clear and swept of all atavistic dust; where neither prejudice nor convention raised any walls, and the harshest logic always found a hospitable path stretching implacably to an infinite remove.

"And that," he concluded, "is how we have once again traded winter there for summer here. A difference of thirty degrees centigrade. I know women who wouldn't have survived the adventure."

"What women?" asked Mévil.

"Those who had fallen in love and now found themselves left behind, to weep for our absent caress. — Sad."

"Did you have a mousmé in Nagasaki?"

"I had all the mousmés in Maruyama. Maruyama, should you be unaware, is Nagasaki's Yoshiwara.[5] As a quarter it's proper and decent, like all things Japanese, where lots of nicely decked-out young girls smile at passers-by from behind bamboo gates. You can look and touch: it costs nothing to look and little to touch. The whole is inexpensive, refreshing, and almost pleasant."

"Japan has hardly changed."

"It has, actually, and quite a bit. Its morals, customs, and very nature

---

5 The red-light district, established in 1617, of Edo (now Tokyo), capital of the Tokugawa shogunate, which licensed this and two others: Shimabara, in Kyoto, and Shinmachi, in Osaka.

have conformed to Western ways, but the race has suffered almost no admixture, and the Japanese brain remains intact. The cerebral mechanism works the same way, and the new ideas it generates share the form of the ideas of times past. — The Japanese have remarked that their prostitution differs from European prostitution; but they have been unable to compel a resemblance, because their women preserve, and will long continue to preserve, the sort of modesty that is proper to their race, and sensibly refuse to conceal behind closed shutters what to them has always seemed licit and honorable. And they're right, by the way."

"Certainly," agreed Torral.

"And so — without enthusiasm, of course! — I arranged my life to match the resources of the land. Still, when we up and had to leave, all of a sudden — the way we always leave — it upset me, and almost made me sad."

"You're too high-strung," said Mévil.

"Too young," said Torral.

"Yes," Fierce admitted. "It's a disease. I don't like goodbyes; they're like little scratches on a patch of my skin. — Bah! Here we are in Saigon, so let us live in Saigon."

"No Yoshiwara here," said Mévil. "You need a mistress, the only admissible distraction for the afternoon nap. If you had the time, the world here would offer a wide enough selection, but for a tourist like you, no sooner arrived than shipping off again, the world here is like an overcrowded brothel; you're likely to end up waiting around and finding nothing to your taste. — So you're left with the professionals. The whites are both high in price and long in the tooth. I wouldn't advise them. On the other hand, we have a nice supply of Annamites, half-breeds, Japanese, and even Chinese — all of them young and fresh, if not pretty."

"I'll take an Annamite," said Fierce. "I've observed that one mustn't overdo it with exports. — I'll take an Annamite, or several. — In any case, we'll talk it over again. I'll ask you both for an opinion."

"Not mine," said Torral. The issue of women falls outside my purview…"

"Really now? Don't you still live down in that nice little neighborhood, on Rue…"

"Rue Némésis. I'm unafraid to utter the name, even in our present chic surroundings. Rue Némésis, formerly called Rue du Numéro Trente, which was symbolic. — Yes, and yet I've renounced Satan! I've been touched by grace!"

Fierce, astonished, just looked at him. Mévil chuckled, with a sly look in his eye, the way he chuckled with women when uttering improprieties. Then Torral came clean, explaining:

"I have removed the coefficient of love from my equation, because it was forever perturbing the harmony of my sums; the terms it multiplied were increased out of proportion and all of life deformed. Consider, too, the difficulty, even for the most civilized man in the world, to omit love and retain the female! The simplest thing was to eliminate the one along with the other. And that is what I have done."

"Are you taking drugs?"

"No. I am not damming the flow. I am diverting it."

"A derivative?"[6]

"Kind sir," said Mévil in a very soft voice, "it is vulgar to require the dotting of an unambiguous *i*. You cannot be unaware that we are in Sodom."

Without batting an eye, Fierce chose a cigar, lit it, and let the smoke rise in the most indifferent spiral. Saigon's repugnant vice did not offend him.

"That's one way," he said, "but I couldn't eat of that bread at every meal. As an extra, by happenstance, yes…"

"It's common nourishment here."

"Not for me," murmured Mévil. "I've tried it. Torral's mathematical equation is correct: women clutter one's life — clutter *my* life; but I cannot … I cannot forgo women…"

Torral rose from the table.

"Neither of you," he said, "has yet reached the highest point of the curve. You're civilized, but not civilized enough. Less than I. Bah! It's fine enough you're the people you are."

They left.

---

6 *Dérivatif*: an old medical term for the drawing of a humor away from some part of the body. Some derivatives are known as revulsives (*révulsifs*). Despite the talk of equations that proceeds it, this is probably not a pun on the mathematical derivative (*dérivée*).

IV

It was Saigonese night, with twinkling stars and the heat of a summer's day in the West.

They walked without a word, Mévil's victoria following behind. The street an avenue, what with its vault of interlacing trees and its electric globes hanging from the foliage — not to mention its silence and solitude. A mediocre capital, Saigon confined its ruckus to a single, central street, the Rue Catinat — and to a few other, more discreet places, of which the wholesome feigned ignorance.

The bustle of Rue Catinat is of a proper, socialite sort — yet admirably free and impudent, because the sovereign law of land and climate trumped imported custom. In the raw light of electric street lamps, between the houses, with verandas masked by greenery and gardens, a motley crowd concerned only with its pleasure passes back and forth. In it are people of all countries. Europeans, especially Frenchmen, brush past the native with the kindly insolence of conquerors; and Frenchwomen in evening gowns slowly parade their shoulders beneath the lusts of men.

— Asians from all over Asia: Chinese from the north, big, glabrous, and dressed in blue silk; Chinese from the south, small, yellow, and vivacious; Malabars, rapacious and indolent. As well as Siamese, Cambodians, Moi, Laotians, Tonkinese. — And, finally, Annamites, men and women so alike that one would fail to tell them apart at first, and soon pretend to confuse them.

One walks along with an idle step, chatting and laughing, in a languor born of the day's overwhelming heat. One exchanges greetings and rubs elbows, and women proffer damp hands burning with fever. Bodices exude strong perfumes, which fans blend and propel into one's face. A common sensual pleasure expands every eye, and the same thought brings a blush and a smile to every woman's face: the thought that, beneath the thin cloth of white tuxedos, beneath the light silk of pale gowns, there lies nothing: not skirts or corsets, not jackets or shirts — that one is naked, everyone naked…

Torral, Mévil, and Fierce went down Rue Catinat and took seats on the terrace of a big café, with a commanding view of the crowd.

The boys hopped to orders, with exaggerated, derisive respect.

"Rainbows," said Fierce.

He was brought champagne flutes and seven bottles, each containing a different liquor. Into each glass he poured from all the bottles in succession. Drop by drop he poured, the densest drugs first, to prevent their mixing and instead to stack them in layers of alcohol, each with its own color — hence rainbows. — And when finished he drank his down in a gulp, like a drunkard. Mévil was delicate, using a straw and tasting each flavor in turn. Torral declared that an expert palate ought to appreciate the various notes of the spirituous chord all at once, as a musician savors all the instruments of a concerto. He drank his down like Fierce.

Mévil gestured broadly at the crowd.

"This," he said, "is Saigon." — "Behold, Fierce. Women yellow, blue, black, green — and even white. Think them the same as the multicolored women you meet elsewhere on this round earth? You are mistaken. These differ from the rest on the inside: they are not hypocrites. All are for sale — as in Europe — but for money, and not for the tricky, Tartuffian coin known as pleasure, vanity, prestige, or tenderness.[7] — It's an open-air market here, with rates spelled out. All those half-naked arms that gleam like pearl in the sleepless night are so many sensual necklaces ready close around your

---

7 Allusion to *Tartuffe ou l'Imposteur* (*Tartuffe, or The Imposter, or The Hypocrite*), a comedy by Molière first performed in 1664.

neck; you may choose. Me, I've chosen whenever it has so pleased me. — Just today I left the settled price on my mistress's mantel, and every month I forget a billfold at every house I've enjoyed. — A market for women, the best supplied and most impudent in the universe, the most delicious, and the only one worthy to draw such buyers as us, men without faith or law, without prejudice or morality, true believers in the sublime religion of the senses, whose temple is Saigon. — I blasphemed earlier: women do not clutter one's life; they furnish it, adorn the walls with hangings, and make it habitable for the wholesome. I owe them luxurious, upholstered lodgings, which my egoism tolerates. Save for a day's migraine or a night's nightmare, I've always slept more delicately in those lodgings than the late Montaigne on his skeptic's pillow."[8]

"Incomplete," said Torral.

He repeated Mévil's sweeping gesture at the people, who continued their languorous stroll like a slow waltz.

"Saigon," he proclaimed, "the world capital of civilization, by the grace of its propitious climate and the unconscious will of all the races gathered to commingle within it. You understand, Fierce: each has brought with him his law, his religion, and his modesty — and no two modesties are the same, nor any two laws or religions. — One day the people took note of this. So they burst out laughing at one another, and in this mirth all beliefs shattered to pieces. Later, with brake removed and yoke slipped, they began to live by the good rule: minimal effort for maximal pleasure. Human respect was no bother to them, for each in his mind deemed himself superior to the rest, because his skin was of another color, and lived as if he'd lived alone. No voyeurs: universal license instead, and a normal, logical development of all the instincts that social convention would have pent up, diverted, or eliminated. In short, an incredible advance of civilization, and a unique opportunity for all of the aforementioned people, and they alone on the earth, to achieve happiness. They have failed, for lack of intelligence, but we, living on their fringes, will manage it — are managing it. We need only do as we please, with no concern for anything or anyone — with no concern for the maleficent chimeras christened 'good' and 'evil.' This man here tastes only of women's love? Let him forge a paradise of warm thighs and moist mouths, without scruple for faithfulness or loyalty. — Have I chosen for my lot

---

8 Michel de Montaigne (1533–92), erudite humanist whose wide-ranging *Essays* (1580–95) set judgment (individual thought) ahead of learning.

perfect numbers and transcendental curves? Well, I do mathematics, and my intimate boy, with no prompting from me, will settle my nerves and restore the necessary calm. — As for you, I've no doubt that, like us, you have your legitimate passions or pet hobby, and I firmly believe that you'll achieve absolute happiness in abandoning yourself to it without reserve."

"It's beautiful," said Fierce, "to have a stalwart belief in something."

They drank more rainbows and went to the theater.

V

"ll Saigon?" Fierce asked, looking at the boxes, half of them empty.

"All Saigon," said Mévil. "The theater is too big for its public. It's rather well worked out, in fact, as the ratio of size to public keeps down the heat. — The hall's usually almost empty. But tonight we have a premiere audience: a singer's making her debut, and although she'll no doubt be bad, as all of them are, it's good manners to come watch, if not listen."

Paying no mind to the raised curtain, or to the actors, Mévil reclined in his seat and said, "Let me play the mahout,"[9] and for Fierce's benefit proceeded to point an impertinent finger at each box in turn.

"Right of proscenium, between the tricolor flags: H.E. the governor-general of Indochina — common citizen in mainland France but here proconsul of the Republic and viceroy. — Yes, the little old man with the weasel's snout. — His neighbor, the noble figure of senescence à la Tour de Nesles,[10] is unknown to me, I regret to say."

---

9   Keeper or driver of an elephant. Let me play the guide, Mévil means.

10   A sneer at bygone grandeur. The tower in question — usually called Nesle, not Nesles — stood near what is now the Institut de France and once formed part of the wall of Philip Augustus

"That's my admiral," said Fierce, "old-man d'Orvilliers."

"A newcomer; all is revealed. To continue. Left of proscenium, facing our politico-military powers, are our — more stable — economo-financial powers. That enormous brute, square all over, with the wolf's teeth and the fearsome hands, is Mr. Malais, farmer of rice, tea, and opium, and my particular enemy; forty million in the coin of the realm, all of it ill gotten. Next to him: his wife, blonder, pinker, and skinnier than is apparent from here, and, alas, too rich for my purse, or I'd already have left my billfold on the tea table in her veranda. Moving on. The central boxes, semi-official. To the left: that pile of sumptuously embroidered green brocade, with the tiny brown hand peeking out of the pagoda sleeve, is Mademoiselle Jeanne Nguyen-Hoc, only daughter to the new Phou[11] of Cholon, a strange and mysterious little animal who's either more European in appearance or more Asiatic in reality: one doesn't know which. To the right: Lieutenant-Governor Abel, our beloved sub-potentate, lording it in familial manner between his first daughter and his second wife, whom one might fairly take to be sisters: one pretty, the other ugly."

"A harsh prettiness to the pretty one," observed Fierce. "An alabaster sphinx, with eyes of black diamond…"

"Too girlish, and her stepmother of insufficient plasticity. Holds no interest. Look on if you seek beauties of rank: the mauve bodice and the pearl-grey hat, next to that lemon-yellow caricature of a lawyer… Madame Ariette, wife to a sly man of the law, and sly herself."

"Mévil is paid to know such things," said Torral from his seat, not bothering to turn around.

---

around Paris. It was the site of the adulteries of the three daughters-in-law of Philip IV of France, in the fourteenth century. The scandal inspired, among other works, a play by Alexandre Dumas and Théodore Frédéric Gaillardet called *La Tour de Nesle* (1832), about Marguerite de Bourgogne, Buridan and the d'Aunay brothers. Henry Llewellyn Williams rewrote the play as a novel, *The Tower of Nesle, or The Queen's Intrigue* (1904).

11 As Farrère himself writes in another novel, *Une jeune fille voyagea* (1925): "A Phou in Annam is not exactly the same thing as a *fou* [madman] in France…, or at least only comic philosophers would accept the equivalency. An Annamite Phou is a civil servant of fairly high rank whose duties are more or less comparable to those of our prefects, or of our mayors… I say "more or less" because I know no better, and it doesn't matter in any case. The only thing we need to specify for the clarity of this account is that in Indochina a great many Phous of curiously varied origin have led careers of no less variety, and thus among these magistrates whom we would like to believe uniformly respectable we can find former bandits become wholesome people, and formerly wholesome people whose wholesomeness has somewhat withered. After all… are we certain that things are so very different in France… and that we couldn't ferret out here and there a few mayors and prefects worthy of promotion to Phou in Indochina? But what's the use of blaspheming, right?"

"I am not paid," rectified the doctor. "I *have* paid … and am paying still. Bah! The she-devil is pretty, and it would amuse me to see her chaste visage on my pillow. As I was saying just now: all the women here have their price … Eh?"

He turned to face the stage.

The new singer, no doubt gone hoarse, had come to a sudden stop. Vexed and confused, she remained there, arms dangling, caught between the satisfied irony of her fellow treaders of the boards and the scornful curiosity of the audience. She was a lovely buxom girl with red hair and laughing eyes.

A whistle in the hall, then an outbreak of laughter. No, the new singer had not gone hoarse. It was a simpler problem than that. She had no voice, no voice at all. She possessed other attributes — attractive arms, round shoulders, a toned rump — and had no doubt come to Saigon in the hopes that these would be enough. In truth, Saigon usually asked no more. But tonight the hall seemed, as it were, to have caught the musical bug. It was just about demanding that she sing.

Coldly, the actress set her resolve and crossed the stage, dragging her skirts. She stopped stage-left, faced the audience, and once more essayed the rebel phrase. It was, alas, too high. Insolently, then, with no regard for the orchestra, she changed the note. Now it was too low. Whistles again. She stopped a second time, set her fists on her hips, and, phlegmatic and philosophical, uttered in a hush that snaked its way into every hostile ear the word *m——*, before turning her back.

There was a moment's stifled silence and then, suddenly, someone's furious applause, and the singer, more surprised than anyone else, turned back around, agape. She saw a handsome, elegant young man devouring her with his eyes and fraying his silk gloves. Charmed, she blew him a kiss mid-curtsey. In this moment of caprice the kiss hit Mévil like the lash of a whip. He tore the orchid from his boutonniere and tossed it to the girl's feet. They beheld each other, smiling, as if it were already agreed that they would lie together.

This two-character comedy proved as good as any other. Drawn in, the audience began to laugh and was soon applauding. The men, with quickened eyes, elbowed one another; the women, scornful and jealous, tossed their flowers to the heroine, lest their jealousy show. It was a sort of theatrical hit that the two lovers could relish together.

Mévil nevertheless asked:

"Who is she? What's her name?"

A spectator hastened to reply, eager to partake in the adventure.

"Her name, sir, is Hélène Liseron. Pray, do me the honor of taking my program."

"Liseron?" said Fierce. "Then I know her. Last year she was the mistress of my shipmate What's-his-name, in Constantinople, and when he was believed killed in the famous Bulgarian attack she shot herself three times in the chest with a revolver, just like that.[12] As luck would have it, not one bullet hit anything vital. They ended up convalescing side by side in the hospital, and so loved each other that everyone predicted marriage. The lay nurses wept with tenderness. Three weeks later the pair had a terrible falling out, for reasons unknown, and went their separate ways."

"Very good," said Torral.

Not listening, Mévil scribbled a card, which he read out in an undertone:

DOCTOR RAYMOND MÉVIL HOPES MOST FERVENTLY THAT THE EXQUISITE HÉLÈNE LISERON WILL PRESENTLY DEIGN ALLOW HIS CARRIAGE TO CONVEY HER TO HER RESIDENCE BY THE LONGEST OF ROUTES.

"And now," he said, "out we go. Come along: especially you, Fierce. A first Saigonese night, on me, with the kind of people who won't sleep it through. We'll kidnap that charming woman and head first for Cholon, a fitting place for the sort of party I have in mind. After Cholon, anywhere. And I'd like us to see the dawn tomorrow, in the manner of the virtuous."

They rose. Fierce took a last look at the boxes: at Ariette the lawyer, yellower than before; at his wife, still chaste and magnificently indifferent to her lover's public infidelity; at the Abels, decently attentive to the show… The young daughter, like a sphinx, was so still that the image returned to Fierce's mind of an alabaster statue inlaid with diamond eyes.

"My friend," he said to Mévil, ready to go, "you're quite mistaken to disdain that child. She's easily the prettiest woman in the hall."

---

12 It is hard to say which attack is being referred to. The 1890s were a time of tense, low-level conflict between Bulgaria and the Ottoman Empire. Macedonia, then an Ottoman territory, had a mixed population of Bulgarians, Greeks, Serbs, and Turks, and every Balkan nation advanced a claim to it.

Bulgaria supported the Internal Macedonian Revolutionary Organization (IMRO), which sought Macedonian autonomy, with a view toward reunion with Bulgaria. It supplied arms, trained men, and sometimes even sent volunteers to fight alongside the IMRO. The Ottomans, naturally, sought to suppress these uprisings. Their forces would clash with IMRO rebels (who often enjoyed Bulgarian backing) along the border. The Ottomans were often brutal, their civilian massacres inflaming Bulgarian public opinion and increasing support for the IMRO.

"The little Abel girl?" jeered Mévil. "You're always ready with a good one!"

He looked again, though, with disdain.

Had he never considered her? Was he taken aback by the uncommon beauty that now beset his eyes? Was he rather, as he later maintained, dazzled into a stupor by the electric arc of a lamp he had mindlessly stared at? He looked to be turned to stone. No part of his body moved. His hand, squeezed by Fierce, dangled insensible. Only a blow brought him back to his senses.

His two disconcerted friends looked him over. He lowered his gaze to them, bleary-eyed and disturbed.

"Foolish," he muttered, imperceptibly.

He passed a hand over his brow and walked to the door without another word.

Outside, however, he spoke naturally, as if nothing had happened.

"In fact, you're right. She's not such a little girl anymore. She's going to make a very pretty lady."

VI

No bigger than donkeys, and as skittish as squirrels, the Annamite horses pulled the victoria at madcap speed, kicking and leaping. The native *sais* drove the beasts hard, because the broad street ahead lay vacant in the electric light. Also, he held the white men in contempt, never turning to look at them.

They had waited a long time at the theater's door. Mévil, not yet come around from his mysterious spell, had paced the sidewalk in a fever. When she finally showed up, hesitant and mischievous, he had set right on Hélène Liseron, curiously eager, dragging her off like prey. The four of them had squeezed into the narrow carriage. There had been brief introductions, and thereafter no one had said a word.

Mévil, thirsty, had first conquered the woman's lips. Rather than play the flirt, she had caressed him right back. They remained in their embrace, teeth clicking with every jolt — even as Torral and Fierce, both cold, looked on.

Torral lit a cigarette, careful to burn no one, as they were piled in. Fierce saw that one of Hélène Liseron's hands was hanging limp, forsaken. He took it, caressed it, leaned in to press his mouth to the palm — then let it go, and stared in a trance at Torral's cigarette, a red beacon in the night.

The victoria left the streets and entered a zoo — unlike any other on the three continents. All four shuddered. An Asiatic odor, of flowers, pepper, wildcats, and rotten incense, flowed in like a tide — and engulfed them. There was no breeze, but the bamboo leaves rustled nonetheless, and the noise was shrill, like the kiss of the two, still-conjoined lovers. From behind the bushes and bars, as the team of horses passed, came the snorts of tigers, panthers, elephants, and other imprisoned beasts, only half asleep in their cages. There were husky exhalations and phosphorescent pupils. The horses whinnied and stepped up their trot.

Hélène separated her mouth from Raymond long enough to stammer a few words that no one understood. Torral and Fierce, feigning nonchalance, looked outside for a minute. Then Fierce leaned in for a light off Torral's cigarette, both men retaining a stony demeanor. — Hélène, arms visible round her lover's neck, was in slow, rhythmic motion, emitting great sighs and moans… A carriage approached and crossed their path in a flash. Others came up. The road turned left and fed into a park avenue, charmingly hemmed with lawns and groves. This was the Inspection — the Acacias[13] of Saigon, where it was customary to stroll by night or by day. — The gleam of many lanterns produced a vague, intermittent half-light. The victorias advanced at a walking pace, in two files. One could make out people's faces; for discretion's sake, however, no greetings were exchanged.

With a thrust of the lower back and wrists Hélène sat up. She breathed deep and fanned her face. Tending to decency, Fierce reached out a hand and arranged the folds of her dress. In so doing he brushed the young woman's wrist, and she gave his fingers a harsh squeeze, as though to relax her still-frayed nerves. Mévil, head back in the corner of the cushions, lay as still as a dead man.

"Stupid of us," Hélène said after a moment's pause. "All those people could see."

She was pointing with her chin at the carriages in the other lane.

"Now have a look at *them*," said Torral with a shrug.

In every carriage was a man and a woman, or two women, or now and then a man and a boy. — And every couple, without exception, was engaged in a tighter embrace than they would have permitted themselves before sundown, and took a thousand liberties that the night could veil only about three-quarters of the way.

"Lovely town," said Hélène Liseron. "Revolting."

---

13 Probable reference to the once elegant and tree-lined Allée des Acacias in Paris's Bois de Boulogne, since paved for motorized traffic and renamed Allée de Longchamp.

"Not at all," said Fierce, with scorn and indulgence. "It's simply natural, and sets a good example for the hypocrites who pretend to prudery. Besides, my dear, it's a foolish prejudice to shroud love and sex in mystery. Glimpsing you just now, frankly, I thought you weren't at all subject to it. I myself and many of my friends observe no great delicacy in the matter. Don't look over there, where things occur that evidently displease you, and instead lend an ear to a tale — indeed, a true story: A few years ago, by chance and because we had similar tastes, I befriended a certain Rodolphe Hafner, diplomat and perfect man. At the time this Hafner had a pretty mistress whom he valued highly and whose praises he liked to sing me. I heard so much good of her that I fell in love myself. Hafner took note, said nothing, and played the neatest trick of friendship I've ever been privy to. He invited me one night to dine with him and his mistress. That evening, once he'd plied us with enough drink, he went off to the opium den and began playing the piano. He had a passion for music, and I knew that once he got going no thunderclap would tear him from his stool. On he played, then, and what he played was languorous as the devil: so languorous that the mistress and I didn't listen to the end. — The adventure reached its conclusion on an the softest of Turkish divans, which was not, I believe, there by chance."

"I would hope not," said Torral, "but your Hafner was rotten with elegance and stuffed with idealism. Had the boy been of the purely civilized, with no frills, he'd have put things clearly: 'You want her? There she is.' — When I was working on the viaduct of Sassenage, in the Dauphiné, I had two colleagues whose company I miss to this day: they died in the landslide at Engiens.[14] We were young, level headed, and broke, and the three of us had a woman: just the one. We'd chipped in to cover her passage from Grenoble. She was nothing special — I mean as far as brains go — but we trained her. Every night one of us would take her to bed. — We'd take turns. — The four of us would spend our evenings together by the fireplace. — It's colder there than here. — We'd do mechanics and calculus. The girl would listen, forbidden her to open her trap. — At midnight, for her trouble, the evening's lover would crack open a sentimental novel and read aloud for a spell. It wouldn't take long. The

---

14 The Dauphiné is a former region of southeastern France, Sassenage was once the seat of one of the Dauphiné's four baronies, and Engiens, generally spelled Engins, was once a dependency of the Sassenage family's.

silly words would work on her like an infusion of Spanish Fly.[15] Two pages
in she'd be astride the man — that day's lover. — In spite of this — pray,
believe me — we'd continue to read through the chapter without a flinch.
Confound it! There's nothing shameful about making children, as far as I
know, and I don't see why one should take cover when going about it — or
pretending to go about it."

Liseron sat up to look at Torral.

"You are abominable," she said, and then turned tenderly towards
Raymond: "Isn't that so, my friend?"

"Yes," said Mévil in the low, flat voice — the voice of those who reply
without listening. — He remained in a heap on his seat, his face hidden in
shadow. Fierce blinked to look him over, heard the free and even sound of
his breathing, and stopping worrying.

"Cholon," cried Torral to the *sais*.

They quit the lane of the promenade. The horses trotted. The road
took a turn through a wood, between dense hedgerows. In an instant all was
silence, solitude, and darkness. They traveled a long stretch through sleepy
countryside and, when the wood petered out, entered a great plain.

They had stopped talking as soon as they were alone — muzzled, as
it were, by the black night of the groves. The plain, less somber, gleamed
faintly beneath the stars, for it was bare of trees and bushes alike; regardless,
though, one felt no inclination to speak on this plain: the Plain of Tombs.[16]
— In every direction, as far as the eye could see, the land was dimpled with
regular little mounds, all alike and close together, handfuls of dust above
with handfuls of dust asleep below, all of it impossibly old and anonymous,
exuding oblivion and void. — No stones or epitaphs. At long intervals
there would be a broken, crumbling brick, a pebble greyed with lichen.
And always, stretching off to infinity, the uniform tombs — countless and
monotonous as the waves of the sea. — Countless: the Asian dead possess
their funerary dwellings for eternity; they are never expelled, even after
centuries upon centuries; never do old bones make way for new: all rest in
peace, side by side, and it is a long journey across their domain.

The *sais* halted halfway through, a lantern having gone out. They had

---

15 A diuretic and urogenital stimulant or irritant prepared from the dried bodies of the Spanish
fly (family *Meloidae*, not *Cantharidae*) that was once used as an aphrodisiac, though its primary
component, cantharidin, is a potent poison.

16 See Expansive Notes, in the appendix, page 237.

ridden in complete silence for an hour: the mortuary plain weighed on them like a shroud over corpses. — Torral shook off his torpor and leaned for a look outside. At a hundred paces, silhouetted against the black sky, stood a formless grey structure, alone amid the tombs, and itself a tomb: the grave of the Bishop of Adran.[17] Torral named it aloud, just to say something, just to break the intolerable silence with some human sound. But he received no reply, and the *sais* whipped the horses. On they went for a long, long while. Fierce, lulled almost to sleep, passed the time with a fantasy: they were, he dreamed, wandering a labyrinth in Hades, never again to rejoin the land of the living…

They rejoined said land abruptly, like a train bursting from a tunnel. Cholon broke out from the shadows, surging up around them. With no transition they found themselves in the middle of a city: a Chinese one, incredible in its blare and bustle, with busy shops, bamboo lanterns big as pumpkins, shop windows of lacy gilded wood, blue houses smelling of opium and rot, food stalls open to every wind, lit by oil lamp, and selling comestibles with no name we can utter. The streets swarmed with men, women, and children, all laughing and shouting in joyous tumult. All the men wore long ponytails tied off with silk, all the women gleaming buns adorned with green beads — for they were Chinese and not Annamite. There are no Annamites in Cholon. This is why Saigon's subsidiary is not a brown, delicate, melancholy city but a yellow, exuberant, coarse one, like the southern cities of Kouang-Tong and Kouang-Si.[18]

The *sais* cracked his whip to cleave a path through the crowd, and the horses stepped in place. Torral began whistling a tune, and Fierce reached with his cane to repel a child who was diving under the wheels. All took it upon themselves to lighten the mood and turn garrulous, superstitiously relieved to have escaped the Tombs and the Silence. They chattered and laughed. Mévil snapped awake from his torpor and kissed his companion on

---

17   Pierre Pigneaux de Betraine (1741–99), Bishop of Adran, missionary to Indochina. Savior in 1777 of Nguyễn Ánh, whose family was killed in the Tây Sơn revolt. Nguyễn Ánh's uncle, king Hien Vuong, was among the slain. The bishop took Nguyễn Ánh's son to Paris, to solicit help from Louis XVI. Nguyễn Ánh in time defeated the Tây Sơn and went on to reign from 1804 to 1820 as Gia Long, founder of the Nguyễn dynasty. In 1787 the bishop negotiated a military alliance between the France of Louis XVI and Gia Long. The bishop's tomb, in the form of pagoda, was erected in 1799 at the behest of emperor Gia Long, who delivered a eulogy. France took possession of the tomb in 1861. According to the *Monde illustré*, "the tomb has always been respected by the Annamites, and even during the most recent persecutions anyone who had dared to destroy it would have been looked upon as a profaner."

18   Guangdong and Guangxi.

the mouth, with a coaxing that she mistook for tenderness. Once through
the crowd they arrived at the fashionable cabaret, took their supper, and
whipped themselves into a froth of gaiety.

Torral remarked that it was one o'clock in the morning, an hour when
it was ridiculous to be in Cholon and not be intoxicated — with alcohol,
opium, or something else. Fierce was prompt to select liquors, mix them,
and set about drinking, having observed that the place was ill suited to the
highs either of opium, which require the reflective atmosphere of a chaste,
philosophical den, or of ether, which thrive in alcoves, in complicit loving
mouths, and under bedsheets drawn over one's head. — He drank as if
numb, in shots, once he had lifted his glass to the lamplight to review the
colors of his drugs. He would set the glass down empty and, head titled to
the left, brow furrowed, survey the bottles as a painter surveys his palette.

Torral, disapproving of any and all excess, shrugged and ordered dry
champagne, excellent for a momentary and quickly calmed high. Mévil
said but two words to the boy-chef, who went off to prepare for Hélène an
iced beverage, soft and treacherous, that went down like water and gave
no warning — and for him a tall glass of brown, opaque filth that stank
of pepper. The doctor coughed twice as he emptied the glass, and in an
instant was tipsy in the most sparkling way, and as fresh and alert as he had
been prostrate in the carriage after taking his first pleasure from his mistress
— and now, with a deft hand, set out to tease the young woman, whose
modesty seemed to melt away as if by magic with every swallow of her
drink.

All were drunk, each in his way. Torral broke glasses, and Fierce caned
one of the boys, who had dared to look at him and laugh.

They clambered back aboard the victoria and returned to Saigon in full-
throated song, behind the silhouette of the *sais*, stony and wry on his seat. —
They returned by the high road, the one most redolent of magnolias.

VII

In Saigon they alighted, descending from the carriage without knowing why, and set out on foot in a random direction, continuing to sing.

"It is good not to know where one is," declared Torral, interrupting his marvelously obscene refrain. "It is in the character of civilized men to act the sage by day and the fool by night. A little of everything is needful."

He took up a new couplet, which, doubtless in repudiation of modern psychological literature, sinned by an excess of clarity.

The stroll had, in their present state of mind, a definite end, and that end lay hard by the quarter where Torral lived. But they lost their way; this ought not to have surprised them but did. Having gone quite a ways they found themselves in the middle of a now deserted Rue Catinat. Mévil was first to realize their error.

"Drat," he said. "This is not where we were going. Oh, to hell with it. I live right around the corner and am going home. What I need right now is a bed."

His arms secure around his mistress's waist, the two walked off joined at the mouth, not without stumbles.

"You're drunk," said Torral. "We are not splitting up. Everyone, follow me."

He took the lead, but went up the street instead of down it. A cat, spooked by their cries, sprang from the shadows of a door, brushing past Hélène, who let out a piercing shriek. Fierce, bringing up the rear, threw his cane at the fleeing beast, which crumpled to the ground, its back broken. Torral turned aside to finish it off, stomping with his heel, then picked it up by the tail, whirled it around, and reckoned the circumference aloud. They were now reaching the cathedral and came to halt before it, stupefied not to be where they thought they were.

"The house of so-called God?" shouted Torral, as if furious over a stupid joke. "This is too much!"

He twirled the cat's corpse and flung it at top speed against the church. Calmer now, he got his bearings and set out in the opposite direction — the others still following without complaint. They did not turn to see the two dark, disdainful spires sink into the night behind them.

This time they got where they were going. Elsewhere the city slept, but here every house glowed red from an open door, and peals of drunken laughter rang out generally. Triumphant, Torral speechified. He was *ichiban* — number one — among guides, and the world of sensual delights now lay open before them. All they had to say was "Open sesame"[19]… Fierce, ever more taciturn as the night air deepened his inebriation, replied with a single word, calling for Japanese women. They invaded a little white house that had the feel of a rustic villa, and sat clamorously down amid a circle of trinket-girls. These were draped in robes with big flowers on them and laughed in giggles with great decency and politesse.

Fierce, a connoisseur in the matter, chose the prettiest of the Japanese and followed her into a cell so clean that he left his shoes at the threshold. She thanked him for this courtesy, proper to a well-mannered man by the customs of Japan. They engaged in idle talk. She listened to him in earnest, attentive to understand his sluggish voice and taking pains to maintain a correct, reserved smile on her painted lips.

He spoke good Japanese, and made faces to express his admiration. She told him her name: Otake-San, Mademoiselle Bamboo. He understood Otaki-San, Mademoiselle Wellspring,[20] and at this her eyes watered with laughter. She told him also her age, thirteen years. She feared he would think her too young,

---

19   "*Sésame, ouvre-toi*" is a magical phrase in the French translation by Antoine Galland (1646–1715) of "Ali Baba and the Forty Thieves," in the *One Thousand and One Nights*.

20   The author writes "source," wellspring, but *otaki* appears to mean waterfall, cascade, rapids.

knowing that in Europe women would wait until they were old so as not to be "pure like Fousi-San[21] very pure." But he explained that he had developed a taste in Hong Kong for ten-year-old Chinese girls, and that in fact she seemed to him a very mature person. So she took a seat on his lap, and they made some gestures. That is, he did, and she, docile, like a good little girl, tried to imitate them — until a picture of abominable things began to form in her mind, and she raised indignant protest. Now it was his turn to laugh, and he swore that he had not mistaken her "for a Frenchwoman." She now consented to some natural, albeit warped, games and even made an effort to simulate not an unseemly and unlikely ardor but a tasteful indifference, free of irony.

The big room was in turmoil on their return. Mévil, prey to baroque imaginings, was intent on coupling in illicit postures with poor Liseron, flabbergasted and sobbing, and with several stupefied, scandalized Japanese. Fierce restored the peace, though he too could no longer walk straight, and was now seeing two Otake-Sans instead of one. At last they left. Torral, bored with the Japanese women, was waiting at the door, seated on the sidewalk's curb. He rose, and the others followed. He alone, thanks to the dry champagne, could still find his way.

At the far end of a black alley they reached a hut of worm-eaten planks and rotten straw, shadier and more tragic-looking than a melodrama's inn. The door, propped with two sticks, seemed to have been shut over the scene of a murder. One could easily believe as much on entering, as the floor, of bare dirt and mud, was strewn with lying bodies. But these were merely the bodies of drunks.

Opening to the left and right were doghouses, with slatted doors to shut them off. These were in fact bedrooms for lovemaking — because one made love in this sty. One would make love with drunken women who sprawled on the ground and whom one could not at first make out, by the smoky light of the single oil lamp, always on the verge of being snuffed, but whom one would soon verify were indeed women, some young and some old, the latter more hideous, though not by much, and more experienced. All were drinking rice wine, and playing with *boys*, lads of some age yet prepubescent — the establishment's repugnant draw.

At the moment the place had a second draw, though one absent from the menu. — Sitting on the floor, back to the wall, was a man — a Westerner, a Frenchman. He was laughing in little hiccups, like a clucking hen. He drank

---

21   Perhaps an alternate spelling of Fuji-san, as in Mt. Fuji.

nothing, smoked no opium, had neither woman nor boy. — No. He only watched, looking straight ahead, dull-eyed. This was the only place in the world where he felt content. — He watched and laughed, stupidly.

The Civilized recognized him on entering — knew him for one of their own. For his name was Claude Rochet, and he had been the colony's most dread pamphleteer — many a governor having quaked before his pen. Today he was old — forty years! — and wasted, empty, finished, imbecilic — yet remained nonetheless one of the three or four masters of Saigon and Hanoi, thanks to terror he could still command through the newspapers. He had boasted his whole life, and in supreme moments of lucidity boasted still, that he followed neither God nor master nor law.

Ah, but he had lived! By the maxim — without prejudice, convention, or superstition — by the dictates of his whim — his every whim — and even today, old and nearing the grave, or the hospice, he retained the courage and will of his olden days: he could still seek his pleasure where he found it, even in a hovel — right here! Torral, in passing, greeted the man. — Then he went into one of the kennels, having crooked a finger to summon two *boys*, who ran right over; and he did not come back out.

Hélène Liseron, drunk and weary, was falling asleep against her lover's shoulder. Mévil had stayed by the door. A rickshaw runner called to him from the street. He unthinkingly turned around and let himself be taken home with the singer, forgetting about Fierce.

Fierce was alone, standing amid the sewer. Four women, clinging to his clothes, were dragging him down to their mats.

He wasn't thinking much anymore, or clearly, yet an idea surfaced nonetheless in the shipwreck of his brain — a stupid idea, but tenacious as a migraine… This Rochet fellow, ten years back, must have been an intelligent, proud young man… Funny he had turned into this…!

Rochet clucked and drooled. Wriggling his shoulders, Fierce muttered: "Ugh!"

He looked at the females — monkeys, to be sure. "Ugh!" he repeated. — He selected two, the youngest and the oldest. — Then he collapsed onto the mat, gathering all his saliva to utter a distinct, imperious command:

"Opium."

VIII

even o'clock in the morning. In his officer's quarters, aboard his naval cruiser, the *Bayard*,[22] Fierce — Jacques-Raoul-Gaston de Civadière, count of Fierce — lies asleep on his bunk.

Nice quarters. The quarters of an aide-de-camp — vast, ten feet long, eight wide, six tall — and magnificently bright: two portholes, the size of pocket handkerchiefs, for opening in fine weather. — Four walls, of corrugated steel; an armoire and desk, of smooth steel;

---

22   After the Pierre Terrail, seigneur de Bayard or, commonly, Chevalier de Bayard, the "knight without fear and beyond reproach" (ca. 1476 – 1524). Bayard served two French kings, Charles VIII and Louis XII, distinguishing himself in many battles. He also famously defeated in a duel one Alonso de Sotomayor, a Spanish knight who had insulted Bayard's hospitality. In William Gilmore Simms's account, Bayard accorded to Alonso, his prisoner of war, "one of the handsomest apartments in his household, supplied his wardrobe, and, upon the pledge of honor of the captive not to quit the castle, gave him the entire freedom of the garrison, putting no guard upon his footsteps." Alonso agreed to purchase his own freedom for one thousand crowns and sent for the ransom. During the wait, however, Alonso contrived to escape, bribing a groom. He was recaptured and insisted that he had had no intention of defrauding his captor, for the ransom was on its way. Alonso was then shut up in a tower, and the ransom arrived in a fortnight. When at last back home Alonso spoke highly of Bayard's courage and virtue but complained of his treatment. Word of this reached Bayard, who, though ill, dispatched a challenge. In the ensuing duel Bayard killed Alonso, though the means are in dispute. For example, in Simms it was a dagger thrust "to the hilt, through the gorget, and into the neck"; in Edward Walford it was the thrust of a poignard into face, between the nose and the left eye; and in Jacques de Mailles it was a dagger thrust through the nostril.

a basin and commode, of rounded steel; a bed, of linear tubes of steel. — And that is all, quarters now full. — In France, at Cherbourg or Toulon, Fierce, being rich and delicate, would repudiate any such dwelling as this tin can. On land he would instead maintain, on some discreet and respectable street, the sort of tasteful, Paris-styled hovel that cannot be done without in squadron life, where one can lament without too much bitterness one's bachelor flat on Rue de Magdebourg. — Here, unable to escape, he had resigned himself to upholstering his cage. The upholstery is artistically done. The bars are now invisible. Sheet metal of all varieties has vanished beneath an alternation of pearl-grey seersucker and iron-grey velvet. Too much grey, but it is in grey that the sleeper thinks, there on his bunk, with its curtains of grey muslin.

He is calm in his sleep — has about him the purity of one who has not in the least gone to bed long after dawn, soused in the most ignominious manner. His eyelids are a shade dark, to be sure, but his brown curls spread chastely on his forehead, and his chest rises as peaceably as the flat chest of an innocent pensioner on a convent cot.

Jacques-Raoul-Gaston de Civadière, count of Fierce. — Azure, a chevron or, three boats of the same color set on seas argent, two and one. — Born in Paris, on 3 December 19–; only son to the late Count Fred-Raoul de Civadière de Fierce and the late Simone de Marroy, his wife. — There is at least the civil register to attest to this unlikely conjugal collaboration: the Fierces had too good an upbringing to open themselves to ridicule for the joint production of a child in their eighth year of marriage. As is proper, they had been lovers for four months — their four months in Tyrol and Hungary, after a cardinal in the family had bestowed a luxurious blessing on them at Sainte-Clothilde — and spouses beyond reproach thereafter, without a hint of untoward intimacy. — Jacques de Fierce was thus probably the fruit of whim compounded by distraction. No matter, though. Whatever her whims, Madame de Fierce knew better than to depart from custom; her son is in consequence a true gentleman. This is, besides, the least of his concerns.

Jacques de Fierce began like a weed sprouting in a prison yard — on the fourth floor of the family townhouse, in the moralizing company of a German maid, several lackeys, and many toys.

Such was life up to the age of six, year of his first notable memory — a winter's late afternoon — snow fallen on the sills: all of the details are etched sharp into the young brain: little Monsieur Jacques escapes his maid and scampers through the house. — It is five o'clock; Mother is probably taking her tea, and there must be excellent cakes to go with the tea. — Monsieur Jacques descends three flights and slips into his mother's room, none too sure of his way. One door — two doors — three doors, closed — a folding screen: Monsieur Jacques forges ahead, sneakier than a mouse. — And there is Mother, lying back in a wing chair, clasping a man in her arms; nothing to be seen but the man's back and Mother's arms, and the wing chair, squeaking like a box spring, scoots back a bit with every thrust. — Monsieur Jacques is astonished and troubled, withdraws on tiptoe, and goes to inquire diplomatically of the menials, who supply explanations, copious ones.

A first tutor at the age of seven, with many others to follow. This first is a priest, an honest and virtuous man, who instills in him an enduring disgust for virtue. By some mystery of atavism, Monsieur Jacques turns out to be an exceptionally sincere and forthright child — and no fool, to boot. The contrast is too stark between what he is taught and what he sees. — It is all lies. — Monsieur Jacques comes to doubt a great many things. By their educational methods, all different and particular, his successive tutors manage to convince him that life is a sort of colossal sham and the world a well-appointed stage for *comédies-bouffes*.

Age thirteen. Little Fierce, attending a religious secondary school in Belgium, spends the Easter fortnight in Paris, with his parents. There he would grow ill with boredom if not for little Troarn, a schoolmate whose company he is permitted to keep. Free and curious, the two secondary-schoolers explore Paris. On 11 March — these things deserve a date — Fierce and Troarn venture to Rue de Moscou, where dwells an elegant person by the name of Madame d'Harteval, whose fame has reached even their ears. She turns out to be a pretty if slovenly girl, who, for appearances, pretends to be offended before consenting, indulgently, to what they desire. Somewhat unsettled as he lies down, Fierce rises in mild disappointment, and, out of countenance before the young lady's mocking eyes, takes the sensible path of bursting into laughter. The deed is done.

Age eighteen. Fierce has decided to become a sailor the way his friends decide to be cavalrymen or diplomats. The Naval Academy serves him as an unexpected but precious and crucial refuge from the dangers of his own nature, which is exacting and admits of no regulation. Fierce has just spent three brilliant, wearying years in Paris: brilliant by the number and quality of intrigues pursued, wearying because these monotonous intrigues have spurred him to more varied, less anodyne entertainments. At just the right time, then, he finds himself confined, at the far reaches of Brittany, to a crude, dour, cold vessel, far from the professional and society skirts that in previous winters had welcomed him all too well — far from the rousing caress of some little cousin he was initiating on holiday at his château in Anjou — far from the backrooms for senators and the English bars for foreign diplomats to which his stubborn desire for all things new and forbidden had led him. — Monsieur de Fierce is a naval officer, and the rank is a momentary sheath against various untoward maladies, senility and ataxia being of their honorable number.

And now Fierce roams the world.

It is not much fun. It is, however, more fun — more eclectic and less false — than Parisian life. — In substance Parisian debauchery falls little short of the exotic kind, but it labors under the hypocrisy of closed shutters and dimmed lamps. Elsewhere sensual gestures fear not the sun, and Fierce continues to set sincerity above all else.

He has made it his trade to seek after it everywhere — in China, Sumatra, and the Antilles — in the philosophers bound in grey velvet that line the shelf above his bed — on the brown or pink lips of many a mistress caressed at some port of call — in the bottoms of too many flasks and bottles, and in every kind of smoke known to this petty world: opium, hashish, ether — in the positive and rigorous theories of a Torral, in the Epicurean egotism of a Mévil, in his own impulsive, indifferent conduct. No scrap of truth discovered, no patch of veil torn off, has managed to satisfy. He has tasted of all things, and come to a universal disgust. He continues nonetheless to live, and he abuses life, for it is, he finds, insipid merely to use it.

His father and mother are dead. From this double mourning he has drawn a measure of melancholy and little sadness. Free and rich, he follows the same path, knowing of none better, though suffering a vague desire for one.

An old admiral, idealistic and candid, has taken a shine to him, having perceived him through some purifying prism; he loves him like a son and treats him like a hero; Fierce repays this with a bit of scornful friendship.

Fierce roams the world, ferrying from one climate to the next his disdain for all laws, his irony for all religions, his hatred for all lies, and his hunger and thirst for all the novel and miraculous nourishment that life promises and never delivers.

IX

ierce's orderly — a small, barefoot sailor in a striped, short-sleeved polo — entered the sleep-bound room and, silent as a mouse, straightened it up. The room was a mess. There had no doubt been some blind stumbling about on the way to bed, a heedless tearing off and casting aside of clothes, and as little care over the flipped armchair. An instant later, though, order reigned. The armchair had been set right and draped with other, immaculate clothes: a freshly ironed jacket adorned, as per regulation, with its epaulette *attentes* of gold, its stripes, and its anchor buttons. There was water for the lavabo and in the tub, the sponges were free of their nets, and the bottles stood in a neat row. Now that all was laid out the small sailor spoke, in a Breton voice:

"Lieutenant! Seven-thirty."

The violet eyelids fluttered, and the eyes gleamed like lamps in the night. Fierce snapped to lucidity, his mind clear: opium is a passable antidote to alcohol, combatting hangovers with nausea. The innocence and serenity vanished from the awakened face, now once again weary and unsated.

The small sailor had gone away. Slightly pale, his temples damp, Fierce rose and began by downing half the bottle of coffee he kept in reserve among his perfumes. Then, less unsettled in the gut, he doffed his white pajamas and entered the tub. Afterwards, skin dripping deliciously, he let the morning breeze dry his shoulders, and looked into the mirror. While not given to coquetry, he had a judicious appreciation for the advantages in life of a well-built body and an affable face. Despite twenty-six years lived in full, he was pleased to note, his belly remained flat and his forehead smooth. He sat up, nude and lazy.

He laid his nape against the back of the armchair. The opium still weighed on his appendages. There was an iron ring clamped around his head, and his chest was empty, void of heart and lungs. He had no doubt risen too early from the den's mats. — A pretty little den, by the by; truly an elegant door through which to escape life and enter the dream of the gods! — Yes, he had most certainly risen too early. But he'd had to get back — back aboard, back to life. Here, now, he must dress and go, give orders and receive them, bestir himself with the silly and vain affairs of men. He must forget the sovereign quietude of the night's opium, and the bibulous, lubricious orgy that had ensued; forget the golden wings on which he had soared over the earth, and the marvelous kisses that a fairy princess had piously heaped at his, the smoker's, feet... In fact, it had been that ignoble little Annamite she-monkey; she'd had a nice, catlike way, though, of squatting between your legs — discreet...

Risen too early, no doubt about it. A little more coffee, to dry up the accursed sweat. — Sad such returns aboard as the previous night's. Sad the jolting, rickety rickshaws, and the damp sampans smelling of rot, and the nausea that sways the gut like a swing...

Before donning the suit jacket, with its gold ornament, he wet his hand and set it on the narrow of his waist: the same freshness yesterday in the caress of the little Japanese, Otake-San. One after another, in memory of her, he dug every fingernail into his skin. Then he donned the jacket and attached a collar and cuffs, to counterfeit a shirt, and spare himself another layer of fabric. The heat was starting to rise.

He powdered his livid eyelids a bit and rubbed his cheeks red, giving himself a look of absolute readiness, and left his quarters.

On deck the tents had been pitched and the curtains lowered, and the strakes were being washing down. The admiralty's band was assembled. A helmsman was minding the binnacle chronometer. Sentries at the gangways were loading their rifles for the morning's colors.

Fierce checked the time and had the tricolor signal-pennant struck. At port were two cruisers and the full division of Saigon's gunboats and coast guard. Clarion calls sounded from ship to ship. Repeated signals clattered from the tops of the masts.

The chronometer's hand advanced to eight o'clock. The regulation orders followed solemnly at a signal from the aide-de-camp:

"Attention for the colors!"

"Haul down the signal!"

"Admiral hoists!"

"Hoist!"

Rifle shots at the gangways produced blue puffs. The band played to the flag. The sailors saluted, doffing their caps. Fierce removed his helmet, with disdain for the sunshine that leaked between the panels of the tents. — The French flag, as proud as on the evening of Austerlitz,[23] rose slowly at the poop. — And Fierce gazed upon it, and smiled with an imperceptible shrug, and murmured by rote, for the appearance of sincerity, seven words from a book he liked: cholera blue, famine white, fresh-blood red. — He put his helmet back on and turned his back, to pay a visit down below to the admiral.

Monsieur d'Orvilliers, duke and peer, rear admiral commanding a division of the China squadron, was in body a marshal of the First Empire, taller, leaner, and more heroic than the men of today, his aspect hardened by a ruder mustache of grey and thicker white hair; but his eyes, doubtless for never having seen battle, had gone tender and soft, and were ever directed straight ahead, with an honest, candid, somewhat chimeric gaze. In spirit Monsieur d'Orvilliers was like his eyes.

He proffered a hand to his aide-de-camp, and looked him over with love, admiring of his youth and beauty, his superior intelligence and wit. Indeed, the good fellow was convinced that Fierce was above reproach in every thought and gesture. Fierce shook the hand,

---

23   A town in southeast Czech Republic where, in 1805, Napoleon defeated the Russian and Austrian armies.

replied elliptically to a few paternal questions about his evening and night, then cut short the man's counsel on discretion and prudence by asking for the day's orders. Monsieur d'Orvillier darkened in mood and informed his aide-de-camp of the serious political and maritime situation. Long familiar with the old man's pessimism, Fierce paid no heed. — Monsieur d'Orvilliers went into specifics, spoke of England and Japan, shook his head over France's policy of effacement, and concluded with a prediction. There would be war, no doubt deadly war, within three months.

"In March," Fierce matter-of-factly observed. It was late December.

"In April or May," the admiral affirmed, gravely. Still gentle and placid, and in no way emphatic, he added: "Not one of us will be coming back, probably; but at my age death is the inn where one will be taking one's dinner, like it or not; the dinner hour itself is of no concern. I'll have attained one of my greatest joys, and the least deserved, if I die in the manner of Brueys, Nelson, and Ruyter…"[24]

Respectful and melancholic, Fierce counted in his head to twenty-one and returned to the original question:

"So, today's orders, Admiral?"

Monsieur d'Orvilliers gave them. He needed a landau for three o'clock. Fierce pointed out that the sun would be hot. But the admiral averred that the sun would not prevent his parleys first with the governor, then with the defense council and the commanders of the navy and the troops. Finally, he was expecting numerous dispatches, which the aide-de-camp was to decipher himself before disembarking, if he felt like a walk before noon.

"Very good," said Fierce.

A first telegram, the weather bulletin from Shanghai, was awaiting in his quarters. He laughed.

"No doubt the very belligerent symptoms we're so worried about: rough seas off Formosa, typhoon over Manila. — In jolly good form, good-old d'Orvilliers: England's war, nothing else…"

---

24 François -Paul Brueys d'Aigalliers (1753–98), French naval officer in the American Revolution, French commander in the French Revolutionary Wars, leader under Napoleon of the French expedition to Egypt. Defeated by Nelson and killed at the Battle of the Nile (1798).

Horatio Nelson (1758–1805), vice admiral in the Royal Navy. Hero of the Battle of Trafalgar (1805), where he perished.

Michiel de Ruyter (1607–76), admiral of the Dutch navy during the Anglo-Dutch Wars.

He looked over his bibelots, his book-bindings, his Venus of Syracuse,[25] its amber marble gleaming in a corner.

…"Add an artillery shell to the collection? That'd fill some space."

He thought no more about it and took up a book.

…"If the dispatches arrive in time I'll go attend Mevil's levee. The lovely Hélène must be charming in bed… And as long as the old man leaves me free this evening, even if only for an hour… Eight months since I've made the rounds here, the Inspection…"

The dispatches arrived. The last cruiser sent to China had just reached Djibouti. But the minister was recalling it to France.

"Why the devil…?"

Next, fifteen tight lines from Hong Kong, all figures. Dispirited, Fierce let his hands fall into his lap, then gathered his courage and looked for the consular dictionary.

"No doubt an English cruiser's changed its moorings… or the royal governor's horse has suffered a sprain…"

He penciled his translation:

"Squadron … Yangtze … collected … sixteen ships … — Come on! — *London … Bulwark … Venerable … Duncan … Cornwallis … Exmouth …* — Six battleships, six … — *Cressy … Aboukir … Hogue … Drake … King Alfred … Africa … Kent … Essex … Bedford* — Nine armored cruisers, fifteen, all stronger than us, of course."

He set down the pencil and once more looked around his quarters:

"An artillery shell, yes. That'd do nicely."

He carried the dispatch to the admiral. D'Orvilliers read it without surprise or disquiet, satisfied.

"Just as I was saying."

Fierce walked away serene, so much the fatalist that no news could disturb his peace, and a physiologically courageous specimen besides. He smiled as he mused on the admiral.

----

25   No doubt a knickknack copy of the *Aphrodite of Syracuse*, sculpted by an anonymous hand in the second century AD and now preserved at Greece's National Archaeological Museum, in Athens. The statue was discovered at Baiae, in the Bay of Naples, and restored, as it were, by Antonio Canova (1757–1822), who supplied the missing head and arm. It depicts Venus almost in the nude, with some drapery to cover her pudenda. The anonymous sculptor is said to have taken inspiration from Praxiteles (fourth century BC), author of the *Aphrodite of Cnidus*, said to be the first female nude at scale.

We note with surprise that Fierce has not selected for his quarters' decor the Callipygian Venus: literally, the Venus (or Aphrodite) of the beautiful buttocks.

"A man escaped from the previous century who's unwittingly missed out on life. Under Napoleon he'd have been some manner of great man. Today he's grotesque. But a pleasant fellow, all things considered. I like him the way he is, mock him though I might."

At about ten o'clock, duties done, Fierce found himself on the wharf — in uniform; he had not taken the time to change clothes. A rather lively breeze happened to be blowing the heat off the streets, and it was still pleasant to walk — in the shade.

Fierce set out, keeping to the leafy trees and the arcaded houses. Having been away from Saigon for eight months, he felt a traveler's joy in recognizing every corner of the city; at the same time, the hard contrast between the Saigonese summer of today and the Japanese winter he had just left behind made him ill with something close to pain, but he savored it, knowing it to be rare. All of this together made for a charming stroll. He reached the Jardin untroubled by the dust or the sun. He trod the red sand of the paths, between the lawns and the sinuous arroyo, on whose banks the reeds and ferns grew so thick as to conceal the water of its meandering rivulets. The trees of the tropics blended into a miraculous forest that shut out the sun. But the loveliest ornaments in this peerless park were the clusters of bamboo, whose slender stems, as if bound is fasciae, bloomed higher than the tops of the arecas and the tamarinds; from afar every bouquet seemed a single tree, vaporous as lace, and colossal.

The red paths were deserted; a sampan, silent beneath its lid of woven straw, drifted along the arroyo.

Fierce wended his pleasant way through the exotic forest. A path struck his fancy, because its multiform fronds had interlaced into a vault, producing a green tunnel, and because every ten paces this twisty tunnel would run up against a bush and come to a dead end. A culvert prolonged it past a stagnant, lotus-spotted pool, framed with a great bristle of iron bars: breaking the surface at the center was the flat head of a crocodile, still as a tree trunk. Fierce sniffed the fetid odor, drowned in the despotic fragrance of magnolias; and farther off, too, he could smell another, muskier scent.

The magnolias and palms were now thinning out. The path gave yet another turn, and the wood came to an end. A big cage was backed against the last trees, and natives, soldiers, and women — three bright European parasols — were looking on.

It was the tiger cage. There were only two tigers in view, but they were formidable specimens, indescribable in their majesty and size. The female was pretending to sleep, lying on her belly, head between her paws. Feigned sleep, coquetry for the male: claws protruding from their velvety sheaths and craftily poking holes in the ground, shivers undulating beneath the striped pelt.

The male, still as a tiger of stone, watched her. He was much taller and longer than any lion. His breast, white as snow, swelled powerfully as he sniffed the other, prone beast.

A pink parasol rose to meet Fierce at the crackle of his step on the gravel.

"Look who's here! Come to see great beasts perform their horrors?"

Fierce saw Hélène Liseron, fresh under a cloud of powder, with but the faintest rings around her eyes.

"What have you done with Raymond?"

She had extended a hand; he squeezed and, as was his wont, caressed it with all his fingers, one after another. She chuckled.

"Ask instead what he's done with me…"

"Well?"

She laughed, this time with some heart, and pouted.

"Not much!"

The tiger began to roar, pausing to consider the weaklings surveilling him; then he turned his snout aside, with slow disdain, and marched to the tigress. He pushed her with his head; she played dead, refusing to budge. Anger, a second attempt, and he rolled her as one would roll over a kitten. Now she grew cross; she pounced at him, claws out. He did not retreat, however, and she took fright at the fixed eyes, flaming like twin green lanterns. She bent down, flattened herself, went soft. He delivered a brutal swat of the paw, cast her to the ground, and covered her. The coupling beasts went still. The tiger, triumphant, continued to growl.

Excited and frightened, eyeing the scene, Liseron squeezed Fierce's hand, and panted a bit. Every roar drove her nails in deeper, and when at last the tigress obtained her modesty's reward the scratched palm began to bleed.

Fierce looked at his hand, then at the young woman.

"You wouldn't mind being a tigress…"

She hit his arm with her fan.

"Quiet, you!"

It was over in the cage. Silent, proud, glazed eyes looking straight ahead, the tiger had taken a seat, some four paces from the lying female.

"Have you come on foot?" asked Fierce.

"Of course not. My coach is on the path. Do you have yours?"

"No. I'm out for a stroll."

"You're not walking back in this sun, are you?"

"I'll have to walk."

"You're mad. People drop like flies out here… I'd offer you a ride if you weren't in uniform."

"So why won't you?"

"Everyone will see you, by God."

"And so?"

"Really, it doesn't bother you?"

"What nonsense!"

In the coach he slipped his hand around Hélène's waist — to smooth the folds of the bodice.

"Where shall I drop you?" she asked.

"Your place. On your way back to Raymond's?"

"No, silly. I'm going back to my hotel, on Rue Catinat."

"Rue Catinat, then."

The coach set off.

"So Raymond just let you fly off, at dawn?"

She pouted again.

"He'd have had trouble holding me back. He was so asleep, he's probably still unaware I've left."

"Oh yes? You tired him out that much?"

"Really! First of all, that's none of your business."

But there was a smile at the corner of her mouth, and Fierce's hand was caressing her shoulders. They laughed, both thinking the same things.

"It's funny," she murmured. "He's young and tall and strong … and …"

"And he tires so fast."

She nodded and modestly lowered her lashes.

"By God," explained Fierce. "Call him young if you like, my dear, but he's thirty."

"So?"

"…Thirty years, an adventure or two — I imagine I shatter no illusions if I tell you you're not his first lover… An adventure or two, as I've said.

A little spice here and there… He's no longer spanking new. The object's faded, been a bit too long on display."

"At thirty!?"

"Alas. I'm only twenty-seven myself, and, believe me, I've had some rather trying nights…"

"Oh, come now. What tales are you spinning? I too am thirty, sir… It's an age one can readily admit to, and I assure you these thirty years weigh as lightly on me as if they were twenty…"

"That has nothing to do with it."

"…And I know very serious men — mature, let's call them — men fifty years of age! — who, by golly, are worth more than your friend."

Fierce mimed his impotence in the matter and sought to make no reply. One aged quickly, to be sure, living the sort of life they all lived: Mévil, Torral, and he himself. — The degraded, ignoble image of Rochet befouled his mind, and to chase it away he tightened the hold of his arm around his companion's shoulders. A slight desire snaked its way into his sinews, and he was relieved to find he was young and strong before the pretty woman.

The carriage came to a halt.

"Shall I drop you here?"

"Is it not permitted to go up with you?"

"Oh, certainly, by God, but things are a mess… I'm just passing through."

There was nothing stylish about the hotel room. The plaster walls were bare, and there was no mat over the floor tiles. But the big bed, thin, hard, and fresh, looked comfortable beneath a carefully closed mosquito net of tulle, and bath robes lay pell-mell on a rattan chaise-longue.

"If you don't mind," said Hélène Liseron.

Standing before a mirror, she raised her arms and unpinned her hat. He took a seat and watched. The red hair came fluttering down, and the plump nape gleamed as under a hairnet of pure gold. The firm, fatty arms blossomed from short sleeves, with a warm dew pearling on the skin. Fingers in the hair loosed a violent, delicate fragrance.

In the mirror Fierce caught a sly look, then an odd smile. So he rose and just seized her bodily. She was stunned, or pretended to be.

"Well, now. What's come over you?"

He made no reply whatsoever, having sunk his gluttonous teeth into the golden down of her neck. He was everywhere up against her, his knees poking in behind hers, his chest against her shoulders.

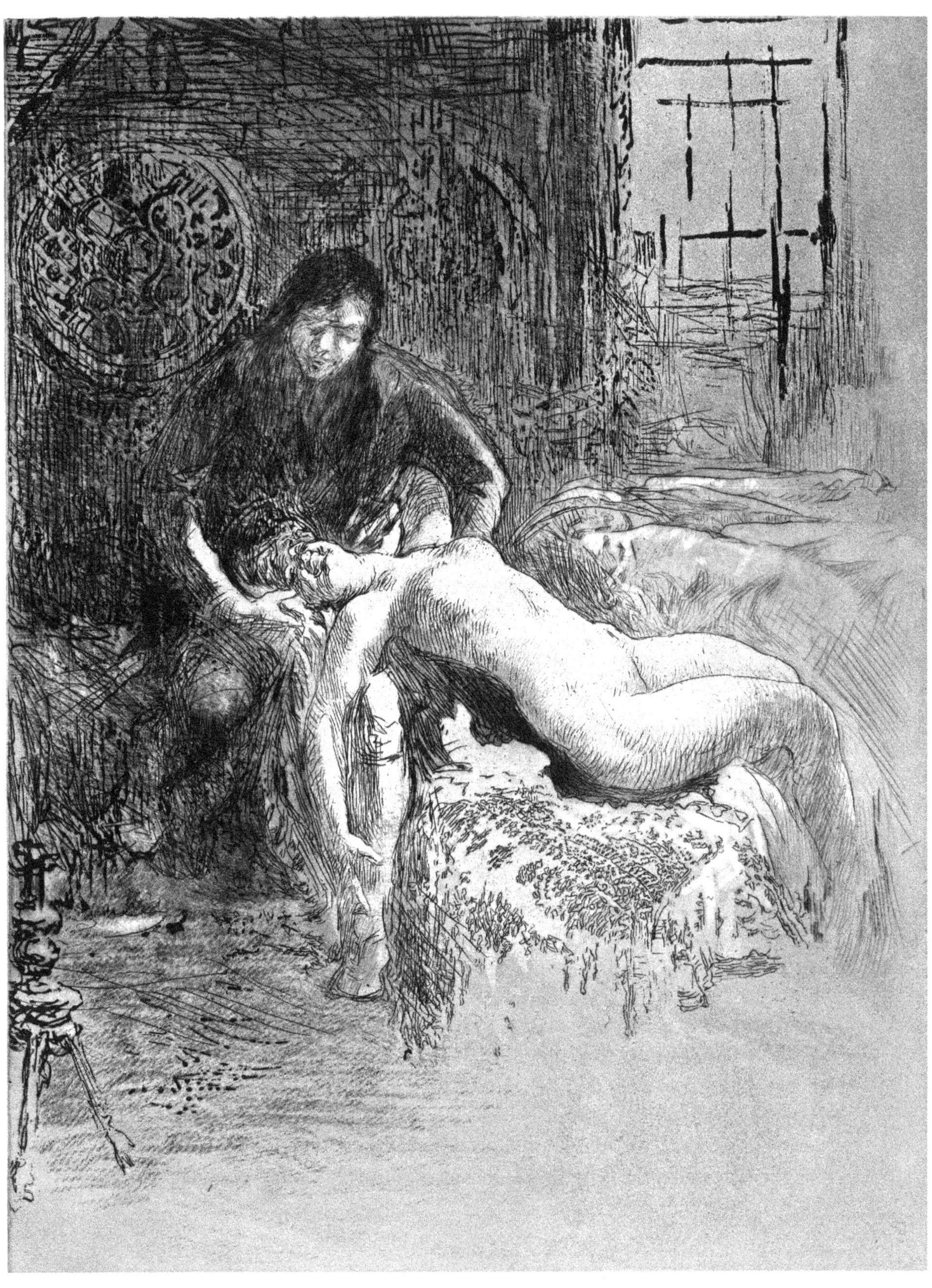

"Are you going to let me go?" she cried.

He did the opposite; he took her up like a doll, one hand at the waist, the other under the thighs, and tipped her into the chaise-longue, amid the rustling silks. Now she put up a genuine defense — not for long.

"Finish up, why don't you!"

"I'm finishing."

And finish he did — in his way — and rose, calm as could be, instantly genteel.

Without a word she returned to the mirror and smoothed her hair, then laughed, good-naturedly. Teasing, he had gotten behind her again to nibble her scented hair.

"What about Raymond?" she broke in.

"What about him?"

"You have no regrets?"

He was very kind:

"You're far too pretty."

With a flattered, incredulous pout, she insisted:

"But you're great friends, you two, aren't you?"

"Yes indeed."

"Well, what if he found out? He'd be furious…"

He held back a guffaw. Jealousy is not among the civilized sentiments; and Mévil worried not a whit about any of his mistresses.

She looked at him tenderly, seeking a kiss. It was obvious that she judged Fierce's betrayal of Mévil severely, and the blackness of the crime tickled her vanity. He granted the kiss, obliging if ironic. Besides, now that he had had her she was an object of utter indifference. In truth, why the devil had he leaped on her before? Bah!

At noon he was back aboard for lunch. A helmsman was on the lookout for him, to get him to initial some freshly signed orders. He read:

> THE COUNTER ADMIRAL COMMANDING THE SECOND
> DIVISION OF THE CHINA SQUADRON
>
>   ORDERS:
>
>   FROM THIS DAY THE ELEMENTARY SCHOOL AND
> GYMNASIUM SHALL CEASE TO OPERATE ON THE SHIPS OF
> THE DIVISION.
>
>   IN THEIR STEAD THE COMMANDERS SHALL SEE TO

THE EXECUTION, ALTERNATELY, AND BY ALL MEN IN THEIR CREW, OF THE ORDINARY EXERCISE AND GENERAL EXERCISE OF THE CANNON.

FURTHERMORE, EVERY EVENING, AFTER THE BEAT TO GENERAL QUARTERS, THERE SHALL BE EXERCISES FOR NOCTURNAL AIMING.

THE ADMIRAL INSISTS ON THE EXTREME IMPORTANCE OF THE AFOREMENTIONED EXERCISES AND RELIES ON THE ZEAL AND PATRIOTISM OF ALL PROMPTLY TO MULTIPLY THE EFFICACIOUS FORCE OF THE SHIPS ENTRUSTED TO HIM BY THE REPUBLIC.

D'ORVILLIERS

ABOARD THE *BAYARD*

27 DECEMBER 19—

"So," thought Fierce, "the tomfoolery begins."

X[A]

Eight days later, risen in the morning, Fierce leaned at the gunport, resting on his elbows.

By some quirk of the season, it had rained during the night — a brief deluge, as comes down once a month in the thick of the dry season. There was a spring freshness in the air, though the sun was already setting the sky aflame. Fierce observed that the left bank of the Donai, buried in verdure, consisted of stacked layers. At bottom, hanging over the current, were the reeds, the bananas, the dwarf palms: piled in tight, with nary a hole, nary a slit, in their dark hedge. Magnolias, banyans, acacias, and tamarinds alternated above with shoots of bamboo, all in a blend of finely nuanced color: the tender grey of the bamboo, the gleaming green of the mandarins, the metallic brown of the round-leaved spindle-trees. Myriad flowers — white, yellow, and especially red: poppy-ruddy poinciana, carmine hibiscus — peppered the foliage. Still higher waved palms of all kinds, their delicate stems cutting fantastical, complicated shadows against the sparkle of sky. The long fronds of airy arecas mixed with the broad fronds of fan palm, and the intercut fronds of coconut, heavy with fruit. All of this hovering over the forest, fairy bouquets on the tips of stipes slender and white like Ionic columns.

Yellow water lapped the hull beneath the cruiser's gunport, slipped swiftly by, hasty and worrisome, ferrying half-sunken trunks, leaves, planks, debris come from far away, the uncertain wrecks of Asia's great unknown. The sun had laid a dazzling sheet on the river, blinding all to the black whirlpools that snatched at things as they floated past.

"All good, this," said Fierce.

He was in excellent spirits, having smoked no opium the night before.

It had been a propitious week. Faster than expected, Saigon had favored him with tolerable hospitality: an agreeable inn, joyful suppers, and the rest. The inn was a mere napping room, furnished with nothing but a horsehair bed, a mosquito net, and a punkah operated by a *boy*. The windows showed a leaning poinciana pushing forth its branches and shaking off flowers. Outside lay the old Tuduc quarter, with its half-Chinese, brown, fragrant streets, lively with shops and laundries. It was pleasant to sleep in this airy room during the torrid hours of the afternoon, while the cruiser's sheet-metal expanded and creaked under an atrocious sun, flaking the white paint and oozing globs of molten pitch. At such times Fierce would stretch out nude beneath the mosquito net, skin damp from one of his frequent baths, and dream of his Saigonese life, taking care not to stir, for if he so much as stretched out a hand his whole arm would stream with sweat.

At supper he would have Mévil and Torral's company. For these three every night resembled the first, varying only in detail. The mixture was always of women, opium, and alcohol, in unequal proportions, their entr'actes strolls by night through the swarming Chinese city or the lonely slumbering countryside.

The "rest," finally, Hélène Liseron would supply. Not that Fierce had made her his formal mistress or kept some ridiculous faith with her. But they had developed a taste for each other with their first adventure and were now carrying on in secret. This had the benefit for Fierce of simplifying his life. It is a comfortable station to be second lover to a woman one makes love to without attachments. As for the obligatory stew of exotic sensualities, daily suppers in Cholon supplied the proper condiments: Japanese, Annamite, or Chinese.

In all this Hélène entrusted herself to her fate, and saw no harm in it. Two generous lovers were better than one. Besides, Fierce and Mévil avenged her each in turn on the other. Hélène, with a fairly primitive feeling, liked both well enough to be jealous. It injured her pride and sensuality to see them make love to other women. Fierce would make the

most cursory efforts to conceal his Asian flings, and Mévil would announce his trysts and fortuitous beddings. So Hélène, knowingly betrayed, delighted in betrayals of her own, and looked forward to the day when she would dare admit to each of her lovers that the other was her favorite. As it happens, Mévil knew nothing of his counterpart. Fierce, out of consideration for her, kept Hélène's secret, and indulged her occasional threats to "tell all," out of jealousy or sadism…. Nice inn, joyful suppers, and the rest…

Above all, the specious gratification of having an objective in life and a road leading to it. For many years Fierce had lived by his senses, seeking only to satisfy them as best he could. But Mévil and Torral's company was leading him now to believe that nothing better existed in the world, that the thing-beyond for which he had been hoping was chimerical, and that he would do well to abide henceforth by the civilized way: maximal pleasure with minimal effort. — The proposal had a scientific frankness he found seductive.

He liked no less the precision with which his friends hewed to their maxims. Mévil, whose exclusive tastes ran towards love alone, had an official tally of five mistresses — and neglected for their sake not one of the supplemental voluptuous encounters that chance brought his way. No prejudice held sway over his choices, and his kiss felt the same draw from every mouth, as long as it was young and described the proper arc. — An operetta singer — a *mondaine*,[26] wife to a renowned lawyer — an Annamite *congaï* in his employ: more servant-slave than servant-mistress, by the way — a Japanese pensioner at a brothel, summoned on Tuesdays for a weekly delight — a young girl of candid repute who performed her debaucheries incognito. Five women, then — each of whom would likely have disdained the four others, for their different destinies — were equally valued, flattered, caressed, and disdained by a professional lover never once troubled by preference. — Therein lay the evident wisdom. — Torral, eclectic, resorted to an Epicurean arithmetic to balance his pleasures,[27] and it was his boast thereby to express all of the happiness that life contained. This objective being needful to achieve,

---

26 Socialite, or society woman, as opposed to *demi-mondaine*, or half-worldly woman. The latter became synonymous with prostitutes, ladies of pleasure, or women-for-hire.

27 An epicure is fond of or accustomed to luxury or indulgence in sensual pleasures, but Epicureanism relates to the philosophy of Epicurus, a Greek who flourished in the fourth century B.C. For Epicurus the good amounts to pleasure in the sense of fear or pain's absence. Such pleasure is achieved through intellect, virtue, and moderation. The Epicurean arithmetic, then, is a careful balance of such pleasures.

the opinions of others did not exist in his eyes. He would parade in the street even his masculine liaisons, and take his promenade through the Inspection in the company of his two intimate *boys*, Ba and Sao. — This too, perhaps, was wisdom, heightened by a perhaps courageous cynicism.

So Fierce enjoyed his Saigonese life, and enjoyed as well the soundness of his pleasure.

He took a last look at the forest-lined river.

"Good town, Saigon…"

X[B]

t was Sunday, the second of January. The admiral was to host an intimate luncheon. Though averse to such society servitudes, Fierce had accepted this particular invitation, because the Abel girl was to attend — the lieutenant-governor's daughter, the delicious sphinx-eyed alabaster statue who had struck his fancy on the first day, and tempted him more with every encounter. — A strange girl, he thought: still waters that made you feel like tossing in a stone, to see what might rise to the surface. — Also attending, in addition to the Abels, were the governor-general, old friend to the Duke d'Orvilliers, and a pupil of his, a young girl whose mother, a blind widow, would never accompany her in society. In the dining room, already set, Fierce looked to the flowers, searching the shelves for the admiral's Japanese cloisonné enamels to fill them with roses and orchids. Setting down corsage bouquets, he read the ladies' calligraphed names off the menus, and paused at the setting for the governor's pupil, memory failing him — Mademoiselle Silva? — Silva? — He asked the admiral, who was in his study folding maps of batteries.

"You mean you don't remember?" said d'Orvilliers. "You must know your history!"

He told the tale:

Mademoiselle Sylva was no less than the daughter of the famous Colonel Sylva, of the Chasseurs d'Afrique, killed at El-Arar[28] in the most epic charge of the century. As soon as he mentioned this Monsieur d'Orvilliers forgot the daughter for the father, and delivered unto his respectfully aloof aide-de-camp a minute account of the aforementioned

---

28 There appears to be a wadi (riverbed) called El-Arar in a region of Morocco called Drâa-Tafilalet, which borders on Algeria.

battle, and of the glory secured on the occasion by the Chasseurs d'Afrique under hero Sylva's command. Like it or not, Fierce would learn that the brigade had been betrayed and surrounded at the Moroccan border and miraculously rescued by two squadrons dispatched on reconnaissance and believed by all to have been wiped out. Colonel Sylva was in command of those squadrons. He himself had been surrounded at the center of a province in revolt, had broken free with a prodigious charge, and had ridden for three days through cloud after cloud of enemy forces, never once returning sword to scabbard. On the third day he surged up behind the Moroccans, already sure they would prevail, and turned their victory into defeat. Afterwards, his sky-blue dolman gone purple under so many blows, he had led the victorious cavalrymen to the French tents, cried "Halt!" — and died on the spot.

Fierce, artiste in spirit, admired the act, and the variegated splendor of the red and blue squadrons cutting and thrusting through the crush of brown burnooses.[29] Then he smiled out of pity, weighing the foolishness of the whole affair. What had come of it? Widows and orphans, under the pompous label "family of heroes" — and free to starve under universal admiration. — He imagined little Sylva, a skinny brunette, with a profile fit to be struck on a medal, angular, exalted, weepy, and stupid as a cud-chewing beast — with the makings of a spinster. — The admiral, staring into the distance, dreamed of epics; the aide-de-camp, shoulders in something of a shrug, murmured: "Poor bastards — and poor lass."

The clock striking eleven, the helmsmen announced the governor's approach, and the officer of the watch summoned the guard, who took up a post by the gangway. Fierce climbed to the bottom of the ladder, to help the ladies aboard. The polished brass of the dinghy being hauled in gleamed with sunlight, blinding the eye to all else.

The dinghy reached the gangway. Fierce saw the governor's white, weasel-like head, Abel's grey and grave head, and three parasols: pink, mauve, and blue. The mauve parasol was lowered. Fierce took the arm of Madame Abel, who hopped lightly onto the first steps; she seemed to him her usual self: not pretty but smiling and good-natured — she was likable.

---

29 A long circular, hooded cloak worn by Arabs.

Mademoiselle Abel — of the pink parasol — was the second aboard. She had preserved her mysterious sphinx's gaze. She took the proffered hand but made little use of its support, giving no squeeze with her cool, slender fingers. Fierce admired the fragile wrist, which one might have mistaken for Saxony porcelain.

Beneath the blue parasol, finally, appeared Mademoiselle Sylva.

Here Fierce was astonished, as she in no way resembled the picture he had formed of her.

Mademoiselle Sylva was neither skinny nor a brunette nor marked by fate but pink and blond all over. The grey eyes[30] stood out first, for their size and forthright gaze.

She leapt aboard, intrepid, never touching his hand. Fierce observed that she was supple and robust, though delicate. He came aboard behind her and, on deck, offered his arm. The bugles sounded *aux champs*,[31] for the governor. She came to a halt, raising her eyes to the badge of the ship's arms, and Fierce heard her sound out the motto: WITHOUT FEAR AND BEYOND REPROACH.[32]

He looked at her as they walked: there was pastel in her complexion, purity in her forehead, pride and malice in her mouth — and on top of it all a pervasive charm of youth, grace, and sincerity. Right away he found her delicious, and forgot Mademoiselle Abel. When he saw them side by side in the lounge of the poop, however, he had to admit there was no contest: the alabaster sphinx, with her regular beauty and the enigmatic depth of her eyes, carried the day. But he was secretly aggrieved, as if at some failure of his own — and later smiled with a sort of pride on observing that Mademoiselle Sylva, though less beautiful, remained the prettier, because more lively, more womanly, and less of a statue.

They were neighbors at table. The admiral's dining room was ventilated by two corner gunports, embrasures for the rearward cannons. They cluttered the room a bit, these cannons, but to a woman's eye they were curios, and drew Mademoiselle Sylva's admiration. Obligingly, Fierce supplied some interesting explanations, and the ice was broken. Mademoiselle Sylva was curious and did not conceal her

---

30   The author's adjective, *pers*, is the traditional French translation of γλαυκῶπις in Homer, as in the epithet "grey-eyed Athena." The grey of Athena's eyes is in fact a blue-green.

31   Literally "to the fields." A ceremonial military call.

32   Or, in Edward Walford's tidy translation, "fearless and spotless." See note 22.

curiosity. The wall-hangings of asbestos fabric, the family china with its ducal arms, the Japanese screens with their orchids all in turn brought forth questions that from a less seductive mouth Fierce would have found childish. In this instance, though, he was delighted to reply, and their talk was soon lively indeed. Cheer suited Mademoiselle Sylva, who had the prettiest laugh in the world, and Fierce, under its charm, took every opportunity to stoke it. The young lady, for her part, was as pleased as could be with her companion.

They chattered away. Fierce knew nothing of young ladies; in fact, he doubted their very existence. The creatures so named whom he had encountered here and there, on his voyages, or when stationed in France, and at the four Parisian salons where he would still put in the occasional appearance, had left behind unpleasant memories; they had been the mere germs of women, yet more depraved and more likely to lie. He could appreciate their prettiness as he might that of delicate knickknacks, impish and unfinished; and he looked on them with pleasure at first and with scorn as soon as they opened their mouth. Unlike these disdained partial virgins, however, Mademoiselle Sylva struck him chiefly as being frank and candid — as a young lady, that is, in the old sense of the term. It was surprising and satisfying, though he was not yet convinced of this candor and frankness.

"I'm in luck," Mademoiselle Sylva was saying cheerfully. "Until this morning I was sure that some snag would prevent this lovely luncheon from occurring and relegate it to my dreams."

"Thank goodness for the luncheon," says Fierce with a laugh. "So it was tempting for you, Mademoiselle, to come sample this cage of ours."

"First of all, your cage is delicious… This is a darling dining room, so simple and yet so fit for a grand personage…."

"And we have a view of the sea!"

"You're poking fun. Very naughty of you. — Yes, I absolutely wanted to come aboard the famous *Bayard*. It's the talk of all Saigon. You're all over the newspapers… And a military luncheon: a veritable party for a little girl!"

"Is she so little?"

"I still play with my dolls… Ssh! Don't say a word. But I so love a ship, and sailors, and all of it…"

Fierce holds back a smile.

"You like sailors? Why do you like sailors?"

"Because…" — Mademoiselle Sylva reflected for a moment — "…because they're not like other men."

"Ah…. Very good."

"No… They're not like other men today … Soldiers aren't either, in fact…. They roam the world. They set forth on a voyage or go off to fight any which place, whatever the country or the enemy…. And they don't worry over money, for they could earn fortune if they wanted to; but they *don't* want to. They'd rather keep being soldiers or sailors. They're men from another time…"

Fierce ponders.

"And that," concludes Mademoiselle Sylva, "is why I'm happy to be here, having greatly feared that I would not be."

Fierce emerges from his reverie.

"Greatly feared? Do you mean to say that we seriously risked missing out on your company?"

"I wouldn't have come if mother had been ill."

"I believe your mother is very old, no?"

"Not very old, but enfeebled, especially in this stifling heat. She misses me quite a bit when I'm not at her side. You know she's been blind for three years!"

"I know. Life mustn't always be much fun for you, Mademoiselle."

"But in fact yes! When you meet Mother — and you *will* meet her, as she's an old friend of Monsieur d'Orvillier's — you shall see that it's impossible to be sad in her company. She's so good and joyful, so perfect…"

"You love her well!"

"Oh yes. In fact, I think it impossible to love someone more than I love Mother…. It's rather natural, wouldn't you say? Even if I weren't her daughter, though, I'd love her just as much and be just as happy to live under the same roof."

"I didn't know the admiral was a friend of Madame Sylva's."

They met a long time ago and lost touch, but only after having been on quite intimate terms. It all happened well before I entered this nether world. I myself laid eyes on Monsieur d'Orvilliers for the first time just now. But I love him in advance, Mother having spoken of him so often. I know how good he is, and of what good character…"

Fierce shot a glance at the admiral, whose candid eyes belied the high, rude face.

"As you said earlier, he's a man from another time."

"Yes… Another time better than the present."

"Perhaps," said Fierce. "So, Mademoiselle, you live in Saigon, almost as a nurse, and you are content with your lot. You never get bored?"

"Never! I'm always busy, as you can image!"

"True. You have your doll…"

"Shush! Is this how you keep the state secrets you're entrusted with? It's my honor at stake. You know I'll be twenty years old next month? — Let's leave 'my daughter' in peace. I play at motherhood for a lark, but I'm the genuine mistress of the house."

"True enough."

"And I'm a good mistress of the house, I'll have you believe. — The house, readings, and drives: these make up our life, a full and in no way boring life… A hearth is so good, Monsieur, even when the fire is mythical, as it is here!"

"That," said Fierce, "is a joy that sailors sometimes fail to appreciate, but I can imagine it. — Do you dislike society altogether?"

"Of course not! The very idea! The hearth does not exclude society. I love balls, soirees, parties, dresses, and especially uniforms. And I'm mad for dancing. Monsieur, we shall waltz together in a week at the Government Palace: my guardian will receive in the *Bayard*'s honor, and I'll save you the first line in my dance card."

"It's a deal. A thousand thanks. You know, Mademoiselle, you are a most eclectic young lady. The hearth, society life, uniforms, sailors — what else? — you like it all, without preference."

"What else can one do, alas? If you think about it, life is not so very droll… You must make the most of it. I'm reminded of the ship that brought Mother and me over from France, four years ago: thirty days at sea. At first it seemed impossibly long and monotonous, but the ship was full of charming people, and we'd soon set up games, readings, and tea parties; we had dancing on the spar deck in the evening; we'd rehearse a comedy after supper; in the end, the cruise went by like a dream. Life is just like that: a sea crossing. You must make the most of it."

"You're a philosopher."

"Not at all. I abhor grand, hair-splitting arguments. I find it stupid and absurd to quibble endlessly about the soul, eternity, the infinite, without ever arriving at anything common-sensical… Marthe and I are always quarreling over this."

"Marthe?"

"Marthe Abel. Didn't you know her name was Marthe? People are always calling her by nicknames…"

"Do tell."

"Oh, no." She smiled. "Better if you don't know them."

"You're a discreet little friend."

"Friend … more or less. But always discreet."

"Friend more or less?"

"We're friendly. I don't have a young-lady friend. Young ladies abhor me. It seems I lack refinement, and proper upbringing,…"

"Anything else, Madam?"

"I assure you. Is it not written all over my face? — I'm the balding, mangy mongrel. Marthe more or less puts up with me, but we are not of one mind…"

"Where do you differ?"

"Well, for one thing, she's philosophical. She reasons things out, speculates. She reads enormous German tomes, full of upsetting ideas. She does not attend Mass; she's an atheist; and I find all that terribly shocking."

Curiosity piqued, Fierce turns to look at the strange, sphinx-like girl. Mademoiselle Abel hardly speaks; she listens and observes. Her black eyes, deep as lakes, gleam serenely in her alabaster face, framed by heavy headbands with a blue sheen. It is most impossible to fathom those eyes, and discover the thought that lurks in the depths of their still waters… "Me," continues Mademoiselle Sylva, "I don't read Schopenhauer, and I go to Confession."

Fierce turns his gaze back to the pretty blond child, who has eyes the color of time, and still plays with dolls.

"You're content with the Catechism?"

"Entirely content."

"And you are very pious?"

"Not pious: I don't spend my life in church. But I'm a good Catholic, very much practicing."

Fierce does not shrug. Mademoiselle Sylva continues:

"You yourself must be religious, Monsieur. All sailors are. Besides, one would have to be mad to deny God… The main thing, though, is that I find an atheist woman to be a sort of monster. It's inelegant, atheism is. I think it should be limited to old gentlemen, to grouchy, fusspot, foolish, bald, and pusillanimous bachelors."

"Absolutely," said Fierce, not bothering to hold back a laugh. "But it's an old theory you're repeating there, Mademoiselle. Have you read Musset?"[33]

"I've half-read him. Mother used to clip together many pages, and I've never since wanted to read those pages. — I'll wait until I'm married."

"That will be soon."

"Pray believe me, I'm in no hurry. I'm very happy at present, and I could certainly be no happier…"

They pursue their intimate chat, look at each other, and smile — with no ulterior motive. They found a friendship. Mademoiselle Sylva babbles and confides. Fierce listens and dares not interrupt. Mademoiselle Sylva treats her cavalier as an old crony, as a compatriot in race and soul, almost as a brother whose thought, faith, and ideal one knows to be identical to one's own ideal, one's own thought and faith. Fierce divines the young girl's credulous illusion, and blushes in secret for not dissipating it. At times, as she passes from one thing to another, he reproves his silence, likening it to a lie. — He would like to be frank, certainly — would like to say: "I am not what you think I am. There is nothing in my heart or mind that you could love or comprehend. My innards, were you to glimpse them, would horrify you. I am a jaded man, a skeptic, an infidel. I believe in neither good nor evil, neither God nor the Devil. I have been all over, and have thus returned from all things. Swayed by the grace of my uniform, you have heaped on me a full lot of archaic virtues that are not my own and that I despise. The only cult I keep, the bitter cult of impudent truth, would strike you with horror as a blasphemy. We hold nothing in common." — But he utters not a word of this, for he lacks the courage — and for the third time the Japanese maître d'hôtel carries away an untouched dish. From the far end of the table the admiral smiles towards his aide-de-camp.

"My dear Governor, I hereby address to your Excellency an official complaint: my little Fierce is neglecting to eat, the better to court your pretty little pupil."

"He is mistaken," declares the governor. "One does not court Mademoiselle Sélysette. Mademoiselle Sélysette is not a young girl: she is a

---

33   Alfred de Musset (1810–57), French playwright, poet, and novelist. Author of *La Confession d'un enfant du siècle* (1836) and lover of novelist George Sand. Influenced by Romanticism and something of a libertine with respect to drink and sex (said to have been bisexual). Elected to the Académie Française in 1852.

boy, and I would defy Don Juan himself to note that she is wearing a skirt.
— Besides, Monsieur de Fierce is addressing a frightfully mocking little pest,
and I advise him to desist."

Mademoiselle Sylva protests and laughs. Fierce watches her turn
pink: her prompt, vermillion blood shows through her tenuous skin. In his
remotest childhood, he muses, he imagined fairies to be just so, in their
palaces of gemstone…

"Your name is Sélysette? How pretty and unusual."

"Too unusual! But my father liked the name, and though I have three
or four others to choose from I will bear no name but the one he gave me."

Fierce begins to muse once more — and does not think to be struck
by the paradoxical pleasure he is savoring from the tiny little girl of the
primitive notions — he the civilized man, friend to Mévil and Torral, friend
to Rochet…

All rose from the table. In the parlor Fierce left his neighbor's side to
proffer cups of tea: a green tea from Szechuan[34] in handle-less cups from
Sadzouma.[35] — The governor, an orator of talent who remembers the
Chamber[36] — where has served and will serve again — holds forth on the
colony's morals — both indigenous and imported.

"The Chinaman is a thief and the Japanese an assassin. The
Annamite is both. That said, I acknowledge out loud that the three races
have virtues unknown to Europe, and civilizations more advanced than
ours in the West. It would therefore behoove us, as masters of those who
should be our masters, to surpass them at least in our social morality. It
would behoove us, the colonizers, to be neither assassins nor thieves. But
that is utopian."

The admiral ventures a courteous protest. The governor insists:

"Utopian. I shall not review for you, my dear Admiral, the belabored
humanitarian follies of colonial conquest. I have no wish to indict the
colonies. I indict the colonists themselves, our French colonists, who are
veritably of far too inferior a quality."

"Why?" someone asks.

"Because, in the unanimous view of the French nation, the colonies
are reputed to be the last resource and supreme asylum for reprobates

---

34 Chinese province of Sichuan.

35 Province in southern Kyūshū, Japan. Its pottery became popular with European collectors in
the late nineteenth century.

36 Chamber of Deputies, France's parliament under the Third Republic (1875–1940).

of every class and ex-convicts of every court. Accordingly, the homeland keeps carefully to itself all recruits of value and exports only the rejects of its contingent. Here we shelter the rogues and the wastrels, the scroungers and the pick-pockets. — Those who clear scrub in Indo-China have proved indifferent tillers in France; the traffickers here were bankrupt there; those who hold command over lettered mandarins and secondary-school dropouts; and some of those who judge and sentence have themselves been judged and sentenced. It ought therefore not to surprise us that in this land the Westerner should be inferior morally to the Asiatic, as he is intellectually in all countries…"

Lieutenant-Governor Abel spoke in turn, the sweet, ironic voice contrasting with the rigid magistrate's face, incapable of laughter.

"Governor, at the risk of pleading against my own chapel — the colonial chapel — I would like to support your words with an anecdote. Do you know Portalière?"

"The Portalière who's chancellor of the Residency at Tonkin?"

"The very one. Do you know his story?"

"I know he's incompetent. Dubois, the former minister, made us a sad gift of him last year."

"Yes. And now let me tell you the story behind it; I know of none more instructive when it comes to the recruitment of colonists. In former days Portalière was a reporter writing in the back pages of a rag that scraped by on blackmail…"

"All right."

"He was starving…"

"Shame it didn't kill him off!"

"God does not seek the sinner's death. Just as he was reaching the end of his tether providence saw fit to have Portalière to cross paths with the famous Madame Dupont, wife of the former minister of justice. You have heard of Madame Dupont?"

"She's a…"

"You have heard of her. Now, Portalière was both a fool and smug…"

"An exemplary colonist."

"…And these qualities endeared him to women. You can infer the rest. One fine morning Portalière was provided with a desirable sinecure: in Paris, of course. Things proceeded apace for a few months. Then Madame Dupont passed to another reporter, and the sinecure to another occupant. Portalière, finding himself back in the gutter, raised a complaint, in ungrateful words that sounded like threats."

"He was thinking of his old newspaper."

"Probably. Dupont, who detests a ruckus, resolved to condemn her former protégé to an amicable exile. The Pavillon de Flore[37] is not far from Place Vendôme. Dupont paid a visit to Dubois and held forth as follows:

"'I've got an imbecile to get rid of. Do you have some corner somewhere, preferably far off?'

"'Do I ever!' says Dubois. 'Bring the imbecile on by.'

"Portalière's brought in, with ambitions on his lips.

"'What can you do?' asked Dubois.

"'A little bit of everything.'

"'So nothing. Have you obtained your baccalaureate?'

"'No.'

"'Perfect. I've got a clerkship for you, in the civil service in Indo-China. You find this suitable, I hope?'

"'Hardly', says Portalière with scorn. 'Clerkship! Phooey! Don't you have anything better?'

"'You're put off! Well, let's see if we can't oblige Dupont… How would you like to earn six thousand francs in a nice, salubrious country?'

"'Where?'

"'In Annam.'

"'The Annam in Africa?'

"'Yes.'

"'Six thousand… I won't say no… Six thousand to start? What would I be doing?'

"'You'd be chancellor of the Residency.'

"Portalière's face lights up instantly.

"'Chancellor?' he says. 'That I'll accept. A position sort of like Bismarck's, no?'"[38]

The governor does not deign to laugh.

"This is the way of things! Such are our aspiring colonists — rotten, and ignorant, to boot — and ready, whatever the circumstances, to play Napoleon at a moment's notice. They're already blemished, often defective, by the time they get to Saigon, and the double influence of abnormal surroundings and a depressing climate rounds them out and does them in.

---

37 The part of the Louvre Palace where the French Ministry of the Colonies had its seat. It now forms part of the museum.

38 Otto von Bismarck (1815–98), prime minister of Prussia, chancellor of the German Empire.

They promptly spurn our principles and amplify our prejudices, and, unlike those who lived through 1815,[39] they soon forgot everything, while learning nothing. — It's a human dunghill. — And perhaps it's for the best…"

"A paradox?"

"Surely not! It is perhaps best that over these colonial lands, freshly plowed and tilled beneath the stomping of the many races that mix here, some human manure be spread, so that from the purulent rot of old ideas and old morals the lands might yield future civilizations."

In a corner of the parlor Fierce wields a palm frond with a tortoiseshell handle to fan Mademoiselle Sylva, who is taking tea. On hearing the word *civilization* he looks up. The governor finishes his speech:

"Amid these contemptible colonial plebs I have glimpsed a few superior individuals. These have drawn benefit from the milieu and climate, and have become, as it were, the forerunners of tomorrow's civilizations. They live on the margins of our overly conventional lives, they have renounced all our fanaticisms and religions, and if they abide by our penal code it is, I believe, in a conciliatory spirit. Such men could thrive only in an Indo-China at once very old and very new: it required the ambiance of the Aryan, Chinese, and Malay philosophies ground slowly together; it required the corruption of a society in which European morals had collapsed; it required the burning humidity of Saigon, where all things — energies, beliefs, the sense of good and evil — melt and dissolve in the sun! These men who have leapt ahead of our century are civilized. We are barbarians."

The soft voice of the lieutenant-governor concludes:

"So much the better for us."

Madame Abel, aware of Saigonese life, and no fool, though good at heart, murmurs in turn:

"Yes. It is good, perhaps, neither to lag behind nor to get ahead of one's time."

Riveted to the wall at the far end of the parlor is a bronze plaque. Admiral d'Orvilliers has gone to lean against the wall nearby.

"I understand none of this," he says, "yet here is a barbarian I like better than your civilized men."

He reads the plaque's engraved inscription:

---

39   Year of the Battle of Waterloo.

✚

*

*   *

IN MEMORY

OF VICE ADMIRAL COURBET40

COMMANDER-IN-CHIEF OF THE FAR EAST SQUADRON

HERE WERE INTERRED FOR THEIR RETURN TO FRANCE

IN MOURNING

THE MORTAL REMAINS OF THE ILLUSTRIOUS SAILOR

[HORIZONTAL LINE]

THUAN-AN, SON-TAY, FOULCHEU, KELUNG, SHEÏPOO,

PESCADORES

1883–1884–1885

Mademoiselle Sylva rises and approaches the epitaph. She reads it to herself, then asks in reverent contemplation, like one kneeling before the Sacred Table to receive First Communion:

"Was it here that he died?"

"No," replies d'Orvilliers. "He died aboard another *Bayard*, since decommissioned.[41] But what does it matter! Old folks like me believe in ghosts, and I'm convinced that the old ship's soul lives on in this new hull — who knows? — perhaps the old admiral's as well."

"A very great admiral," the governor politely proclaims.

"Yes. An admiral such as we no longer have. An admiral of olden days, cousin to the pirate captains who ruled the sea — a barbarian, in short — nothing like today's soldier; not one of the civilized at all — quite the opposite…

"A matter of taste! You may prefer your men of tomorrow, my dear Governor. I prefer their forebears, as is proper to one of my age. Unquestionably, those forebears were unrefined, even somewhat savage; they took after primitive man, kept the simple instincts, the brutalities, the

---

40   Anatole-Amédée-Prosper Courbet (1827–85), vice admiral of the French navy. Participant in the Revolution of 1848 as a student at the École Polytechnique, Paris. Victor in the Tonkin Campaign (1883–86) against the Vietnamese (Annamites), the Black Flag Army of Liu Yongfu, and the Chinese armies of Guanxi and Yunnan. Distinguished himself also in the Sino-French War (1884–85).

41   This was an ironclad, under sail, that had served in the Sino-French War. Courbet died aboard her of cholera in the Pescadores Islands, about three months after the Pescadores Campaign, one of the war's last. The ship was launched in 1880 and scrapped in 1910.

sincerities as well; they were unsubtle, and they were intolerant; they neither understood nor put up with any contradiction, and in their naive pride held the rest of the world in scorn. Their ideal was to do battle, and they conceived of nothing more beautiful than to be soldiers…

"And, upon my faith, they were indeed beautiful soldiers. They bore no resemblance to the soldiers of today: they were neither literary nor musical nor artistic. On the battlefield, though, the enemy was afraid of them. They were boors almost to a man and would insolently flout constitutions and laws, but when the time came they would lay down their lives for the same laws they'd scoffed at before.

"We don't have people like that anymore: the race is dead. For better or worse, as you like. They were a barbarian race, clashing with the modern world, but a picturesque one and glorious, a race of soldiers. There are no soldiers anymore. I knew the last of them: Courbet, Sylva,…"

Monsieur d'Orvilliers breaks off, for Mademoiselle Sylva is right next to him. He had forgotten her in the heat of his speech. Mademoiselle Sylva, however, is impassive, although pallid. Fierce, eyes locked on her, can just make out the tremble of her proud lip and the feverish fingers clasping her handkerchief.

The governor, skeptical and courteous, objects:

"No soldiers anymore? My dear Admiral, just consider that right has never been more aligned with might than at present, through parliaments and majorities. Never have soldiers been more necessary. I concede that they do not resemble the soldiers of old, or that they are, if you insist, literary, artistic, and philosophical. But do you believe they are therefore poorer soldiers?"

A pout spread beneath Monsieur d'Orvilliers's shaggy mustache.

"It is a question of manner," he murmurs.

And he yielded the point, with melancholic cheer:

"In fact, you are right. One must be optimistic. Besides, the new generations are not to be disdained…"

He takes three steps and lays a hand on Fierce's shoulder.

"Here is proof. Behold this lad: nurse fed, versifying, sonata-composing — tainted with every vice. — But do not be fooled by the goody-goody face: I know full well that at the right time my little Fierce will not shilly-shally, and will teach me a lesson in honor."

Phlegmatic and resigned, Fierce does not flinch. He restrains with respect an ironic grimace. This is not the first time he has stonily endured the praise of his candid superior. Though at times it tests his loyalty, he always bears the praise in silence, out of friendly pity for its source. Not that he would ever endeavor to take the old man's medieval fanaticism further! But why upset people?

Now, however, he looks up, and what should he meet but the gaze — warm with admiration — of Sélysette Sylva. Mademoiselle Sylva has taken the dithyrambic couplet seriously. Monsieur de Fierce is now set up for her as a hero…

And suddenly, without knowing why, Monsieur de Fierce blushes with shame.

An hour and a half. The guests take their leave, early, because of the afternoon nap. The parasols are brought in. With a pretty flourish Mademoiselle Sylva taps her hair, tousled in the currents of the punkahs.

"A mirror?" Fierce suggests.

He leads her to his room, nearby, and sets her before the big mirror of his armoire, draped in grey velvet. Mademoiselle Sylva is all admiration.

"What stylish quarters you have! All these silks and muslins! All these little books with plush bindings! Are they for young ladies? May one have a look?"

"One may not," says Fierce, laughing.

"Ah. I shall have to wait until I'm married. — Your quarters are a little paradise. And yet…"

"And yet?"

"Are they not a bit sad, in the long run, what with all the grey hangings?"

Fierce smiles.

"You do not like sad things, Mademoiselle?"

"Not much… I especially find that life is sad enough without our fashioning artificially sad things. You would be wise, Monsieur, to send all these things to a dyer, so that he might send them back sky blue."

"The color of your eyes."

"What nonsense! My eyes are green…"[42]

She shrugs, with no hint of coquetry, and gives him her still-gloved hand.

"Au revoir, and thank you very much."

He takes the hand, pretty and frank, with nothing limp or wavering in

---

42 As explained in note 30, her eyes are *pers*, grey: that is, blue-green.

its boyish grip. Seized with a sudden desire, he leans toward the hand and tries to raise it to his lips.

It is of little account to kiss a young girl's fingers. Still, Mademoiselle Sylva balks — she is discreet but clear. — One does not touch Mademoiselle Sylva.

Who knows, Monsieur de Fierce? Perhaps this failed kiss, the unknown taste of it, will disturb many of your nights.

XI

ierce signed the report he had been writing and slipped it into an envelope, then opened a box and looked over some Japanese prints. It was past six o'clock: the day's task was done.

The prints were ingeniously obscene. Indeed, Fierce collected no other kind: it pleased him so to honor artists who had not burdened themselves with lies and modesty. He venerated Hokusai and Utamaro.[43]

---

43 Two masters of Japan's *ukiyo-e* (pictures of the floating world) style of woodblock prints and painting. Hokusai (1760–1849) is the better known today, especially for his *Thirty-Six Views of Mount Fuji*. Utamaro (1753–1806) is known best for depicting women.

He leafed through. Amid cherry trees in blossom and azure-tinged horizons mousmés made wholesome love with samurai clad for war. There was nudity only in spots, but it was of the most realistic sort. Fierce engaged in monologue.

"A most curious art. The exactitude! The flights of sensuality! No irony, never a joke or a snigger or a smile. Men and women going at it, pouring in their heart and muscle…"

With a fingernail he traced the lumps of biceps and calf. Overstretched, robes and kimonos tore apart in the fury of the clasping. A woman's head caught his eye. It was a modern print, and the artist, rather than imitate the long, disdainful beauty of a Japanese lady, or slap on the plain, simple little smile of a mousmé, had sought for inspiration in the West. Fierce smiled. The grey eyes and finger-flick upturned nose recalled for him the pleasant profile of Mademoiselle Sylva.

"This woman here," he thought, "is less pretty, though it's true I don't have such plunging evidence for the young Sélysette…"

The print's heroine, skirts hiked up, lay on her back in a flowery field, while an excited young man hastened towards her. The young man was fussily drawn. Displeased, Fierce turned the page.

"No indeed," he repeated," these things have nothing to do with Chinese indecencies. In fact…"

He took up a Chinese album, bound in old silk.

"…There! This girl on all fours, waiting at the pleasure of an ill-disposed old man — a Japanese would never do this. For one thing, the subject, chock full of irony as it is, would never tempt him. Worse, he'd never think to sully a sensual engraving with a grimace like that, mocking pleasure and partner alike."

He looked for Hokusai's famous *Dream*.[44]

"… This is what he'd imagine: an impossible scuffle of faceless beings. And he'd give ten pudenda to each, to fit sixty couplings onto the page instead of six."

He admired the prodigious print for a good while, then rose and dressed to go out.

As he was going to trade his uniform jacket for a white tuxedo, he paused to look again at the Japanese image resembling Sélysette Sylva, taking secret pleasure in concealing with his hand the figure of

---

44   The *Dream of the Fisherman's Wife*, or *Octopi and the Shell Diver*, a woodblock print depicting a woman and two octopi in the throes of oral sex.

the realistic male lover, as well as the disorder of the female, so as to see nothing but a malicious face smiling up at him. Then he donned the tuxedo and grabbed a straw hat: the sun was going down, so he could spare himself the helmet.

"In fact," he said aloud, breaking the silence, "it's stupid to have all this grey in my quarters. I've been splenetic all morning. Out with it."

He left.

On the wharf he hesitated between various distractions. He had had a glum day, unable to avoid fixating on the inanity of his pleasures and of his life; and by an ironic, absurd contrast the image of, Sélysette Sylva, that girl unknown to him two days earlier, had danced before his eyes some twenty times, the bloom of happiness on her every smile. Seen in repetition, the image did not fail to irritate, agreeable as it was to look upon. Now Fierce wanted to push it aside, to taste a sort of revenge, with an earnest plunge into the delights of the *Thousand Nights and a Night*,[45] forever prohibited to innocent young maidens, and outside their knowledge.

But when the time came he found he lacked the enthusiasm to carry out his plan.

Debauchery is not much fun when your heart isn't in it. The hour had passed, he thought, to go see Liseron, his mistress: Mévil might come by, and Liseron hated to be caught in the act. The hour had passed, also, to seek among the *congaï* or the métisses of Tân-Dĩnh or Hóc-Môn for a willing companion before dinner: all of them were no doubt parading their Asian graces in the victorias of the Inspection. The wharf was deserted. Fierce deemed himself alone in the world, and unable to join another's solitude to his own. He stopped a passing empty carriage and had himself conveyed to the club.

It was on such days of boredom that Fierce would repair to the club. There was nothing charming for him in colonial society per se: it was too much the human dunghill described by the governor-general. Many of the club's members were of a dubious sort, admitted for lack of competition, and respected above all for their happy impunity — moreover, men of the world, or striving to seem so, and putting a happy face on the ravages of foolhardy living — convivial rogues, able in every mediocre circumstance

---

45 The most common contemporary French translation of the *Arabian Nights* is by Antoine Gallande (*Les Mille et une nuits*), but the translation that an English-speaking libertine like Fierce just might have is the one cited here, published in 1888, unabridged, unexpurgated, and with much commentary, by polyglot, explorer, ethnologist, and force of nature Richard F. Burton.

to make a show of honor, even honesty. Fierce, jaded, paid no more heed to this comic stew.

It is true that certain individuals stood out from the crowd. Dr. Mévil would sometimes show up at the club — when some new intrigue obliged him to dine with a husband. — Torral would frequent the casino, where he could see a maximum of Saigonese in one place, the better to disdain them at a stroke. And still other remarkable men, civilized or barbaric, would put in an appearance: Rochet the journalist, Malais the banker, Ariette the attorney — all who had risen above the hoi polloi and attained the aristocracy of freebooters; all who had made their fortunes, and achieved varying degrees of sumptuousness, with something more than simple fraud; all who had shown the skill or daring to mint their money while abiding by the law, although at the expense of others. These were pleasing to Fierce, and as his carriage rolled towards the club he looked forward to running across a few of them.

Fortune smiled on him. Malais was reading the evening editions in the newspaper room. At first Fierce saw only the stack of papers, but at his approach the stack fell over to reveal the banker, already standing. By turns a soldier, sailor, typographer, businessman, and colonist, Malais had retained from his many trades an active energy that showed forth in both his rare, brusque gestures and his sober, prompt words.

"I trust Madame Malais is well," said Fierce. — He had encountered the young woman twice at the theater and had not courted her, though he thought her what she was: delicious.

"My wife is well, and without cocaine," said the banker, laughing.

Fierce raised his eyebrows.

"Ah yes. You're unaware. Your friend Mévil wanted to prescribe for her his favorite regimen. That ingenious boy has been drugging most of the women here. It serves him as a pretext to gain their favor. With those pills of his, imported from parts unknown, he renders his patients numb to the heat — not without certain nervous inconveniences, of course; but one does not look too closely in Saigon. — As he finds my wife not unpleasing, our friend Mévil endeavored to fly to the rescue, cocaine in tow. Well, I put a stop to that: not that I hold anything against him, mind you."

Fierce smiled.

"Are you dining here?" asked the banker.

"Yes, I think I am."

"I am as well. Do me honor of sharing my table. I've put in a hard day's work, and deserve the reward of such good company as yours."

They sat. Malais kicked aside the newspapers lying around him.

"The idiots at these rags! They fill column after column with the governor's latest visit to some hospice or other, and print not a syllable on English affairs! Gang of ruffians!"

His eyes snapped to Fierce and fixed him, scrutinizing.

"But you, the aide-de-camp: you should know…"

"Nothing at all," said Fierce in sincerity. "You mean the diplomatic tensions? I think it's nothing serious, but I have no information on the matter myself. Besides, the cables are English, and if the impossible were to occur and war broke out we'd learn of it from the enemy squadron tasked with our destruction."

"Quite the pickle you're in," observed the banker.

He reflected for a moment and shrugged.

"No matter, anyway. I've got nothing to gain from it, or to lose."

"Even in case of war?"

"Here I am a banker, an administrator, and a tax farmer, by golly. All of the country's affairs pass through my hands: and what's a war to me? Let the government change hands; I'll be indispensable no matter who takes charge."

When the hour struck they dined. Malais drank nothing but a dry champagne sent to him from America, and which Fierce liked. Wine, at any rate, seemed to Fierce a convenient refuge from his present melancholy. Later a few opium pipes managed to restore his optimism. He entered into a mild intoxication.

Boys cleared the table. On the terrace Malais ordered more of his champagne. They continued to drink while smoking Turkish cigarettes. Fierce admired the blue smoke as it swirled through the motes in the electric lamplight, like the swirling clouds round a ride of the Valkyries.

"Do you enjoy a daydream?" asked Malais.

"You do not."

"No. I don't like bastard things. Daydreaming is neither work nor rest."

"You're a man of action."

Fierce was smiling, and there was scorn in his smile, but Malais seemed not to notice.

"You too! A sailor?"

"No," replied Fierce, still smiling. "I wear the livery but lack the soul. I'm more of a friend to Raymond Mévil than you think."

"Too bad" was the flat reply.

But he maintained the cordialities. Fierce pleased him as he was, and he said so.

"You're worth more than your friend. You're more intelligent."

"What do you know of it?"

"I know."

He tossed away his cigarette with a frown of disdain for blond tobacco — or for something else — and selected a cigar from Manilla, then continued:

"Raymond Mévil lives for and through women. I reproach him for that, as it is at once degrading and inept."

Fierce did not deign to protest. He was growing curious:

"Now that you mention it," he said, "you seem well informed on the matter of Raymond's pretty friends."

Malais laughed.

"You are as well informed as I. It seems to me, you have at least one mistress in common."

"Tut," said Fierce, denying nothing. "That one hardly counts. I wanted to speak of the others — the ones one does not remunerate, or at least not officially."

"Tut," Malais repeated. "Those hardly count more. Their names should be known to you. They're so many open secrets. The lovely Liseron can tell you more than I, and her revelations will likely come with some spice…"

Fierce shrugged and poured out drinks.

"I prefer this," he said, raising his glass, "to matters of women."

"Right you are," said Malais. "It's at once less dangerous and less silly."

Fierce drank.

"There's nothing silly about it," he said, filling his empty glass. "There are different brains and dissimilar men. I like this," he said, tapping the bottle with his finger and producing a hollow sound, "and this," he said, puffing his cigarette. "That's the thing for me. Mévil prefers dark or light hair, green or violet eyes, pink or brown breasts. That's the thing for him. You, my friend, are happy to levy taxes, manage a bank, or make a loan. That's the thing for you. It's all valid. There's nothing silly."

"Sure," said Malais, "but harken nevertheless to this, Monsieur de Fierce. Sooner or later you will find that the Turkish tobacco has become insipid, that the wine has turned; sooner or later you will see your friend

Mévil leave behind his cortege of women pink, brown, and violet and take a seat in the little car for ataxics. Whereas I will never — you hear me? never! — cease to find my life of travails and battles, my life of motion and action, to be good and flavorful, because it is in harmony with what is strongest and healthiest in man: the combative instinct, the instinct for self-preservation. — My word, you have me philosophizing. Me, philosophizing!"

He burst into laughter and rose to his feet. Through its French windows the casino sent the glitter of lights and clink of piled piasters onto the terrace.

"Monsieur de Fierce," Malais announced, "this evening I'm going to initiate you into the life that is mine. Come. We'll play. We'll play seriously, like men who are out not to kill time but to win a fortune. I promise you powerful emotions and vigorous joys, without the slightest frisson of neurosis. Come."

Fierce upended the last bottle: it was empty. He rose and followed Malais without a word. He was drunk, and still speaking little.

Seven, eight, nine poker tables, and a *baccara automobile*[46] — in all, ten mats of green felt laid out under the electric chandelier. Despite the fans at the room's four corners, and the punkahs on the ceiling, and although all the windows were open to let in the night air, it was hotter than a forge in the casino; hair stuck to temples, shirt fronts imbued tuxedos with their damp, and the needful pushing and dragging of bets brought sweat and suffering to every face.

Malais crossed the room, his vigorous step clashing with the ardent torpor of the scene. A gambler rose from the last table, and Fierce was astonished to recognize Torral. The engineer gambled but rarely, and then only to test, cards in hand, his favorite theories on the calculus of probabilities. His test was no doubt complete, as he refused to sit back down. His partners

---

46 Baccara automobile — a term the translator has found once outside the present novel — appears to be a joke referring to the *chemin-de-fer* (literally *railroad*) variety of baccarat.

The following item ran in the French daily *Le Journal* on 14 April 1899: "In yesterday's *Vélo* [a periodical titled *Bicycle*] we find some complementary information on the famous race whose organization the Automobile-Club de France is supposed to have entrusted to a morning daily newspaper, under the condition that the newspaper give twenty-five thousand francs for the prizes. Only the A.C.F.'s board knows that the prizes have been provided by the gambling houses of the cities that the projected race crosses. Therefore, as one of our spiritual fellows was saying to us yesterday, we are going to de-christen baccara chemin-de-fer and henceforth call it baccara... automobile.

"Jokes aside, we have a hard time seeing the Automobile-Club de France sponsor this race-advertisement, and an even harder time seeing the sort of gentlemen who at present partake in Automobile sport lend their support to such a scheme.

"Let us nevertheless await the decision of the A.C.F.'s board on the matter."

were Ariette, Abel, and a German by the name of Schmidt, owner of flour mills. The soft-voiced lieutenant-governor welcomed the new arrivals, and the still lemon-colored attorney flashed a somber smile on his glabrous face.

"Monsieur de Fierce is playing, and I'm backing him halfway," Malais announced. "We'll be playing for high stakes, gentlemen. You've been warned."

"I'll stay to watch, then," said Torral.

He took a seat beside the banker, behind Fierce. Fierce, silent, shuffled and dealt.

The green tables tinkled with piastres amid the rustle of bank notes. The piasters made more noise and took up more space than the discreet gold coins of Europe would have done; they stood in well for the heavy riches of the trafficking, speculating Far East. There were piastres from Indochina, struck with a sedentary Republic — piastres from England, with Albion's helmeted effigy — Japanese yen and Chinese taels, with nightmarish twining dragons — and especially Mexican piastres, with liberty's eagle in triumph over the serpent and, on the reverse, the Phrygian cap radiant — all of them big, thick coins worth their weight in pure silver. Many of them were new, because Mexico spills the excess from its mines onto the two shores of the Pacific, but most were old, worn, blackened, spotted with the greasy inks of the Chinese moneychangers' mysterious stamps; these latter coins had of course passed through many yellow, rapacious hands, lain hidden in the depths of many extraordinary purses, purchased many goods unknown to Europe, and served for strange bargains outside Western imagining. They came perhaps from frozen Chihli,[47] or from Kwangtung,[48] where the women do not bind their feet — they came from arid Yunnan,[49] or from Chin-King,[50] birthplace of emperors — they came perhaps from farther afield, from the remote, secret provinces of the oldest parts of China, from Szechuan, where men proliferate, from nearly Tartar Kansu,[51] from Shensi,[52] a cemetery of prehistoric capitals — they came from every corner of the colossal empire where countless Chinamen bustle and sell and buy, unflagging in their quest for riches.

---

47   Or Zhili. A region of China that was dissolved in 1911 and is now called Hebei.

48   Guangdong, a Chinese province on the South China Sea.

49   A mountainous Chinese province bordering on the countries of Indochina.

50   Perhaps Chonqing.

51   Chinese province of Gansu.

52   Chinese province of Shaanxi.

"You who've made a profession of disdaining men," muttered Malais to Torral, "look upon the poker players: you shall find in them food for your pessimism. The high-society sheen flakes right off the face of men who win or lose money. Even as they feign boredom or a smile their every gesture lays them bare." He lowered his voice. "Look at Schmidt: he may be a millionaire, but the shop he comes out of has shrunken his eyes and his belly; he stacks his piastres and counts them with hooked fingers. Look at Abel: the honorable figure of the French civil servant, accustomed to juggling other people's money; for him the words *ten, twenty, thousand* do not differ in their definition; his concern is the cards, not the stakes. And look especially at Ariette: he pleads and quibbles with himself, weighs the pros and cons of every hand, gauges his adversaries at a glance, and closes his eyes lest they read something in his look — as at court when defending a bad cause; he seeks only to win."

"You're a good psychologist," said Torral.

"Yes. A tax farmer had better be."

Malais smiled. Torral indicated Fierce with his eyes.

"And this one?"

"This one," said Malais, "is a sick man. The natural instincts have waned in him. But gambling is a good healer: soon you shall see the sick man revive, bestir himself, seize his ordinary mask of skepticism, and cast it aside."

"It is no mask."

"We shall see."

Luck was on Fierce's side. He won every other hand, and the pile of coins and notes before him grew to impertinent dimensions.

"I believe," said Malais to Torral, "that you have made a special study of the laws and phenomena of chance. How do you account for the fact observed by gamblers that streaks come in series rather than intermittently?"

The financier enjoyed plying specialists with questions. But Torral, brutal as always, shrugged and said:

"The explanation would be lost on you. You wouldn't understand."

"Thank you," said Malais, without annoyance. "Explain nonetheless."

"All right. Listen. All games played since the beginning of the world form a whole, do they not? A finite and determined whole. Well, then, let n be the number of games."

"N?"

"I said you wouldn't understand… Each of these n hands could be won or lost, and so the set has a number of solutions equal to 2^n."

"Ah…?"

"Only one of those 2^n solutions has occurred — naturally. And it so happens that this unique solution has admitted series and rejected intermittencies. Which is what we have set out to demonstrate."

Malais raised his eyebrows. Torral, more ironical, continued in professorial tone:

"Corollary: at the limit — that is, in the eternity of centuries — n tends toward infinity, as does 2^n, and the probability of the realized hypothesis tends toward zero. So the hypothesis does not exist. Therefore, poker has never been played. It is an illusion…"

"Huh?"

"An illusion."

"You're right," said Malais with a shrug. "I don't understand."

He turned back to the game. At the far end of the room the clock struck eleven.

"Gentlemen," said Abel, "if you wish, we shall limit our play to four more hands. It's getting late."

No one complained. Abel dealt the cards. Schmidt took a few notes from his basket and slipped them into his pocket. Ariette took successive glances at Fierce, as if to reckon his winnings, perhaps to plan their appropriation.

But Fierce won twice, one hand after the other.

Ariette dealt in turn — for the penultimate hand — and laid down a considerable pot.[53] Schmidt took fright and folded. Abel and Fierce stayed in. The attorney raised and doubled. But Fierce beat three aces and won again.

"What insolent luck," said Malais.

Fierce turned to smile.

"I'm ashamed."

He could not have been calmer.

"As you can see," said Torral, "it's no mask."

They ante'd for the last time.

"Fifty piastres," said Abel.

"A hundred," said Fierce.

"Yes. A hundred."

"Two hundred," said Ariette.

---

53 The word appears in English.

All stayed in. On to the cards.

"Three cards."

"One."

"There you go," said the attorney.

He'd given his cards a long look. Malais, curious, was staring at him. But Ariette, eyes closed, seemed a faithful if ugly caricature of mystery itself.

"Is he bluffing?" whispered Torral, taking an interest despite his disdain.

"I don't think so," the banker whispered back.

Fierce checked his last card and passed. Schmidt opened the betting. Abel raised.

"I raise two hundred piastres," said Ariette, in the most colorless voice.

Fierce pushed in some notes.

"I see your two hundred and raise four hundred."

Abel and Schmidt folded, one with a smile, the other with a sigh.

"I see your four hundred and raise a thousand," said Ariette, never opening his eyes.

Several players from neighboring tables made their way over. For Saigon this was a big pot: the equivalent of four hundred French louis.

Fierce turned to Malais.

"I beg your pardon," he said. "I am ill serving your interests, but I am also truly ashamed of my streak."

He laid his cards on the table.

"I'm sticking, without raising: royal flush."

"He had the ace, the king, the queen, the jack, and the ten of hearts — the unbeatable hand. Ariette went pale after his fashion, lemon turning to straw. Cries of admiration saluted the winner. His fingers not trembling at all, Fierce drew the pot to himself and mixed it into his pile of notes. He then divvied it all into two equal mounds and asked Malais to choose.

Ariette, meanwhile, had in the blink of an eye returned to his senses.

"My dear sir," he said, "I bet a thousand piastres on my word, and I owe them to you. You shall have them tomorrow morning…"

"Not too early, I beg you," said the lieutenant, laughing. "I am at times not a morning person."

Ariette, with infinite grace, summoned a laugh.

"In that case," he said, "I'll do you one better. I never break my fast before noon. Is that late enough? And will you do me the honor of sitting at my table? There I'll settle our little difference, and you will spare me a maritime voyage, which I would I find frightful. Your *Bayard* is anchored so far from the wharf!"

"A hundred twenty meters out," thought Fierce. But he didn't hesitate.

"You are too kind. I accept."

"Until tomorrow, then," said Ariette, and set off with a smile on his lips. Many people admired his nerve; he had lost at least four thousand piastres.

Fierce lit a cigarette. Malais looked him over attentively.

"I fear you're sicker than I thought. My remedy has failed to work."

Fierce smiled.

"Were you hoping to see him dance with joy over his pile of piastres?" said Torral. "Too civilized for that, Fierce is!"

"Too sick," Malais repeated. "Incurable."

He held out his broad hand to the lieutenant.

"Good evening, partner. Try to have a nightmare; it'd be the best thing that could happen to you."

"Going home so early?"

"It's not so early. Do you know that by five o'clock every morning I'm out on the steeplechase track riding my horse? No better prelude to a day's work. Good evening."

Torral sniggered.

"Quite the life you lead. All those millions of yours, and yet you have to go to bed before sleep has hit you, and right when the city turns pleasant!"

The banker turned back and delivered his riposte:

"A matter of taste. You sleep during the day, I during the night. This shocks you?"

"No," said the engineer, "but I work to live, and you live to work. *That* shocks me."

"I'm sorry you see it that way," Malais coldly said. "You'll pardon me if I continue, however, as I find it suits me. What would you have me do? You must take me as I am or leave me. I'm not a civilized man of your kind: my life is simpler and ruled like score paper. I earn money and sleep with my wife."

"And you provide her with children."

"When I can."

They smiled upon each other in reciprocal contempt.

"In fact," jeered Malais, "it's why my race is superior to yours. Yours will die out; mine will endure."

"The pride of the civilized," said Torral, "lies in leaving no successors. The task is done. What need for other laborers?"

"Pride of the mad."

"You think me mad, do you?"

"Yes… And a malefactor too."

Torral shrugged. Malais left.

Fierce, silent, lit another cigarette. The engineer turned toward him.

"Coming?"

"Where you like."

They went out together. Fierce's piastres rang in his heavy pocket. He considered not without melancholy that all these winnings gave him no joy.

"Two, three thousand piastres," he thought. "At the ordinary rate for women there's enough here to fund the spasm for a regiment…"

"Where are we going," asked Torral.

"To the devil! Life is stupid."

XII[A]

ierce peered into the shop window, forehead to the glass, at the fashionable jeweler's.

He was looking through the open jewel cases for one case in particular. There were too many things on display: too many rings and bracelets, and especially too much of that thin, dented silverware they make in Hong Kong. Amid the dazzle of thimbles, cups, saucers, and ewers he could not find what he was after.

He entered the shop. Fernande the Jewess, a celebrity in Saigon, approached and greeted him with her discreet smile.

"I'm looking for a bracelet," Fierce explained, "a circle of gold and emeralds. You had it out the other day…"

The door suddenly opened again, and the tall figure of Malais appeared in its frame. Fierce hadn't seen the banker in two days — since the poker game.

"Well," said Malais familiarly, "what are you doing here? Getting a plaything for Liseron, I'll wager…"

He called over the Jewess, who was searching through the jewel cases.

"Fernande! My fan? I suppose it's ready this time?"

He turned to Fierce.

"A gift from my wife to Madame Abel. Think it's in good taste?"

Fierce took the fan with admiration.

"Wow, it's fit for adoration! Where'd you steal these feathers from?"

The fan was of marabou and mother-of-pearl. A golden vine, inlaid on the flat, carried black pearls in lieu of grapes.

"You know," said Fierce with a laugh, "this vine here is indiscreet: it bespeaks a *pot-de-vin*."[54]

"And that bracelet there: what does *it* bespeak?"

The bracelet was a slave ring, weighty and enriched with big cabochons. The Jewess read the price off the label: two thousand piastres.

"A ready investment for your winnings of two days ago."

Fierce smiled. Malais slapped his forehead.

"But of course! This stone-stuffed ingot is headed to Rue Chasseloup-Laubat!"

Fierce pretended to search his memory.

"Rue Chasseloup…?"

"Go ahead, play the innocent. To Madame Ariette's."

"I entreat you…," began the officer, curtly.

But Malais shrugged.

"It's no use taking offense, my friend! You're going to make Fernande laugh. Discretion would be misplaced here…"

Fierce thought of Mévil and decided his play: not to deny it.

"Devil of a man! How did you know?"

"Because you're the twentieth man it's happened to."

Malais had taken a seat, after a glance at his watch. He doubtless had some time on his hands, and paused for some talk.

"The twentieth. Oh, you've entered into a typical family. Old acquaintances of mine. I met the Ariettes at Nouméa,[55] eight years ago.

54　A bribe. A *pot-de-vin* is literally a jar of wine, figuratively a sum that would allow one to purchase a jar of wine, and by extension a reward. Here the *vin* relates to the jewelry's vine.

55　The capital of New Caledonia, a French territory in the southwest Pacific Ocean, about 750

They were newlyweds, and their honeymoon turned out to be russet.[56]
They didn't like each other, for lack of familiarity, but they soon became
familiar…

"The woman was as pretty then as she is now. Someone took note,
and this someone was an archbishop's son, and suitably rich — one of your
comrades, the ship-of-the-line lieutenant in command of the stationary
ship[57] at Caledonia. What happened is what always happens: one fine
evening Ariette timed things out and caught them in the throes of love.
A tactful man, he made no fuss, and accepted fifty thousand francs not to
make any."

"He paid, this archbishop's son?"

"Madame Ariette made him pay. You are familiar with her method, I
suppose."

"Then what?"

"Then husband and wife struck a bargain: all liaisons were henceforth
permitted to both parties, on condition that they prove profitable, and the
gains are split, honestly."

"Tut!" said Fierce. "It's modern, and there's no hypocrisy in it."

He paid for the bracelet.

"Two thousand piastres," said Malais, curious… "Is it worth that much?"

Fierce thought for a moment.

"No… And yet…"

He explained:

"No woman is worth two thousand piastres, or even two hundred. The
pleasant — and, in fact, monotone — sensation that our fair collaborators
provide for us in our most intimate moments ought reasonably to be
reckoned at a much lower price. To my taste, however, that overly vaunted
sensation is but one of the prurient pleasures. Indeed, I confess that I have
not desired to request it of Madame Ariette."

"How come?"

"No… We have… No matter. What *is* worth two thousand piastres,
perhaps, is the decor and the incidentals; it's the piquant contrast of the

---

miles east of Australia. It is an archipelago whose main island is Grande Terre.

56   A *lune rousse* (russet moon), as one dictionary puts it, is a full moon in April or May said to
forebode late frosts, which then turn sprouting plants red. The Fierces' honeymoon, by implication,
began cool but turned passionate.

57   A *stationnaire* is a small warship moored at the entrance to a roadstead and surveilling the
maritime traffic.

luncheon I was invited to and of the dessert I tasted of on the chaise-longue; it's the spice of the virtuous prologue: the family dining room, the husband, the four-year-old child…"

"Eight. Eight-year-old."

"Four, I tell you! It's written all over his face."

"Eight. You're forgetting the climate, which will stunt a lad, even as it works to the advantage of the mother, who grows younger in proportion."

Malais rose. Obsequious, the Jewess hastened to get the door. Fierce caressed her breast as she passed, because she was a pretty one.

"This Fernande, by the way: are you sure of her?"

"Of her discretion? She's a Jewess, for crying out loud! She's too cunning and rapacious to betray a customer if there's no profit in it. Besides, one scandal more, one scandal less: what's it to her? All the adulteries and bribes of Saigon pass through her hands. Nothing but filth in this nest of wickedness!"

"For instance, a bracelet and a fan."

"Correct! Adultery and a bribe — although my bribe is baptized, plastered,[58] sugar-coated for the mouth of semi-wholesome man Abel, whereas your adultery, as you've told me, is…"

"The sort of thing proper to little girls at a convent."

Malais's hand came to rest on Fierce's shoulder.

"This amuses you?"

"What? Convent adultery?"

"No. The life you're living, the role you're forever playing: that of the vicious braggart?"

"It does not amuse me. But you're in error. I'm not playing a role."

They walked side by side. Following behind was Malais's carriage, drawn by a splendid team of black Australians, each twice as big as an Indochinese pony.

"You embody," said the banker suddenly, "the race I most detest: the race of elegant anarchists. And yet I like you. In fact, I'd like to help you out of the quagmire you're in — yes, a quagmire; don't deny it… Now, would you mind a bit of advice? Take leave of your usual crowd and begin to frequent other people. It'd be no sacrifice for you, and you'd risk nothing in the exchange. You have no attachment to the Ariettes, the Rochets, and their band. If you only knew the sinister collection of rogues that lie

---

58 Covered with a medicative plaster.

beneath the honorable whitewash! Rochet? A blackmailer gone senile. Ariette? At once a ruffian and a liar for hire. His wife? A duplicitous whore. I prefer your Liseron a hundred times over. She doesn't hide, doesn't try to fool anyone, and doesn't demand respect…

"I'll say nothing of Torral and Mévil: they are your friends… Besides, I don't confuse them with the colonial clique; they're a whit better — and a whit worse: intelligent men gone astray. — No matter. What I want to say is that there are other people, people you don't know, and whom you might enjoy meeting: wholesome people. They exist. There aren't many, but there are some. Would you like to see them? Come to my house. I'm no wholesome man myself, by golly!"

"No?"

"No. — I'm a bandit, dear sir. I've robbed, pillaged, ransomed. I've earned money, and within that phrase lie a host of small turpitudes that tally up to both a criminal and a millionaire. However, because of these very turpitudes, of which I've had my fill, and which have turned my stomach, I have the tenderest of spots for all things wholesome. At my house, Monsieur de Fierce, you will shake no dubious hand. It's a great luxury in Saigon to refuse such handshakes, but I'm rich enough to afford such privileges. Here as elsewhere, my wife suffers only clean persons."

"And you're not afraid," Fierce teased, "that I'll be a blemish?"

"That is my affair. Come."

"When?"

"Whenever you like. There's no day set aside for the prodigal…"

They were walking past the *Hong Kong* and the *Shanghai*. With his characteristic promptitude, Malais shook his companion's hand and vanished into the porte-cochère.

Fierce walked away pensive. Red flowers rained down from the ironical poinciana overhead.

Lost in reverie, he failed to notice this as a turning of his back to his path — because the clock at the post office was striking five, the hour for the Inspection, and his victoria would be waiting on Rue Tuduc. Rue Tuduc lay near the Donnai, and Fierce, headed nowhere in particular, was walking away from the river.

He left behind the loud central streets. Shady, contemplative thoroughfares run through Saigon's northern districts. Fierce crossed Rue Chasseloup-Laubat, the Ariettes' street, without registering it; he was too busy savoring the green cool of villas hidden away in their gardens, behind wooden gates; he was unaware that one of these little houses sheltered a woman and a sofa he was intimately familiar with. His reflections were of another order.

He continued on his way, disregarding the spectacle of the street. A young, pretty *congaï* standing at the threshold of a rich Indochinese house and knocking at the door broke into a high-pitched laugh, to draw his attention. But he went on by, head down. Saigon is the best of cities if one wishes to forget all things: the excessive, damp heat numbs the senses, and the red dust of the streets mutes all living sounds.

"Life is stupid," muttered Fierce. He was sorting through all manner of messy thoughts, all pessimistic. It was beyond debate that the people he spent his time with were not only crooked by the light of conventional morality but also of the most tiresome monotony. Just as monotonous, stomach-churningly so, was his own existence; and monotonous and soon insipid were the pleasures with which he tried to spice it up. "It does not amuse me," he repeated, as he had earlier. How incredibly poor, he reflected, was the catalogue of human joys. In all and for all purposes there were five sensations deemed to be pleasant. No more than five! And the best of them, the tactile sensation, love, fit whole within its medical definition: contact between two epidermises. Nothing more, nothing better. — "Epidermises?" Fierce corrected himself: "Not even. Mucous membranes!" Four square decimeters of skin. — "And the variants? Literature! It's humiliating." His scorn flitted from Mévil, crazy enough to enjoy love, to Torral, silly enough to reduce happiness to a formula: maximum enjoyment… — "There is no enjoyment. An illusion… But what if there were? What if there were unknown joys?"

XII[B]

 ray from the already low sun struck his face. He tilted his helmet and looked around mechanically. A sign bore the street name: Rue des Moïs. The Moi are an ancient Indochinese people. — Fierce saw two rows of old trees, lined with gardens. The houses thinned out, became few and far between. The nearest was a villa in the Annamite style, broad and low, with brick walls and an overhanging roof; a big ebony veranda hid behind a curtain of creeper vine, and tall banyans cast their shadows over the varnished tiles.

A victoria was waiting at the door. A tiny *boy* kept the horses in order: horses fit for a maiden or an old woman. The street, the house, the carriage, and the solemn, pretty garden visible through the open gate existed in an exquisite harmony of simplicity and peace.

Fierce thought: "Must be nice to live there — away from all our drunkenness and all our rutting…"

He had stopped near the gate. Two women emerged from the house, and Fierce felt a secret discharge in his breast, sharp as a pistol shot. Mademoiselle Sylva was headed his way, leading towards the victoria a shuffling, white-haired old woman.

A blind woman: her mother, of course — a soft face, pale and smiling, beautiful despite the shut eyelids.

Mademoiselle Sylva, attentive and tender, carries the two parasols and a light coat for the twilight hour. The blind woman climbs aboard. The young woman helps and settles her in, then turns and notices the officer, four paces off.

"Monsieur de Fierce!"

An exclamation of frank pleasure. The quick little hand extends, wide open. Introductions ensue.

"Mama, it's Monsieur d'Orvilliers's aide-de-camp. Monsieur, Mama knows you well already. I've spoken to her at length about your ship — and about you…"

Fierce bows low. Entering the carriage has now slipped Mademoiselle Sylva's mind. She babbles joyously, delighted to see once more a gentleman who struck her fancy. Madame Sylva, judging the street an unsuitable parlor, desires to rise and receive the visitor inside the villa.

"Pray be so gracious as not to treat me as an importunate guest," protests Fierce. "No need to delay your drive on my account. Nor have I any right to your welcome, Madame, for chance alone has led me to your door. I was unaware that you lived here."

"Then chance has smiled upon us," graciously replies Madame Sylva. "But if you absolutely do not wish to enter under our roof, ride aboard the carriage with us. We shall drop you where you like…"

A final appeal from Mademoiselle Sylva:

"And that will count as a visit. We mustn't allow chance to have operated in vain."

"You make a very tempting offer," says Fierce, "but I'm certain I would only encumber you."

"Not at all! We have an excellent jump-seat, and I adore jump-seats…"

"If it's as good as all that, I'll take it for myself."

He steps nimbly aboard and sits. The carriage departs. Fierce's knees are caught between the blue skirt and the black skirt, the one and the other troubling him with the same — infinitely chaste — emotion.

"Have you nothing to do?" asks Madame Sylva. "Accompany us out to Tuduc, then. We'll be back in town before seven o'clock."

Fierce agrees, and gives warmer thanks than courtesy requires. In truth, he finds the unexpected drive enchanting. Malais's words have been clouding his thoughts for an hour, and a curiosity has taken root in him for these wholesome people whom he does not know, whom he has never known… Never, anywhere. Who can tell? Perhaps they will turn out to be more amusing and less monotonous than his usual circle of civilized — all too civilized — strumpets, spongers, and nihilists. Having sat next to this girl of true purity and candor (he never doubts her for a second), Fierce imagines that he has taken refuge — after a long, feverish season of gambling dens, little theaters, supper clubs, and brothels — atop some Alpine pinnacle and is chastely breathing the virgin air of glaciers.

…And Mademoiselle Sélysette's smile and babble are fresh and soothing — and Madame Sylva's calm visage and voice sweet and pacifying.

Monsieur de Fierce, bound up in well-being, heart benumbed with warmth, speaks not a word. The carriage rounds the old citadel on country roads and passes the arroyo at the Jardin's bridge. The bridge is empty, like the russet lanes that sleep between their hedgerows of bamboo and magnolia. Saigon is out at the Inspection, for a stroll and a flirt, and no one takes a turn through the Jardin before sundown.

Mademoiselle Sylva inquires:

"You know Tuduc, of course?"

"Tuduc…?" Fierce tears free of his soft tranquility to answer. "Tuduc? No…"

Mademoiselle Sylva shrieks, indignant, scandalized.

"You don't know Tuduc! But, good God, what have you been up to in the fortnight since the *Bayard* sailed into Saigon?"

No easy thing to say what he has been up to!

"Not much good. I always go out very late. My *saïs*[59] takes me where he likes — and it's always the Inspection…"

"The Inspection is intolerable," announces Mademoiselle Sylva, brooking no dispute. There are too many carriages, too many dresses, too many chic people on that silly, dead-straight lane. You can't even get to a trot. See if the road to Tuduc isn't a hundred times lovelier…"

Fierce is already convinced. Near the bridge the road to Tuduc is nothing more than a pleasant path snaking through rice fields and dense magnolias, but the rice fields are greener than an Irish meadow, and from their every bloom the magnolias emit an intoxicating fragrance.

"Nowhere else are there such fragrant paths," says Fierce. "Saigon is a cassolette."[60]

"Nowhere else?" asks Mademoiselle Sylva. "True, you've been to every country. Tell me about your voyages…"

Fierce, docile, tells. He has been all over the world. His eye is keen for peoples and landscapes, and from a hundred picturesque possibilities he can pick out the most novel, the most piquant detail.

He describes Japan, where he has just been. He tells of houses of white wood that seem forever new, and of the overly big trees that envelop them in mysterious coats of green. He tells of arched bridges over dry torrents, and of the rustic *ochaya* where a traveler can always find a steaming cup of

---

59 Coachman.

60 A small porcelain, glass, or metal container used for cooking and the serving of individual dishes. Saigon, then, is a compact, redolent dish.

tea, a tender *castella* cake, and the well-bred smile of a shuffling servant-girl.
He sketches the profile of peaked Fuji-san, and the processions of yellow,
blue, and mauve pilgrims that speckle its snowy cloak. — And he neglects
to mention the bamboo-fenced *yoshiwara*, the candidly hospitable mousmés,
and the *sukebē*[61] in Japan. — His neglect is effortless: Mademoiselle Sylva
exudes a contagious air of chastity.

The carriage crosses a stream on a bridge of pink brick.

"Are Japanese bridges like this one?" asks Mademoiselle Sylva.

"Not at all. There are a thousand differences — so many that I
couldn't explain. But just by looking at this stream and arch I know I'm in
Cochin-China and nowhere else. No two countries are alike the world over,
for eyes that can see."

"How fascinating," sighs the young lady, "to have seen so many things,
and then to preserve them in memory like so many photographs! — Your
head must be like an album."

"Fascinating — and sad too," objects Madame Sylva, in a pensive
voice. "The nostalgia of sailors, forever exiled from all the countries they've
loved, must be as extensive as their travels…"

Just the other week Torral was scoffing at Fierce's melancholy mood.
Fierce remembers, and Madame Sylva's sympathy is all the sweeter for it.

"So much nostalgia does not amount to sadness. We preserve a clear,
charming picture of the countries in our past, but we rarely miss them,
because today's countries are just as good. One nail drives out another.
How would you have me look back with regret on anything when I'm in this
forest of blooming magnolias?"

Mademoiselle Sylva nods her blond head.

"And tomorrow, in another forest, you'll forget this one. It's
inconstancy."

"I admit, but if I were constant I'd be unhappy."

For the first time in his life he forgets himself and dreams aloud:

"One can be inconstant without being unfaithful. I remain grateful for
the sweet moments of yesterday, but those moments are dead. Why should
their ghost ruin the sweet moments of today? When I turn the page in life
I try to look upon the next page with fresh eyes. It's easy, because no two

---

61 All things obscene. [Author's note.]

     Editor's note: Yoshiwara was a red-light district in Edo, present-day Tokyo (see note 5).
Mousmés are the girls who work in such districts, comparable with Saigon's congais, while *sukebē*
are the lechers, like Fierce, who frequent them.

pages are ever alike. In Saigon I am no longer the Japanese Fierce of two months ago, and that Japanese Fierce did not resemble the Parisian Fierce of last year, or the Turkish or Tahitian Fierce of times past…"

Amused, Mademoiselle Sylva laughs.

"Tell us of all these Fierces who are no longer you."

"They seem to me intimate friends I was once very fond of, and I sometimes imagine they still live in the countries where I knew them. The Tahitian Fierce, for instance, was a contemplative character. He liked nothing more than trees, meadows, and streams. Every day he'd walk through the countryside, wearing a *pareo* of blue canvas and a big straw hat — barefoot, naturally. In the village of Papeete, which he pompously referred to as the capital, he'd rented a small hut in the middle of a garden of coconut palms. And once a month, when letters and newspapers would arrive, covered with colorful stamps and French seals, he would leave the letters unopened and tear up the newspapers to use for kindling in his kitchen."

"And the Turkish Fierce?"

"He was a very observant Moslem, who wouldn't let a week go by without praying to Allah at some notable mosque in Istanbul. Afterwards he'd sit in silence on the terrace of an Osmanli café and contemplate the Bosporus. And every Friday — a day off — he'd go to the cemetery in Scutari[62] and daydream for four hours straight."

"Has there been a Chinese Fierce?"

"Certainly! That one would spend all his days swelled with pride over his race, the oldest in the world, and his philosophy, the most clairvoyant and ironic. He was an unbearable man: he cared only for his rice paper and his ink brushes, and held all the earth in contempt."

Mademoiselle Sylva began herself to daydream.

"Brain after brain in the same head! It's disturbing to think about. Tomorrow you'll have changed again, and if we run into each other in Paris or Japan we shall have to start fresh…"

"Perhaps. I imagine myself as a photographic plate: hit me with a ray of sunshine, and the impressed image will fade; but just apply a fixative to produce an inalterable print."

---

62 A district, now called Üsküdar, of Istanbul, and renowned to this day for its Great Cemetery, filled with cypress trees. People in this region have traditionally planted a tree at the birth and another for the death of their relations. The graves are marked with a stone at the head and a tree at the foot, and the cemetery's trees are constantly rejuvenated.

"And what fixative is that?"

"I've yet to find it."

A long silence. The road has wound its way into the areca woods by Tuduc; there are no more magnolias or rice fields or motes of red dust in the sunlight. There are nothing but arecas now, crowding their straight, slender trunks together, interlacing their open fronds fifty feet from the ground. The result is a somber temple vault resting on countless Ionic columns. The ground between the trees is brown and gleams with puddles. There is a hush over the whole forest.

Mademoiselle Sylva, hands joined on her lap, looks avidly around and says nothing. Fierce admires the grave grey eyes, and is surprised that a girl can perceive the beauty of a wood without flowers, birds, or sunlight.

"Monsieur," says the blind woman, "I believe you did not tell us everything just now. I can easily understand that with every new country you would discover a sort of new soul within yourself, but it seems to me that you would everywhere remember home, your family. And this uninterrupted memory must maintain a bond, establish a common descent, between all the different men you believe yourself in turn to be."

"I have neither family nor home," says Fierce.

"No one?"

"No one."

"That is sad at your age."

Fierce thinks. A home is a prison, and this prison is complexified with chains: parents, friends — none of that has ever tempted him. — A family? Monsieur, Madame, and the other. — Squealing, sloppy kids. — A bit of servitude, a bit of ridicule, a bit of dishonor: seductive mixture! — Fierce is about to laugh. But, raising his eyes, he sees the family before him, astonishing and disquieting: the tender, smiling mother, the pure, delicious daughter… And in sincerity he replies:

"Yes, sad — sometimes: when, wandering Jew that I am, I halt in my travels and happen upon warm and pleasant house, and through an open door spy contented husbands, beloved wives, lovely children. On such evenings my ship is sullen, my solitude heavy, and in spite of myself I wish bad things on those too-happy people. Man is an ugly, envious beast, who takes his pleasure only from the misfortunes of others, and vice versa."

The romantic legend of the errant sailor, an exile wherever he roams, nursing in silence a mortal nostalgia for tenderness and home, is a well-worn lie: a lie that will nonetheless and forever fool all women, because beneath the varied polish of their educations, fashions, and poses they all conceal an identical core of sentimental gullibility. — Monsieur de Fierce is an orphan; Monsieur de Fierce has no house, almost no country. The two sympathetic women listening to him seek delicately to soften his hard solitude.

"Monsieur," says Madame Sylva, "I fear that after all your voyages you have never yet known the most comforting thing in life — the hearth! If you like, you shall come to know ours. You are almost a son to my old friend d'Orvilliers, who was my husband's dearest companion. My house is your house…"

She raises an old hand, still soft and white, and Fierce lays upon it a welcome kiss. Mademoiselle Sélysette joyously approves.

"You are hereby enrolled! Oh, we're a very small but hand-picked band. We do not flirt or pose or gossip — three exceptions in Saigon. We play tennis — real, serious tennis. — We read, we chat, we take walks, long walks, and we shut the door to disagreeable people. A very, very small band: the governor, the Abels, Madame Malais.

"Madame Malais?"

"You know her?"

"Very little. I'm more familiar with her husband, who just today was asking me to pay him regular visits."

"Perfect timing. You'll see Madame Malais at our house, and you'll see us at hers. She's an utterly perfect friend…"

Mademoiselle Sélysette details the perfections of Madame Malais. Fierce reflects that chance can at times assume providential proportions. Yesterday's events, as if by miracle, served to render his old life tiresome, sickening; today's conspire to draw him into a new life. Yesterday his usual world laid out, like a coquette, all of its defects and blemishes; today a new and seductive world shows him its biggest door, flinging open both leaves. He will enter…

The carriage comes to a stop. The drive is over. The road has come to an end at the river, and there is no bridge or wharf. There is a ferry, and on the far bank Tuduc lies concealed amid the arecas; only three *cai-nhas*,[63] of cob and thatch, are visible.

The river slicing through like a giant lane, the forest hangs thick over the two banks. Tree roots wade all the way into the current, and a

---

63   The *cai-nha* (*cañha* in the French) is the Annamite house, as Farrère himself explains in another novel, *Une jeune fille voyagea* (1925).

moiré of green lies upon the yellow water. In this way the arecas hem the Donnai between two dense hedgerows, two palisades of pressed trunks crowned with a frieze of fronds in panache. The sun, excluded from the forest, takes its revenge between the hedgerows, along the liquid lane, and the water blazes…

The horses rest. The indifferent *saïs* knots his lash anew.

"Those undulating fronds," mutters Sélysette Sylva, "are standards planted on the forest's roof…"

The ferry drifts mid-current. Like shadow puppets, rowers appear as slender silhouettes against the ember-colored water; a *congaï* is seated at the front, feet in the water, and chirps out a discordant, plaintive song.

The sun is declining. It is time to head home. Night begins beneath the arecas. And, as droplets of six-o'clock dew begin to settle all around, Mademoiselle Sylva prudently, with a mama's care, wraps the blind woman in her coat.

…Beneath the arecas night begins…

"When I was little," Sélysette Sylva dreams aloud, "the trees in our garden seemed very tall, and the garden immense. These arecas, and this whole forest, are miniscule by comparison with my memory…"

The horses' hooves make no sound on the soft earth. The twilight invites contemplation, and confidences.

"…We lived in an old house that looked like a farmhouse. We called it the castle, because of its pointed tower. It was in the Périgord.[64] There were a lot of flowers, and a herd of goats on the hill, and little goatherd with a red beret. The walls were all covered with wisteria, and the peasants would hang lanterns and bunting from it every year when Papa would return from Africa, for the harvest… How cheery the house was when he was there! His blue dolman would spread sunshine all over… Those were some wonderful harvests! When he'd leave we'd keep a place for him at table. His plate and cutlery would be set out for every meal, as if he were present. — And then he never came back…"

Speaking low, Fierce asked:

"Is that when you left France?"

Madame Sylva's even voice replied:

"The year after. I was a widow and my daughter already grown. Her tutor was named governor in Saigon, and we followed. And I did

---

64   Former province of southwestern France, more or less coextensive with the present-day département of the Dordogne.

right, because six months later, my already ailing eyes shut forever. A blind mother, an absent tutor — my poor Sélysette would have died of boredom over there…"

Fierce looks at the white hair and unwrinkled face. In just a few years, then, the entirety of this woman's happy life had collapsed, been lopped off like a ripe ear of grain. She has lost her husband, her house, her country, and the sweet light of day. Yet she smiles. All the bitterness has not soured her courage; and for love of her daughter she has smothered her tears, stoically.

"When I was little…"

Mademoiselle Sylva recounts lovely memories of childhood. In the back of his own memory Fierce sees his own childhood, sad and lean. Tenderness swells within him for this trusting girl who with such grace is opening her little box of secrets for him.

… The magnolias, more fragrant in the dusk — the arroyo and little bridge, whose pink bricks have turned grey — the garden, where the elephants trumpet in their cages — back to town they go …

"We'll see you soon, shall we not? Very soon?"

"Tomorrow, if you'll permit me."

He walks back, through the scintillating night. The warm air is strangely brisk.

A hail from Torral on Rue Catinat.

"Cholon tonight?"

Drink, bawl, goose some girls in Cholon?

"No. I can't…" — He is lying of a sudden, without meaning to lie. — "I can't. I've been walking all afternoon and am worn out. I'm going back aboard."

XIII

n Rue Catinat, at the Inspection hour, Torral ran across Mévil, who was on foot, arms swinging loose. He was surprised, ironical.

"Where's your carriage? What the devil are you doing here when all the women are out on the Allée des Poteaux?"[65]

"I don't know."

Mévil seemed tired and dull. Torral took his arm.

"And Fierce, what's up with him? Eight days since I saw him last. The that last time was here, in the evening. He was running about like a foal. I invite him out for the night, and he yells that he can't, he's all tuckered out, and speeds off. Gone ever since."

"I glimpsed him yesterday, from afar, in the Malais's landau."

"He's gone in for that!"

Astonishment had brought Torral to a stop.

"Yes. They speak of him often in that house, and in others."

"I'd thought him less foolish."

---

65   Probable reference to the Allée des Poteaux in the Bois de Boulogne, Paris: itself a lane for carriage rides.

They walked side by side.

"Malais," said Torral, "is at the moment earning a fortune on that rice business. The levying of the tax was conceded to him for a mere four million, because the governor didn't dare levy it himself. But Malais dares. He's hired two thousand rascals armed with Winchesters, and the tax is going to earn him eight million. — On the other hand, we're going to have a revolt."

Mévil made a gesture of indifference.

"It's troublesome to have a revolt," Torral insisted. "They might mobilize us."

He was a reserve officer, and designated, if necessary, to command one of the batteries at Cap Saint-Jacques.[66]

Mévil wasn't listening and walked eyes to the ground.

"What's eating *you?*" the engineer broke in.

The physician slowly shrugged.

"Woes…"

He was loath to speak.

"…Woes. There's a woman I want — who doesn't want me. There are two women I want…"

"Which ones?"

"Malais — Abel."

"Mother Abel?"

"No. Marthe."

"The little one? You'll find her slight."

"Yes. But I get dizzy when I look at her. You remember that evening at the theater? I almost fainted. She dazzles me like an electric lamp. I've searched my books and found no analogous malady. I don't know how to cure myself…"

He stopped for a moment.

"I'll marry her," he said, with finality.

"You're mad," said Torral.

"Maybe so."

Torral thought.

"Two women who don't want you. That's a lot for Saigon. Have you tried everything?"

"I've tried nothing. All I do is hit a wall. Marthe has me scared and paralyzed. The other is scared of *me* and shuts her door."

---

66 A significant port city in the south of Vietnam, as detailed in note 3.

"She likes you, then."

"Fat lot of good it does me!"

They lit cigarettes. Mévil let his go out.

"There are other women," the engineer advised. "Here or there, the spasm's the same."

Mévil nodded.

"I can't. Lord knows there are other women — more than I want, more than I can take. — In fact, I'm expected this very moment at Cholon, and if I'm on foot it's because I don't want a coachman conveying me to my appointment, for a discreet adventure: a girl…"

"Makes no difference to me. And…?"

"And she's not the one I want. Neither are the others."

"Beware. If that's where you're at, you're in peril."

They had walked as far as the cathedral and now stopped before the door.

"Remember the cat I hurled against that heap of gravel one evening? It was the day Fierce arrived. — That imbecile of a Fierce! — We were drunk, and looking for the Boresse quarter, that quarter of good repute.[67] There's philosophy in this tale — and medicine, the sort of medicine your case requires. Alcohol and coitus. Your dizzy spells will pass."

"No," said the physician. "I've tried it. When I'm gripped with desire for a woman nothing will distract me. I've given in to such desires too often. I've become their slave. This time too I must obey, or…"

They were on the red sand of the street. A victoria passed within inches, wheels grating. Mévil did not move. An axle brushed his leg.

"Careful!" the engineer had cried, with a backwards leap.

Mévil looked at him with an air of surprise, then made a blithe gesture.

"There's no danger," he muttered.

They stepped back down onto the street.

"There," said the physician.

"Nothing's lost," said Torral. "The Malais woman probably likes you. Woo her. Use that imbecile Fierce, since he's always visiting. Meet her,

---

67 In 1905 the large, low-lying quarter of La Boresse lay on the western periphery of Saigon, along the route to the distinct city of Cholon. Before a major land reclamation it was largely undrained marshland. Such areas were characterized by poor sanitation and makeshift housing (i.e. huts on stilts over stagnant water) and were often inhabited by the city's poor. These conditions and its fringe location gave it a "notorious" reputation among colonials, who associated it with poverty, disease, and crime, as it lay outside the immediate oversight of the city administration. In 1909–10 the entire district underwent extensive drainage and filling, which fundamentally altered its character and brought it into the urban landscape.

anywhere. Watch her, track her, lie in wait for her! And, as for the other one — for crying out loud, you don't love her! Bedazzlement isn't rutting."

"If I can't sleep with Marthe Abel," declared Mévil, headstrong, "I'm not through with bedazzlement, and it's going to kill me."

"Everything has an end," said Torral. "See you tonight, at the club."

He walked off, then returned.

"And, for God's sake, look out for carriages. You walk at unfortunate tangents to the trajectories of wheels, and that's worse than inner bedazzlement."

XIV[A]

orral's den was dark, because the big louvers of his shades were blocking out the two-o'clock sun. A single opium lamp yellowed the ceiling, and heavy brown volutes curled in the drug-soaked air. The slight sizzle of the pipes alternated with silence. Torral was smoking, his *boys* asleep at his feet.

The torrid hour of the knock-out, dreamless nap. Saigon sleeps, and a murderous sun rules the empty streets. Smokers alone continue to live, shut within their dens: their trains of thought, miraculously lulled by the opium, stretch beyond the human world, all the way to goodly, lucid regions that in former days Khoung-tseu[68] sought to open to his disciples.

Lying on his left side, his right hand presenting the needle to the lamp, Torral prepared his sixth pipe. Beneath him he had piled Cambodian cushions, of fresh rice straw; his open pajama exposed a brown torso too narrow for the big head: a torso at once robust and rickety, the torso of a civilized man forever refining his hereditary brains while scorning his body, abandoning it to debauchery. — Torral smoked his sixth pipe.

He sucked in all the black smoke in one breath and let himself suffocate rather than expel it. His head, tilted back, hit a cushion, and he

------

68 Confucius.

stiffened in sensuous pleasure, every sense twanging like a bowstring. The drug's warm odor filled his nostrils, and the smoky lamp befuddled his metallic eyes. The gentle breathing of the sleeping *boys* tickled his ears, like the exquisite plaint of a violin.

There were footfalls outside, far off on a street as silent as the Sahara — and audible at first to no one but a smoker. Torral listened with curiosity to the man's approach — a man's, because the step was a long and unhurried. Amused, the smoker brought his keen perspicacity to bear. The man stopped, then set off again. As a heel collided with the stone of the sidewalk Torral inferred the reason for the brief pause: to cross the road the man had been obliged to quit the shade of the trees. The steps stopped before the door, and from the single-fingered knock Torral recognized Fierce, though Fierce had never before braved the pavement under the worst of the day's sun.

Torral kicked the heap of sleeping brown flesh. The *boys* disentangled themselves and stretched. They had looked like recumbent little bronzes. Sao rose to his feet, his eyes red and opium-swelled. He was looking about for his white canvas *cai-hao*, tossed into a corner for the nap, when Fierce grew impatient and knocked again. So the *boy* went out naked to answer the door, bothering only to tuck his long hair under a black turban.

Fierce entered, tossed aside his helmet, and sat, in silence.

"What?" asked the smoker.

"Nothing."

He stretched out to the right of the lamp. Torral prepared a pipe and offered it to him. Fierce refused with a shake of the head. Torral smoked alone, and afterwards they nodded off. The *boys* too had fallen asleep.

The black smoke began again to smudge the rice mats on the walls. The equations on the slate gleamed through the dense volutes, and the smoker sought to read in them the silver verses of an irrevocable gospel.

At the strike of four Torral rose, his face and hands blackened by the drug's soot. He rubbed them with cologne and held out the bottle to Fierce.

"Ten pipes, and two hours' rest after the tenth. One must avoid excess in all things."

He removed his pajama and dressed. Fierce had lit a cigarette. Torral straddled the one folding chair.

"Why take your nap here?"

"I've been chased out."

"Who?"

"Liseron."

Torral awaited an explanation. Fierce ground out his cigarette on the opium platter.

"It's a simple story. Every now and then I flirt with this girl, who is kept in the main by Mévil. Mévil knows nothing, of course…"

"Hardly matters."

"And, all endings being good, I've sought over the past few days to liquidate Liseron. Difficulties have arisen."

"It takes two to divorce."

"I am but one, and she's decided to cling. It's amused her to cheat on Mévil with me. I began to space out my visits; she began coming to my domicile. I contrived absences; she would wait at my door. Yesterday evening, having tired of all this, I wrote her."

"A clear letter?"

"Not clear enough. I begged her never to return. And just now, during the nap, she dropped by."

"Like socialism on the bourgeois."

"It's not funny. I was in my pajamas. I was sleeping. I had to get up and answer."

"A nuisance."

"She comes in, and I'm instantly hit in the face with three hundred piastres — the ones I'd sent with my letter the day before. Then the entr'acte: a nude woman in my arms. She'd come in her peignoir."

"And you complain!"

"I abhor rapes. I did what I could to extricate myself. I threw on a jacket, and here I am. — She raged, but it'll pass. I told her so."

He smiled. No hard feelings.

"Is your furniture fragile?" Torral asked.

"Nothing but an iron bed."

He took a second cigarette. The blue puffs rose calmly to the ceiling.

"You were a boor," Torral indulgently judged. The opium was still coursing through his veins, tempering his usual harshness.

"I was a boor," Fierce conceded.

He went to the slate and looked over the analytic formulas. Torral pivoted on the folding chair to follow him with his eyes.

"You've vanished for ten days," he broke in.

Fierce blushed.

"Been tired."

"Yet you look hale!"

He could not have been more hale — complexion clear, eyelids unblemished, no cosmetics or powder. Torral began to smile.

"Whom have you found to replace Liseron?"

"No one. I'm going on holiday for a while."

"Very good. This evening I'll be dining at the cabaret in Cholon — all on the up and up. This should suit you. Care to come?"

Fierce blushed some more.

"I can't. I've accepted a dinner invitation in town."

"In town?"

"At the Malais'."

Torral feigned excessive surprise.

"The Malais? You're paying a visit to those chic people?"

He burst into laughter and folded his arms.

"My poor old boy! So it's true. I'd been told, but I didn't believe it. You, a civilized man, a solider fighting in our van, have turned into that grotesque specter: a man of the world! Look at you: in thrall to women's skirts, strapped down in a foul milieu of courtesies, elegance, and snobbery! Skirts that aren't even worth the trouble to hike up! Bowing and scraping that won't get you more than a bow in return! False merchandise, false coin. And for a barbaric, noxious stew of falsehoods you spit out the savor of our rational, straightforward lives — our mathematical lives! It's been ten days since you turned your back on us, ten days since you repudiated our reasonable manly ideal. What chimera, what tomfoolery, are you chasing now? What lying quagmire are you bogging yourself down in? You, a man of sincerity. You're mad or a renegade."

"You exaggerate," said Fierce.

He'd taken the rebuke without protest. Before the philosopher, whom he did not try to refute, he felt uncomfortable and shy. But the new life he had tasted over these past ten days had shackled him with too many sweet delights. He could not renounce it now.

"I live by your formula," he pleaded. "Without any effort I've found pleasures to my liking, and now I'm gathering them. I'm living as I please, without care for any*thing* or any*one*. This is the program you yourself laid out for me!"

"Imbecile!"

Torral leveled his abuse without anger, with a frown of pity.

"Imbecile! Let's not talk about it. — Are you in love? It wouldn't excuse anything, but it would explain…"

Revolt surged up in Fierce. All the reproach, all the jeering he took with bowed head, but the name of Sélysette Sylva profaned here? Never! — However — he suddenly reflected — why get irritated? Who was speaking of Sélysette? He was not in love, no more with her than with any other woman in the world. He laughed.

"In love! And you?"

Torral fixed him with a scrutinizing eye. But Fierce was not lying; his good faith was smiling all over his face. Torral did not insist.

"I'm going to Mévil's," he said, taking up the clothes he had shed for the nap. "Coming?"

Fierce looked at his watch.

"Yes. I've got time."

"Time? What do you have planned?"

"A tennis match."

"Where?"

"At the Malais'."

Fierce was no longer blushing. He was not in love; that point, clearly articulated, reassured and stilled his conscience. He shrugged when Torral stubbornly declared:

"Once it ceases to be rutting, love is an anemia of the intellect."

XIV[B]

They walked to Mévil's. Rue Némésis was redolent of indigenous odors. They turned onto Rue d'Espagne at its end and arrived in a quarter-hour. The doctor's gate was open, and in the courtyard with the big poincianas stood the lacquered and silvered rickshaw, awaiting the master.

"Pretty *cai-nha*," said Fierce before entering.

"Appealing and discreet: a woman trap."

Torral esteemed it as a painter or algebraist, with tilted head and a squint. Mévil's house lay in ambush behind a rampart of trees, and from every story jutted a veranda masked with creeper vine and resembling a shield. Just past the gate the lane turned toward the oblique front stairs. From the first step a visitor would vanish.

"The temple of love-rutting," Torral said again. "Inside are chaises-longues tailored to all womanly dimensions. The women to whom you pay your respects every day with a visit, at Malais's house or elsewhere, either have lain or will lie on those chaises."

"Perhaps," Fierce dryly said.

They entered.

Mévil was alone, his last (female) patient having left. His office, though vast, managed to seem intimate, thanks to the dimness and muffled silence. The French doors seemed small through their tulle shades, which the breeze passed through without lifting. The walls lay buried beneath an overly long and wide mauve muslin, spilling over everywhere in trailing folds, and the same muslin draped the rattan love-seats and sofas, and was attached curtain-like, with loose tie-backs, to the two perennially closed doors. — All this soft fabric functioned like a sieve, lending the room an air of secrecy and security. Whatever was said and done within those silken walls stayed within those silken walls; the complicit rustle of the hangings stifled gestures and words alike. And many women would repair to this confessional to admit and relieve the bothersome injury to which almost all of Saigon was resigned; and many, unhurt or cured, would accept or request other treatments, on the ever-receptive sofas.

A confessional, not a doctor's office — a confessional for very high-society sins. No books, papers, or medical bag; instead, knickknacks, scents, fans, and the usual liqueurs and confections for refreshment.

Mévil, in a chaise-longue, was watching his cigarette go out in his ashtray. Scampering about on the felted mats was the *congaï*: the half-servant, half-wife Annamite girl indispensable to the furnishings of a European man's Indochinese house — fourteen years of age, mellow-eyed, long and obscene in the mouth, her slender hands deft in all things. She was as pretty as could be for her bastard race — an unfortunate blend of the incompatible Hindu bronze and Chinese amber.

"Is it you?" said Mévil, without getting up, as Torral and Fierce entered.

The *congaï*, now snuggled against the master, smiled at the friendly visitors, with a grimace on her lips and coquetry on her lashes.

There was no gush of cordiality between the friends when they gathered. Their friendship was but a concordance of opinions and intelligences, an association of parallel egoisms, arrived at without tenderness to expedite the pursuit of maximum enjoyment. Why bother with the falseness and puerility of handshakes?

"Family portrait," jeered Torral while looking at the *congaï*.

They spoke of this and that. Fierce delivered the day's political news: not good, according to old-man d'Orvilliers, who continued to prophesy fire and flame. Without cease the men aboard the *Bayard* were conducting military exercises of all kinds. The whole squadron was in a tumult of war.

"Senile trepidation?" asked Torral.

Fierce made a pout of indecision.

"I thought so at first. Now I don't know…"

He was surprised at how persistent the alarming rumors were, and even more at the building concentration of English squadrons in all the world's oceans.

"England," he concluded, "might after all be mulling a blow. It wouldn't be completely unexpected."

"Yeah!" said Torral.

He was considering the possible mobilizations, and the battery awaiting him, on the cliffs of Cap Saint-Jacques, with the enemy's

bombardments incoming… He laid out his other worry, an eventual revolt of the natives, should Malais prove too merciless in the collection of his tax.

Mévil shuddered at the mention of Malais's name.

The engineer interrupted himself. "Speaking of Malais," he said, "what's new with you in that house?"

"Nothing," Mévil murmured.

Torral observed the rings around his eyes, the white lips, the sunken cheeks.

"Sick?"

"No."

Fierce intervened.

"Tired, at least. Take a break. Believe me."

Mévil, ironic, smiled.

"It's been eight days now — eight days! — and my chances seem worse than Saint Joseph's."

Torral frowned.

"The devil you say. Still?"

"Still."

"What?" asked Fierce.

Torral snickered.

"This is outside your bailiwick, man of the world! Mévil, here, is in love, but his love, tenacious as it is, does not stray into Platonism, and his dream is but to bed the object of his wishes. Too simple for your new mentality."

Fierce shrugged in annoyance. He was going to reply when the *boy* in charge of the door entered to speak with the master. Mévil dismissed him with a nod.

"It's just Liseron," he said. "It's her day. She'll be mistaken, poor thing…"

Torral hoped to take in a comedy. Mévil, an instinctive flirt, smoothed his canvas jacket. Fierce, thinking only of his tennis match, fretted over the time.

Liseron entered, smiling. Fierce, probably, was no longer on her mind, or perhaps she was out for the instinctive revenge of a woman betrayed, but it was him she saw first, and all the anger that had just subsided within her rose back up to stick in her craw. She came to an instant halt. Fierce was looking at her with apathy. Her female pride having been injured a mere hour ago, she took his apathy like a lash to the face. Her color gone, she pounced, seized Fierce by the arm, wrenched him from his chair, and set him before a surprised Mévil.

"Know what? I'm sleeping with him!"

Then, in triumph, avenged and rabid, she awaited the catastrophe. Her simple brain thought the furor of a cheated male was sure to come, ineluctable and tragic, but hereditary civilization had yanked from Mévil every last root of that bestial emotion known as jealousy. Without a flinch he smiled. Liseron released Fierce's arm, stunned, stupefied, her rage squelched. — Fierce, serene, retook his seat.

"Truer words never spoken," he declared.

He hunted for some apt quip, but none came to mind. Mévil, curious, raised his eyebrows, for the scene had intrigued him like a charade. Fierce explained:

"The tragedy renewed of the Egyptian story of Potiphar and the stripped garment…"[69]

"My poor girl!" commiserated Mévil. "You just had to belong to last century!"

They were laughing in her face, both of them — all three. She thought she had gone mad. "I've slept with him…" she repeated. "I've slept with him…" Her anger surged, once again gained the upper hand, this time mixed with a singular indignation.

"Cowards!" she spat. "You don't give a damn that your women sleep with the first pigs to come along? Well, I, a whore, am going to call you what you are: wet rags, the lot of you — a bunch of hollow, rotten men. You wouldn't feel a slap to the face, because that's not blood coursing through your bellies. It's…"

The filth would not land, would slide off on their irony. Torral most of all relished the insults as a barbarous homage to his superiority. — It is a philosopher's pleasure to contemplate the free play of a naked instinct. — Torral laughed without anger or indulgence. Hardly less shielded, Mévil listened phlegmatic to the end, then rose and threw the woman out — not that he was in any way offended; it was unseemly, he thought, that a mistress should dare to speak to him with anything but servility. Meanwhile Liseron, a slave in revolt, was near to shrieking and defending herself, but she looked into her lover's eyes, bad eyes that counseled obedience, and fled, banging her shoulders on the leaves of the door. Mévil returned to his chaise-longue and yawned.

---

69 Quran (Surah Yusuf). Also Genesis 39 (see Expansive Notes, in the appendix, page 238).

Only Fierce had turned red. He said nothing and lifted not a finger, but a strange shame rose to his face. He could muster no scorn for the low injury. It had cut into him like an etcher's mordant, like the truth: he was unsure that it was *not* the truth.

… The *congaï*, frightened and huddled behind the chaise-longue, had fallen silent while Liseron spoke. Later she hazarded a high laugh, which Mévil cut short with a rap. And with that there was no further comment on the adventure. Torral continued with his counsel, taking up his sentence right where he had left off.

"You're wrong not to react against your obsession," he said to Mévil. "I'll be dining at Cholon this evening. I've invited Fierce, who's turned me down over a case of intellectual anemia, so nothing's preventing us from a proper debauch, in moderation. Eight days' chastity is an extravagance."

"Whom is he in love with?" asked Fierce.

"With Madame Malais," said Torral, looking at him.

Fierce did not budge.

"…With Mademoiselle Abel too."

"You could name every woman on earth…," Fierce teased.

Yet he had feared another name, though he would not admit it to himself.

"Five o'clock," he said. "So long."

"Where are you off to?" asked Mévil.

"To play tennis."

Mévil stood.

"Take me along."

"Ah, no!"

He wouldn't have been able to say why, but Mévil seemed the last person he ought to introduce to the people he was going to see.

"Why not?" said Torral. "Go together. Mévil knows all of Saigon. There'd be no introduction. It'll do him some good to go there — and do *you* some good to see him there…"

Fierce shook his head. Torral persuaded him with an ironic quotation: "Jealousy, Monsieur? At first but a rustle…"[70]

____

70   The original lines are spoken by Basile in Act II, Scene 8, of Beaumarchais's *The Barber of Seville*. They concern not jealousy but calumny, or slander (altered translation of Arthur B. Myrick): "Slander, sir? [*La calomnie, monsieur ?*] You hardly know what you despise. I have seen it all but crush the best of men. There is, believe me, no outright wickedness, no horror, no absurd tale that one cannot fasten upon the idle residents of a great city if one goes about it the right way — and we have some deft hands around here!… At first but a rustle [*D'abord un bruit leger*], skimming the ground like the swallow before the storm, murmurs *pianissimo*, and flies, and sows as it speeds along its poisonous seed. Soon it finds its way into some mouth or other, and is adroitly deposited *pian*

"Imbecile!" said the other, and gave in. Mévil dressed faster than usual. Torral accompanied them as far as Rue d'Espagne.

"Here our paths diverge."

He looked at Fierce.

"…Diverge even more than it would seem. That way lies the road to foolishness — this way the road to reason."

He took the road to reason.

"I no longer know which way to go," joked Mévil, hesitating.

He nonetheless followed Fierce down the road to foolishness.

---

piano into your ear. The evil is done…."

XV

évil was first up the front stairs, but Fierce hurried past him in the entrance hall and showed him the way. It displeased him that under that roof Mévil had assumed the air of a regular visitor.

The entrance hall gave on to the veranda and the veranda on to the garden. The tennis court was a lawn hedged by groves. The arecas grouped next to it formed a natural tent, beneath which a circle in pale dresses and white clothes was engaged in chitchat. Here and there lay balls and racquets. It was time for a rest.

Fierce and Mévil advanced. Madame Malais came to meet them. She sparkled with beauty; the open air suited her blonde-marquise delicacy; amid the lawn and the great trees, and despite the bothersome helmet that the climate required, Fierce believed he was seeing a Watteau[71] come to life and smile at him. He kissed the proffered hand, uttered a phrase

---

71 Jean-Antoine Watteau (1684–1721), French painter of theatrical inspiration (commedia dell'arte, ballet). Credited with a revival of the waning Baroque style. Took his inspiration from original works by Correggio and Rubens in the collection of his patron, Pierre Crozat.

of introduction for Mévil, and left him to essay his courtship. He himself, meanwhile, hurried to the arecas: he had already spied a blue dress, and it drew him like a magnet.

Madame Malais endeavored to receive Mévil as she had received Fierce, but the handsome doctor kissed her wrist instead of her fingers, and she lost her composure, for she was in fact scared of him, with an anguished fear that was perhaps indeed some manner of love. Honest, and ably sheltered by her husband against Saigon's perverse contagion, she found it terrifying that someone would dare to besiege her, and trembled lest she give purchase to the enemy; she was wracked, too, with a secret shame, for what indignation she could feel over this intrepid pursuit lacked vehemence.

Mévil took advantage of her distress, speaking affectionate words to soothe her as they followed Fierce towards the arecas — and deepening her distress. Then he suddenly fell silent: Marthe Abel was approaching. He blanched, bowed before the young women, babbled a few words, and beat a retreat — all in the blink of an eye. — Relieved of her fear, Madame Malais pressed Marthe's hand. The young woman watched in astonishment as the man fled.

Mévil, however, was regaining his composure, cross with himself. With a furious effort he joined the chitchat circle and, playing along, dazzled with his wit. The fluid frivolity of his character once again served his purpose. All of the women listened to him, and Fierce was eclipsed.

Rather than go right to the one he was seeking, Sélysette Sylva, Fierce succumbed to some obscure sense of modesty and veered off to greet those to whom he was indifferent. As soon as a few words had been exchanged and a few hands kissed, however, he ended up, as if by chance, choosing a chair at her side. Mademoiselle Sylva was still holding her racquet; her cheeks were purple, her forehead damp; she joyfully stretched out her warm hand and chided:

"This is how you get here early? I've already lost a match without you!"

He took her in, intoxicated with her grace and the force of her youth. He felt in his confusion that a great gulf lay between them — he the bitter, skeptical civilized man, she the fresh-souled girl. It made him sad. She laughed heartily with him, but he saw her stop to catch a witticism from Mévil, and a jealous anguish caught in his throat. Torral's ironies ran through his mind: in love? He wondered, filled with turmoil, and could not at first read his own heart.

The tennis began again. Girlishly, Mademoiselle Sylva struck the net with her racquet.

"Bet you won't jump it!"

He forgot Torral.

"And you?"

"Don't dare me!"

She was already gathering her skirts. He teased her, calling her a little goat, and looking at her ankles. She laughed, in confusion.

"Shall we play?" someone asked.

Marthe Abel stood up. Madame Malais stayed in her seat. Mévil hesitated, but the blonde marquise was affecting a confidential chat with her neighbor; he followed Marthe.

"We must draw lots," declared Mademoiselle Sylva. "And let's hurry. The sun's going down."

They drew the players, then the doubles. As things turned out, it was Marthe and Mévil against Fierce and Sélysette. Happy, Mademoiselle Sylva shook her partner's hand as they crossed to their side of the court.

"Is he a strong player, your Monsieur Mévil?"

"Very strong. He plays day and night at the houses of all the chic women of Saigon."

"It's me who's going to regret this pairing if you make me lose!"

"Naughty girl."

He was laughing in the lips, but his jealousy was rekindled.

Across the net Mévil and Marthe took their places. Mévil was looking at his partner. He dared to speak to her:

"This evening I'll set a white stone on my table:[72] two hours ago I had no notion of the good fortune I was about to enjoy, to play at your side, Mademoiselle…"

He had used his most seductive voice — warm, with affectionate inflections. But Mademoiselle Abel, despite her black eyes and white complexion, was a skeptical philosopher by trade, and not to be swayed by a few courteous words. She observed the coldest gentility and directed her gaze nonchalantly at Madame Malais.

---

72   Revelation 2:17 (King James translation): "He that hath an ear, let him hear what the Spirit saith unto the churches; To him that overcometh will I give to eat of the hidden manna, and will give him a white stone, and in the stone a new name written, which no man knoweth saving he that receiveth it."

Biblical scholars differ in their interpretations. Here it refers to the ancient Roman custom of awarding white stones to the victors of athletic games.

"Ready!"[73] cried Sélysette.

Mévil raised his racquet to serve. Stung by his partner's indifference, he sought now to dazzle her by playing a brilliant game. Standing on the lawn as in a stadium, arm lifted to the sky, he seemed a young god. All eyes followed his serve. Fierce saw Sélysette's attention: her admiration, perhaps? — Every fiber of his being shuddered. That look she was giving the enemy he felt to have been robbed from him. He was run through with a bolt of anger, and he squeezed his racquet with a duelist's grip. He would play as one would fight.

"Play!" Mévil warned.

His serve went off like a shot, and Mademoiselle Sylva could not return it. But Fierce set up in turn, and the second serve, though faster than the first, was returned with such precision that Mévil let it go by.

From then on it was a hard-fought duel. The young ladies hardly took part, disconcerted by the fire and severity of the shots. Quiet reigned beneath the arecas. The spectators, almost grave, watched in surprise; each vaguely glimpsed a mystery, a secret match for which tennis served as a mask. The game continued nonetheless in silence, and the general attention paid to it became a bother, almost a source of anxiety.

Balls sailed over the net to sharp or tricky rebounds. Mévil would aim for the corners and focus his attacks on Sélysette, a weaker player than her partner. This made for an irregular, oblique match, a dangerous match with a likeness to its player. Fierce did not at first know how to parry. More loyal, unwilling to respond with an attack on Marthe Abel, he lost point after point for several games.

But he did not lose heart. Beside him Mademoiselle Sylva was putting her soul into the match, helping him, defending him, supporting him with the fidelity of a brother in arms. They were two beings with a single soul between them. He felt that she was all his, and a passionate tenderness warmed his heart. In that moment of physical violence and sincerity he came to the marvelous understanding that he loved her with a great love, and that life at her side would be sweet. He hoped that she would love him, that she loved him already. He felt a surge of energy in his veins.

He redoubled his efforts. Simple, hard play was tiring Mévil out, whereas he himself was not tiring. They traded advantage. Now Sélysette was applauding his shots. He took pride in this, and became more daring.

---

73 In English in the original text.

Across the net Marthe Abel remained indifferent and cold. The luck of the shots mattered nothing to her. Bored with the long match, she hardly helped her partner, watching the balls go by without deigning to stretch out her arm. Mévil felt this nonchalance weigh on him, heavy as scorn.

He was less spirited, less spry, less beautiful. One could sense his defeat. His arm could hardly return the ball now, and sweat was pearling on his temples. — It was the end. — Games flashed by, all of them lost, and the match point hit him in the body, frustrating his return. He let his racquet drop and tripped when picking it up.

Bravos rang out to celebrate Fierce. He did not hear: Sélysette had cried victory and was running to him. He saw her precious eyes shine with a childlike joy; he received her warm little hand, thrust frankly into his. She thanked him up close, familiar and delicious.

"You made me win… Aren't you just the nicest!"

Mévil was crossing the lawn. Mademoiselle Abel, all courtesy, apologized for her clumsiness: without her he would surely have won. He was not listening. He was watching Fierce and Sélysette, hand in hand. — Something cold penetrated his heart.

Fierce was drunk, drunk on the love that was now streaming from his chest, like a pond filled to overflowing by hidden springs. In Sélysette's amiable gaze he read a promise of love returned, and his exaltation swelled to a frenzy. At the start, because she was squeezing his hand, he adored her like a Madonna, and kept himself in check, lest he drop to his knees and kiss her hem.

The sun blazed in a ruddy sunset, bloodying the earth. Like bolts of lightning, reflections issued from the stream-like sidewalks and the house windows. The road was a triumphal way, lined with gold, paved with purple.

It seemed to Fierce, bedazzled with his love, that life had now opened up to him, radiant as that road.

XVI

his morning I crossed the Bosporus on a caïque.[74] I had spent the night at my harem in Scutari[75] and was heading back to my house in Istanbul, where am I writing this book. My caikdjis[76] rowed in silence, the muscles of their arms swelling their white sleeves, and the caïque glided along, leaving not a wrinkle on the water.

The sun was already high, but a band of clouds had concealed it, and the morning light was dim and gloomy. Lying between a pale sky and a grey sea, Istanbul was like a town in the north of France.

Gigantic Hagia Sophia,[77] buttressed with its ramparts of yellow and red, was nonetheless in view; I could see the stony poem of Byzantine walls that men have crenelated from above, the sea from

---

74 A skiff typical of the Bosporus.

75 See note 62 for details on this part of Istanbul.

76 Boatmen.

77 Istanbul's iconic structure par excellence. Built as a Greek Orthodox church in the fourth century, it was converted into a mosque in the fifteenth century, into a museum in 1935, and back into a mosque in 2020.

below; I could see the infinity of Turkish houses, their old planks turned violet like autumnal undergrowth; and I could see the mosques, unparalleled the world over, every one having voided the coffers of an emperor: Achmedje, its hundred domes like bubbles of marble[78] — Mehmedje, which the Sultan Conqueror made robust[79] — Suleimanje, which the Sultan Magnificent made pompous[80] — Bayazidje, chosen by the pigeons of Allah[81] — Şehzade, which expiates a sin of Roxelana's[82] — so many others. The grey cupolas cluster like desert dunes heaped up by the simoom;[83] the minarets pointed skyward like the lances that conquered Istanbul for the Prophet. And the city came to an end amid the old seraglio's black cypress trees, a melancholic shroud for the beautiful, empty kiosks[84] of the sultans.

But the sun was absent, and Istanbul's soul with it. Its color washed out and sullen, Istanbul was like a town in the north of France.

Then the sun broke through the clouds. I felt its warm caress on my shoulders and nape, and I saw the sea light up around me, as if a sheet of rays had spread over the water, speeding faster than the caïque towards Istanbul. Shadows fled before it, and the city was conquered in a bound under the sun's assault. — It was a miracle. The palaces, the mosques, and the houses, with every stone of the ramparts and

---

78   Officially the Sultan Ahmed Mosque, more popularly the Blue Mosque, for the hand-painted blue tiles of its interior walls. Built in the early seventeenth century by Sultan Ahmed I, whose tomb it contains.

79   Built in the late fifteenth century, the Fait Mosque, or Conqueror's Mosque, is named for the Ottoman sultan Mehmed the Conqueror, who conquered Constantinople in 1453.

80   A sixteenth-century Ottoman imperial mosque commissioned by Suleiman the Magnificent. It contains a mausoleums for the sultan and his wife Hurrem Sultan (Roxelana; see note 82). For 462 years it was the largest mosque in the city.

81   The Bayezid II Mosque is an early sixteenth-century imperial mosque commissioned by the Ottoman sultan Bayezid II. In nineteenth- and early-twentieth-century accounts of the city (like this one) it is often referred to as the Pigeon Mosque, for the many birds that would congregate nearby to be fed by worshippers.

82   Roxelana (1505–58), possibly named Aleksandra Lisovska at birth, known in Turkish as Hürrem ("joyful one"), of Slavic and perhaps Ruthenian origin. Captured as a girl by Tartars, sold at a slave market in Constantinople (Istanbul), and taken into the harem of Ottoman sultan Suleiman the Magnificent, or the Lawgiver (1494/95–1566), in time becoming his concubine and then his wife, and bearing him at least five sons. So skilled at palace intrigue that she was thought a witch. Thought also to have plotted the execution of the sultan's grand vizier, Ibrahim Pasha (1493–1536). Like Roxelana, the vizier had been born a Christian and enslaved.

83   A strong, hot, dry, dust-laden wind, particularly a local wind in the Sahara, Israel, Palestine, Jordan, Iraq, Syria, and the deserts of the Arabian Peninsula.

84   From the Persian *kūshk*. Kiosks were originally small garden pavilions open on some or all sides. They were common in Persia, the Indian subcontinent, and the Ottoman Empire from the thirteenth century on.

every leaf of the gardens, were so many living, quivering creatures in the golden light. The bronze crescents atop the minarets' points scintillated like stars in the blue sky; a sea bluer than the sky reflected the whole white, green, and violet city as in a mirror of sapphire. And the sacred hills of Eyüp,[85] invisible not long before, cut a noble and bold profile above the boat-packed Golden Horn. — It was a miracle: a resurrection, so prompt a resurrection that I marveled in a stupor. — A ray of sunlight had sufficed…

In like fashion the love of Sélysette Sylva, shining rays of sunlight into his heart, at first metamorphosed the whole of Fierce's life.

In truth Fierce had never yet lived, for he had tasted neither joy nor suffering. It is in fact this aloofness-by-design that sums up the effort of civilizations; and Fierce, being among the civilized, had so let his primitive instincts wither that he could strike from his life every semblance of emotion — no more woes or joys, no more pleasures or cares: the ones differing so little from the others. — The procession of human chills no longer penetrated to his marrow; only one, the most potent, the chill of love, could still move and rattle him.

A weak rattling, probably. Too cerebral, Fierce was no doubt less smitten than one of the sailors of his ship would have been. But he had never been rattled, even a little; with no point of comparison, this rattling seemed to him violent indeed. It revolutionized the nauseous monotony of his destiny, to his surprise and delight. He took pleasure in the notion, the inexact notion, that his love was like that of an innocent stripling, and so he neglected to be what he had always been: his own psychologist. He lived without observing himself live. The new game taught him to savor life, and, though his palate was suitably dry, he marveled at this new taste.

With relish he came to know the young joy of hopes and illusions, and the exquisite, throttling anguish one feels when the beloved appears. His illusions were, incidentally, simple and his hopes modest: he desired nothing more than Sélysette's smile and friendship. Too many women, all objects of his contempt, had passed through his bed for him to wish his one idol to lie in it.

---

85   Also called Eyüpsultan. District of Istanbul province extending from the Golden Horn to the shore of the Black Sea.

03♦80

When Fierce paid his visits to the villa on Rue des Moïs — he went often, contriving to find Madame Sylva and her daughter alone — he would pass through the gate, always open, and reach the garden without crossing through the house. At about four o'clock, before the drive, Madame Sylva would almost always sit beneath the banyans of her terrace and breathe an air that the dense trees would keep cool. Fierce would find the blind woman there, on the same rattan chair, her old hands busy with the same grey woolen knit, and Mademoiselle Sylva, ever her faithful companion, babbling or reading aloud.

He was now the best friend, the one most joyfully welcomed, the one who would never disturb mother and daughter's tender tête-à-tête. They would make room for him, invite him along for the drive, or prolong into the evening for him their intimate garden chat. He would talk of the news, and they would initiate him into the serious trifles of family life; with Sélysette he would discourse on gentilities in a teasing way that would tickle the girl's verve and cheer; and the blind woman would bring to bear on all things her gentle gravity, along with the exquisite docility of old women who have suffered much but whose wracked hearts have not turned bitter and whom mourning and resignation have improved and sublimated.

At times they would still be in the garden at nightfall, and Madame Sylva would take Fierce's arm to go back inside the house. The lamps would go on, lending Sélysette's cheeks a pearly pink hue. And before he left Fierce would ask to have the piano opened. Mademoiselle Sylva was not a great artist, but her tuneful, rustic voice was so pure in tone as to recall vibrant gold.

Old songs, rhythmic legends redolent of bards and the land. Ironical, depraved Fierce would listen to the candid refrains with an emotion that moistened his eyes.

On his way back through the brown night he would be overcome with melancholy. The farther he got from the cherished house the heavier it would become. The road would seem long, his legs grow weak; sometimes he would hail a late rickshaw. He was freer to daydream in the silent little conveyance, and there he would admit without shame that all his happiness lay imprisoned behind him — back there, with the adorable girl who had stolen his heart. What would his life be now, far from her? A voyage with no destination, in no way worth taking up again.

◌◦◦◌

The two Chinese upholsterers — fat Cantonese with fine ponytails and white stockings ending in black, felt-soled slippers — listen to Fierce's orders in the small room aboard the *Bayard*.

… "Tear all the grey silk from the walls. Same with the velvet. — In their place put this."

This is a light-blue Chinese seersucker with a greenish sheen. — It comes from Shanghai; Fierce has taken pains to find this color, the one he had to have.

… "Frame signs with that."

Pagoda sleeves unsewn from old Chinese dresses. An embroidery of ten thousand butterflies — wings of every shape, of every shade of blue — crowding a narrow black band of satin. Mademoiselle Sylva had marveled over it at the merchant's in Cholon.

… "And hide all the nails well. Any way to have it for this evening, all finished?"

A nod, a smile on the glabrous faces. There is always a way. *Impossible* is not a word in the Chinese lexicon of commerce.

"Careful nothing gets dirty. How much?"

A brief reckoning, a brief colloquy in Cantonese patois. Notebooks of silk paper emerge from pockets. — This much. Nothing to haggle over, as it's a one-off job. Fierce is accustomed and knows. He agrees and leaves.

It is of no use whatsoever to surveil a Chinaman's work. He will do what is required, scrupulously, and refuse any pay rather than suffer reproach.

The grey room has now become blue — the color of Sélysette's eyes. Happy, Fierce surveys the friendly hue — then sits at his table. The books remain open to the same pages: the meticulous Chinamen have returned everything to its exact place.

There are books on tactics, lighthouse lists, nautical instructions. From closed drawers Fierce now produces the secret plans of the batteries and forts. He spreads out the nautical map of the Donnai and the coasts of Saint-Jacques.

It is a matter of combined blockades. He is not working under orders. To assuage his own patriotic anxieties, Fierce studies for himself the surest means to defend Saigon against enemy attack.

— "No attempting anything against Saint-Jacques," he murmurs, "unless the enemy's manifestly mad, and his punishment will be swift… But a landing from the west is possible — yes. On the very first night, then, he'd have to break the blockade. — Breaking the blockade: it all comes down to that. Will we have enough torpedo boats?"

He pauses, raises his eyes. His books, a collection of strong libertine bent, now seem a blemish, with their grey plush spines, on the wrought-iron shelf that serves as his bookcase. He smiles: how surprised he would have been back when he read such things had some sorcerer predicted to him that he would one day substitute Commodore Mahan[86] for the Marquis de Sade![87] He half-sings a couplet:

"For love of a blonde,
A blue-eyed blonde…"

It is a song of Sélysette's. He stops, turns serious:
"…One thing is clear: I will never again be able to do without her…"

ೞ◆ಔ

Madame Abel, the lieutenant-governor's wife, would receive on Tuesdays, from six to seven. Fierce would attend regularly, first out of professional duty — the admiral's aide-de-camp owed a visit to Saigon's second magistrate — but also because he liked the amiable woman, one of Madame Sylva's intimate friends. Madame Abel was better than her stepdaughter. Fierce disliked the polite coldness about Marthe, with her underlying thoughts forever unknown, whereas her stepmother, neither silly nor naïve, would confide in and even let loose with her friends.

One Tuesday Fierce mistook the time and arrived too early. The road was deserted, the usual carriages absent, and the Tonkinese sentry asleep in his box. Distracted, Fierce noticed none of this as he passed. The residence of Saigon's lieutenant-governor is an imitation of a German temple in the new Athens: ugly and rich, with Corinthian

---

86 Alfred Thayer Mahan (1840–1914), American Navy man who was alive at the time of the novel's setting and publication, fought in the U.S. Civil War, and wrote a number of books on naval history and the influence of sea power.

87 Donatien-Alphonse-François, count of Sade (1740–1814), French libertine and writer of erotica, some of it composed in prison.

columns. Fierce climbed the front steps: the Annamite boys watched in surprise and let him enter: a native mustn't dare to stop a European, even under his master's roof. Fierce met no obstacle as far as the parlor; only there, before the empty chairs, did he understand his mistake: the clock on the false fireplace showed five to five o'clock.

"Stupid of me," he thought. "What to do?"

It occurred to him that a *boy* might have gone to warn the mistress; he was known to all in the house. — He waited just in case, ready with an apology. He wandered around the parlor without taking a seat. The pictures on the walls were uninteresting. He made his way to the pedestal table, covered with Tonkinese embroidery, and removed an album from its sleeve, for perusal — a beautiful lacquered album, with Japanese binding. He touched the lacquer with a finger: it was thick and without flaw, brown, covered with peach blossoms. He thought of Nagasaki, where such lacquers come from, and Shirayama-San, who makes them in her brown shop amid the twitter of mousmés…

… Japan, pretty and clean. Sélysette would like that country…

He thumbed through the album. It contained photographs, portraits; he took no heed of the odd face he recognized as the pages turned under his finger: he was thinking he should leave without further delay, and looked up at the open door.

Then a sudden shudder: as he was about to close the album he spied a photograph of Mademoiselle Sylva.

He had never seen one before: this was the first. She was loyal and lovely; it was like seeing Sélysette herself, and he felt the slight anguish in his throat that would always trouble him when she appeared.

… Sélysette herself; her favorite dress, with its plunging neckline of muslin lapels; her capricious hair of pale gold, and her smile, and the reverie in her eyes…

Lowered shutters kept the room dark.

Without hesitation, Fierce stole the photograph from the album. — His fingers trembled somewhat: he was obliged to remove his gloves, because the paper wouldn't slide well through the slit of the page.

He then raised his head and looked towards the door; there were footfalls outside. He slipped the portrait into his bust — under his shirt, against the skin: the portrait could hear the thud of his heart, beating with fear and daring — and he quickly escaped, like the thief that he was.

However, back aboard the ship, locked in his greenish-blue room, he felt so drunk with joy before the conquered portrait — trophy, treasure, relic — and wept such crazy tears over Sélysette his prisoner, who would forever henceforth be sharing his life, that he was overcome with superstitious fear and sealed the image in an envelope — as Polycrates,[88] tyrant of Samos, once sacrificed his most precious ring to Adrasteia.[89]

---

88   See Expansive Notes, in the appendix, page 239.

89   Ash-nymph, daughter to Melisseus, sister to Io, and nurse to Zeus, whose mother, Rhea, had hidden him from his father, Cronus, lest he be eaten like his siblings.

Robert Graves, in *The Greek Myths*, writes: "Amalthea's name, 'tender', shows her to have been a maiden goddess; Io was an orgiastic nymph-goddess; Adrasteia means 'the Inescapable One', the oracular Crone of autumn. Together they formed the usual Moon-triad. The later Greeks identified Adrasteia with the pastoral goddess Nemesis, of the rain-making ash-tree, who had become a goddess of vengeance."

"The philosophical Nemesis was worshipped at Rhamnus where, according to Pausanias, the Persian commander-in-chief, who had intended to set up a white marble trophy in celebration of his conquest of Attica, was forced to retire by news of a naval defeat at Salamis; the marble was used instead for an image of the local Nymph-goddess Nemesis. It is supposed to have been from this event that Nemesis came to personify 'Divine vengeance', rather than the 'due enactment' of the annual death drama; since to Homer, at any rate, *nemesis* had been merely a warm human feeling that payment should be duly made, or a task duly performed. But Nemesis the Nymph-goddess bore the title Adrasteia ('inescapable' – Strabo: xiii. I. 13), which was also the name of Zeus's foster-nurse, an ash-nymph; and since the ash-nymphs and the Erinnyes were sisters, born from the blood of Uranus, this may have been how Nemesis came to embody the idea of vengeance. The ash-tree was one of the goddess's seasonal disguises, and an important one to her pastoral devotees, because of its association with thunderstorms and with the lambing month, the third of the sacral year. / Nemesis is called a daughter of Oceanus, because as the Nymph-goddess with the apple-bough she was also the sea-borne Aphrodite, sister of the Erinnyes."

XVII

ademoiselle Sylva and Mademoiselle Abel, the one kept for lunch by her tutor, the other paying a visit, strolled through the grounds of the government palace.

There was no intimacy between them, because Marthe thought Sélysette too young and Sélysette thought Marthe too old. Both were twenty years of age but at different maturities.

They walked at leisure, without much talk, through the English lanes, between the lovely, thick copses that make the park into a wood — a wood no bigger than a garden but so thick that the walls remain out of sight.

"Sélysette," broke in Mademoiselle Abel, "what's happening with your flirt?"

"What flirt?" said Sélysette, with sincerity.

"Why, Monsieur de Fierce, of course."

"That's not a flirt, Marthe. He's just a friend. I assure you he's not courting me at all…"

Mademoiselle Abel flashed her sphinx smile.

"Your photograph has been stolen from my album. What do you say to that?"

"My photograph's been stolen? By whom?"

"I don't know, naturally. An admirer, I suppose."

"That would be dreadful," Mademoiselle Sylva indignantly declared, "but I suspect it's more likely been lost. I'll send you another."

She spotted a stone bench along the lane's edge and, tiring of the slow walk, cleared it with a leap.

"How young you are!" said Mademoiselle Abel, in the same clear, crystalline voice she used for all her utterances.

Mademoiselle Sylva returned to her side.

"*I* ought to be the one asking for news of *your* admirer, Marthe. Has Dr. Mévil not been tending to you?"

Marthe looked at the lane's red sand.

"Yes … perhaps; and to many others as well. It's not very interesting, this matter with Dr. Mévil."

"I thought…" Mademoiselle Sylva hesitated to recall something Fierce had said. "I thought he was tending more to you than to the others…"

"He'd be mistaken if so." Mademoiselle Abel's indifference was at its coldest. "Who told you that?"

"No one," Sélysette lied, blushing scarlet. "You don't find him pleasing?"

Marthe Abel pursed her lips and seemed to ponder distant things.

"I prefer Monsieur Rochet," she said suddenly, with a strange laugh.

"The old newspaperman? You're mad!" said Sélysette, scandalized.

They sat down on the stone bench.

"Sélysette, what do you think of Monsieur de Fierce?"

"Nothing, nothing in particular. He's charming, very delicate, and a good companion. You know this as well as I do."

"Does he please you?"

"Marthe, why are you teasing me? I assure you, there's nothing going on between us, absolutely nothing…"

"You're a darling girl," ruled Mademoiselle Abel, before taking Sélysette's hands in her own for a squeeze: an extraordinary show of sympathy for one so chill by custom.

"I'm certain," — she pressed — "*certain*, that there's nothing going on. But tell me anyway. Does he please you?"

"Why not?"

"Do you love him?"

"You're being absurd!"

Mademoiselle Sylva rose to her feet, almost angry.

"Don't get cross," Marthe implored her. "I swear to you, Sélysette, I am not, absolutely not, trying to cause you pain. On the contrary…."

"I know," muttered Sélysette, becalmed.

"Listen," said Marthe, trying again. "You're young, very young, and so kind that I'm very fond of you. We were just speaking of Dr. Mévil. He's close friends with Monsieur de Fierce…"

"Yes," said Sélysette, blushing again over the lie she had told a moment ago.

"Well, see if … how shall I put it? … if you can't make them less-good friends…"

"But how do you expect me…?"

"Try and see, Sélysette. I'm fonder of you than you think, much fonder…."

♦€

The hibiscus were in bloom in the garden of the Rue des Moïs, and all the bushes were red.

That same day Admiral d'Orvilliers was paying a visit to Madame Sylva, who was alone in the house. Sélysette, retained by the governor, had not yet returned.

The two armchairs were adjacent beneath the banyans of the terrace, and the tiny *boy* with the silken chignon had set by the admiral's side a big whisky-soda with plenty of ice.

"I've missed listening to a lovely voice I enjoy sing me my old songs," he said.

"Sélysette won't be long," said the blind woman. Madame Sylva was smiling, because just hearing her daughter's name gave her pleasure.

They waited. The admiral had taken one of his old friend's hands in his own, kissed it, and kept it, in friendly fashion.

"Would you believe," he suddenly said, "that I deem you to be happier than I, despite all your sorrows and miseries? You have your Sélysette; whereas I have a great hole in my old, solitary life: no daughter of my own to love me."

Madame Sylva gently pressed the hand that held hers.

"A twenty-year-old girl," murmured the admiral, and blurted, "When is she getting married?"

Madame Sylva shrugged her spare shoulders.

"When God wills it. Mothers are all the same, and my child shall not leave me without rending my hoary heart. But I'm not egotistical. Besides, my daughter must marry, to provide me with grandchildren."

"Are there husbands to be had in Saigon?"

"Far too many, because my Sélysette is rich. But we shall choose at our leisure. I'd prefer a husband who was not a colonist."

"Such husbands can be found," said d'Orvilliers. "What does Sélysette think?"

"Nothing at all as yet."

"You think so? Girls have their little secrets."

"Not mine," declared Madame Sylva.

She explained her belief.

"My daughter is not a girl of today. I've raised her to be like me, and as my own mother once was. I do not find that there's been progress in women's education. People disparage the white geese[90] of yesterday, but I've seen the new generation: it is less white and more goose."

"I have little experience in the matter, but what you say seems reasonable to me."

"Without a doubt. These days we initiate girls into all of life's ugliest parts. And how do we do it? Through novels and newspapers, on the street, with flirts. Are we to believe that they draw profitable knowledge from this? Are we to believe that if sullied in advance they'll have an easier walk down the muddy path? The smith learns his craft only at the smithy. We teach these children that the world operates only by dint of calculation, but they're no more skillful for being less naive, and when the time comes they miscalculate, and end up in unwise marriages."

"And back in the day?"

"Back in the day mothers would calculate on their daughters' behalf. Things were cleaner and less foolish. I will handle the calculation for Sélysette. I will reckon the sincerest and most honest among those who strike her fancy. She will marry him through her trust in me, and will love him with all her heart. And they will live happily…"

"Unless…"

"Unless something unexpected happens. But what can you do? She will play the great lottery with the best numbers. If the wheel takes an

---

90 In France a "little white goose" is an innocent girl raised in the old manner. Madame Sylva is contrasting traditional virtues against the moral decay of modern society.

unfortunate turn, she'll still have her Christian faith, and she'll bear all her crosses, just as I have borne mine."

"We shall speak of these things again someday," said the admiral, "and I'll impart an old idea that this old brain has produced."

Mademoiselle Sylva, pink-cheeked, burst in like a gust of wind.

"Mama, Mama! It's been a year since I saw you last…"

She gave her an eager kiss.

"It just wouldn't end at the governor's. There was a crush of people — Marthe Abel…"

Monsieur d'Orvilliers rose to his feet.

"I've seen the prodigal and am content. I'll be leaving."

"Not yet!" Sélysette begged.

She went over to a hibiscus, stripped it, and offered the old friend two handfuls of red flowers with golden pistils.

"For your lovely parlor, arrayed with sabers and bayonets — and so that you'll think of us more often down there!"

Monsieur d'Orvilliers took the flowers and caressed the little hands.

"Thank you. You'll permit me to give some to Fierce, in consolation for his not having accompanied me today?"

"Hmm, I'll have to think about that!" joked Mademoiselle Sylva. "Where *is* Monsieur de Fierce?"

"Reveling," the admiral gravely affirmed.

The blond brow knitted — imperceptibly.

"At a nautical party," Monsieur d'Orvilliers specified, with a laugh. "He took passage on one of the torpedo boats of the mobile defense and is busy with exercises off Cap Saint-Jacques: all out of pure and simple zeal, which is to his credit. There is inclement weather today at sea."

03 ◆ 80

That same evening before bed Mademoiselle Sylva went to the veranda for a breath of air.

The warm night was rife with fragrance. Every flower on every clod of humid, odorous earth sent forth troubling exhalations.

Mademoiselle Sylva shivered in that living shadow. The veranda was low and the horizon limited, but the murk of night gave the illusion of a vast black expanse. Mademoiselle Sylva dreamed that the entirety of Saigon was in view, along with the river, with its ships and junks. In her dream a torpedo boat passed, white with foam.

Fierce was at the same moment returning aboard the *Bayard*.

He was weary and sore, and soaked to the bone with the spray of the open sea. The salt of the waves lay like a stinging powder on his face and burned his eyes.

But a wholesome joy coursed through his arteries. — Memories would at times besiege his idle hours, memories from before Sélysette, memories of debauchery and skepticism — and not unlike nostalgia — but the day's rude gusts had blown the foul nostalgia far away. He was back in his blue room now, at bedtime, simple and innocent of heart and mind — uncivilized — in love.

He was under the spell of a singular intoxication. He had a vague notion that he was evading a strange malady — Civilization. — He believed himself a convalescent; he was reckoning on the future, a future in which he would be cured and enjoy radiant health.

From the wall, in a bizarre and sumptuous frame, made with the fur of a black panther, a pastel smiled down — Sélysette Sylva, sketched after the photograph stolen the other week. Religiously, Fierce knelt before his physician, plumbed his memory for adoring words, and prayed — for the first time, to be sure, since his earliest childhood.

XVIII

fortnight later the governor-general, set to depart for Hanoi on his spring tour, threw the last ball of the winter, inviting all of Saigon. Vast as the palace of the viceroy of Indochina was, they had to light up the grounds and hide an orchestra amid the trees.

The guests began to arrive at about ten o'clock and were received by ordinance officers and the residential staff. The governor being a bachelor, Madame Abel, the woman of highest rank in Saigon, took charge of the women, and sought to ensure that all was for the best.

The governor — a most radical former member of parliament — excelled in matters of pomp. He made his entrance at eleven o'clock, his Tonkinese lancers marching ahead of him through the park, torches in hand. He himself was unaccompanied, on a sovereign's parade among the guests. Bare shoulders bowed in courtly reverence. White tuxedos folded the shirt fronts within, already damp with sweat. The sovereign passed, all nonchalance, offering two fingers for shake, flashing a smile. Over his back the broad diagonal of the great sash of Annam completed the aristocratic profile: a profile calculated and purposeful — and, in Asian countries, politically astute. He withdrew to a secured parlor.

Admiral d'Orvilliers joined him there alone with the general-in-chief. One could make them out from afar, through the open windows. They spoke without gestures. The Tonkinese stood guard outside, sabers out.

Then began the dances, and the flirts as well. On the marble flagstones of the grand hall — which, tall as a church, collects through its vast windows all the cool that a Saigon night can produce — they danced till dawn, though couples would stray into the garden's thickets. Pale dresses blended with white uniforms, and the ball sparkled, spared the mournful black attire of Europe. Out on the grounds, beneath the flat light of the bamboo lanterns, the slow rotation of strolling couples took on a lunar shade, like a nocturne by Watteau.[91]

All of Saigon was on hand. Although it was a European party, a party of conquerors enjoying their victory in the conquered capital, natives too had been invited, flexible mandarins who had rallied to the Republic, and whom their old subjects cursed from the depths of their *cai-nhas*. The Tong-Doc of Cholon[92] talked taxes with Malais; the ambassador of the king of Siam evaded the lieutenant-governor's questions. Mademoiselle Jeanne Nguyen-Hoc, the new Phou's[93] only daughter, stonily endured the courting of the captains and lieutenants gathered about her person. Pretty and delicate in spite of her simian race, but more mysterious and closed than an ancient Egyptian statue, she faced the world with a smooth brow and cold eyes, the thoughts behind them forever beyond apprehension; and there was perhaps nothing beating beneath the magnificently embroidered green satin that covered her narrow chest — or at least nothing comprehensible to European men. Born French and baptized Catholic, properly raised in a worldly convent, she could waltz, flirt, still her mind to listen to Beethoven; hands supple and lips thin, she knew, too, all that is known to the demi-virgins of Europe, as was writ beneath the ambiguous irony of her smile. But all of this: so much clothing. Clothing too the ambition she never concealed to choose a French husband, who would give her legitimacy within the conquering nation — clothing of Parisian fabric, under which her Asian soul would hunker down and defy all violation — for the Asian soul, too old, too crystallized in its millenary refinement, will never be modified or decrypted. No Western philosopher, no master psychologist could discern even the form of one Phou Nguyen-Hoc's daughter's Annamite dreams.

----

91 See note 71 for details on this French painter.

92 A tong-doc is a provincial governor. The association with Cholon, then its own city (it was fused with Saigon in 1931), is unclear.

93 See note 11 for an explanation of this Vietnamese title.

… All of Saigon was on hand, and it was a prodigious pell-mell of people who were wholesome and people who were not — the latter being in the majority, because the French colonies are a proper sewage farm for all the excrement and rot that the mainland spews and expels. — To be found there were dubious men in infinite number, men whom the penal code, that slack spiderweb, had failed to retain in its weft: bankrupts, adventurers, blackmailers, able husbands, and some spies. — There was a crush of more-than-easy women, all capable of a copious debauch in any of a hundred ways, adultery being the most virtuous. — This cesspool was marred by the rare instance of probity, of pudeur. — This disgrace, though known, spread, and displayed, was accepted, welcomed. Clean hands shook the dirty without disgust. — When far from home the European, king of the world in its entirety, likes to declare himself above laws and morals, violate them with pride. The secret life of Paris or London is perhaps more repugnant than life in Saigon, but it is secret, lived with the shutters down. Colonial defects fear not the light of day. And why condemn their frankness? Houses of glass require no expense of illusion and hypocrisy.

Dr. Raymond Mévil arrived late and did not dance. He hardly made an appearance in the sitting rooms and selected the grounds for his base of feminine operations. He was not content this night to hunt whatever game happened to come his way. He lay in wait for Marthe Abel and Madame Malais alone, resolved to act against one or the other. But fortune proved hostile to his designs. It was Madame Ariette whom he ran across, at a bend in a lane with no crossroads. For four weeks he had been missing their weekly tryst, and now could not avoid giving account.

Madame Ariette was a proper woman, and by reputation Saigon's greatest prude. A lover's betrayal could not much move her; she was most susceptible in the purse, where the betrayal was leaving a void.

"It would seem," she calmly said, "that my society displeases you. Why? We no longer mean anything to each other, as you have led me to understand in no uncertain terms. And, though I'd have preferred a more loyal adieu, you may rest assured that I will not try to bring you to my bed."

Resignedly, Mévil undertook to find an excuse.

"Let's have none of that, if you please. I haven't the slightest ill feeling towards you. You love me no more, and I did not love you. Let's remain good friends. Just one final word. Yesterday I was expecting your visit on my day…"

Mévil understood.

"Correct," he insolently replied. "I owe you the term's rent, because I have neglected to serve notice…"

He counted out bills under the Chinese lantern; she smiled, too adept to grow cross.

"Might one know," she murmured in a delicate voice, "whether you've chosen your new … apartment? I do not doubt your taste, but perhaps you've run into trouble … moving? Might I be useful, as a friend? I can provide such services."

"I've never doubted it," said the doctor ironically.

A Nile-green dress passed at the lane's end. Mévil thought he recognized Madame Malais.

"Here," he promptly said, handing over the bills. "I believe this settles things. As for the other matter, no need to worry. I always work alone."

They separated. Madame Ariette returned to her husband in the game room.

"My pocket is torn," she said. "Would you keep my purse?"

The lemon-yellow attorney nonchalantly took the purse — and kissed the hand.

Meanwhile Raymond Mévil pursued the green dress. The woman passed before a lighted window; it was not Madame Malais. Disappointed, the doctor searched the far reaches of the grounds.

On a lonely bench — but not a dark one — he saw a couple seated in silence, Mademoiselle Sylva and Fierce, and felt a sad jealousy run him through like a sword.

He picked up his pace on the deserted lane. A man leaning against a tree gave him a tap as he passed. Surprised, Mévil recognized Claude Rochet, the newspaperman, who for one night had left his vile hovel in the Boresse quarter.[94] He was chuckling out his clucking mouth, and tripped as he recovered a glove that had slipped from his grasp — a woman's glove; Mévil observed the numerous buttons. A flirt for Rochet, this brute reverted to childhood — although a rich brute, with millions… — Curiosity piqued, Mévil ran to the end of the lane, but there he found several women and several gentlemen in group conversation, with Marthe Abel at the center of their circle. Many hands were bare. — Mévil forgot Rochet.

Later he joined Madame Malais in an empty sitting room. He had given up trying for a tête-à-tête with Marthe. She was dancing the night

---

94   See note 67 for a description of La Boresse.

away, her card full and all caps[95] accepted. — The blond marquise, lovely in her Louis XVI dress, was at a mirror touching up her hair. She suddenly spied Mévil up close behind her, and turned as if in a fright.

"Have I scared you?" he said, most respectfully.

She forced a smile.

"No, but you've surprised me… It's late, and I'm looking for my husband, so we can go home."

"Not before granting me a turn through the grounds?" He was begging. "Just one turn. I haven't kissed your hand at all this evening, and I am here for you alone."

She retreated, babbling. A large silhouette filled the frame of the door. Malais entered, ironic and cordial.

"Ah! Bah? You, Doctor? I haven't seen you all evening. Found the Ring of Gyges,[96] have you? — Shall we go, my dear?"

"Oh yes!" she said.

Alone, Mévil wandered the grounds before departing in turn.

"Rotten day," he murmured.

The bench with Sélysette and Fierce was now empty. Drooling Claude Rochet had fallen asleep against his tree trunk.

"Rotten day," Mévil repeated. — And with that he left, imbued with the sadness of the vanquished.

On their bench — the bench that she had one day cleared with a little girl's bound — Sélysette and Fierce had for two hours forgotten the rest of the earth.

They had taken refuge there from the start. Because she was miraculously pretty in a white dress wrapped with a bramble in bloom, all had wanted a dance with her, so many that she had feigned a twisted ankle to evade unwelcome requests. From then on the need to keep up appearances kept her pinned to the bench, which she had not the slightest desire to leave.

He had taken a seat right next to her. They spoke of banalities, and often fell silent — distraction breaking their sentences into absurd bits. They hardly noticed; their eyes, friendly, would meet, and this language was as good as another. The chaste evening buzzed with crickets in the dew-laden trees. Filtered through the opacities of the lanterns, the light cast a bedroom-yellow pallor on the bench. The ball was far away, hard to hear through the leaves.

____

95 *Casquettes*: literally, caps. By metonymy, military men.

96 See appendices.

Fierce was thinking back over his life — going back through the dead years, the forgotten travels, the drab adolescence, the neglected childhood in an indifferent house. — Never before, nowhere before, the memory of so sweet an evening. A befuddled gratitude swelled his heart and melted his marrow. There rose to his lips a violent, timid desire to exclaim to his companion frantic words of enslavement and adoration.

She, pensive, had let the fan drop from her open hand. Perhaps at times, in her virginal reveries, she had imagined such a park, and a solitary bench, where someone would swear unknown oaths to her. — She did not withdraw her hand when he took it. She did not interrupt his halting words. A shiver went through her shoulders, and a flush rose to her cheeks.

He spoke, very low. — The hibiscus themselves, tilting their curious corollas towards his mouth, could not make out his voice. This was no civilized man artfully courting a new sensation. Lips were in all sincerity babbling a fearful confession, and it was a thing more chaste than a mother's kiss for her child.

"This hand" — he could barely bring himself to touch its fingers — "will soon bear a band of gold. You will choose the least unworthy from among those who love you … Would you like … would you like him to be me?"

A terrible anguish coursed through his veins. His legs grew weak. He was on his knees before her.

She was panting like a doe at bay. Her lowered eyes stared obstinately at the sand.

The crackle of a step sounded at the far end of the lane. In an instant both had leapt to their feet. They dared to look each other in the face. Fierce held out his hand.

"Sélysette…?"

Mademoiselle Sylva blushed deeper. She timidly reached out her damp little hand, then tremulously stepped back with a lovely smile of confusion. The hibiscus snagged her white dress. She murmured:

"If Mama likes…"

XIX

The morrow was a blue day that seemed to smile upon all the hopes of men. — Admiral Duke d'Orvilliers paid an official visit on behalf of his aide-de-camp, Jacques de Fierce, to ask for Mademoiselle Sélysette Sylva's hand in marriage.

Madame Sylva was in her garden, seated amid the banyans. Summoned, Sélysette listened, frightened and blushing, from over by the hibiscus. When her mother consented she silently granted her hand. And the two promises were exchanged.

Mademoiselle Sylva agreed, happily, to become Madame de Fierce. Placing absolute trust in her betrothed, she gave herself over without reserve; and nothing seemed better or more certain to her than the love of that honorable man, whom she held in high esteem and fancied with all her kindly heart.

That evening they exchanged their kiss of betrothal. The evening ran late on the creeper-veiled veranda. At midnight Fierce walked back to the somnolent wharf. The *Bayard* cut a long black silhouette against the blue horizon. The masts, the smokestacks, the gangways, the blockhouses — all seemed a muddle of bizarre timber-work. In the background, amid the arecas of the eastern bank, floated a yellow crescent moon, like a shadow-puppet lantern.

Fierce was astonished to see four columns of smoke rising from the cruiser's smokestacks. So the fires of all the boilers had been lit, but why? Up the gangway he went, hastening his step. A helmsman had been on the lookout for Fierce. The admiral was expecting him, at a table covered with orders and dispatches.

"Out of luck, Fierce my boy. We're off to Hong Kong presently. — Orders from Paris. — Don't get upset, though. Perhaps it'll only be for a week or two…"

The grey moustache was stark against the surly old visage, but the gentle eyes were tender with compassion.

Without a word Fierce went to his room and closed the door. The sentry in the corridor heard the bed creak as he sat and saw no light emerge from the air vent. Head in hands, Fierce daydreamed in the gloomy night.

He did not lie down. He was like a convalescent who feels, in the blunt thud of his temples, the sudden return an ill-extinguished fever.

The *Bayard* cast off for the six o'clock tide.

XX

he *Bayard* entered Hong Kong through the western pass, its keen hull slicing through the water without an eddy. The crowd of sampans and junks milled about to make room, and the cannons at the fort replied to its salute.

Mountains hemmed in the harbor like a lake. At this lake, it seemed, all the world's ships had scheduled to meet, and Hong Kong was an Asian caravanserai between America and Europe. Sailboats, enormous three-masters laden with rice, lay at anchor along the cliffs at the entrance, their hulls of green, pink, white, or sky-blue reflected in the calm sea — a mottle of impressionist watercolor. Next came the inky-black colliers, hugging the first wharves of the outer ports, and so low to the water that only their masts and smokestacks showed. These served as avant-garde to the steamships. The preponderance followed, scattered throughout the harbor. — Hideous, dirty steamships, some of them unloading with a bustle and din onto barges or junks, most of them as dead and inert as abandoned factories. White cruise ships, agleam like yachts, lay here and there like castles among the factories.

The swift *Bayard* made way towards the wharf for warships, visible at the far end of the harbor, neatly aligned and prideful.

Sampans squeaking past churned water with the heavy blow of their sculls. Sails of woven bamboo hung from the yards, and one could make out the repugnant Chinese riverboat-women, their smooth hair constellated with green jewelry. Yellow babes wallowed at their feet on dirty planks, amid rice and upset drinking bowls. A nauseous stench wafted from these cesspools.

Now that the *Bayard* was on approach, however, no one had eyes for anything but the land. Hong Kong's mountains seemed to burst from the sea, single slopes stretching all the way to the summits. On the far side the continental coast rose in layers towards a blue range that fused with the sky, whereas the island was cut steep and straight as a crater; the villas scrutable halfway up seemed to have alighted on the rock like so many birds.

There were a great many such villas. Their staged terraces peopled the mountain. Joining them together were catwalks undergirded by grand arches, lending them an air of Roman aqueducts. A terrifying funicular, vertical as a tower, scaled the tallest peak. And the city, hemmed between sea and mountain, stretched as far as the eye could see along the shore, its colorful houses clinging wherever they could find purchase, and mounting their assault on the foothills.

It was a lovely city, this Hong Kong, flirtatiously veiled in great trees, coiffed with its extravagant green hat of a mountain. It thrived on an exuberant life, with its busy docks, its noisy arsenal, its conveyances, its launches, and its wharves yellow with Chinamen.

The look of a great maritime city is striking, spellbinding. No spectacle could take better hold of an anxious or ailing mind, or better serve to entertain or distract it.

From the *Bayard*'s poop, elbows resting on the gunwale, Fierce watched the city of Hong Kong come to him.

XXI

onsieur Jacques de Fierce to Mademoiselle Sélysette Sylva.

"Sélysette, my love, I'd have liked every evening to send you the sort of kiss I set on your forehead on the eve of my sad departure. And even that slim joy, the only joy that would have softened my exile, I must renounce: no cruise ship to Saigon for many days yet; the Cochin-China post left Hong Kong before the *Bayard*'s arrival; I'm not sure you'll even read this letter: how and when will it leave?

"And what of your letters? Will they reach me? I so need them! You are to me like the lighthouse that guided us along Hainan[97] the other night: without it who knows what shoals our *Bayard* would have run up on; without you I have no notion where my life would lead. I shudder even to conjecture, it so frightens me. I was a sick man, and you have been my healer; but now, absent my physician, it seems to me that my fever is going to take hold once more…

____

97 Island off Guangdong, in the South China Sea.

"This is nonsense I'm writing you, of course; don't laugh. I've a right to rave a bit at this distance from you. My little fiancée, do you know how much I love you? You must understand, I'd never loved anyone before meeting you, and had never had a sister, or a friend. And my mother never cared to caress me, nor did my father pay me any heed except to select my middle schools, all far away. What I bring you is a brand-new heart, a heart that has never been put to use; and though you be a little saint and I a miscreant, of the two of us it is I who am the more naive and less jaded, for even these words I write you now, words that can never be tender enough, I knew nothing of as late as yesterday.

"I'm writing you from my room — now blue, as you wanted it — near the portrait that one day I stole from you, and which I will return to you honestly the day I have you in exchange. For the moment, and in spite of your anger, I lack the courage to deprive myself of the image — my talisman, my fetish, all that remains to me of you. — Seven days already since I left you behind! And how many more before we meet again? We're at Hong Kong, as I now know, because England and we have had a spat, and we're trying to remedy things with handshakes and evening balls. Who knows how many handshakes[98] and how many balls will prove necessary? I want nothing to do with it, and I shut myself up aboard ship like a sick man wearied by the noise. Still, I am not entirely free of obligations. Yesterday I had to pay official visits to the garrison's English mess, and Admiral Hawke's[99] battleship is preparing a colossal party for us that, like it or not, I shall have to attend. — Yes, I set foot on land yesterday for the first time and, I hope, the last time, for my heart was heavy throughout the ride…. You see, my palanquin — carriages are rarer here than in Venice — was conveying me to the upper city on roads consisting of stairs, and I thought I'd walk a bit to stretch my legs. I reached a genuine park lane up on the mountainside, through a dry riverbed; a green, wooded lane so well hidden among the trees that it seemed a path to some fairy castle; it runs along the ravine, crosses it here and there over a mossy little bridge, and has a rustic parapet; with their Gothic arches, the little bridges look like doorways to dilapidated abbeys; the parapet is a crude earthen structure, with yellow

---

98   *Shake-hands* in the French text.

99   This appears to be a fictional admiral. The famous admiral by that name was before Fierce's time. This was Edward Hawke (1705–81), who took part in the Battle of Toulon (1744, War of the Austrian Succession) and won a great victory over the French at the Battle of Quiberon (1759, Seven Years' War). For his trouble he was raised to the peerage as the 1st Baron Hawke.

balustrades and green balusters. It's all silent, mysterious, narrow — all the more narrow because through the hedgerow of palms and ferns one can glimpse the massive harbor sleeping at the foot of the mountain. I felt much more alone and much farther from you now on this lovers' path than I had the instant before — and so sad that I produced my handkerchief. The palanquin-bearers thought I was wiping my forehead…."

XXII

everal squadrons — English, German, Russian, American — had gathered at Hong Kong, and the war harbor, cluttered with ships, seemed a cosmopolitan city, an international Venice, with all of the world's flags flying over an archipelago of steel palaces. Battleships and cruisers lay side by side, in amicable alignment, unconcerned with old quarrels or forthcoming wars. The winds were blowing peace; it was time to fraternize.

Dinghies, patrol boats, whalers came and went without cease, crossing paths in every direction. Visits were paid, salutations delivered, bits of information gathered; the parade of aides-de-camp choked the gangways; the messes and wardrooms[100] were society parlors, where champagne flowed in infinite streams; and one spoke English, French, Russian, even Japanese, as in a modern Tower of Babel.

---

100   In the original text this word appears in English.

This would last all day, and evening would see even greater bustle in the fevered fleet and city. When the sun sank into the pink sea the flags would make their pompous descent down crutches[101] and masts, glorified to the sounds of clarions, rifles, and drums; and national anthems would play in the twilight — each ship playing first its own, then all the others, out of courtesy. Thus the day — the official day — would come to an end in a welter and confusion of melody.

But then the other life, nocturnal, would commence. The lighthouses, the beacons, the lanterns, and every window in the city would come to life. The suburbs would encircle the harbor with light, and the ships, in the center, would reply on every side with their electric beams. Here and there on the water would run a trail of sparks from steam-driven boats. And the squadrons, in launch after packed launch, would dispatch their tumultuous horde of sailors on shore leave to mount their assault on the city.

The wharves gleamed, white as snow under the voltaic streetlamps. To reach them one would climb stone steps, which the boats would crowd in to accost. The white, red, and green beacons would dance a luminous polka at the foot of the steps; up top, meanwhile, the rickshaw- and palanquin-men would be at loggerheads, heaping Asian abuse on one another and shaking their mottled lanterns. Running, singing sailors would pile into the vehicles with cries and whistles and calls — all this din drowned in an immense Chinese clamor that would only redouble — hoarse, singsong, mysterious.

The gallop of runners and porters sank into the zebra-striped night of light and shadow. Up the sloping alleys and endless stairs they went, all the way to the heart of the Chinese city, which knows no sleep. The banks, clubs, and European counters of Hong Kong run along a single street, parallel to the wharf. Queen's Road, as it is called, aside from a few details of overly local color, could exist in any English colonial city. Step away from it, however, and Chinese Hong Kong — prodigious Chinese Hong Kong — begins. It is not Chinese only: it is Parsee, Tagal, Macau, Japanese, cross-bred. From dusk to dawn its maze of streets, streets like basement stairs, furiously swarm; the city swarms with mobs, brawls, scuffles, and the frightful concert of a hundred thousand voices crying themselves hoarse. The Sikh policemen, huge beneath their red turbans, concern themselves only with injury by club or knife. The rest is licit; and every night is like a riot.

----

101   *Corne (de vergue)*: The *crutch* or *cheeks* fixed on the inner end or a gaff or boom, which embraces, and slides along, the mast of a small vessel as the sail is hoisted or lowered. (See A. Boyer, *Dictionnaire royal françois anglois et anglois-françois*.)

In this pandemonium sailors thirsty for wine, cries, women, and copious orgies would find satisfaction. In the black night all would begin their festivities.

Later, after dinner, the staff boats would set out and the officers invade the land in turn — a second invasion hardly less noisy than the first. The sailors of various squadrons would not mix, because of their different languages; only as the night drew to its drunken end would they congeal into cosmopolitan bands. The officers, however, were polyglot enough to fraternize with gusto. Soldiers by trade to a man, and trained to kill one another at the first order, they displayed an intimate camaraderie, the cordiality of condottieri,[102] ready to slit one another's throat out of loyalty but with no hatred in their heart, and with deep ignorance of and disdain for the quarrels whose purpose they served. They laughed, drank, swore together; they shared bottles and mistresses alike.

These were joyous nights indeed. First they wore themselves out on carefree hikes high and low all over the city. Then they gathered by the mass in the propitious quarter of Cochrane Street, for an assault on its houses of ill repute. The doors would yield to blows, the wooden stairs resound like drums under galloping boot heels, and the women, piled into dirty parlors, emit cries of fright and servile laughter.

Their debauchery was excessive, prideful; they paraded their force and violence; they sought the illusion of being in a conquered and sacked city: they shattered glasses against walls and let fly piasters by the handful. The women, accustomed to maritime shore leaves, bent the back and held out a hand; and all of them, all of them — the yellow Cantonese of narrow bare feet, the northern Chinese coiffed with pearls, the round and made-up Japanese, the Spanish-eyed Macau, the Moldo-Vlachs of European aspect — accepted without repugnance the Western soldiers' rapid clutch. Open windows gave a view of the orgies across the way; the half-nude couples in one house would address those in another. And the tumult rose from the street, with provocative calls, obscene cries, and furious scuffles.

The city of Hong Kong occupies only the first slopes of its mountain. Higher up are the villas, great trees, and silence. Shady paths look down

---

102 Italian captains in command of mercenary companies in the Middle Ages and of multinational armies in the early modern period. In medieval Italian a *condottiero* was a contractor; the *condotta* was the contract by which he would enter into the service and payroll of a city or lord.

on terraces, and on a serene night the moon will sift through the leaves and shine a mosaic of light and shadow on the white ground.

To these terraces, with their exquisite cool and milky calm, Fierce would often repair to dream away his first nocturnal hours. But to get back aboard he would cross the shrieking city, in full rut. And as he brushed past the ill-shut doors of the dives, and the oozing debauchery within wafted into his face, blunt memories would rise in his mind and shoot through his skin — unwholesome reminiscences smacking of nostalgia.

XXIII

I t was a magnificent party thrown for the French aboard Admiral Hawke's battleship, the *King Edward*, a colossus beside which the *Bayard* was but a yacht.

This was one of those enormous celebrations whose recipe is known only in exotic lands. It began with a matinee, with a concert and comedy — savory stew in a city where theaters are unknown; there followed a dinner, or rather a banquet, fit for Pantagruel;[103] and the ball was opened by couples already tipsy and roused; the dancing went on until morning, with furious flirting on gangways that had been left in the dark for the occasion. Not until daybreak — after the hoisting of the colors and the eight o'clock "God Save the King" — did the last boat ferry off the last guest. The supper at small tables had turned into a proper orgy, and the battleship was as maculate as a sailors' bordello.

Admiral d'Orvilliers put his best foot forward, arriving early and leaving after dawn. His aides-de-camp, under orders, danced without

---

103 The giant son of another giant, Gargantua, in Rabelais's pentalogy of satirical novels, *The Lives and Deeds of Gargantua and Pantagruel* (1532–64). The authorship of the fifth book, published after Rabelais's death, is debated.

quarter and gave lavishly of themselves. The opposing camp had been just
as dead set, and the result had been an assault of cordialities and courtesies.
The instruction had evidently been to exaggerate. All these people knew,
more or less, how close they had come to battle, and the terrible specter
of a war barely averted hung over the party, deepening the stupor and
drunkenness. The women especially, the lovely Englishwomen whom the
French officers had gallantly clasped, never forgot that the very gentlemen
now fawning over their graces had considered and perhaps planned an
inexpiable massacre of their fiancés and lovers, and the heady odor of blood
nearly spilled in rivers did not fail to tickle their sensual nostrils.

A tropical climate will soften and depress males, whereas in females it
will whip up a thirst for pleasures — all pleasures. There is no society woman
in Saigon who will consent to go home from the theater after the fifth act, take
no supper, turn in before dawn; no woman who will not require, in addition
to nocturnal caresses, the treat of frequent naps for two. Shutters will close
at balls lest sunlight flush out the dancers, and the baccarat table will not
always be empty at the stroke of noon. — It was delicious to be aboard the
King Edward, where pleasure donned the mask of patriotic duty. By the second
quadrille[104] all the flowers had been stolen, all hands freed of their gloves, all
waists secured in a clasp. By supper the flirts had taken on an air of bedroom
rendezvous. A vessel serves the purpose, with its many discreet corners,
sheltered from lamps and searchlights. There, at leisure, demi-virgins can pick
the petals of their demi-virtue, and women can yield still more. What peace
of mind, too, to have a sailor for a partner, a transient ready to vanish, whose
fleeting kiss, free of consequence, will remain forever secret, null, inexistent!

The English had invited the whole of their cosmopolitan city. Women
of all countries were present — Westerners, fresh from prudish Europe, but
already well loosened up after their four-week cruise — colonials, every one
an honest lady, according to Brantôme[105]: girls from Hong Kong, where
the air is feverish; girls from Shanghai, where every house has two doors;
girls from Nagasaki, where the Japanese example is perfidious; girls from
Singapore, where the flowers are too fragrant; and, finally, girls from Hanoi
and from Saigon, which initiates at times call Sodom and Gomorrah.

There were others, come from farther afield: immigrants,
contributing to the candidly perverse Far East their own picturesque

---

104   Formal dance performed by four couples in a rectangular formation.

105   Pierre de Brantôme, author of *Mémoires de Messire Pierre de Bourdeilles* (1665–66), which
contains, among other books, *Les Vies des dames galantes* and *Les Vies des dames illustres*.

perversions: Americans, flirtatious and frivolous; Creoles from Cuba, nymphomaniac; Australians, with lower necklines than are dared even in New York; and the legion of travelers of all races, rendered skeptical and libertine by the contrast of too many countries, and who endlessly roam the world, so as to be ensnared by the moral prejudices of no country.

Among these women was one who took charge of Fierce. Chance had set them side by side at table. They first revealed their name, their country, their race — to make each other's exact acquaintance — with the prompt curiosity of nomads, lacking the time to bother with needless discretion. — Her name was Maud Ivory; she was an American from New Orleans — orphaned and free — unmarried; she had been traveling for three years, in the company of a friend of the same age, Alix Routh, betrothed at Bombay, and who would probably marry once they reached India. Miss Ivory would thereafter be alone, and would savor no less her easy existence as a tourist avid for pleasures and the open air.

"We're fresh from Australia and New Zealand," she said, "and when Alix marries I'll go to Egypt — for a first stop."

Curious, Fierce asked:

"Always on the move, then? No rest? What about home?"[106]

"Later — later."

Deep in his heart he saw a hearth he knew well.

"And love?"

"Love?" — She looked at him, provocative. "When it pleases me."

This manner of love he had never considered.

After dinner they went for a walk on the spar-deck, which had been made into a garden. She breathed deep, like a hardy, sensual girl, her chest raising her corsage, her hand heavy on the supporting arm. He would look at her from time to time, and could not help but find her lovely, with that fauness profile, those hard, voluptuous eyes, and that prideful, unfurling golden fleece.

The friend betrothed at Bombay, hanging on the arm of a lieutenant, joined them. All four leaned on the stern rail. The fire-dotted harbor was warm and fragrant; the palms and ferns heaped on the bridge instilled a sense of solitude and secrecy. A Nordenfeldt gun[107] nested nearby on its

---

106 *Home* appears in English.

107 A multi-barreled gun designed by Swedish engineer Helge Palmcrantz and patented in 1873. The weapon's manufacture was underwritten by Thorsten Nordenfelt, a Swedish steel producer, banker, and (later) weapons-maker. In an early demonstration a ten-barreled version fired three

corbel, the steel of its long, fine barrel gleaming like silver.

The Englishman, tall, strapping, and ruddy, began to lay siege to his partner. Miss Routh put up no fierce resistance. Night served as obliging mediator. Kisses were stolen, the beginnings of gestures made. Miss Ivory's hand stiffened on Fierce's arm.

Fierce felt a distressing tide rise in his veins. He wished to cast it back, react. He joked:

"Beware, Sir. Miss Alix's heart is no longer at liberty…"

"Bah!" needled Miss Ivory. "*Bombay est loin* — far from here!"[108]

Yes. Other cities as well, and other pledges.

Miss Routh, however, perhaps startled by a caress too well placed, suddenly repulsed her companion, and drew Miss Ivory in for a conference. Huddled together, elbows on the rail, the two young women whispered. The Englishman, sheepish before Fierce, sought to put a brave face on things, and mechanically opened the Nordenfeldt gun's breech.

"A nice piece," said Fierce, to break the silence.

"Nice," repeated the Englishman.

They gave no thought to their words; as they were only waiting for the Americans to finish their low Mass, they talked shop, absentmindedly.

"Twenty-four pounds?"

"Yes."

"How many cannons like it?"

"Sixteen. A good battery against torpedo boats…"

Fierce grabbed the breech levers; the block pivoted, slid along its shaft. The bore, round and black, with parabolic striations, came into view. — The cannon's parts moved easily, as under a friendly hand. — A slight effort would raise the block, or press it once more against the closed hole; steel hit steel with a muted thud. Fierce sought the pistol and pressed the trigger; the spring clicked.

The space all around was plentiful and sheltered from the wind. One would no doubt be comfortable on this well-appointed bridge — even on a lugubrious night of battle — when hunting down torpedo boats, when lying in ambush for miserable walnuts shells cast about in the waves, smarting, streaming, vanquished from the start…

---

thousand rifle-caliber rounds in three minutes and three seconds without stoppage or failure. The Maxim gun in time made the Nordenfelt obsolete, but in 1888 the Nordenfelt company and the Maxim Gun Company merged into Maxim Nordenfelt Guns and Ammunition Company Limited.

108   "Far from here" appears in English. To retain the effect of a switch of language we retain the French for "Bombay is far off."

At the sound of the cannon's manipulation the Americans approached, curious. The Englishman closed the breech.

"Things of war — humbug."[109]

He marked his words with derision and, laughing, retook Miss Routh's arm. Fierce was distracted for a moment, and an old, ill-forgotten gesture made its return beneath his notice; rather than offer it, he used his right arm to encircle Miss Ivory's waist, while his left hand pressed her fingers. She gave herself over, and he no longer dared to release her obliging waist. He was remorseful nonetheless.

Now the American, surprised and pricked by her gentleman's reserve, deployed her own coquettish arts, engaging him with flirtatious phrases that turned into declarations. She stirred him with scabrous words, feigned resistance the better to yield, excited him, drove him to distraction, brought his blood to a boil, and turned his head around. The other couple, meanwhile, was no longer holding out against libertine desires, and the Englishman's ruddy face would at intervals turn pale. The two girls, hardened to the game and cold as cats, eyed each other and laughed, and spurred each other on.

There was a table nearby; they supped. A few extinguished lamps produced a chiaroscuro. Glasses were immediately exchanged, knees pressed together. With a sudden lean, Miss Routh offered her gentleman half the litchi she had clasped in her lips. The kiss lasted a while, with the click of teeth.

"A fiancée!" exclaimed Miss Ivory with mock indignation, her arm reaching for a pickle, and brushing slowly past Fierce's mouth.

Fierce passed up a kiss on the arm. — Fiancé. — The word was a shaft through the heart. A dreadful shame burst upon his conscience. So this was all it took? He could fall into the grip of his filthy past just like that? Was he truly, truly incurable? A dog that must return to his mud for a wallow? A gangrenous appendage, to be lopped off?

A thigh had come to rest, heavy, on his own thigh; semi-naked flesh was in contact with his privy flesh, lying astride him, possessing him.

But tears of disgust were welling in his eyes, and he went no further that night in his betrayal.

---

109   These words appear in English, in a slightly different position.

XXIV

onsieur Georges Torral to Monsieur Jacques de Fierce.

"Little one, you left Saigon ill in spirit. — As far as I can judge, I no longer have the honor of being in your confidence. I nevertheless claim to be your friend, and I come with medical intent. Here is my remedy: a pill of true truth. Swallow and be not afraid; it is not bitter. It concerns Mévil; you are in the clear. But *hodie mihi, cras tibi,*[110] eh? Mévil is at the moment piteously ruining his life, and a lovely and intelligent life it was – like mine. The life of a Civilized man. The boy is trading away reason for instinct. Harken to his tale, and profit from it if you can.

"Mévil was once a sensible man, who loved women — all women, without the ineptitude of a preference for this one or that. Logical and precise, his desire sought in them only what they were made for: coitus. — This was, indisputably, a reasonable taste. Growing into it, Mévil was for a

---

110 "Today me, tomorrow you." A popular epitaph in medieval times.

fair number of years very happy. The other month, however, he developed a desire for one woman — after many others — and this woman, unlike the rest, pushed him away. You know who: the chaste friend, spouse to that brute of a tax farmer now stirring up revolution in the country. — It is of little account, in any case. — Mévil, holding to his peculiar notions, grew stubborn. It went too far, but more or less everyone goes too far. Me, I sometimes get it into my head to work out useless solutions in pure geometry. There's no great harm in that. The harm began when Mévil, for the sake of this mistress he could not have, tossed his other mistresses out into the street. — A fine start down the road to madness. Women have no variety of spasms at our service, so what does the merchant matter if the merchandise is the same? Preference, which must be founded in a detail or an accessory, should not encumber as we deal with the essential — with the coupling. — Mévil was going off the rails of good sense, and he soon derailed further.

"He went gaga for a second woman — the Abel girl; and this time his madness was complete. Absurd as it was, his love for the Malais girl still had a reasonable end: desire; he wanted her in his bed. It was glorified rutting, but rutting nonetheless. With the Abel girl he veered into Platonism. He loved her without knowing why, with an aimless love bordering on mental alienation. Now, I'm the most tolerant of men, and I admit of Platonic love, which is a kind of friendship: the intimate friendship of two beings who could lie together but would rather philosophize in unison. — But Mévil's love for Marthe Abel? Oh no! It is to laugh. They saw each other at the ball, at the tennis court; he heard her cry *play* and *ready*,[111] and noted that she waltzed out of time. The belief that this is a sound foundation for friendship, for intimacy, for any exchange whatever of cerebral sensations, is the figment of a man who carries in his pocket a one-way ticket to Charenton.[112]

"That is how far gone Mévil is.

"I see him every day, and study him with infinite curiosity: he is a lovely pathological case. The two passions gnaw at him like two dogs set on the same bone. In the morning he is subject to the influence of his imbecilically chaste night: his thoughts turn chiefly to the Malais woman, and he devises rather naive plans against her: his former deftness has evaporated along with his good sense; his imagination is now limited to

---

111   The two words appear in English.

112   The French equivalent of Bedlam. An asylum founded in the seventeenth century by the Hospitaller Order of the Brothers of Saint John of God.

kidnapping and rape; and, no joke, I think the Court of Assizes[113] has him under surveillance. — End of the day, same old tune to play[114]: setting sun, red sky between the black trees, languid breeze laden with heavy fragrance — Mévil turns poetic, dons a dead-leaf tie and hits the Inspection in his silvered rickshaw, to greet Marthe Abel with his pensive eyes. At nightfall he heads home, dines poorly, and goes to bed alone. This diet is not fattening. Nothing worse for an alcoholic than to be weaned at a stroke from alcohol; and Mévil is a kind of alcoholic, who has chosen women for his eau-de-vie.

"There you have it, little one: the story of a man who was once happy, because properly behaved, and is now unhappy, *very unhappy*, because mad. Life has proved insufficient for him. He has sought a taste of the chimerical — a noxious drug, poisonous to people. Mévil has been poisoned, and I know not whether he will recover, though I proffer him my antidotes. As for you … get this tale through your head, and think hard on it."

---

113 The criminal court, the police.

114 "*Le soir, autre guitare*": curious locution where *guitar* means something like *same old, same old*, but in this case with a rhyme.

XXV

Torral's letter did not reach Fierce, nor did a voluminous letter from Mademoiselle Sylva, which left on the same first cruise ship. The *Bayard*, suddenly hastening its departure by several days, had set sail from Hong Kong without news from Saigon. Such surprises are common at sea, and sailors pay them no heed. Fierce was nevertheless sorry to have no letters; it was hard to leave like that, going who knew where — to a secret destination — without the viaticum of a few sweet sentences, a tender thought, a scrap of paper touched by the betrothed. The longed-for letter's urgent remedy he would have to set forth without, uncured. He set forth, then, feverish and upset, his flesh in revolt, his mind unsteady. All of his former skepticism, all of his former nihilism, had been laying siege to him since the Englishmen's party. Despite his betrothal, despite the pure and deep love burning in his heart, one libertine encounter and a meddling moment had sufficed to bring him within a hair's breadth of betrayal — to crumble his will and send it sliding down into debauchery. — He now had bitter doubts about himself. Had his former life not irredeemably rotted him out? That supreme civilization, the civilization of the Torrals, the Mévils, the Rochets, the rationalist civilization of men without God, without a master, without a code: was it not a mysterious mental ailment, a gangrene of the soul, that would release no prey it had once bitten? All of his life — twenty-six years — Fierce had been courting pure reason; today he deemed it vain and deleterious; but could he flush it from his brain? Would it suffice for this cure to be in love with an ingenuous and faithful virgin? The love of Sélysette Sylva was like a sunbeam within him; but his thoughts turned to the tubercular, who in a warm and dry climate could at times put off their doom: a chill wind, a few rainstorms, and death quickens its pace; not for a minute must the ailing evade the sun their savior.

The *Bayard* left Hong Kong without a sound, furtively, as if escaping. An unplanned, mysterious departure, the result of a sudden decision over there, in Paris, in ministerial chambers where perhaps frightful questions of peace and war were being bandied about. Unease loomed over the harbor, among the ships under various flags that watched the French admiral leave. The *Bayard* passed the poop of the *King Edward*; fraternal the evening before, united in all matters festive and orgiastic, the two ships now exchanged a stiff salute, cannons sounding their brief note, white sailors and red soldiers coldly aligned face to face, the rising son splashing blood on the bayonets.

The *Bayard* put some sea behind it. Hong Kong sank below the horizon. The ship steamed west. The Chinese coast turned blue to starboard. At dusk Lei-Chao[115] emerged from the setting sun; Mount Jacquelin rose up, in yellow and black: sands below, brush above. At the next dawn the *Bayard* entered the Maxie river and steamed up the Kwangchowan[116] estuary, between two green banks, lined with protective shoals and peppered with tree-cloaked villages. The French town[117] had its barracks, its docks, and its schools — all empty. A cruiser lay at anchor at the port. The *Bayard* stopped and signaled; the other ship weighed anchor, and the two steamed back down the river in Indian file.

Fierce was counting the days. Another three before Saigon — if the route was direct. But no: they passed the Hainan Strait; d'Orvilliers's

---

115 Leizhou Peninsula, Guangdong province, west of Hong Kong, east of Vietnam (Annam). Also known as Aberdeen Island, because it lies next to Aberdeen Harbour. It now covers about half a square mile, after some land reclamation, and is one of the world's most densely populated islands, with a population of more than ten thousand.

116 Guangzhouwan, territory on the coast of Zhanjiang, China. Leased from 1898 to 1946 by France, which gave its capital, Zhanjiang, a new name: Fort-Bayard.

117 Fort-Bayard.

division was to concentrate at Tonkin, in Halong Bay. Fierce despaired. The charm was now broken that had renewed him in Sélysette's proximity, restored his youth, made him chaste and ingenuous — and happy; alone, far from her, he was once again old, debauched, skeptical — civilized. In vain did he look with fervor upon the cherished stolen portrait, which had so often served him as a protective talisman. — The charm was broken. — The portrait of Sélysette was now but an impotent image; he needed her very presence, her voice, her hand, her soul — quick, before the incurable relapse.

The *Bayard* penetrated the Tonkinese mists. The sea, suddenly shrunk, was glaucous and flat as a pond; and strange rocks as tall as Gothic towers bristled in the fog. The ship advanced amid the fantastical forms, a blend of clouds and islands. It was a nightmare archipelago, a petrified legion of giants emerging bit by bit all around to surround the ships. From the leaden sky fell a fine, steady rain, a drizzle that felt eternal.

Ahead, drowned in the mist, lay Halong Bay. A long phantom, hard to catch sight of through the obfuscating rain, floated upon the water: the cruiser they were seeking. They halted for two days. Coal barges, invisible even when close, came over from the port, to fill the holds. Then the division steamed off towards the open sea. Still the grey sky wept its grey mist onto the grey rocks.

Outside Halong the sea lapped and the monsoon whipped the sea-washed hulls with its foam. The sun lighted the Annamite coast, abrupt and golden. The division made headway towards Saigon, but slowly; the ships crawled along the shore, hugged every promontory, entered every bay. The idea, it seemed, was to parade the ships, show the cannons — and the tricolor flag — all along the land. They dropped anchor several times: at Thuận An, at Tourane, at Quy Nhon, at Nha Trang; these were lost hours. But on the tenth night, at last, they passed the lighthouse at Padaran, then the lighthouse at Saint-Jacques; and awakening Saigon once again saw upon its river the masts and hulls of its cruisers reflected in the current. The absence had lasted thirty-one days.

Impatient, Fierce looked at the city, but first he had to open and decipher the accumulated mail. On top of the month's usual dispatches — which had not been forwarded — there were the military and diplomatic orders that had arrived on the eve and on the day before that. The staff spent four hours on the task. Every aide-de-camp separately, in the isolation of his room, dug in to his share of the texts, and the worked-through translations arrived one by one to the admiral's table, where all was coordinated and took on sense. Fierce deciphered his lot without reviewing the whole; it mattered little to him whether the wind was turning to peace or war; he was dreaming of the Rue des Moïs.

There he sped, taking the first staff boat, the three-o'clock sun exerting no check on him. He set off on foot rather than wait for a carriage, and his heart pounded warm when he caught sight of the villa and the cherished veranda of his betrothal. A shudder of happiness shot through his marrow: he still loved her, so nothing had been lost, nothing compromised; these thirty days of murk and obsession would vanish like a bad dream at the first smile from his fiancée. He rang at the gate and was met by a lazybones of a *boy*, who, recognizing him, went off to fetch a letter; Fierce, astonished, anxious, tore open the envelope — and stood there dumbfounded, the letter in his fingers: Sélysette was not in Saigon; her mother had been compelled to leave the city for the sanatorium at Cap Saint-Jacques.

Fierce was deeply disappointed but reassured: he had been gripped with fear while unfolding the ill-omened letter. — After all, the cape is not far from Saigon; the boats of the river service make the journey there every day in two hours. — Fierce reread the letter, two pretty pages scratched out in a hurry, at the moment of departure: Madame Sylva had suffered through the overly humid heat of late April, and Sélysette, ever prudent and maternal, had mandated a few weeks in the mountains. The governor, it so happened, was at Tonkin and his villa on the cape vacant; they would settle in there summarily, and Fierce would have a room; they would expect him as soon as Hong Kong had at last finished with the poor *Bayard*.

"Tomorrow," he thought, "I'll ask for leave, and I'll dine at the cape."

Comforted with this certainty, he observed that the sun was high and his helmet thin. He hailed a malabar (Saigon's lousy answer to the fiacre), took shelter in it, and resigned himself to going back aboard the ship. On Rue Catinat he stopped for some shopping; after thirty days' absence it was time for some provisions.

Saigon was unchanged. He observed this without displeasure, and it served to distract him from his discomfiture. At the laundry the same Chinese figures were bent over the wash, their cheeks swelled with water, to moisten it with a vaporous rain before setting down the heavy, ember-laden irons. At the tailor's the same shears were cutting the same white fabric, six times folded over: this to expedite the manufacture of clothing, a half-dozen articles at once. Fierce entered A-Kong, shop of his favorite merchant, and the old Cantonese ran to greet him, the broad smile slicing open his face like a lemon. — A cup of tea — "Real Foochow,[118] Cap'taine! — And what you want? You arrive from Hong Kong? What the English do? When you fight?"

"You're an old scoundrel," said Fierce with a laugh. "There will be no fighting. — Send me over some rice powder, some extra-dry champagne, some Pedro Ximénez,[119] and some cello strings."

Right away, confidentially, A-Kong proposed a new quality of rice paper — "very excellent" — and some tennis balls in red and white — "good for to see on the ground — By way, what new with Cap'taine Malais, by Great Lake?"[120]

"What do you mean? The rice tax?"

"Nothing, nothing…"

The old man prudently changed the subject, turning his phrases with a diplomat's skill. The Chinese, silent conquerors, have spread their business network through all the cities and villages of Indo-China; marvelously informed through their secret freemasonry, they get wind of coming events from a long way off; so keen is their flair that, amid the indolence of Annamites and the astonishment of Westerners, they infallibly and ironically profit from every last thing, and never cease to enrich themselves.

The clock struck five. Fierce was hot, and the *Bayard*, roasting in the still-high sun, was no doubt a furnace. This was no time to hurry home. Better to mill about in a carriage for a couple of hours — till dusk. Fierce paid off his malabar and selected a well-hitched victoria. Without taking the trouble to inquire, the *saïs* set off down the usual path: it was time for the Inspection. Fierce left the man to his business.

Saigon was on parade on the Allée des Poteaux. The men and women alike were there, and Fierce recognized all with whom in his former life he had crossed paths or rubbed shoulders — at a supper, at a ball, at a gambling den, or in a bed. — Odd! The life of sensuality and skepticism that he had been leading he had now left behind, far behind, so far that it had vanished from view, and even from memory. It existed nonetheless; it continued to go its licentious and welcoming way; it was there, in carriages laden with flesh to sell and consciences to be bought — ready to take hold

------

118 After Fuzhou, capital of Fujian province, China.

119 A sherry from Jerez, Spain.

120 The Tonlé Sap, in present-day Cambodia.

of him once more, whenever he so wished. On an impulse, Fierce bade his coachman to step up the pace, but nothing doing; the road was clogged with vehicles.

They came up to a two-wheeled carriage hitched to a single pony. Torral sat within, beside one of his *boys*: he took occasional pleasure in exhibiting his vice in the city, out of cynicism, and a scornful hatred for the people he shocked. He saw Fierce and yelled a greeting; then, the traffic carrying him along in the opposite direction, he turned to ask whether Fierce had received his letter; but Fierce was already distant and failed to understand; he was looking forwards.

At the far end of the Allée des Poteaux stands a small brick bridge; by the dictates of fashion, this was as far as carriages could go; it was there that they would turn around. This exit had become Fierce's objective, a way out of the crowd. There would be open air beyond, far from these wicked and jaded men, far from these painted women in their soft dresses.

But a hand came to rest on his arm: Dr. Mévil, on his bicycle, had made his way up to him, skirting many a wheel – rather imprudently. Fierce had not read Torral's letter, and was surprised to see the doctor's haggard face: Mévil had turned the color of wax, and his widened blue eyes seemed open onto a void; his mouth, once red, as if bloodied by the impact of feminine teeth, had faded to pink; his pale moustache of Gallic decadence was ill stiffened despite the cosmetics. Fierce asked after his health: he shrugged without reply; but his hand sought the hand of his friend in thanks.

"What have you been up to?" said Fierce.

"Nothing."

They rode along for a moment, side by side, in silence. They suddenly met Hélène Liseron, in her victoria. She had no doubt reconciled with Mévil, and was now pursing her lips as if for a kiss; she had in fact never been able to hold a grudge against anybody; and, recognizing Fierce, she stuck out her tongue and laughed.

"Have you taken her back?" Fierce asked.

"No," said the other, with a shake of the head. He spoke in monosyllables, like a man exhausted.

He suddenly looked Fierce in the eye.

"Say, is it true you're to marry Mademoiselle Sylva?"

A shade of singular respect, and gloomy sadness, had come into his voice. Moved, Fierce pressed his hand.

"Yes," he said, "and I'm very happy…"

They were approaching the brick bridge. The victorias were turning around to head back, still at a walking pace. The women inside smiled, vain in their dresses. — Mévil looked at them, and then, slowly, shrugged. With a murmured "adieu" he leaned, cut the corner, and set off fast in the opposite direction — in pursuit of the women, this one or that, or perhaps some other not on hand. Fierce, pensive, looked at the flooded rice field, and at the setting sun, sprinkling its rubies over the water.

He had the carriage stop past the bridge, where the road had emptied out. A few trees cast some shade, and he liked the spot, especially as it was there that he had paused the other month with Sélysette and fireflies had whirled around them. — Full of the memory, he alighted, and soon came to regret it: the Ariettes' carriage came to a stop at the same time, and he could not escape a meeting. The young attorney grimaced with his most amiable smile; Fierce was obliged to go to the door; Madame Ariette, as if distracted, stripped the glove from her hand for a kiss.

"You're back from Hong Kong? How long a voyage it was!"

Ariette seemed delighted to reunite with his excellent friend; he invited him to dine that very evening — without the slightest ceremony.

"I can't," Fierce dryly said. "I'm a bit ill, and am leaving tomorrow for the sanatorium…"

"All the more reason: you require a family dinner, and an evening of calm that will not last too long. Come, then!"

"It will give us such pleasure," Madame Ariette sweetly urged, never raising her eyes.

He had to accept.

And it was a perilous and murky dinner. Madame Ariette's lovely, supple fingers played gently with the tablecloth, bending and curving as if engaged in a secret caress; and Fierce, in spite of himself, recalled the giving and receiving of such caresses. A foot touched his foot beneath the table; he responded unwittingly to the pressure. A desire made its sinuous way into his sinews; his long continence rose up against him.

He took fright, and withdrew: the attorney alleged a defense to reread, so as to leave his wife and guest alone; Fierce produced his watch, exclaimed how late it was, and took his leave — failing to observe the look of disappointment exchanged by husband and wife.

"I'll accompany you to the wharf," Ariette suddenly announced. "My defense can wait."

The streets were white with moonshine, and the night warm. They walked slowly. Before the club Ariette so insisted on going inside that Fierce acquiesced.

The poker games were in swing. Fierce was obliged to become a fourth player. It was a big pot, and Ariette contrived to raise the stakes. Fierce lost, and got into the game. His luck did not change; he continued to lose, played on till dawn, and emerged tired and bitter. For four hours, cards in hand, he had forgotten Sélysette. He climbed the *Bayard*'s gangway rueful and upset, seized with a sense of foreboding.

He was nevertheless unprepared for the coming blow.

A paper awaited on his table, a big official sheet stamped with the administrative seal. He read it stupefied:

IT IS HEREBY ORDERED THAT

ship's lieutenant Monsieur Jacques de Fierce shall disembark from the *Bayard* on the date of 20 April 19… and on the same day board, on temporary reassignment, the *Avalanche*.

Monsieur de Fierce shall take command of the *Avalanche*, which shall be fitted out on the date of 20 April.

Aboard the *Bayard*, 20 April 19…

Counter Admiral and subordinate commander

d'Orvilliers.

All was in order. Baffled, he ran to the admiral's quarters.

"You've received a command," said d'Orvilliers. "Not bad at your age…"

Fierce's anxious face gave him pause.

"You've seen Mademoiselle Sylva, I trust?"

"No. She's at the cape…"

"Ah, well. It seems you're jinxed, my poor boy. At the cape! You won't have time to get there. The arsenal has fitted out your *Avalanche*, and you set sail tonight."

"I'm leaving?"

"For the Great Lake. Cambodia's a mass of fire and blood, and the Siamese are meddling. The dispatches arrived this evening. A serious revolt, and all too sudden: there's English money behind it. I predicted as much; it's the beginning of the end…"

He climbed onto his favorite hobby-horse and prophesied catastrophes. Sélysette's betrothed, still and silent, did not hear.

"Admiral," he broke in, "is the *Bayard* to stay at Saigon? You'll see Mademoiselle Sylva…"

The old man came to an instant halt and, tenderly, laid his two hands on Fierce's shoulders.

"I shall see her. Go on in peace: she'll know; she'll wait."

It was not, alas, *her* patience or fidelity that he doubted.

XXVI

he *Avalanche*, a tiny gunboat with twenty-five hands, weighed anchor two hours before sunset and steamed up-river. Saigon hid behind its forests of areca, with only the two spires of its cathedral long remaining over the horizon, like two pointy islands in a sea of trees. The river meandered. On the bridge the Annamite helmsman demonstrated the practicable channel with motions of his hand, and the gunboat would at times hug one of the banks. When it did the crowded trunks showed distinctly, as did the swampy land between them; here and there a rice field gleamed green amid the brown trees; natives, having emerged from a few invisible *cai-nhas*, watched in silence as the boat passed.

Night fell, without a dusk. Unsure of his route, Fierce dropped anchor mid-current. The night wood emitted a stronger redolence, and the forest din filled the darkness.

Fierce paced the bridge all night long, hungry for some cool.

A bit of fever coursed through him with the beat of his pulse. He felt

superstitious and fearful. It was obvious, the obstinate fate that for a month
had kept him apart from Sélysette defied the possibilities of mere chance.
There was something inexplicable in it; the shadowy work of some hostile
genie, perhaps now haunting the environs, in the unsettled night — ready to
pummel him with still more blows.

At dawn the *Avalanche* set forth again.

Days passed, all of them the same.

The native revolt had caught fire all of a sudden and overrun the country
like a trail of powder. Two provinces had risen up in two days, burning
down their villages, mutilating their colonists, mounting assaults on
residencies and defended posts. Much blood had been shed quickly. Then,
with the French counteroffensive, when the colonists came forth to face
down the rebels, the tumult had given way to a sudden silence, and a void
had formed before the invasion: Oriental war — devious and headstrong —
had commenced.

There was no combat. Ambushes, nothing but ambushes — a rifle shot
from a hedge, a sentinel's throat slit in his box. — The soldiers grew anxious
in their struggle against a disembodied enemy; the only good fighters were
the Annamite infantrymen, as patient and cold as the enemy — the same.
Indeed, they fought ferociously, because fighting against their countrymen,
and because civil wars in Asia — as in Europe — are inexpiable.

The gunboats roamed from arroyo to arroyo; sometimes — rarely
— they would sound the woods with a few shells. The insurgents feared
the boats and would keep away; they held the bullets and cannon fire in
contempt, but their popular theology — always respected and nourished
by their men of letters — looked upon these floating machines, with their
sparks and smoky panaches, as filled with hostile demons. — The gunboats
came and went in vain: they inspired flight.

These were thus long, useless treks, undertaken on false intelligence
from false spies. — The village to be bombed was nowhere to be found,
unless it was already in cinders; the war sampans said to lie at the far end of
a blind branch of the river would magically turn into a few rotting planks. —
The exasperated captains would now and then try a substantial operation:
surround some country with a fifteen-league perimeter; fortify the lines and
double the guard; set a gunboat to block every arroyo; and advance only after
a thousand precautions: march in silence through the empty woods, the circle
tightening: nothing. Night would fall, however, and in the black thickets tardy

rifle-fire would break out; the bullets would whistle all the way to the river, and set the metal ringing on the gunboats; the cannons would enter the fray; there would at last be a real battle, lasting till dawn. But at dawn the shots would suddenly cease, because things would become clear: there would be no enemy. Gone astray or betrayed, the French would have fired on themselves, massacred themselves by mistake. There would be ten or twenty dead men on the ground. The living would bury them — and move on to other errors. They would kill and die without glory, weary and bored.

The soldiers were the wearier and the sailors the more bored. The gunboats were like cloistered convents, with no way out, and no word from the outside world coming in. Every evening, in ignorance of the day's events, they lay at anchor in isolation, smack in the middle of the river, far from the treacherous banks, source of the nocturnal boarding parties — silent and bloody. However far off they lay, though, they could not escape the humid warmth of the forest, or its sensual odor, the fragrance pumped out every which way by all its flowers and leaves, and the feverish effluvium of fermenting soil. The nights were alive, full of rustlings and shudders. The forest crawled with secret things, their stirrings, breaths, and pants within earshot. A formidable murmur rose from that sea of trees; and at times there would be some ruckus, to inspire anguish through its proximity: a gallop on the ground, a splash into the river, the cries of beasts on the hunt or in their amours. Nothing in the world lives more sensually than a tropical forest.

Fierce, on his watch, listened to and breathed in the forest.

He had been chaste for three months. Faithfully and with pride he was saving himself for his wife-to-be. His month of absence and exile had weighed heavily on his constancy: doubt and nihilism were back snapping at his heels; but not debauchery; he had scarce known the rare temptation, quickly gone. And his continence was a recent source of pride, kept him from believing that he would relapse for good. At least his flesh remained worthy of Sélysette. This new life that he had glimpsed, this chaste and faithful life — he was still capable of living it. He had one chance left.

XXVII

ow, the revolt of the Great Lake had a leader. A prince of imperial blood, the distant descendant of a forgotten dynasty, had mysteriously arisen among his people. His name and history were unknown. A virgin, they said, had prophesied his coming; and at the appointed time he had appeared; and the virgin had recognized, designated, and proclaimed him among the crowd. He bore the stigmata of his race; the priests had prostrated themselves before him, and the people had taken up arms. Now he was fighting with an army and a court; his prudence and daring were fearsome, and his fanatical partisans had named him Hong-Kop, the Tiger. His imperial name would be proclaimed later, after the definitive victories, amid triumphs and genuflections.

One night, however, Hong-Kop was betrayed.

The story has remained obscure. The Asian soul never unveils itself but by half. — Vengeance, ambition, jealousy? Other unknown motives, incomprehensible to barbarous Europe? — An anonymous warning, written in good classical Latin, reached headquarters. Two columns were dispatched in haste, and at the indicated village the prince was caught unawares in the company of a weak escort. These intrigues were never elucidated.

The village was surrounded with rice fields and stood near a thick wood, suitable refuge for flight. At the first noise Hong-Kop sought to escape. But the French were guarding the wood; in the moonshine were two lines, their men numerous and vigilant. — The attacking columns advanced through the rice fields; bayonets gleamed in Indian file on each of the paths. Every retreat was cut off. Hong-Kop understood that he was lost, and resigned himself to it. On his order his men returned to the village, and the dynastic tragedy's somber, disdainful fifth act played out. The emperor took a seat amid his court — the neighboring *cai-nhas*, set alight, were already in flames — and, without declamations or tears, but with a smile, drank the tea of deliverance. Now that he was dead none rose to imitate him, because it befits not men to set themselves equal to princes; rather, all waited around the dead man for the enemy to begin his massacre. They were fifty-eight men and two children. They put up no futile resistance, wary of tiring themselves before death. The order from Paris was in fact to massacre the *pirates*, and the order was executed.

They were led out of the village, into the rice fields, because the village was now but a single flame. They were not bound; they knelt on their own, properly, in two lines; the rice field was in flood, its water reaching their calves; a few raised their black robes, the robes of lettered men, to avoid the mud. The executioner arrived, an infantryman like the condemned, a smooth-bunned Annamite with the air of a girl; and he took up the broad sabre, apt for beheadings, while all bared their neck, obligingly. The burning village lit the strange scene and reddened the wet grass, stage for a baroque dance of shadows. The victorious officers, pallid, could see the indifferent, ironical eyes of the victims. One head rolled — two heads — forty; the executioner paused to hone his blade; the forty-first rebel watched him with curiosity; the sharpened sabre returned to its work; and the two children went last.

Then the infantrymen planted the heads — to serve as an example — on the pickets of a fence that the fire had neglected. A tiger in the nearby wood, frightened by the red fire, barked like a dog.

Fierce was there. It had been necessary to act quickly, not to wait for help from the distant groups: to make a show of numbers, half the gunboat crews had been disembarked. Fierce was in command of this contingent.

The stroke of midnight. The men made camp on the spot, in sections, the sailors lying closest to the wood. There seemed to be nothing to fear. Only double sentinels were posted, and the camp lit fires, too excited and disturbed to sleep. Nostrils obsessed over the smell of blood, and also of the Asian village, an abominable mixture of pepper, incense, and rot.

There was a sudden rifle shot from the wood.

A tumult ensued; the men ran to arms. Other explosions rang out. A sergeant, his thigh broken by a bullet, screamed in pain. A sentinel, his throat mysteriously cut, fell without anyone's seeing the cutthroat. The men all but broke into panic, but the officers thrust themselves to the front, and their example urged on the rest. Fierce was the first to head under the trees, sword low. A savage wrath was driving him, the wrath of a big cat disturbed in its sleep. In a rage he sought an adversary.

But the enemy had fled. The empty wood was as calm as a graveyard. An arroyo flowed through the middle: perhaps sampans had carried off the fleeing men. There was nothing to be found but a few black *cai-nhas* looming over the water. No noise came from inside. In their disappointed fury and thirst for violence the sailors broke down the doors nonetheless. They rushed inside, yelling and swinging.

There were women in the *cai-nhas* — *congaïs* holed up like hunted beasts, females without force, mute and half-dead with terror. The sailors killed them, without seeing that they were women. Murderous wrath was carrying along all of these people — the little Breton fishermen and the tranquil peasants of France. — They killed for the sake of killing. The bloody contagion drove their brains to madness. Fierce too, in his fury, broke down a door and sought some living prey. He found it behind two upright planks serving as a barricade, in a roofless nook bathed in pitiless moonshine: an Annamite girl hidden under mats. Once discovered she sprang to her feet, so terrified she could emit no cry.

He raised his sabre. But she was almost a child, and almost naked. Her breasts and pubis were in view. She was pretty and frail, with supplicating, weeping eyes.

He stopped. She threw herself at his feet, kissing him on the hips and knees; she begged him with sobs and caresses; he could feel her, warm and palpitating, clinging to him.

He shivered from head to toe. His hands, hesitant, touched the smooth hair, the brown, polished shoulders, the breasts. She squeezed him with all the strength in her bony hands, drawing him to herself, offering herself in ransom for her life. He tripped, fell onto his prey.

The crumpled mats rustled softly, and the worm-eaten planks creaked. A cloud passed over the moon. The warm *cai-nha* was like an alcove.

Outside the sailors cries grew faint, and the tiger's bark drew nearer.

XXVIII

I n Saigon the early anxiety had turned to curiosity, which then turned to indifference.

It was taking too long, this revolt — and the war, now, seemed stuck forever in the far reaches of Cambodia, in swampy forests no one had ever seen. — For a week people had been concerned, yielded even to worry. Now life was starting up again, carefree and nonchalant.

The hot season was approaching, the season of rain, malaria, and dysentery. Saigon would soon be a bog — its lovely ruddy roads mired in muck, its gardens soiled with yellow water; there would be two rains a day, morning and evening, at fixed hours; coach-rides, tennis, and balls under the stars would come to an end. The time had come to seize the last of the fine days, to get one's fill of parties and joys. Seize them people did.

Saigon lived in gluttony. The history of cities is fertile with examples of this fact: that imminent catastrophe engenders in every city a mad rush for pleasure and debauchery, a rush born of fatalism. For Saigon the native revolt posed a threat and served perhaps as an omen — the dark omen of a more terrible peril, some unknown thunderbolt hanging over Gomorrah. Unwittingly savvy, the Saigonese indulged in befuddlement and toxins.

Doctor Raymond Mévil did not take part in the general mania. He was now more and more often sick, in body and mind alike. Madame Malais and Marthe Abel had become the two poles of his life, two equally inaccessible poles; he would neglect to eat and drink, and, worse, to love. Torral had judged right to declare him a kind of alcoholic who took women for alcohol: cut off suddenly from his eau-de-vie, Mévil was wasting away.

A pathological case, in sum. Mévil had debauched himself for a long, long time without seeming to impair or spoil his youth. He had nonetheless worn out his marrow with the perpetual labor. It was, moreover, not healthy marrow, the marrow of wholesome, normal humanity: Mévil was one of the Civilized: that is, a hothouse plant, modified, deformed, atrophied by fussy cultivation, and now become monstrous, with dwarf leaves, overly big flowers, and petals instead of stamens — with speculation instead of instinct, and a brain at once admirable and deformed. This brain had at first ensconced itself in a comfortable egotism, leaving the senses at liberty, and taking no part in their games; but the gangrene of the nerves had one day reached it a last. Come to the end of his truncated youth, to the end of his dulled sensations, Mévil had wholly and in one go broken down and gone soft. His appetites of yore had now given way to deep and sickly passions. — The hothouse plant was indeed coming into bloom, a strange and tragic bloom, fed on fertilizers of skillful rot.

Madame Malais, an honest bourgeoise with a great lady's countenance, and a French provincial saved by her husband from colonial contagions, was the most difficult woman to seduce. In her the senses, like the imagination, conveyed nothing; she offered no purchase; on top of it all, she loved her husband. Mévil wore himself out in pursuit of her, a pursuit all the more arduous because in it he was investing head and heart together, and because he sought not only to possess this Galatea[121] but also to bring her to life, awaken her, transform her. He managed only to unsettle and frighten her. She sensed in her socialite suitor a dangerous and mysterious being, a magician who could, in spite of her efforts, draw her into a forbidden realm, where

---

121   In Greek myth, the statue carved by Pygmalion that comes to life.

the conjugal fidelity she took such pride in would perish. — Modest, though perhaps tempted, she skirted his attacks, and closed her door to the assailant.

Mévil now saw her only from afar, at the market, at the theater, out for a drive. She would turn away on seeing him and withdraw if he tried to approach. The game drove him to exasperation. Torral, the drama's attentive observer, expected violence and scandal to ensue. But Mévil already lacked the energy for violence.

He was hunting two preys, and was incapable of abandoning the one to force the other. They dragged him — dogged, mad — down two different paths: Madame Malais represented for him a sensual ideal never yet attained, while Marthe Abel stirred fibers within him that he knew nothing of, and whose vibration shot him through with fear: mystic and superstitious fibers — the fibers of a pallid, icy love — mortal love. — He thought of the love of nuns for the Christ in their cells. — That white, serene girl, that alabaster statue, the Egyptian sphinx magically brought to life appeared to him as an enigma he wanted to decipher, or else die in the attempt.

He did not court her: one does not court an enigma. He laid no manner of siege. The notion never occurred to him that she was made like a woman, and could serve to give pleasure. He loved her more chastely than Fierce loved Mademoiselle Sylva, and when he contemplated marrying her he did not think of their honeymoon night: had he thought of it he would perhaps have retreated, taking fright.

Marry Marthe Abel. — Mévil first fashioned this figment at a feverish hour. Marriage arrived amid the principles and rules of his life like a dog amid ninepins. The very word made Torral burst into laughter; shamefaced, Mévil relegated the idea to his drawer of follies.

But soon rules and principles amounted to nothing much for him. In love as he was with two, and chaste with respect to both, he had suddenly become impotent before all other women. He could no longer love. At first it had been a repugnance that he did not seek to overcome; but he soon realized that it was worse: an impossibility. Torral, ministering to him as a friend, had demanded that he keep a few mistresses: he resorted to them like an old man. — He was but thirty years of age; but his countenance was older, and the disarray in his marrow was now reflected therein. — The face was still beautiful, but worn out.

So he came to understand that he was headed for an impasse, and that any door would serve for an escape. At the same time, the news of Fierce's marriage came to seem an example to follow. He took up his project, grew accustomed to it, and had soon deemed it excellent and reasonable, in conformity with all his wishes, however vague. He thenceforth sought to undertake the affair. But at his first approach he saw the eyes of the sphinx, fixing him with their immobile gaze, was dazzled, spoke not a word, and departed.

The eyes of Marthe Abel. — Alone, Mévil considered them for the first time. What lay behind those cold, black lamps? — He had loved many women, had watched them live and stir; he knew their usual motives, which are ambition, vanity, sensuality — and venality, the sum of the rest. What lay behind the eyes of Marthe Abel? She was a sphinx, within and without. He gave up trying to fathom her and took heart in practical reasoning. Mademoiselle Abel was twenty years old; she was an only child, well brought up, very pretty — yes, but without a dowry — the lieutenant-governor buried in debt — without a dowry, and of too original a beauty, unsettling rather than attractive — in sum, difficult to marry off. He, Mévil, was young, had a clientele, a reputation, and something of a fortune — a good match, no question. Why would she not accept?

Why? — He looked at himself in a mirror: he was handsome, as beautiful as she was. — He returned that very evening to Marthe's — and retreated again, in fear.

But two days later, treading the cobbles by morning, he ran into Torral, on his way home for lunch.

"Fierce arrives tonight with his *Avalanche*," said the engineer. "I stopped by the governor's palace a little while ago: the revolt is over, or at least so they're saying."

"Ah!" said Mévil. "Fierce is coming back?"

The Fierce-Sylva wedding was no longer a mystery; the banns had just been published.

"Yes," Torral repeated. "Fierce is coming back, the poor old sod. The Sylvas got back yesterday from Cap Saint-Jacques. He's sure to spend the evening *en famille*. Fierce *en famille*! Ah! I thought him made of tougher stuff. Well, let's speak of it no more. Tonight, the two of us, dinner together?"

"I don't know."

"If you don't know it's yes. You need some shaking up, my little friend. Eight o'clock at the club, or a little earlier on Rue Catinat."

Alone at home Mévil took a seat, cheek on fist.

Fierce was coming back; Fierce was going to get married. So it was possible for the Civilized, in spite of the debauchery, in spite of the fatigue, to select a virgin and marry her, as the barbarians do. — It was possible. — For hours he sank this certainty into his skull. — At four o'clock he called for his rickshaw. Now that he was ready to leave it occurred to him how very like a duel this request he was going to make was. — He had been present for a few such encounters; he knew the sympathetic drugs that steel a faltering heart; he drank a phial — at random. — The Tonkinese runners ran fast, too fast.

The weather was stormy, the sky low. It had rained that morning — the first shower of the monsoon; and the evening's rain was in preparation. The streets were muddy; the runners stopped to raise the top and turn down the leather foot-cover; it seemed to Mévil a brief halt. The first drops of rain fell as the rickshaw was pulling up to the palace. But the Tonkinese, with an effort, climbed the front steps, and the master alighted under the colonnade of the portico, without wetting his canvas shoes. The guard brought his heels together and stiffened, weapon to his shoulder. A *boy* emerging from the hall drew back in haste to let the European pass.

Mévil entered. The hall was empty, the door to the little parlor open — he advanced. The downed phial warmed his blood; he felt almost no fear on seeing Marthe. She was there, alone, seated at the piano; she was reading through a score without playing, her slender, slender hands poised over the keys. The mats over the flagstones crackled under Mévil's step. She turned her head and approached the visitor, holding out her hand. They took a seat face to face. Polite, she thanked him for having braved the rainstorm: water was now streaming down the windows, and the parlor, usually dark, in the manner of Annamite parlors, began to seem a crypt or cavern. And perhaps, thought Mévil, that was what it was, the cavern of the sphinx, where her victims were torn apart.

Still he maneuvered for an attack. Rather than head straight in, though, he sought for a deft oblique to take. The Fierce-Sylva wedding came to mind.

"Jacques de Fierce," he said, "is arriving tonight from Cambodia."

The news surprised Mademoiselle Abel.

"Are you sure? I took my breakfast this morning at Sélysette's, who knew not word of this."

"The news comes from the Governor's."

"Too bad: the Sylvas have just left for Mytho and won't be back until after dinner."

"Bah! They'll see each other tomorrow."

The sentences were hard to connect. He made an effort. — The decisive question seemed a mountain to lift.

"A nice marriage, don't you think?"

"Very nice."

"And it will be a happy one."

She mimed her ignorance of the future.

"You don't know Fierce. He's been my friend for more than ten years, and he's loyalty, sincerity itself."

"So much the better for Sélysette, who deserves to be happy."

Mévil looked at the clock: already ten minutes wasted. It suddenly occurred to him that a visitor could appear. The breach was there that he had to rush into. He got his running start.

"A marriage is an example to be followed. What do you think?"

"A good example or a bad one?"

She was laughing her peculiar laugh, brief and free of mirth.

"A good one," Mévil averred. "When will you be following it?"

"Me? I'm not yet giving it any consideration — not at all."

"Others are perhaps considering it, with you in view."

"Do you think so?" she said, indifferent.

He burned his ships.

"I know of … at least one … who aspires to win only you and dreams only of you."

She looked at him, scrutinizing.

"And you know who," he concluded, rising to his feet.

"Might it perchance be you?" — She began laughing again.

"It's me."

She did not hesitate for a second.

"My God! You ought to have warned me. Is this a declaration? Are you asking for my hand officially?"

"Both."

She was still laughing, as calm as could be.

"Let's set all this to music, shall we?"

She took a seat at the piano, played two chords, and set her fingers to a saraband with a burlesque tune and brought it to a sudden close with a mysterious phrase in minor.

She was mocking him; he grew irritated.

"I know nothing of sonatas. What does this one mean? Yes, or no?"

She pivoted on her stool and faced him.

"Are you serious?"

"More serious than I've ever been."

"You want to marry me?"

"I want nothing else."

"For keeps, no kidding around?"

He thought she was being flirtatious.

"On my honor," he said warmly, "in granting me that hand you would be doing me the most royal charity of love that a woman could ever do!"

She pouted in polite regret.

"Well, that is a shame, for that is a charity I cannot grant you."

"Why?"

"Because. — In truth, I cannot."

He was not expecting her to fall into his arms. Women say yes only once; he knew it better than anyone.

"Mademoiselle," — he was on his feet, ready to withdraw — "deign to listen to me. This is no game; it concerns my happiness and perhaps yours as well. You know who I am, my name, my situation, my life; I have money, if not a fortune; the woman I marry will be happy in more than one way. That woman will be you, or none other, because I love you passionately, as I have never loved before. — Do not respond! Not yet. — There is nothing in my words to offend you. Think well; take your time; ask for counsel. I will wait two days, three days, a week… And consider above all that my life is yours, and my fate lies in your hands."

He bowed low and walked towards the door. On her feet, brow knitted, Marthe Abel had let him have his say. She called him back.

"Do not wait, Monsieur. There is no point." — Her words were clear, her eyes set coldly on him. — "I have said no; that no will not change — ever. I am not insensible, believe me, to the honor of your quest; I am even flattered, because I know your name, your life, your fortune, and all the other advantages of yours that you have had the good taste to pass over in silence for me. But I do not want to marry you. — Let us say, for example, if you must have a reason for my refusal, that I am too young."

"Am I too old? I am not yet thirty…"

She smiled, impertinent.

"Ah? I thought older. But let us break off here, please. I presume that this discussion is as painful for you as it is for me. I have said no twice, and I would have thought once would suffice for your self-esteem, if not for your curiosity."

He grew excited.

"It is indeed a matter of my self-esteem! I have been stepping all over it for a long time on your account. For two months I have been as your

shadow, for two months been renouncing my life while loving you, for two months endured Saigon, who knew me proud and disdainful, watch me struggle in a trap. — What does it matter! It is a matter of my heart, not of my vanity — of my heart, which cannot go on without yours, of my heart and my life, for if you push me away I will die!"

She considered him with curiosity and irony.

"You are most eloquent!… I now understand much that had always escaped me… Tell me, do you employ the same phrases when you speak to Madame Malais?"

He went pale. — The Sphinx was victorious; the enigma remained undeciphered. — He stared fixedly into the black eyes. — She did not want to… Why did she not want to?

Exasperation suddenly overtook him at his defeat. He had had at his command, once, the insolent words to injure scornful women. He tried to find them now, to use them.

"Well," said he, stepping back. "You are better informed than I thought. So much the better: since you have decided to be frank, I hope you will be frank to the end. One word, and I will leave — for good. If I kill myself when I leave this place I want to know why. Do me this mercy: the reason for your refusal, the real one."

She sat back down.

… "I have no reason to give you."

"But I, perhaps I can guess one?"

She rose, haughty, and looked for a bell.

"Do not call," snapped Mévil: I can very well disrespect you before your *boys*. Let us be done with it. You do not wish to marry me. Have you reason to be difficult? You're as poor as a beggar, as you know: have you any hope of twice finding the man that I am, ready to take you bare, ready to pay off your father's debts?"

She listened, one tense hand laid upon the other. He saw her suddenly smile, mocking, prideful. He stopped short, an idea having dawned on him.

"What a dolt I am! You've found him, found your dupe. And that's why… Who is it? Who?"

He searched furiously, with the keen lucidity that moments of nervous tension afford.

She shrugged. Having suppressed her initial anger, she had once more become the impassive Sphinx, whom men know not how to offend. She almost felt pity for this man, sputtering with rage before her.

"Go, Monsieur," she said simply; and as he did not budge she herself took two steps towards the door. He dared to lay a hand on her, and held her back by the arm. She wriggled free, quick as lightning, eyes sparking in that pallid face:

"Coward!" she yelled. "Ah! I was not wrong to refuse you just now: I saw through you and judged well: no courage and no honor, vile, withered, ignoble! There you have it! That is why I do not want you; that is why I am horrified by you! Look at yourself in that mirror! Look at yourself! Look!"

He looked in spite of himself.

"The hollow eyes? The green cheeks? Your whole degrading, abject life is written all over that face! It's plain to see, plain to read, that you're not even a man anymore, barely a marionette whose strings have snapped. And you speak of marrying me, of buying me with your pennies. Me, who am young, healthy, and chaste? You, who are older than the old, and will soon be riding the cart with the other paralytics? You're mad! It's more expensive than that to buy a virgin!"

He tried to straighten up, in a panic of shame.

"More expensive? How much? — I demand to know the price! And the name of the buyer! The rich man, the dupe who'll do anything, the happy cuckold! And, by God, I know who it is: it's Rochet; there is no more senile man in Saigon, nor a bigger millionaire. — And I remember well: I saw him drool over your glove one evening, at the governor's!"

She did not blush.

"You saw? So much the better. Yes, I shall marry him, if I like, if I so deign — if the sadness of life obliges me, me, poor as a beggar, to sell myself. The buyer will at least be rich as a king. You…"

She pointed a finger to the door. Her eyes blazed lightning. He retreated in fear.

He retreated, knocking into two chairs. He hit the door leaf on his way out. He looked at the carpet, no longer daring to lift his gaze to her. He felt her without seeing — upright, stiff, and pale, arm held out — terrible.

The rain streamed on down the front steps: he took no notice. He fled.

XXIX

n hour earlier the *Avalanche* had anchored in the river, alongside the *Bayard*.

There were visits, reports, explanations. Things nonetheless proceeded quickly: Fierce found all doors closed. Admiral d'Orvilliers was inspecting the batteries at Saint-Jacques; the arsenal commander, buried in work, was not receiving; the offices, drawn out of their regulatory torpor, were showing zeal and even activity. In less than an hour Fierce managed to find the first mate for the Mobile Defense, and returned his gunboat. He was afterwards free. The port, he observed in crossing it, was in motion, and everything was topsy-turvy; the six torpedo boats were fitting out: the workmen's hammers pounded furiously. He was surprised as he passed, then thought no more of it.

On Rue des Moïs he found the same closed doors. The *boys* were talking of Mỹ Tho[122] in obscure phrases. Called over, the *bep* — cook — confirmed that they would not be dining at the house but would be taking lunch on the morrow. Fierce left.

---

122   City on the Mekong delta, southwest of Saigon.

He was at once feverish and weary. Eight days before, in the pillaging of the village, his fidelity to Sélysette had perished. And since that fatal night not a single other night had passed without its betrayal. Ah, the lascivious smile of Cambodia's *congaïs*, and their spindly, opium-scented nakedness, and the venal curiosity that impelled their sampans towards the gunboat at dusk! Eight evenings, eight episodes of debauchery. — He was up the gills in disgust, in shame; but his strength and will were as nothing to his instinct, loosed like a beast. — Right here, steps from his betrothed, that very night, would he not succumb once more?

He walked fast, fleeing the warm twilight's temptation. The recent shower had whipped the trees around, and the wet flowers were more fragrant.

On Rue de la Grandière — street of the old tribunal, now serving as the lieutenant-governors' palace — he stopped in surprise: a victoria's draft horses were rearing up before a pedestrian, and the *saïs*, clutching his reins, was yelling at the top of his lungs; in spite of it all the man was walking head-down, seeing and hearing nothing, with the stiff step of a sleepwalker. Fierce recognized Mévil and called to him, but the doctor continued on his way. Uneasy, the lieutenant ran after him and clapped him on the shoulder.

"Where are you off to? What's the matter? Do you have sunstroke?"

Mévil gave him a slow look before replying:

"I don't know…"

He took the hand that Fierce was offering him, and suddenly clutched it like a drowning man.

"You're ill," said the other, forgetting his own distress, and led him home, shouldering him along. Mévil walked as directed, docile, saying nothing. Fierce touched his clothes, soaked with rain.

"Were you out in the rain? What the devil's happened to you?"

"Nothing."

On Rue d'Espagne Mévil almost walked past his own door. But in his bedroom, amid his furniture, his knickknacks, his life's familiar decor, imbued with his particular scent, he gradually recovered and regained his senses. Now he replied to Fierce's questions in vague sentences. He had changed clothes and taken a seat, taciturn. Night was falling, and it did not occur to him to get some lights turned on.

Meanwhile Torral arrived. Worried, he had come to fetch his dinner companion at home.

"It's like a tomb in this bedroom!"

He turned the commutator himself, saw Fierce, and greeted him. Mévil was still very pale and hardly speaking. It was Torral's turn to be surprised.

"You seemed well enough earlier. Bah! Come to dinner anyway."

"He can't," said Fierce. "He was staggering in the street just now."

Mévil made an effort, and got to his feet:

"It was a dizzy spell. But it's passed, or just about. Still, I'd rather not head out right away. Let's dine here together, the three of us. How about it?"

They dined. Mévil had dinner served in the bedroom, which resembled his office: the same muslin hangings, too long and broad for the wall — the same low chairs — the same half-light sifted through saffron-colored lamps. The *boys* came and went without a sound on the felt soles of their shoes. The *congaï* made no appearance.

Fierce was somber and Mévil undone. Torral scrutinized each in turn with his piercing eyes.

"Five months ago," he broke in, "we dined together for the first time, at the club. Do you remember? Things were more cheerful then than they are this evening. In those days you were men, not undertakers."

"Yes," said Mévil.

He rubbed his eyes several times. There, engraved on his retinas, was a vision that would not be erased — the vision of a standing woman… — But he endeavored to see no more.

"Yes," he repeated, "but those times will come again."

He called for some Syracusan wine, and began to drink. Fierce had once liked that wine; he too drank of it.

The cheer, however, would not come. They drank in silence around the circular table; and the electric chandeliers cast their big, still shadows onto the wall. The hangings muffled all sound from outside; the bedroom was as mute as a sepulcher.

Two bottles were now empty. Mévil's face, wan a little while back, was bit by bit regaining some color; but he continued to shudder at intervals, and looked with fear into the blackness of the open door.

"So what's over there?" said Torral, catching him.

"There's nothing there."

"So?"

"Remnants of the dizzy spell: I've got ghosts in my head this evening…"

Torral swore and took up a newspaper.

"Last week of the season at the theater. Let's go; better than going loony here. Liseron's playing, in point of fact."

"Well, I'm going back aboard," said Fierce.

Torral mocked him.

"Have they forbidden you to go out alone? Is *Le Petit-Duc*[123] too risqué for you?"

Fierce shrugged and capitulated. The Saigon Opera is just steps away from Rue d'Espagne, but Mévil had the carriage hitched, on account of the mud.

"We'll have the carriage for a trip to Cholon afterwards, if the heart so desires."

Fierce opened his mouth to protest. But he saw the irony in Torral's eyes and was silent, overcome with false shame.

They selected a box in the lowest tier: Fierce did not wish to be seen from anywhere in the house. But they did not escape Liseron's eye: she recognized them, smiled at them. During the entr'acte, on a whim, she dispatched a note: if they were good boys she would permit them to take her to supper afterwards, her and a little friend who had just arrived in Saigon. — As friends, of course; she knew that Monsieur Fierce… And, besides, she was herself back on the straight and narrow, restoring her virginity.

Mévil wrote yes on a card.

"I won't be going," said Fierce, rather firmly.

"He is wise," snorted Torral, "to flee temptation before marriage: it will permit him to succumb afterwards."

"I can't exhibit myself before all of Saigon with two actresses…"

"… In the black night, on deserted roads, inside a closed carriage. You cannot, clearly: Sélysette would feel it in her little finger."

The curtain had risen for the third act. Fierce looked at the singers, and grew curious: which was Liseron's little friend? He supposed it was the cross-dressed brunette.[124] She was slender and annoying; Liseron — the Little Duchess — would brush against her affectionately.

"If I join you," he said haltingly, "it needs to be clear that Torral will deal with that little one…"

---

123 An *opéra comique*, with spoken dialogue and musical numbers, that had its premiere in Paris in 1878. Music by Charles Lecocq, libretto by Henri Meilhac and Ludovic Halévy.

124 The friend is playing the protagonist, the Duc de Parthenay, written for soprano. Duke and Duchess were played by Jeanne Granier and Mily-Meyer at the premiere.

"I'll deal with her. Poor man. All this fuss to sup with two women who say they've restored their maidenhood!"

"Let's go right away," said Mévil. "We'll wait at the stage door, and Fierce shall hide in the carriage."

Onstage the two women paid much attention to the men's box, and little to their dialogue; but Saigon is all about such matters: no one noticed anything.

Four could squeeze into the victoria, and they were five; Mévil spoke of finding a second carriage, but there was none to be found. Fierce, meanwhile, ensconced himself under the victoria's top. They waited a quarter-hour; then the women emerged, scurrying like mice; they had scarce taken the time to remove their stage make-up, and had hooded themselves to the eyes: all of this mystery was most amusing. They poured into the carriage, leaving Fierce no time to rise: they sat next to him, one to his right, the other to his left, while Mévil and Torral took the jump seat. The victoria set off with a jolt. Fierce felt and recognized Hélène's hip against his own; the other woman, meanwhile, held on to his knee, with a malicious, probing hand. — And he, unsettled, felt desire for the one and the other, despite the great, bitter shame bubbling deep within his conscience.

It was a dark night. Bolts of lightning fired in silence to the west. A damp wind was blowing from over there, warm as the breath of a beast.

"I'm suffocating," said the women, and began to unfasten their clothes. A damp breast pressed against Fierce's shoulder; through the thin canvas of his tuxedo he counted the beats of the bare bosom. The sound of kisses sang out in the black carriage: on Hélène's mouth Mévil had gone off in search of his former virility.

All of Fierce's vigor was now channeled into his hands: he was shot through with a furious temptation to seize the other woman, the press her warm flesh, bruise her, and sink in his teeth. — He resisted, though, fingers clutching at one another and squeezed between his knees. — The *saïs* had taken the high road, the shorter one, to Cholon, and they arrived in a half-hour, but Fierce was still at the end of his tether when he set foot on the ground, and staggered in the corridor of the cabaret.

Mévil ordered supper. The Syracusan wine and Hélène's kisses, not without trouble, had dissipated his torpor: he could feel a cloud deep within his head, like wisps neglected by the wind in the hollow of valleys — but a dull fever was heating him up, galvanizing him. He tried madness; he ate

spiced picallillis[125] and drank thunders,[126] which are *flips*[127] with mint instead
of water and red pepper instead of cinnamon. He nevertheless trembled
and jerked and continued to fear the door. In time he was drunk; and
though she supped in his lap he would touch Liseron with his hands alone.

Liseron's little friend looked at Fierce — with the eyes of a cat before
a forbidden saucer of milk; so much so that Torral, who had deigned to go
to some expense for her, soon ordered his dry champagne and narrowed his
concerns to drinking. Fierce put up a desperate defense, endeavoring even
to take refuge in drunkenness, but drunkenness was too late in coming, and
too mild when it arrived. Little by little the girl crept to his side, and was then
on his lap: she drank from his glass; she grew tipsy, and laid into him without
shame. — He somehow rose to his feet, and sought to leave. But all clung to
hold him back; they left the cabaret and climbed back aboard the victoria.

Mévil, his reason gone, ordered the *saïs* to drive straight; indifferent,
the man took them to the suburb's last houses. There, at the *cai-nha* of some
nhà-quês,[128] the burlesque idea occurred to them to ask for drink. A stunned
old man brought them some saké,[129] which tasted bland after their cocktails.
Farther on, at a hovel standing on the edge of a rice field, and frequented
by the dregs of China, Torral, growing bored, selected an Annamite *boy*
and demanded that he be admitted onto the cushions. Now and again the
water-heavy sky spat big rainstorm drops at them, and all squeezed together
under the victoria's top, grasping and caressing. The shower never came;
the heat was rising. The suffocating women, mad with lust, stripped as if in
an alcove, and Fierce, suddenly straddled by a half-naked body, succumbed.

Deep into the countryside they went on the muddy, black road, the sin-
filled carriage like a rolling bordello.

Long did the night hear them sing and shout, in the frenzy of their
rutting and drunkenness. But at last they went hoarse and fell silent — when
fatigue laid them out pell-mell on the cushions and the mats, like soldiers

---

125 Mustard pickles. A British interpretation of south Asian pickles, a relish of chopped and
pickled vegetables and spices.

126 The word appears in English.

127 A hot drink of spiced, sweetened ale or of cider mixed with sweetened calvados.

128 Nhaqués (nia-koués), Annamite peasants [author's note].
     Ñhaqués in the French. *Niakoué*, borrowed from Vietnamese, is a derogatory term in French
for a Vietnamese person, not unlike *gook* in American English, although *gook* has wider application,
having been coined, it seems, during the Philippine insurrection of 1899 and then extended, in
various wars over the twentieth century, to any Southeast Asian and even to Nicaraguans.

129 Saké, eau-de-vie made of rice [author's note].

killed. The orgy came to end in torpor. The women, exhausted, fell asleep despite the jolts; the men, inert, thought no more. And they headed back to Saigon, soft in the body and empty in the head. They had gone far; the road back was long: this was the Plain of Tombs, eternally silent.

To the west the lightning had ceased; the wind had died out.

They were now approaching the tomb of the Bishop of Adran, a vague silhouette on the dark horizon. And something strange and terrible occurred: the horses, stumbling along in their trot, worn out, suddenly leapt in fear, reared up, and retreated. The shock set the carriage athwart the road and all but overturned it. All of the passengers, ripped from their sleep or stupor, sat up with fright and cried out.

The carriage continued to back up, even under the *saïs*'s lash. Sobered up, Torral jumped to the ground. The road ahead was as dark as ink. Fierce, jumping down in turn, grabbed one of the lanterns, and tried to find the invisible obstacle.

"Is there nothing?" he said, turning around.

But now the lantern lit Mévil's face, still thrown back — and, together, Torral and Fierce suppressed a cry:

Mévil's eyes were haggard in a face convulsed with terror and grey as ash — there was no blood in that face anymore, not a drop; the teeth shivered visibly in the hole of his mouth. The lashes too were restless around the eyes, fixed like an owl's, looking into the depths of the night, looking at and *seeing* the Ghastly Thing that the lantern had failed to illuminate.

"There... There...!"

"The ghost... the Bishop of Adran... who bars the road in his shroud... He's signaling to me... to me..."

The women cried out in panic; Fierce felt a cold sweat on his temples; Torral retreated in spite of himself. An indomitable fear passed over them, like a gust through tremulous leaves. The horses seemed riveted to the ground.

Yet there was nothing there, nothing one could see! The night was a void. With a shake, Fierce advanced three steps: a wild pride stirred back to life within him, the hereditary pride of a race that had been strong; and this old pride produced an odd amalgam with the skeptical irony of the Frenchmen of Decadence. On his feet, facing the invisible, Fierce engaged in mock exorcism:

"*In nomine Diaboli*... Bishop, sir, if you please, make way for us honest living men! You are frightening the women, which is most

ungallant of you, and entirely unworthy of your episcopal character. —
If you bring us an ill omen, I shall take it upon myself, and may we let
matters lie there. — Afterwards return home, lest you catch cold! Your
coffin grows chill…"

"Shut up!" fearfully cried one of the women; you're going to bring evil
down upon us!"

Mévil gave a great sigh, and his eyes slid left and right.

"He's going… He's signaled to you too…"

The horses now advanced, with remnants of fear in them.

"No! No!" Hélène violently objected. "Not that way! I don't want to."

"What do you mean not that way?" said Torral, suddenly furious.
"Which way, then? Are you drunk, as well?"

She tried to jump to the ground, but he held her back rudely by the
arm, and the carriage passed the mausoleum, meeting no obstacle. Less
than reassured, the two women clung to Fierce, who seemed to them the
bravest. He was once more sitting quietly, and Mévil, stiff, his eyes still wide,
lay on the cushions like a corpse.

They continued on their way. But the alarm had wiped out the horses,
which now would only walk, even under the lash. The road was endless.
The storm, luckily, had moved away, and the stars twinkled between the
clouds. Broken with fatigue and emotion, and drunk, they gradually nodded
off into a dead sleep.

Night came to an end. Dawn whitened the east; and the sun then rose
without aurora. The morning breeze blew less hot. It was the birth of a
smiling day.

With the caress on his forehead of the air and the sun, Fierce slowly
emerged from his torpor. He sat up. He was still in the full embrace of
the two women, and they were almost naked. The possibility of chance
encounters suddenly occurred to him: it was day, and they were entering the
city; the bridge over the arroyo already lay behind them.

Fierce sought to extricate himself from the restraining arms and jump
to the ground. But they had tightened and tensed up, those arms: they had
him bound; they were like his old life, like his civilized nature, glued to his
flesh. — He struggled to get free; he struggled too late.

Too late. Fate had marked him. As he worked to tear free of the naked
embrace a victoria emerged from a cross street — the Rue des Moïs — and
passed close by, at walking pace: Madame and Mademoiselle Sylva out for
their morning drive.

Sélysette shot to her feet, eyes wide. A cry escaped her — a cry that cut into Fierce's heart like a knife. And that was all; swift, the victoria sped off.

For a full minute Fierce remained on his feet, immobile, like lightning-struck trees that do not fall in the instant. Then, in one terrible motion, he broke the baneful embrace and cast the women aside in a muddle, bloodying one of their foreheads. No matter. He sprang from the carriage and ran off through the streets, mad.

XXX

ike a mortally wounded beast repairing to its den to agonize, Fierce fled all the way to his quarters aboard the *Bayard*. And he sat on his bed, set his elbows on his knees, and rested his head on his fists.

"It's over," he murmured. The words brought forth no thought in him. The turmoil in his head had been too violent at the start: there was nothing left but a total, terrible void. In spite of this he suffered frightfully: his heart was like the prisoner of myriad sharp claws, squeezing and puncturing; and in his thighs and belly he felt the fiendish contraction that only mountain-climbers feel after a great fall. — When this suffering exceeded his strength his head slipped between his hands, and he fell asleep or passed out. — But his sufferings began again as soon as he awoke.

Indeed, he suffered more, because he could think again within his skull. And the notion that Sélysette was dead for him, that he would not see her again — ever! — wrung from him a tortured groan. "It's over," he repeated, this time with clear understanding of his mowed-down life, and compulsory death. Relapse into vice, nihilism, civilization — no. — I still love wine and women, Lorenzaccio[130] would say; this suffices to range me among the debauched, but not to make me wish to be of their number. — Fierce now lacked desire, and courage.

He did not even consider the hope of forgiveness, of pity, from Sélysette: one forgives a guilty man, pities a wretch; one does not marry a fraud who has donned the name and mask of an honest man once loved. Fierce was that fraud, and Sélysette had observed the sham with her own eyes. — What remedy? — Never had a situation been so clear. — Fierce chuckled with impotence and despair: he could write, beg, cry. — But it was over — over — over. He hammered the word into his brain. Afterwards — like the imbecile who wears down his nails on the smooth sides of his drowning well — he wrote, begged, cried. But his letter came back sealed, along with a brief note to sever their engagement — a note that came down on his nape, like the blade of a guillotine.

He had not taken lunch; he did not dine. The clock struck seven, seven in the evening. He realized that a whole day had gone by, from dawn to dusk. In the expanding night he shivered at the thought of being alone; a childish fear chased him from his quarters. The cruiser was already mute and dark. The bugles had sounded to clear the evening's commotion; the crew was on the bridge; the empty battery seemed big, low, and lugubrious, like a cathedral's crypt. Fierce made haste for the gangway, and fled the silence and the shadow. The dark of night was not yet thick on the wharf.

At first he walked at random; but the randomness was sly and led his steps towards Rue de Moïs — and when he noticed where he was going he took fright again and turned around. This time he sought Mévil's house: his distress required help, any help he could get.

But Mévil was not at home. Fierce saw the open gate, and the *boys* huddled at the threshold of the door, astonished and worried. The master had gone out alone after the nap, leaving no orders, and had not returned.

Fierce began to trudge away. He had sought out Mévil, and now he sought out Torral — sought a hand to clutch at.

He crossed Rue Catinat, and some people jostled him as they ran past — without his notice. — The city was in an uproar — and this too he failed to notice. — The crowd, always thick after twilight, seemed driven by a growing emotion. Off in the distance people were hurrying towards the

---

130 Protagonist of Alfred de Musset's play *Lorenzaccio*. In the play, as in life, Lorenzino de' Medici assassinates his cousin, Alessadro de' Medici.

post office, where the agency telegrams are displayed; they were crying out and raising their arms; there were rumors of a riot. Express couriers were galloping past, newspaper vendors were yelling, and the papers ripped from them were being brandished like flags. An anxious fever was spreading even to the Chinese, who were neglecting their tireless labor to converse on the threshold of their shops — even to the white women, drawn out of their Creole indolence, hatless and messy-haired, rushing about over the news. Swept with a mysterious wind of madness and panic, Saigon seemed to have reached a tragic awakening from its eternal *far niente*.[131]

---

131   Italian for idleness. Often *dolce far niente*, sweet idleness.

XXXI

N o, Dr. Mévil had not returned home that evening.

He had gone out early, weary of being alone with his thoughts — his lugubrious thoughts. His drunkenness of the night before had dissipated in the morning; but hallucinations continued to flash before his eyes, terrifying him at intervals. With funereal precision, the nocturnal vision returned to him, sad and terrible, the folds of the shroud floating on the extended arm, and the eyes — the twin fixed eyes of a Sphinx… That vision, and another, the vision of a standing woman…

He felt cold to the marrow, though the heavy heat of day drew feverish sweat from his shoulders and neck. Before going out he powdered himself from the chest up; then, scorning the rickshaw and the victoria alike, he took his bicycle, in the confused hope that he could calm his nerves through muscular fatigue. Wind and sun would be good medicine for his neurosis. He bent over the handlebars and pedaled hard. The bicycle flew over the ruddy roads, which colored the rubber on the rims. A burning breeze had dried up the morning shower, and the mud was already crumbling to dust.

The bicycle had once served Mévil as a discreet vehicle, a vehicle one would use for mysterious and shameful errands whose secret could bear the scrutiny not even of a *saïs*. Among Mévil's many amorous intrigues were some delicate adventures, which for the sake of honor and interest must be hidden from every gaze. A small villa in the village of Tan Hoa, near the Route Haute, had often been the objective of his cycling expeditions. There lived a Saigonese family, the Marneffes, a father, mother, and daughter — he a civil servant, of course; the ladies socialites; and all three spending more than they could have spent without expedients. Poker and naps made up for the deficits: Monsieur played with intelligence, and only discerningly would Madame cease to be virtuous.

Saigon knew this. — Saigon knows many other things. But the daughter, only sixteen years of age, passed for being intact; there were even a few kind souls to pity her for her upbringing, which was bound to corrupt her in time.

The task was done, however.

Mademoiselle Marneffe had long been Dr. Raymond Mévil's mistress. But both had been prudent, and no hint of their affair had filtered out. The villa was isolated and well suited to trysts; Monsieur Marneffe would leave in the morning not to return before evening, thereby preserving a proper ignorance of the comings and goings of his wife, who would often absent herself mysteriously at midday. On such days a maiden's handkerchief would be set out to dry at one of the upper floor's windows, and the gate in the wall would be left unlocked, to spare the *boy* who served as doorman a few steps. — A bicycle was easily hidden in the hibiscus of the garden, and Mévil knew how to climb the brick steps without a sound, and push open the mute door of a virginal bedroom, draped all over in white.

Today Mévil had left the Rue d'Espagne before four o'clock, heading first for the velodrome.[132] But racers were training on the track. He turned off and found himself on the Route Haute. The city was already far behind, and the village of Tan Hoa was upon him, its *cai-nhas* clustered to the left of the path.

Out of habit, Mévil cast a glance at the villa Marneffe: the handkerchief-signal was afloat on a shutter. It had perhaps, Mévil thought,

---

132   A looped, banked track for cycling, often indoor.

been floating there for many days, forgotten by a disappointed hand: it had been two months since his last visit. But Mademoiselle Marneffe was at once depraved and sensible, too sensible to carry a grudge against unfaithful lovers, too depraved to waste in a sulk time that could be better spent. Mévil saw the open gate. He entered.

After all, this was perhaps the best remedy…

But there are ills against which all medicine is vain. An hour later, a bit wearier, a bit more anxious, and, as it were, sore down to his soul, Mévil climbed back onto the saddle. He mistook his route and continued towards Cholon instead of returning to Saigon.

His mistress, exhausted with pleasure, had let him leave without a word, without a look of farewell to filter out through her closed eyelids. He would have liked some tenderness after that libertine and egotistical hour, even if it were spurious. — Tenderness — never in his life, he reflected, had he enjoyed any.

Never — no emotion either, or tears. Everything, down to his oldest memory, was dry. For the past two months, however, he had been catching glimpses of other things, feelings unknown — a better kind of frisson; he could glimpse… He shuddered: the sun was picking out a strange white form on a wall, over there. — He cut a corner and hurried off down a crossroad. At its end lay another road; he took it at random, failing to notice that it led to the Tombs.

The road ran flat and red across the great plain, abounding with burial mounds. A little grass, some low bushes, nothing better to be seen all the way to the horizon, and everything, on account of the dust, was the color of dried-up blood. In the light of day the old necropolis — too old — was neither wild nor sinister, just monotonous; and the very path was not deserted: twice Mévil encountered pedestrians.

Soon he was going less fast. His muscles had long since softened against all fatigue but the amorous kind; and the road was long; he had covered only a third of it; the bishop's tomb had not yet appeared on the horizon.

Now, while he was pedaling softer, a strange physiological change came over him: his thinking matter took leave of his body, separated itself from it, as occurs in sleep and perhaps in death. And the tie between the one substance and the other — the life tie — stretched and turned fragile, while his muscular energy diminished, and his lassitude became overwhelming and painful.

He saw himself doubled, as in a mirror. — He saw his body — or his twin? — crouched on the saddle and bent over the handlebars, elbows pointy, legs stiff. He saw his face, and was distressed at its pallor: What! Was this *his* leaden face, *his* hollow eyes, *his* dull gaze? Were these *his* bloodless lips, whose cold kiss must disgust like the kiss of a man in the throes of death? The throes of death — he repeated the phrase — and *saw* his lips move to pronounce it. — He was a physician, knew well the funereal grimace of men who are about to die; he recognized it — pitiless. Death must be near him; a macabre picture formed in his mind of death pedaling in his shadow, on a bicycle rivetted to his.

His temples were cold. The bond between his body and his double had no doubt lengthened, for now *he saw himself farther off, smaller*. And, in confusion, he could feel that the bond had become less supple: orders from the thinking matter now reached the muscles only with a lag; he was like a machine that has fallen out of alignment, that obeys only with reluctance, and clatters for a good while before stopping or starting. Meanwhile his astral thinking, liberated from his organic brain, was achieving an extraordinary lucidity: agile as never before, it sped from idea to idea, touching in the blink of an eye on a thousand distant and contradictory things, with no visible tie between them. — Opium smokers dream this way. — A forgotten image crossed his memory: the image of Hélène Liseron spitting in his face the day of a quarrel: "One could slap you, and you wouldn't feel it"; and the lifted hand struck his cheek; indeed, he felt nothing…

He murmured: "I've gone the wrong way." — Dear God, were those pedals hard to turn! — He looked steadily at the sun, declining in the west. It was late, too late. Lowering his dazzled eyes, he saw the road, twisting and dark as a tunnel — a tunnel to a dead end. He entered it, irresistibly — and his life too, a life lived the wrong way, entered the dark impasse, full of terrors and phantoms. — He couldn't see!… He made a desperate effort and, slowly, the bedazzlement cleared: the road, the bushes, the tombs, the blood-red dust reappeared — along with the Bishop's Tomb, near, menacing.

A cold sweat poured down the hallucinating man's forehead. He was still going, struggling to push the heavy pedals. On he went — sure that relief awaited on the far side of the Tomb, the terrible Tomb. — He passed it; he took the turn in the road.

Around the corner was a carriage — a victoria hitched to two Australians — proceeding at a fast trot. Mévil moved right and looked: they were Madame Malais's horses — and it was she in the carriage, alone, haughty, and turning away on catching sight of him.

…Thirteen hours ago the Vision had loomed in this very sport…

It seemed to Mévil that his handlebars were veering gently left and right. — His hands were still. — Yet the handlebars were turning, it was certain; the victoria approached, fast, was but ten paces off; he had to bring the handlebars back in line, and lean the body to the right — now. — Mévil tried.

The muscles hesitated. How tiring it was to turn those handlebars! Some mysterious weight had certainly snagged the left side, tipping the whole machine on the sly towards the peril, towards death.

Mévil fought, stiffened — for a half-second, a long half-second…

But what was the use? He was tired, so tired!… It would be easy to seek repose right away, there, on the red path…

The hands let go. The bicycle ran under the horses, which reared up too late. The carriage passed, with a soft jolt…

There was a strange cry, like a moan: Madame Malais leapt from the carriage, before the *saïs*, clutching the reins, could bring it to a stop.

Raymond Mévil lay on his back, arms out crosswise, eyes open wide. On his white garment the dirty wheel had traced a sort of ceremonial sash, in red, from the hip to the shoulder. Indulgent Death had spared the face, on which a supreme beauty of exceeding calm was already spreading.

Madame Malais ran over, knelt, and in hysterics took up the lifeless head. The eyes shifted about somewhat, the lips pursed as if for a kiss — a red and warm kiss, for there was blood tinting the mouth — and that was all; the heart ceased to beat, and the curtain of the eyelids fell.

The tomb-keeper emerged from his house. With the *saïs*'s help, he carried the body under the mausoleum. Silent, Madame Malais produced her handkerchief and covered the dead face. A bit of pink showed through the batiste, marking the bleeding lips.

Madame Malais bent down — and, in pity, or perhaps in love, gently kissed the pink mark…

Then she departed, full of distress; and the perfume of her kiss evaporated from the dead man's lips. Raymond Mévil, cold and stiff, entered into eternal rest.

XXXII

ue Nemesis was silent and black; the Annamite and Japanese brothels had not yet opened their doors or lit their lanterns of oiled bamboo: it was only eight o'clock. Fierce walked the sidewalk with a heavy step; Torral's knocker knocked.

Torral answered the door himself, promptly. He was holding a lamp, with which he first illumined the visitor's face. Having learned who it was, he preceded Fierce into the fumoir. Fierce entered, dragging his soles, like a vanquished soldier.

Torral set the lamp on the floor. The fumoir was empty: no mats or cushions or pipes; three white walls, and the blackboard at the far end, which seemed a gravestone with chalked epitaphs.

The light condensed on the floor. Torral observed Fierce's muddy shoes and the red-speckled canvas of his trousers.

"Where've you come from? What're you doing here at this hour?"

He spoke with an uneasy curtness.

Fierce sought about in his head. He could no longer recall. What indeed was he doing there…? Did he mean to speak of his pain, spread it, bestir it? What was the use, since it was over? He lacked for words, and courage.

He put his back to the wall. Torral weighed his silence and probed his dull eyes; then, with a shrug, he opened his arms to the empty room.

"Do you see? I'm leaving. I'm deserting."

"Oh?" murmured Fierce, indifferent.

Torral repeated his words twice: "I'm deserting." And in the silence that ensued the word penetrated to Fierce's brain, and he slowly understood.

"You're deserting what?" he asked.

"My battery, for crying out loud. Saigon."

"What battery?"

Torral took up the lamp and looked over Fierce's face.

"Sicker than I thought," he judged. "Is it the broken marriage that's reduced you to a stupor? Perhaps you don't realize that war's been declared?"

With head and shoulders Fierce signified that he knew nothing of it, and cared little.

"Declared," repeated Torral, "and the English have been blockading Saigon since noon. The news came in a little while ago, with the cruise ship that took the first of the shelling."

Fierce thought for a moment, trying to imagine any influence all this might have on his own disaster. — No influence, of course. Torral continued:

"Reserve officers are being called up tomorrow morning, and dispatched lickety-split to the front, thank you very much! Batteries are insalubrious places, which my health would be unable to endure. I've retained a cabin aboard the German cruise ship that leaves tonight for Manilla. And I'll leave the fools to gut one another."

Fierce made no objection. Torral's desertion was, without contest, a logical and justifiable act, conceived on the proper grounds: minimum effort, minimum pain. — Expatriate oneself rather than die; it was better, no question. Torral accepted this silent approval, and concluded, less bitterly:

"It's all the same, anyway. So you crossed the city and didn't even hear the caterwauling on Rue Catinat?"

"No, I didn't hear…"

"Very sick…"

He took a little pity, with scorn. But it was the first compassionate word Fierce had heard, and his whole heart melted with pain and acknowledgement.

"Oh, if you only knew…"

Convulsed with suffering, he crimped his hands, joined behind his neck, and stiffened against the wall, as if crucified.

"If you only knew…"

He spoke. The words now rose to his mouth — halting, stuttered, but fervent. He drained his heart, the despair pouring out in spurts of bile. He spoke every which way of his love and indignity, and of the great hope that for a moment had restored youth to his dreary life, and the terrible collapse of his paradise glimpsed and lost. He spoke, and wept as he spoke, wept with great, deep sobs — wept the tears of a barbarian. Torral listened to him with impatience, and scorned him with a hard eye.

"All right, enough's enough," he broke in. "I predicted this, didn't I? That in running off the rails of good sense you'd take a tumble? Stop complaining: you might have fallen from greater heights. Your failed marriage is going to save your life. You are now free, delivered as by miracle from the madhouse you'd likely have ended up in. Imbecile! Instead of weeping, you should laugh. The medicine might be bitter, but you are cured. — There isn't a molecule of sense in all the drivel you've been spilling. Your paradise lost does not exist: it's a land of lies and mirages; you could roam it end to end without ever closing your hand on real happiness. In fact, you now know something about it, don't you. Listen: I'll have left Saigon in an hour, and this is probably the last time in my life I'll ever see you. We've been friends. I'd like to leave you with something better than advice, with a testament: return to good sense. You've been a civilized man, and centuries of indefinitely perfected atavism will not be erased. Return to civilization. Eradicate from your memory the last tufts of prejudice, of convention, of religion. Become once more what you were before the crisis, a man among the children who people the earth. And once more you shall find the sensual delights of men, the wholesome and reasoned delight that consists of not suffering."

He was looking Fierce straight in the eye, and Fierce looked back, pensive. Their two minds bore down on their divergence. Torral rolled a cigarette and lit it.

In the silence they heard the lamp sputter, its oil running low.

"So," Fierce suddenly said, "you enjoy life?"

"Yes."

"You wish for nothing better? It's enough to sleep, eat, drink, smoke tobacco and opium, make love to women — no, to *boys*?"

"Yes."

"From the depths of your sincerity, you believe that evil and good are so much balderdash, and that there is neither god nor law?"

Torral chuckled.

"A lesson in the catechism. I believe in one god: deterministic evolution; I believe in good and evil, as a rule of social utility, the prudent invention of the cunning against the naive; and I believe even that man is composed of a body and a soul, the latter being defined mathematically, as the integral of the former's chemical reactions. — Now, for a more ample commentary, I shall add that this catechism — the catechism of the Civilized — is a secret to be concealed from the earth's peoples, because they are unworthy of it, and to be reserved strictly for the individuals of the elite, to whom I belong. All civilization must be esoteric; and the profanation of its mysteries devolves it to barbarism."

He drew the last puffs from his cigarette and put it out underfoot.

"I imagine, of course, that you know all this as well as I?"

The lamp's flame went down with little convulsions, casting whirls of reddish shadow on the walls. Fierce lowered his head. How to respond? Torral spoke truth, and there was nothing to adduce in opposition to his irrefutable doctrine. Then, amid the phantoms of his mind, Fierce once more had a flash of Mademoiselle Sylva — trusting, believing, absurd, happy.

"Yes!" he suddenly cried. "I know all that. I learned your catechism in middle school; and I practiced it by instinct before I ever learned it: and there is no truth but within its bounds, and all the rest is lies. — Yes, by golly, I know it all. What else? There is no god or law or morality; there is nothing, only everyone's right to take his pleasure wherever he likes, and live off the less strong. — And then? — I've exercised that right; I've mis-exercised it.

And I've made a mistress of the most egotistical and implacable truth: is it my fault if today I'm smothered in her arms? is it my fault if I've found lassitude and nausea where you say happiness lies? Not to suffer — not to feel! That's not enough for me anymore. I'm thirsty for something else. I can no longer resign myself to eating, drinking, and going to bed. And I don't want any more of this truth that has nothing better to offer: I prefer the lie. I prefer its deceits, and its betrayals, and its tears!"

"You're mad."

"No! I see clearly. The truth, what has it do with me? Nothing. Thrice nothing. What I need is happiness. Well, I've seen people live by the lie, amid all the muddles of religion, morals, honor, and virtue: those people were happy…"

"Happy like convicts bound hand and foot…"

"And what of it, if the dungeon is preferable to the open air?"

"Try, and you shall see."

"I can no longer try! You can only exit that dungeon; there's no going in. I've seen the truth, and can no longer return to the lie. But I pine for the lie, and I hate the truth."

"Madman!"

"Truth: what has she made of us, we who have loved her as no Christian loves his Christ? What has she made of Rochet, of Mévil, of me? Sick men, old men, driven to ataxia or suicide."

"Of me she has made a happy man."

"Has she, now? You're a fugitive, an outlaw. Your life is broken like a straw. Tomorrow, dishonored, condemned, chased from every quarter, you'll have no graveyard to rest your bones in!"

"Perhaps. It proves nothing."

It was thoroughly dark now; the lamp was near the end of its grousing, and it was as if a will-o'-the-wisp were still dancing in the blackness. Calm, Torral declared:

"It proves nothing. I am perhaps mistaken; but it's but an error in my reckoning. The problem's method remains correct. I shall start again."

He heard a clock strike the hour.

"I shall start again. It's just a life to begin anew. I am leaving: farewell. I would once have taken you along; we would have deserted together; we would have both emerged alive and strong from this place, which will soon crumble and bury you under its rubble. But you have spat out civilization, you are returning to the barbarians, and I am leaving alone. Farewell."

He walked to the door. The lamp was in his way: he kicked it over.

"Farewell," he said again.

He left.

Fierce, alone in the black fumoir, listened to the fading steps. And, as he was already lending an ear, he shuddered at the sound of a distant murmur — a muffled quivering carried by the southern breeze — the imperceptible thud of English cannon fire, out on the sea.

XXXIII

he 17th of May, 19—. Ten o'clock at night. No moon. Thick sky, heavy with rain.

The torpedo boats of Saigon steam downriver in Indian file, marching towards the enemy. Seven torpedo boats — every bit of the arsenal, catching as catch can: to strike a supreme blow and break the city's blockade before the Hong Kong regiments arrive. Four of the torpedo boats are regularly fitted out; the others have makeshift crews, rounded up as the situation has permitted from the men of the cruisers and the gunboats; and Admiral d'Orvilliers has given them his aides-de-camp to serve as captains.

No headlamps, no signals, nothing that can be seen. The black torpedo boats glide darkly in the night.

A *banc de quart*[133] the size of a tea table, encircled with an iron

---

133 Literally *bench of the watch*. A bench on the aftcastle of a French naval ship where an officer would sit during his watch and the captain would sit during battle. According to the *Nouveau glossaire nautique*, published by De Gruyter, the French navy did away with the *banc de quart* proper by ordinance in 1786, while the English navy never had any such bench on its ships.

guardrail; Fierce is there, hands gripping the wet metal. Below, the helmsman, bent over the compass; right and left, streams of phosphorescent water fleeing past; all around, the warm rain, hissing on the river — the canvas of soaked clothes clings to shoulders.

Fourteen knots. The two banks, flat and the same, go swiftly by. Navigating the sinuous channel requires second-by-second attention. But that is the line commander's affair; Fierce is commanding the *412*, fifth of the line, and needs only to guide his torpedo boat through the luminous wake already traced out ahead.

An easy task — for the moment. — Fierce indicates each turn with a gesture to the helmsman — *left, right, like so* — and dreams, his distracted thoughts removing him far from the time and place.

My God, it is all coming to an end better than he had hoped. In a while he will be dead; and the catastrophe occurred yesterday morning: two days and a night of suffering — not much. — It is all coming to an end better than he had hoped. — Even this death happenstance was supplying, prompt and clean. And it was not easy so to die, without murmur or scandal, with no suffering for Sélysette, without a drop of blood to spatter her white dress! No, not easy: the most well-designed accidents always retain an odor of suicide; and the suicide of a fiancé… — It is all coming to a tidy end. To live on was impossible; impossible any which way; impossible whatever happened…

A funny place to die, this *banc de quart*. Too small by a half to accommodate a cadaver lengthwise. Bah!

Seven torpedo boats: not enough to sink even one battleship; and the semaphore of Saint-Jacques signaling a squadron of three divisions! — Earthen pot meets pot of iron. — So much the better, anyway: the important thing is to die; this battle is a surer way than a revolver blast to the heart. It is all coming to a tidy end. The annoying part is this sailing without lamps: impossible to light a cigarette — the last one for the condemned man, to be smoked during his final freshening up…

Old d'Orvilliers suspected nothing. In the frenzy of declared war he did not even see the Sylvas. And tomorrow, when Fierce is dead, they will of course tell him nothing; they will respect his grief, his illusions. He shall never know. So much the better again: His knowing would have been a drop of bile in the hemlock. Fierce liked the old man. *He* was not of the civilized!

Ah! Civilization! What a failure! Mévil is dead — they had buried him at noon; there had been only Hélène Liseron behind the coffin. — Torral is in flight, and the court martial has condemned him in absentia. — Rochet is living in childhood: they say he is betrothed. — Rochet betrothed!… To whom, in fact? — Bah! — And Fierce… Well, Fierce? Fierce is coming to the best end of all. He's coming to a tidy end, Fierce is.

"Left, helm. Left." Here the channel hugs the bank. The trees exude their warm fragrance in the rainy night. It is like the breath of Saigon, a loving kiss that the soft, redolent city sends to the torpedo men heading to their deaths for her sake.

Jacques-Raoul-Gaston de Civadière, last count of Fierce — killed by the enemy. It is fitting. Mademoiselle Sylva will be able to remember her fiancé without shame. — Mademoiselle Sylva… Ah! It would nonetheless have been sweeter to meet death with the taste of her kiss on his lips… A little while ago, having left his quarters on the *Bayard*, having carefully torn up the pastel portrait — the pieces are there, on his chest, and the empty frame seemed the wide-open door to a sepulcher — having shut his quarters, and thrown the key out a porthole — and why the devil had he done that? — Fierce, in the already black night, snuck all the way out to Rue des Moïs, to feast his eyes on the little light that burned on the windows of the veranda. — The ebony veranda, and its curtain of creeper vine, and the kiss of his betrothal…

To port on the second watch, two points of light in the night — Cap Saint-Jacques. But the river coils in on itself like a serpent, and the target is farther off than it appears.

To die, to sleep. To die — and not to dream. We have come a ways since Shakespeare. Too bad: the false hope of that dream was indeed the only thing that made life tolerable. Ah! Truth, naked truth! A pretty thing to see. — Put on some clothes, you whore!

Another hour yet to live, perhaps two; but not three. Surely not three.

Many lights on the cape. The English have fired their cannons only on the batteries; the villas are all intact. Indeed, the firing ceased at sunset.

She will perhaps weep tomorrow. Nothing better to wish for at the moment. Later she will understand. She will forgive, the beneficent creature. My God, he is hardly to blame, in sum. Whose fault was it if he was of the civilized?

— The other day's betrayal was nothing, but a misstep on his uneven road; and it was not he who had chosen that road. No. Not to blame, nor even to be scorned. The terrible modern equation, the equation of truth, which brings out and determines life's x, had been placed in his hands from childhood. Well, he had solved it, wholly and courageously; that is all. Others, of less probity or greater cowardice, would have hewn to the beneficent lie. He had gotten out, because nobler. He had not stooped to the prudent separation of theory from practice. He had taken the formula from the philosophical laboratory and applied it to life. Is this criminal? No. It is naive. But Tartuffean fate favors not the naive. And Fierce must therefore die.

There is, at bottom, more injustice in this than nihilists have ever redressed with their bombs.

The cape is near, enormous, blacker than the night sky, because of the contrast of the lights, like the silver nails of a pall. Right, right! We've got to round the promontory. — Yes, more injustice in his mowed-down life than in the depths of a coalmine, amid miners in greater bondage than the helots[134] of ancient Sparta!

Not to blame, not to blame. Innocent. Condemned to death nonetheless by civilization, which has robbed him of his share of happiness, his share of love. — Yes, precisely this: hoodwinked, robbed, then killed. A little vengeance, before the end, would be good…

Ah! Corner turned on the cape: here, the sea. Waves lap the stem, and now some foam flies. No more forest, no more stimulating fragrance; the breeze of the open sea, fresh and chaste, hits Fierce on the forehead, dries his damp temples, airs out and calms his thinking. In the distance, nothing but night; the horizon is a poor parting of sea from sky. Yet it is less dark: the rain has stopped, the clouds tear to wisps here and there, and starry gaps appear, the moon slipping through some furtive beams.

The weather is favorable. The enemy will be easily discovered on the lunar water. — Discovering the enemy is always the hardest part: the torpedo boats are so low in the water that their field of vision is limited. Nine times out of ten night maneuvers turn into vain searches. It is fortunate that tonight the moon has intervened. Come, now. All will be well.

A glance at the torpedoes. — The *412* has two tubes of the highest

---

134   The lowest caste of ancient Laconia. Serfs bound to the land and owned by the state.

caliber, 450 millimeters. — More than likely this will do little good: the English cannons will have set things in order before the *412* can get into firing range. — Nine battleships of the line, some hundred fifty three-inch cannons, not to mention the Maxim guns! — And, consider: the *King Edward* is among them. With the greatest clarity Fierce remembers her Nordenfeldt battery, and the ball, and the supper… Baroque. — No, the torpedo tubes will not have much effect. It would be funny, though, to torpedo the *King Edward*, before being sunk oneself. — The torpedoes are ready, loaded, primed, armed. Just a jerk of the cord, and the big steel shark, cast into the sea, will speed towards its prey.

All is in order. Now, his eyes scanning the horizon, Fierce searches — searches for the enemy.

The enemy. — In the brains rendered most effeminate through the heredity of successive civilizations the word is yet wild, still echoes mysteriously with barbarism and violence. — The enemy. — Three curt, rude sounds encapsulating the perennial phantoms of all human ferocities — from the feline battle of two cavemen, which the female contemplates, proud and fearful, from the height of the tree she has scrambled up, to the vast wars of confederations and empires, siccing all their prejudices and appetites upon one another. — The enemy. — The unknown, foreign, different being one fears and hates. — The enemy, to be killed.

Fierce seeks out the enemy — to kill him — and begins to regard him with hatred. — There are surely wild, prehistoric, disperse miasmas in the humid air on this night of battle! A wave of patriotism rises to his head. In former times the lords of Fierce too hunted down the English! Ah! The British battleships have dared to rain cannon fire on French lands? Watch out! Fire! Good Lord, how these preliminaries stir the blood! Are we to play hide-and-seek all night long? — How the sea darkens when a cloud passes in front of the moon! Once, a long time ago, when he was small, Jacques de Fierce feared the dark, feared it with anguish. It was frightful at the old manse in the Faubourg, when the family would gather in the evening, to have to go to the black, black library and retrieve the big picture book that was to teach him the alphabet. — What was the name of that German maid? Something with an A… — What? A fire? Where? No, no. It's nothing. — All the same, these helmsmen: once they've got their eyes open wide in the dark they invariably perceive something, like the proverbial cabin boy saluting the first moonbeam on the horizon: "Red fire dead ahead!" Seamen laughed over this for centuries, and here is Fierce astonished to find himself laughing still on this anxious night.

There is decidedly nothing here. Three times the torpedo boats have rounded Saint-Jacques, in expanding semicircles. This isn't hide-and-seek; it's blind man's bluff. And that moon is exasperating: every five minutes the dregs of a moonbeam scatter fast over the sea, and then right away the darkness grows darker than before. No English. None. To the devil with them! They must have withdrawn from the coast at sunset. We must hunt them in the open sea, and on the indefinite expanse the search will now become perilous. Oh, but they won't hide forever! Is death, liberating death, going to play the flirt, going to refuse herself? Begin life once more tomorrow? Painful life, oh so painful life — chew on all that bitterness again, suffer the ridicule of that abortive combat?… Oh no! No, no, and no…

The torpedo boats, now on the front line, and spread out, cleave through the sea like a giant rake; the enemy could yet be caught between the tines, if he hasn't fled too far into the thick of night. And Fierce, in an anguish of desire, dogged, strains his eyes and falls prey to exasperation. — The cowards. They're scared of battle! — He leans forward, neck craned, hands gripping the rail, teeth biting his tremulous lower lip. The salt air blows in his face, bringing with it strange, prideful hallucinations. It is the whole of Civilization that he pursues, charging after it at the gallop of his vibrating torpedo boat; yes, murderous Civilization, which for twenty-six years has been slowly grinding him, fiber by fiber, nerve by nerve, in its implacable gears, and which in a little while will finish him off with the burst of a shell. — So be it. But beware the vanquished man's supreme convulsion! Those battleships afloat somewhere ahead of his torpedo: on these he will have his vengeance! There is a whole quintessence of civilization shut within their walls, a quintessence of civilization fit for dynamite. — Beware! Beware the kick that the poor human beast in its throes will deliver to the clockwork!

And the Moon, like a pallid goddess, tearing away the clouds that clothe her, suddenly pours her liquid silver all over the sea. And Fierce stifles a wild cry of joy. There! There! Amid the sparkling waves, the night-black battleships have just emerged.

XXXIV

To the Dead of Tsushima[135]

The enemy straight ahead.

And aboard the *412* the orders, delivered sotto voce, came faster and faster.

"Gently. — Both engines, hundred twenty revolutions. — Tube men, arm the hammers."

"And, the rest of you, quiet!"

"Left, five! — Helm amidships. — Can you see, quartermaster? Yes? Steer like that, two points off the front of the line."

"Engines, — ready to maneuver."

The prow cuts through the water without a sound. The *412* sneaks forward. The English battleships show on the grey horizon as a great

---

135   See Expansive Notes, in the appendices, page 242.

muddle. How many miles to go? Two? Three? Nobody knows. Impossible
to judge by night. And a gentle advance is called for. Watch out for sparks!
Watch out for piston slap within long earshot! Must get in close, very close:
the proper distance when things are clearly visible and the target's speed is
known is four hundred meters, but at night it is madness to launch at more
than two hundred. — Fierce knows this, and, without taking his eyes from
the prey, he mutters: "I'll fire when I touch him."

Left and right the other torpedo boats have vanished — melted into
the black distance. — Reckless, the *412* is running towards the enemy alone.

How many miles yet? Two? One? Maybe five minutes before the first
cannon shot. — As fate must have it, the lead battleship, the nearest, is the
King Edward — the admiral's post. Fierce thinks for a moment of Hong
Kong, and of the Nordenfeldt guns wrapped in a garland of roses, and
mutters: "Droll!" Then his thoughts flash back to the great matter at hand:
"I'll fire when I touch him."

"When I touch him." The attentive moon looks upon the field of
battle. Things are visible — too visible. The torpedo boat must itself be a
stark black form on this milky sea...

The battleship's silhouette grows — and grows. Not a firelight or a
reflection on that somber machine; not a sound: it is Sleeping Beauty's
castle.[136] — How many meters now? Fifteen hundred? A thousand? The
English have eyes, don't they? It might as well be the light of day... Ah!
The wait, the oppressive wait for the first shot to go off, unleashing the great
clamor of battle...

In his terrible silence, Fierce hears the pulse in his arteries — loud, so
loud that the enemy too must hear it, from over there... — and he holds
his breath, to the point of suffocation. But in an instant the nightmare is
pulverized in a flash of awakening: arcs of violet electricity spurt from the
King Edward, fly over the sea, strike the dazzled torpedo boat, envelop it,
flood it with a burst of rays, ring it with a halo of funereal glory — while at
the same time the unmuzzled cannons bristle with lightning bolts, and bay
like a pack of dogs.

Fierce can no longer see — struck clean blind by the electric beams
piercing his pupils. Too bad. Onward all the same! He first yells at the
top of his lungs, the better to settle his nerves: "Engines, four hundred
revolutions!" And now, his every fiber bent towards the target, he repeats,

---

136   The tale of Sleeping Beauty was recorded, famously, by Charles Perrault (1628–1703), whose
work laid the foundations for fairy tales as a genre.

repeats to satiety the lesson he has learned: "I'll fire when I touch him. I'll fire when I touch him. I'll fire when I touch him…"

The shells buzz past and slam into the water here and there. Almost all explode on impact, amid the waves, producing huge sprays that fall like rain — liquid ghosts all white under the moon, surging up and vanishing in the same blink of an eye, and converging slyly on the torpedo boat. Yes, they are like nimble specters dancing a round, casting their shrouds on one another — lovely shrouds of snowy foam, with death in their every fold. The circle spins and cinches. But the *412* is now speeding ahead at thirty knots. Through waves and shells it rushes irresistibly, inflexible as the will urging it on. And the churned-up sea leaps and furls, and the bridge, submerged, flows like a torrent bed. The smokestacks blow great flames, which the wind of the boat's speed curves and tears into dazzling panaches.

A shell — the first. Sheet metal rips to shreds. Fierce, turning his head for a moment, sees a gutted man, entrails exposed. A second, better hit: the rear tube and its torpedo are blown to bits, carrying off half the odds of victory. Three ground-up sailors collapse into a red stew. And the *King Edward* is still far off, too far off!

"When I touch him!" The rage of battle has bitten into Fierce's heart, and flashes of clairvoyant hatred furrow his thoughts. There she lies all right, in front of his torpedo — his last torpedo: Civilization! She has beaten and tortured him, seeks to kill him — subjects him to her insults and ridicule, spits into his face all the gusts of furious water that now slap his face and wound his eyes… Ah! Fierce feels himself the weaker party. He persists nonetheless, in a rage. A cry leaps to his lips, the cry of a girl seizing a rival's curls with her fists: "I'll get you, you filthy animal!" Body stiff, eyes wide as can be, mind mad, he desperately keeps the helm straight, dead head.

His body weighs on his hands, which clutch the rail. His support suddenly vanishes, and he falls forward: a blast from the rear has hacked erratically through the railing's steel, and through some flesh along with it. At the end of his arm Fierce sees a dangling red thing — an ill-hewn hand. It does not hurt, not yet. But blood is spurting, and Fierce understands that he is going to die. So he shoots back up to his feet and with all his might cries: "Fire!"

The torpedo, flushed from its tube, dashes away. And the next instant a shell strikes the tube square, breaks it, drives a furrow stem to stern through the torpedo boat, and explodes in the engine room. Rods, men, and cylinders fly to pieces: the air fills with a blend of cries, detonations, hissings;

and from the thunderstruck *412* burst forth great jets of vapor, violently lit, like clouds of apotheosis, by bundles of electric wire.

Rent from hip to shoulder, stunned like an ox beneath the bludgeon, cast down in a puddle of blood, his own blood, which flows like water from a sponge, Fierce nonetheless hears the hurrah of the triumphant English cannoneers; and the certainty of his unavenged disaster galls his heart with a final desperation, though he lies dying bit by bit.

Over there, with the victorious enemy, the cannons persist in their lethal din. Now, at close quarters, it is like a prodigious symphony, with every piece re-bleating its note fortissimo. On a drumroll from the machine guns the three-inch cannons sketch mad arabesques with their staccato scales, and at a deeper roar the medium artillery, ceaseless, lays on wild chords that sustain over the rest of the sonic tumult.

Shells hit everywhere, in this ferocious revel of fire and steel. The sinking bridge of the *412* is but a red rubble where blood-slicked flaps of flesh begin to fry in the flames.

— Yet amid this insolent, triumphal fanfare of cannon fire is a thud, as funereal as the first clod of earth cast onto a coffin. A spray of water bursts from the battleship's flank — and then nothing. As if some unheard-of bolt from the blue had pulverized the cannoneers at their stations, the cannons, all at once, fall silent, muzzled.

And in the sudden silence an immense, clamorous agony issues from the battleship, struck in turn, and rises — hideous — into the night.

XXXV

evenge.

The torpedo has struck the battleship athwart her middle boilers, below the armor of her main belt — twelve feet below her waterline.

An unlatching simple and precise, like a clock bell: the striking point recedes and hits the detonator at the fulminate; the fulminate burns and lights the charge — seventy-five kilograms of flash cotton that explode beneath the ship, like a mine beneath stone. It makes little noise, on account of the muffling layer of water.

A hole forms in the metal, as if by cookie-cutter — a hole four meters tall, seven wide. The pulverized metal vanishes. The sea enters.

Inside is the double hull — a rampart of watertight compartments, like the cells of a hive. All is crushed, torn to shreds; the inner metal, crumpled like paper, frays; and this makes a second hole, a cellar window into the coal holds, which surround the boilers with a black shell. The sea enters and drowns the coal.

A third sheet of metal, separating the boiler rooms. This is the living heart of the ship; the metal envelops the heart like a bosom. But it bends and rends — just a little rent, but a rent in the heart, where a pin prick is worth an axe blow.

The sea slips in, with the light burble of a fountain.

The port-midship boiler room. — Eight boilers aligned before a corridor where the ground coal is heaped. Twenty-six half-naked men toil, brandishing heavy shovels, and hurling the coal onto flaming grills. Lamps hang from the ceiling, their electric whiteness clashing with the bloody shine of the furnaces. A steel ladder descends vertically from the door, a closed hatch — bolted.

The boilermen have heard the explosion. The counter-blow has laid them down like dominoes. They rise, bruised, to their feet and see the water — the lethal water spurting in from the wall. There will be no getting out of the closed boiler room, so they must die like dogs, a stone round their neck. A scene of unspeakable horror.

All at once the men scramble for the ladder — as though it were possible to leave by a hatch that requires ten minutes to unbolt! The water is already knee high. — And the head boilerman, mad with his grotesquely vain duty, cries, "To your posts!," killing one of the deserters, no matter which, with his revolver. Afterwards, in cognizance of the disaster, sure of his impotence, and terrified of the heinous agony he forebodes, he kills himself with a second shot. — The water rises to chest level, and suddenly drowns the eight furnaces. A locomotive hiss smothers all cries, while great jets of boiling water bite furiously into the mass of flesh clutching the ladder.

A monstrous row: all of these human creatures, restored to their ancient ferocity, as if by the waving of a magic wand, smite and tear at one another, tooth and nail, for the laughable right to perish one rung higher. The water covers its first heads. Some men are swimming; others, lacking the know-how, suffer the throes of death at the bottom. The surface boils. At the topmost rung, beneath the hatch, the last man to die clings to the screws and shakes them in desperation; but, in his demented terror, the wretch errs, turning the handles the wrong way.

Now, with the water climbing to the highest reaches, a big, red-haired quartermaster, his strength multiplied by the furor to live, thrashes his way by knifings up the ladder, stabbing the gripping hands until he too can touch the implacable hatch. But the water rises faster than he, and the man stops, vanquished, and lets go of the red knife, and the great, brutal strength wilts into his chest, now heaving with sobs…

It is over; the boiler room is full.

XXXVI

rom the almost-sunken torpedo boat Fierce watches, galvanized, and drinks in his revenge.

The *King Edward* is in her throes. At first there is nothing but a great uproar aboard — cries, whistles, orders, an anguished brouhaha that the breeze carries to the victor's ear like a precious melody. Then the enormous hull undergoes a sudden, prodigious shudder. The electric searchlights, all immobile since the explosion, and casting white beams here and there, into sea or cloud, take up their slow motions once more, all of them together, as if the vessel, on this calm sea, were taken up with an unsettling roll. — Yes, the *King Edward* is rolling. Clusters of men now appear at the railings and throw over a leg, to leap into the sea. — The battleship tilts to starboard, low, very low, lower still, without righting itself. The gunwale dips into the water. For a second the entire bridge comes into view: the ship has capsized onto its flank. — And the next second the bridge goes under, and the bottom of the hull appears — the wale, the keel, the propellers, still turning outside the water. The *King Edward* floats for a minute upside-down, then lurches backwards, the poop going suddenly under, the beakhead emerging to menace the sky. Now upright, like a man diving feet first, the *King Edward* vanishes into the sea.

The torpedo boat too sinks. Fierce, happy, smiling, is half-afloat on the wave-lapped gangway. Too weak, he does not suffer. There is no blood left in his veins. He falls asleep on the lulling sea, and on his lips, like a viaticum, is the name of Sélysette.

… Meanwhile in Saigon, in her room, kneeling beneath her Christ, merciful Mademoiselle Sylva prays for "those at sea."

Istanbul, 1321 *anno hegirae*[137]

---

137 A.D. 1893 or 1894 in the Gregorian calendar.
  The Islamic — or Hijri, or Hegira — calendar is lunar and starts in A.D. 622, date of the Prophet Mohammed's emigration from Mecca to Medina, an event known as the Hijra. The conversion from Hijri to Gregorian years is not straightforward, because the two systems have years of different lengths. The Islamic lunar year is about 354 days long, or about eleven days shorter than the Gregorian solar year. The following formula, however, yields a rough estimate: 622 + (Hijri year x 0.97).

Appendices

Expansive Notes

Civilized Reviews of 1905–06: The Good, the Bad, and the Ugly

Prix Goncourt Origins and the 1905 Farrère Judges

List of Characters

Original Title Pages

Expansive Notes

Footnote 16

From P.-C. Richard, "Saïgon et ses environs au commencement de 1866," in
Revue maritime et coloniale, vol. XVIII (1866):

"North of the Mares [Bogs] lies the Plain of Tombs [Plaine des
Tombeaux]. Some of the countless funerary monuments that it contains are
magnificent; those of the Chinese generally have the shape of a horseshoe;
those of the Annamites are either elongated pyramids or pretty little pagodas
in miniature or else modest tombs affecting the vulgar form of a lying, saddled
horse. All of the little structures in this necropolis are built of brick or earth,
then covered with a thick coat of a sort of plaster mixed with a viscous sap
that one obtains by taking the branches and leaves of a tree the natives call cay
hoïuc and infusing them in water. This plaster, easy to mold and given a brown
color, gets as hard as brick when it dries, and imitates stone so well as to pass
for it at first blush.

"As everywhere else, the poor here have very simple monuments, which
consist of mounds affecting the form of truncated pyramids, on which one
or more tombs are simulated, in accord with the number of persons whose
remains lie under the mound. We've counted as many as ten little tombs on
the upper base of one of these pyramid trunks.

"Beside these monuments one will now and then find cadavers
with a scant covering of earth; sometimes even the coffin is apparent and,
unspeakably, caved in. These coffins were no doubt set down for later covering
with a mound, but the war [the French conquest of Vietnam (1858–85)] has
caused the death or flight of the deceased's relations.

"This vast cemetery is most renowned, and it is an honor to be buried
there; it receives not only the dead of the surrounding country but also the

dead of neighboring provinces who in life had chosen the place for their
burial. This choice is of considerable importance for Annamites; some even
wish to die where they desire to be buried. Among the tombs rove herds of
vultures, vile animals that nature seems to have created to rid the ground of
filth and cadavers, and that carry out to perfection the high mission of hygiene
and public health with which they have been charged.

"This plain is crossed by two fairly busy roads; part of it serves as a
training ground for the troops of the Saigon garrison."

Footnote 69

Genesis 39 (King James translation):

"And Joseph was brought down to Egypt; and Potiphar, an officer of
Pharaoh, captain of the guard, an Egyptian, bought him of the hands of the
Ishmeelites, which had brought him down thither. / And the Lord was with
Joseph, and he was a prosperous man; and he was in the house of his master
the Egyptian. / And his master saw that the Lord was with him, and that the
Lord made all that he did to prosper in his hand. / And Joseph found grace
in his sight, and he served him: and he made him overseer over his house, and
all that he had he put into his hand. / And it came to pass from the time that
he had made him overseer in his house, and over all that he had, that the Lord
blessed the Egyptian's house for Joseph's sake; and the blessing of the Lord
was upon all that he had in the house, and in the field. / And he left all that he
had in Joseph's hand; and he knew not ought he had, save the bread which he
did eat. And Joseph was a goodly person, and well favoured. / And it came to
pass after these things, that his master's wife cast her eyes upon Joseph; and she
said, Lie with me. / But he refused, and said unto his master's wife, Behold, my
master wotteth not what is with me in the house, and he hath committed all that
he hath to my hand; / There is none greater in this house than I; neither hath
he kept back any thing from me but thee, because thou art his wife: how then
can I do this great wickedness, and sin against God? / And it came to pass, as
she spake to Joseph day by day, that he hearkened not unto her, to lie by her,
or to be with her. / And it came to pass about this time, that Joseph went into
the house to do his business; and there was none of the men of the house there
within. / And she caught him by his garment, saying, Lie with me: and he left
his garment in her hand, and fled, and got him out. / And it came to pass, when
she saw that he had left his garment in her hand, and was fled forth, / That she
called unto the men of her house, and spake unto them, saying, See, he hath

brought in an Hebrew unto us to mock us; he came in unto me to lie with me, and I cried with a loud voice: / And it came to pass, when he heard that I lifted up my voice and cried, that he left his garment with me, and fled, and got him out. / And she laid up his garment by her, until his lord came home. / And she spake unto him according to these words, saying, The Hebrew servant, which thou hast brought unto us, came in unto me to mock me: / And it came to pass, as I lifted up my voice and cried, that he left his garment with me, and fled out. / And it came to pass, when his master heard the words of his wife, which she spake unto him, saying, After this manner did thy servant to me; that his wrath was kindled. / And Joseph's master took him, and put him into the prison, a place where the king's prisoners were bound: and he was there in the prison. / But the Lord was with Joseph, and shewed him mercy, and gave him favour in the sight of the keeper of the prison. / And the keeper of the prison committed to Joseph's hand all the prisoners that were in the prison; and whatsoever they did there, he was the doer of it. / The keeper of the prison looked not to any thing that was under his hand; because the Lord was with him, and that which he did, the Lord made it to prosper."

Footnote 88

Polycrates, son of Aeaces (540s–522 BC). Thus Herodotus in Book III of his *Histories* (translation of George Rawlinson):

"The exceeding good fortune of Polycrates [in martial campaigns] did not escape the notice of [his friend] Amasis [king of Egypt], who was much disturbed thereat. When therefore his successes continued increasing, Amasis wrote him the following letter, and sent it to Samos. 'Amasis to Polycrates thus sayeth: It is a pleasure to hear of a friend and ally prospering, but thy exceeding prosperity does not cause me joy, forasmuch as I know that the gods are envious. My wish for myself and for those whom I love is to be now successful, and now to meet with a check; thus passing through life amid alternate good and ill, rather than with perpetual good fortune. For never yet did I hear tell of any one succeeding in all his undertakings, who did not meet with calamity at last, and come to utter ruin. Now, therefore, give ear to my words, and meet thy good luck in this way: bethink thee which of all thy treasures thou valuest most and canst least bear to part with; take it, whatsoever it be, and throw it away, so that it may be sure never to come any more into the sight of man. Then, if thy good fortune be not thenceforth chequered with ill, save thyself from harm by again doing as I have counselled.'

"When Polycrates read this letter, and perceived that the advice of Amasis was good, he considered carefully with himself which of the treasures that he had in store it would grieve him most to lose. After much thought he made up his mind that it was a signet-ring which he was wont to wear, an emerald set in gold, the workmanship of Theodore, son of Telecles, a Samian. So he determined to throw this away; and, manning a penteconter, he went on board, and bade the sailors put out into the open sea. When he was now a long way from the island, he took the ring from his finger, and, in the sight of all those who were on board, flung it into the deep. This done, he returned home, and gave vent to his sorrow.

"Now it happened five or six days afterwards that a fisherman caught a fish so large and beautiful that he thought it well deserved to be made a present of to the king. So he took it with him to the gate of the palace, and said that he wanted to see Polycrates. Then Polycrates allowed him to come in, and the fisherman gave him the fish with these words following- "Sir king, when I took this prize, I thought I would not carry it to market, though I am a poor man who live by my trade. I said to myself, it is worthy of Polycrates and his greatness; and so I brought it here to give it to you." The speech pleased the king, who thus spoke in reply:- "Thou didst right well, friend, and I am doubly indebted, both for the gift, and for the speech. Come now, and sup with me." So the fisherman went home, esteeming it a high honour that he had been asked to sup with the king. Meanwhile the servants, on cutting open the fish, found the signet of their master in its belly. No sooner did they see it than they seized upon it, and hastening to Polycrates with great joy, restored it to him, and told him in what way it had been found. The king, who saw something providential in the matter, forthwith wrote a letter to Amasis, telling him all that had happened, what he had himself done, and what had been the upshot- and despatched the letter to Egypt.

"When Amasis had read the letter of Polycrates, he perceived that it does not belong to man to save his fellow-man from the fate which is in store for him; likewise he felt certain that Polycrates would end ill, as he prospered in everything, even finding what he had thrown away. So he sent a herald to Samos, and dissolved the contract of friendship. This he did, that when the great and heavy misfortune came, he might escape the grief which he would have felt if the sufferer had been his bond-friend.

"It was with this Polycrates, so fortunate in every undertaking, that the Lacedaemonians now went to war."

Footnote 96

According to Glaucon, the main interlocutor of Socrates in Plato's *Republic*, adjustment of this ring would grant invisibility to the wearer. From Book II (Jowett translation):

"The liberty which we are supposing may be most completely given to them in the form of such a power as is said to have been possessed by Gyges the ancestor of Croesus the Lydian. According to the tradition, Gyges was a shepherd in the service of the king of Lydia; there was a great storm, and an earthquake made an opening in the earth at the place where he was feeding his flock. Amazed at the sight, he descended into the opening, where, among other marvels, he beheld a hollow brazen horse, having doors, at which he stooping and looking in saw a dead body of stature, as appeared to him, more than human, and having nothing on but a gold ring; this he took from the finger of the dead and reascended. Now the shepherds met together, according to custom, that they might send their monthly report about the flocks to the king; into their assembly he came having the ring on his finger, and as he was sitting among them he chanced to turn the collet of the ring inside his hand, when instantly he became invisible to the rest of the company and they began to speak of him as if he were no longer present. He was astonished at this, and again touching the ring he turned the collet outwards and reappeared; he made several trials of the ring, and always with the same result-when he turned the collet inwards he became invisible, when outwards he reappeared. Whereupon he contrived to be chosen one of the messengers who were sent to the court; where as soon as he arrived he seduced the queen, and with her help conspired against the king and slew him, and took the kingdom. Suppose now that there were two such magic rings, and the just put on one of them and the unjust the other; no man can be imagined to be of such an iron nature that he would stand fast in justice. No man would keep his hands off what was not his own when he could safely take what he liked out of the market, or go into houses and lie with any one at his pleasure, or kill or release from prison whom he would, and in all respects be like a God among men. Then the actions of the just would be as the actions of the unjust; they would both come at last to the same point. And this we may truly affirm to be a great proof that a man is just, not willingly or because he thinks that justice is any good to him individually, but of necessity, for wherever any one thinks that he can safely be unjust, there he is unjust. For all men believe in their hearts that injustice is far more profitable to the individual than justice, and he who argues as I have been supposing, will say that they are right. If you could imagine any one obtaining this power of becoming invisible, and never doing any wrong or touching what was another's, he would be thought by the lookers-on to be a most wretched idiot, although they would praise him to one another's faces, and keep up appearances with one another from a fear that they too might suffer injustice."

Footnote 135

Battle of Tsushima (27–28 May 1905), between the navies of Russia and Japan, during the Russo-Japanese War. Fought in the Tsushima Strait, between Korea and southern Japan. The Japanese fleet, under Admiral Tōgō Heihachirō, destroyed the Russian fleet, under Admiral Zinovy Rozhestvensky, which had sailed more than 18,000 nautical miles to reach the Far East.

This was the only decisive sea battle ever fought by modern steel battleship fleets, and the first naval battle in which wireless telegraphy (radio) was critical. The victorious Japanese lost 117 dead, 583 wounded, and only three torpedo boats (255 tons); while the Russians lost 5,045 dead, 803 wounded, 6,016 captured, and 26 ships (143,232 tons).

The fleet's destruction embittered the Russian public, which induced a peace treaty in September 1905 without any further battles. In London in 1906 Sir George Sydenham Clarke wrote, "The battle of Tsu-shima is by far the greatest and the most important naval event since Trafalgar."

The Battle of Tsushima occurred just weeks before Claude Farrère finished *The Civilized* and must have affected him, for he devoted his penultimate chapter to it, planting the seed for a subsequent masterpiece. *La Bataille* (*The Battle*) followed in 1909, becoming an international phenomenon, with a million copies sold. Soon readers will be able to experience this classic anew.

DatAsia Press will be releasing the first modern English edition of Farrère's second novel, *The Battle*, in 2025. Meticulously edited by Kent Davis and translated with nuance by Pedro Rodríguez, this volume features detailed annotations, maps, appendices, and 108 painstakingly restored original illustrations by Charles Fouqueray from the lavish 1925 edition.

Civilized Reviews of 1905–06
The Good, the Bad, and the Ugly

A Review of the Reviewers
By Kent Davis

While researching Claude Farrère's novel *Les Civilisés* (*The Civilized*), I've curated an intriguing collection of reviews that appeared in French newspapers and magazines following its publication in late 1905. Now, one hundred twenty years after its debut, Farrère's controversial novel, which won the prestigious Prix Goncourt in December 1905, is finally appearing in English translation. His steamy story of French colonials in Saigon pushing the boundaries of "civilized" behavior sparked intense debate among critics at the time. While some reviewers praised its daring examination of colonial morality, even in the exhilarating atmosphere of Belle Époque Paris, others condemned its frank portrayal of European decadence in Indochina. Personally, I hope this edition inspires some renewed controversy.

In reviewing these historic reviews, I found myself categorizing them with a bit of inspiration from Sergio Leone's 1966 spaghetti Western starring Clint Eastwood. There are:

The Good – Good reviews illuminate a work's themes, plot, characters, and significance. They discuss its literary merits or style, or

---

Important *Caveat* for Readers:

This article, and the antique reviews it includes, contains spoilers that will absolutely ruin your enjoyment of Claude Farrère's book The Civilized, *if you have not already read it. If you haven't seen the original* Star Wars *movie, it will ruin that too! Proceed with caution.*

But after experiencing Farrère's work (and seeing Star Wars*), I think you'll enjoy reading the astute observations, comparisons, insights, and reactions that these contemporary reviewers share.*

explore its cultural and historical importance. But above all, they should help readers figure out if the book is one they would enjoy. Is it worth their time and interest? Will readers experience something unique, informative and/or entertaining within the pages?

The Bad – Bad reviews are exactly like good reviews, except that the reviewer is not impressed, and shares his or her reasons why the book is lacking. Perhaps it doesn't make its points, or it's not accurate or realistic. Perhaps, in the reviewer's eyes, it's flat out boring! Everyone has their own literary tastes, and some reviewers simply didn't like Farrère's book. Which is fine. In fact, one of the bad reviews is among my favorites, because of its vicious, but entertaining, style. Publishers issue a limitless number of books each year, but our time here on Earth is limited. Bad reviews can help us choose wisely.

Whether they're good or bad, the key is creating *useful* reviews, and this is an art that must respect the craft of storytelling itself. Reviewers must walk a fine line between illuminating a work's themes and preserving its discoveries, between analysis and revelation. Which brings us to the third category…

The Ugly – Sigh. Well, I confess that this is a pet peeve. Unfortunately, this review style was in vogue a century ago … and plenty of awful individuals still share ugly reviews, as any reader who got a few episodes behind their friends in *Game of Thrones* can attest!

Ugly reviews ruin the reading by revealing critical plot details with "spoilers," the depressing bane of authors and readers worldwide. Spoilers destroy the author's careful narrative construction as well as the reader's ability to experience the story in a linear fashion. I consider this act nothing short of literary vandalism.

Imagine taking your child to the theater to see *Star Wars* for the first time and saying, "Oh! Before we watch, you need to know that Princess Leia is Luke Skywalker's sister, and Darth Vader is his father!" Now, that's ugly.

To make these good, bad, and ugly reviews accessible to modern English language readers, I've done my best to translate them, adding footnotes explaining now-archaic references and to add historical context. I've also included the original French text in a separate appendix. While my translations aim to capture their meaning and style, Francophones may appreciate untranslatable wordplay and cultural context that I missed.

Most importantly, these reviews represent a fascinating moment in French literary history, when critics grappled with a provocative new voice challenging conventional colonial narratives. Let's explore how these century-old reviewers approached this task — some with admirable skill, others with legitimate criticism, and a few with what modern readers might consider criminal disregard for literary discovery.

Perhaps we need a Reviewer's Hippocratic Oath:

"First, do no harm to the reader's journey of discovery…"

ભ✦ଓ

INDEX of Reviews in this Article

Date	Paper	Words	Author
		The Good	
1905/10/27	*Figaro*	340	Ph.-Emmanuel GLASER
1906/03/13	*L'Idée*	2,100	Yves NILS
1905/12/13	*Gazette*	2,200	Henry DE PÈNE
		The Bad	
1905/12/18	*Midi*	700	Louis ROUBAUD
1905/11/01	*Salon*	1,500	Paul REUSS
		The Ugly	
1905/11/15	*Mercure*	850	RACHILDE
1906/01/01	*National*	2,600	Unknown
1905/11/29	*Gil Blas*	3,300	Louis VAUXCELLES
1905/08/01	*Patria*	600	Charles PONSONAILHE
1906/01/06	*Gironde*	950	Gabriel TRARIEUX

The Good

We begin with a succinct but accurate review by Ph.-Emmanuel Glaser in the *Figaro* newspaper, saying:

"Indeed, the book fulfilled all the promises of its preface and all the threats of its title: disquieting, painful, and feverish, it carried you away through often-admirable pages into a wild whirlwind of phantoms and dreams that both delighted and gripped you while causing exquisite pain."

Next, a literary deep dive from Yves Nils writing in *L'Idée : revue littéraire*. His in-depth review explores literary and philosophical connections to Farrère's plot, and even one of his mentors, Pierre Loti:

"Some critics, whom I poorly understand, have wanted to see in this work reminiscences, or at least the influence of Loti. There are none. Loti writes works of art. This is a work of thought."

The third review in this category examines "Literary Sailors" in the *ancienne Gazette des étrangers*. I credit the unsigned review to the editor in chief, Henry de Pène. In it, he puts Claude Farrère within the context of other naval authors:

"Driven by long reveries, how many sailors have written beautiful verses in the secrecy of their cabins, verses that never saw the light of day! How many have yielded to the demon of the inkwell, writing novels that blend professional knowledge with a love of the palette whose style makes colors shine…"

∞

Source: *Figaro : non-politique* (1905 October 27)
Reviewer: Ph.-Emmanuel Glaser
Title: "Short Chronicle of Letters"

Last year, I mentioned a book in these pages, *Fumée d'opium*, whose author, M. Claude Farrère, entirely unknown in literary circles, presented himself to the public under the aegis of Pierre Louÿs, who had "discovered" his book and introduced it with a preface overflowing with inspired enthusiasm. Indeed, the book fulfilled all the promises of its preface and all the threats of its title: disquieting, painful, and feverish, it carried you away through often-admirable pages into a wild whirlwind of phantoms and dreams that both delighted and gripped you while causing exquisite pain.

M. Claude Farrère, who is nothing less than a professional writer, could not stop there; when one has written such a book, when one has so thoroughly "received heaven's secret influence," one perseveres, and between long-distance voyages or expeditions — for I strongly suspect M. Farrère of being a sailor — one cannot resist the imperious desire to relive and revive, through luminous descriptions and harmonious, sonorous phrases, the emotions one has experienced.

And so it is that M. Claude Farrère publishes this week at Ollendorff *The Civilized*, a novel he has written "for Pierre Louÿs." Entirely different from his previous volume of dreams and phantoms, this is a pure novel that shows us burning, vivid realities. It is in this Far East that he knows so well that M. Claude Farrère shows us "the civilized ones" in the fullness and overflow of their civilization, in antagonism with that of the ancient races upon whom we impose ourselves. And it is in these landscapes of Saigon, which he describes with a rare splendor of imagery and language, that we find an extraordinary tableau of manners, a drama of love and destruction, of sensuality, madness, murder — of civilization, in a word.

ଓ♦ଠ

Source: *L'Idée : revue littéraire* (1906 March 13)
Director: Georges Fagot
Reviewer: Yves Nils

The Civilized! What a magnificent title, profound to the point of abyss, compelling to the point of exclusivity. Claude Farrère has written one volume of it; it would not be too much to dedicate an entire body of work…

But this volume, perhaps the harbinger of a salvation movement (yes, if some event that stirs the elements of a race were to restore to us, for a time, the sensation of equilibrium), this volume is marvelously clear and precise. One watches with horror as it extends over the entire organism of a society, over all the literature of a century, and it is not superfluous to say that contemporary writers, artists, psychologists and philosophers — Loti with his sadness, Bazin with his pity, and Barrès, school leader, launched into full combat, and Daudet, and Serao — we all find ourselves summarized there.[1]

By Jove! The struggle is not new, and it has been many years since Musset, in *L'Enfant du Siècle*, hurled the precursory anathema at the cold goddess Reason. It has been long since Desgenais spoke and his pitiless voice slowly penetrated young hearts. It has been long since the vase of which Renan spoke was empty, but the perfume by which we still lived, the divine perfume is dying… What we will be when it is dead, Farrère's book teaches us.[2]

---

1 All key contemporary writers who, like Farrère, grappled with modernity's spiritual crisis: Pierre Loti (1850–1923) was known for his melancholic exotic novels lamenting the loss of traditional cultures. René Bazin (1853–1932) wrote sympathetically about rural life and social issues, often pitying the impact of modernization on traditional values. Maurice Barrès (1862–1923), described as "school leader, launched into full combat," was a nationalist intellectual who led the anti-Dreyfusard movement and championed what he called "the cult of the self" before turning to political activism — hence the military metaphor of being "launched into combat." Alphonse Daudet (1840–97) wrote naturalist novels often critical of modern society. Matilde Serao (1856–1927), the sole woman and non-French writer mentioned, was an Italian novelist who depicted the moral decay of contemporary Naples.

Together, these writers represented different facets of the period's critique of modern "civilization" — through exoticism (Loti), ruralism (Bazin), nationalism (Barrès), naturalism (Daudet), and urban decay (Serao). The reviewer suggests Farrère's novel synthesizes all these critiques of modernity.

2 This passage weaves together three major French literary responses to the loss of traditional faith and meaning. Alfred de Musset (1810–57), in his autobiographical novel *La Confession d'un enfant du siècle* (1836), portrayed his generation's spiritual malaise following the fall of Napoleon, attacking the Enlightenment's "cold goddess Reason" for destroying traditional beliefs without providing adequate replacement.

Desgenais is a cynical character from this same novel who ruthlessly strips away the protagonist's romantic illusions, representing the voice of disenchanted modernity.

Ernest Renan (1823–92), in works like *L'Avenir de la science* (1890), used the metaphor of an empty vase still retaining the perfume of lost faith to describe how society

Too brutally perhaps, in the needless and cynical exaggeration of a climate that develops vices to the point of frenzy, with wounding insistences that resemble complicity — but also with a boldness and clear-sightedness that none will deny, and with the aid of a composition so strong and learned that very few novelists have perhaps surpassed it.

Some critics, whom I poorly understand, have wanted to see in this work reminiscences, or at least the influence of Loti. There are none. Loti writes works of art. This is a work of thought. Thought so powerful and so apt even that it carries us away, as in Stendhal, well above style.[3] The style, one feels it exact and clear, ingenious in descriptions, and such passages as Fierce's letter to Sélysette show that he could, if he wished, soften to the most exquisite poetry… But it is not poetry that matters here. This is a hasty and anguished document taken from the very entrails of the poisoned one, a brutal diagnosis thrown amid the disquiet of so many irresolute works, and it is also — moreover, it would have been false without this, as false and hideous as *Bel-Ami* — a warning cry before the precipice.[4]

You will have given us a title, Farrère, that could cut like a standard for the combatants of Ancient History, those who still carry a barbarian's heart and who are concerned, moreover, only with the cultivation of sentiments.

---

might preserve some essence of religious feeling even after losing belief in religious doctrine. The reviewer then suggests Farrère's novel shows the final stage of this process — what happens when even this lingering "perfume" of traditional values dissipates, leaving only the empty materialism of the "civilized." This links these earlier critiques of modernity to Farrère's more radical vision of moral collapse in the colonies.

3   This passage contrasts several approaches to writing about modern society's moral decay. The reviewer rejects comparisons to Pierre Loti, whose exotic novels emphasized aesthetic beauty and atmospheric description, arguing instead that Farrère's work is more analytical, like that of Stendhal (1783–1842).

Marie-Henri Beyle, writing as Stendhal, was known for psychologically penetrating novels, like *Le Rouge et le Noir* (1830), that set intellectual insight over stylistic flourishes. This comparison is particularly significant, because Stendhal's clinical approach to analyzing human psychology and social behavior would become hugely influential on later French literature, though this wasn't fully appreciated in his own time. The reviewer seems to be suggesting that Farrère is similarly ahead of his time in diagnosing modern civilization's spiritual crisis.

4   The comparison to Maupassant's *Bel-Ami* (1885) illuminates a key aspect of Farrère's novel. Both works feature ambitious young men navigating a morally corrupt society — Georges Duroy in Paris's journalism world, Fierce in colonial Saigon. However, while Maupassant's hero triumphantly rises through cynical manipulation and seduction, Farrère's protagonist ultimately seeks redemption through heroic death.

This distinction is crucial to the reviewer's argument that *Les Civilisés* transcends mere naturalistic portrayal of corruption (as in *Bel-Ami*) to become a warning cry against civilization's moral decay. Where Maupassant's novel accepts and even celebrates its protagonist's cynical adaptation to modern amorality, Farrère's work suggests that such "civilization" leads only to spiritual death or desperate attempts at redemption through violence.

This elastic and stinging title names the enemy one was searching for, whom Musset endured without seeing, and favors war by illuminating it.[5]

Civilization! Yes, individualism, skepticism, atheism, the self-psychology that devours and freezes intellectuals, the socialism that corrupts the common people's good conscience, this word contains all that. However, there are currents whose mysterious source, forever undiscovered, rolls waves enough to exhaust all courage. And who then will have enough strength, love, and glory to divert this one? When will the new Messiah come who is capable of restoring our equilibrium? Alas! as Musset said, weeping over the same losses:

Where then vibrates in the air a voice more than human,
Who among us, who among us, will become a God?[6]

Yes, it is a God we would need. Just as it is through love alone could Fierce have been saved, unnerved by thirteen years of debauchery and nearly a century of decadence, it is in the footsteps of an adored hero that the faltering race would find its way again. Whether the hero be prophet or soldier, Jesus or Napoleon, matters little; what matters is that the national heart

----

5   Here, the reviewer points to a crucial development in French literary responses to modernity's spiritual crisis. In *La Confession d'un enfant du siècle*, Musset powerfully described his generation's malaise and disillusionment — what he called *"le mal du siècle"* — but portrayed it as a mysterious affliction, a vague spiritual emptiness following the fall of Napoleon and the triumph of rationalism. The reviewer suggests that Farrère's title *"Les Civilisés"* finally names what Musset could only feel: that civilization itself, with its emphasis on reason and progress, is the enemy of authentic human feeling.

The martial metaphor of the title cutting "like a standard" (battle flag) suggests that where Musset could only suffer from modernity's spiritual emptiness, Farrère's generation can actively resist it by championing what the reviewer calls "the barbarian's heart" — those primal human sentiments that civilization suppresses. This reading transforms Farrère's novel from a simple critique of colonial decadence into a call to arms against modern civilization's rationalistic suppression of authentic feeling.

6   This passage draws from another key theme in Musset's work: the desperate search for a new source of transcendent meaning in a post-religious age. The quoted lines come from Musset's "Rolla" (1833), a poem that dramatizes modern spiritual crisis through its protagonist's suicide. The question "Who among us will become a God?" expresses both the need for divine guidance and the impossibility of satisfying it in an age of skepticism.

The reviewer uses this reference to suggest that Farrère's novel, like Musset's poem, diagnoses a fundamental problem of modernity: neither rational thought nor individual willpower can fill the void left by lost religious faith.

This double failure — of both Enlightenment reason and romantic individualism — leads to the next paragraph's suggestion that only a messianic figure — "whether the hero be prophet or soldier, Jesus or Napoleon" — could restore spiritual equilibrium to modern civilization. This linking of religious and secular saviors reflects a particularly French tradition, dating from the French Revolution, of seeking quasi-religious redemption through political or cultural renewal. By connecting Farrère's novel to this tradition, the reviewer suggests that colonial decadence is merely a symptom of a deeper spiritual crisis that requires not reform but redemption.

feel its truths and that there be no higher pleasures for it than those contained in this formula: faith unto devotion, love unto sacrifice.

Among those who followed Jesus on the roads of Galilee and who listened to him for the unknown sweetness of his voice, how few understood him! But all loved him; and this love aroused in all hearts such a pure and intense flowering of sentiments that it is perhaps still this which defends us from the tomb.

But today which temple to choose, which idol to raise up? In the name of what ideal to reawaken the barbarian soul that sleeps beneath the corruption of the civilized? What new muse to present to it, after so many proud dead who aroused its activities? One still remains, and Farrère names it in his preface to Pierre Loti: Beauty.

Beauty! Yes, it would be very French, very elegant, and very haughty that we, the skeptics and materialists, we who no longer believe in the revenge of the beyond, we the faithless, the without-country, the without-scruples, should stop at the edge of evil vestiges uniquely because the ugliness of the fall wounds our aesthetic delicacy. It would be beautiful that we remain heroes through dilettantism and that, having known we worshipped chimeras, we remain faithful to them for the glory of this bitter and disdainful cult. Small group with eyes everywhere disenchanted, let us gather under the columns of Athens and cultivate in ourselves the enthusiasms that lift hearts, that satisfy energies, and that immortalize noble gestures… Let us find their proper resources and constitute for them a field of exercise vast enough to develop completely, without concerning ourselves with an end that constantly refuses itself… And let the sky be empty toward which all dead roses go. What will it matter to us if we have known how to capture the perfume and intoxicate ourselves with it desperately?[7]

---

7   The review's conclusion unites several strands of *fin de siècle* French thought about beauty as a substitute for lost faith. When the reviewer asks "Which temple to choose, which idol to raise up?" he acknowledges the failure of previous attempts to replace religion — whether through nationalism, science, or social progress. The turn to Beauty (with a capital B) as the final refuge represents a distinctly French aesthetic philosophy, influenced by figures like Théophile Gautier's concept of *"l'art pour l'art"* (art for art's sake).

The reference to gathering "under the columns of Athens" suggests a return to classical aesthetic values, while the image of capturing the perfume of "dead roses" echoes Renan's earlier metaphor of the empty vase retaining religion's fragrance.

However, the reviewer gives this aesthetic solution a particularly modern, self-aware twist. His "small group with eyes everywhere disenchanted" knows they worship "chimeras" yet chooses to maintain this "bitter and disdainful cult" on aesthetic principle alone. This position — maintaining noble ideals while acknowledging their artificiality — represents a uniquely decadent response to modern spiritual crisis.

The reviewer suggests that Farrère's novel, by exposing civilization's moral

ঙ•ঌ

Source: ***Ancienne Gazette des étrangers*** (1905 December 13)
Reviewer: Henry de Pène, Editor in Chief (and Managing Director)
Title: ***Literary Sailors***

It is to a man of letters from the navy that the Académie Goncourt has just awarded its annual prose prize.

The French Navy, which takes justifiable pride in having one of its representatives, and not the least distinguished, M. Pierre Loti,[8] in the Académie Française,[9] has produced numerous talented writers. Indeed, many naval officers have written, either while on active duty, under a pseudonym, or after retirement.

M. Bargone, who under the name Claude Farrère has written a biting book, *The Civilized*, which the Académie Goncourt has distinguished above all others, is therefore far from an exception.

Should we conclude that the long hours of solitude facing the ocean and stars are truly made for giving birth to thoughts, sparking ideas, and embedding observations in the mind? No doubt.

Certainly, the life of a naval officer is not idle, but four hours of watch duty on the quarterdeck leave ample room for emotions stirred by nature's grand spectacles: sunsets, starlit tropical nights, islands emerging from the

---

bankruptcy in the colonies, points toward this paradoxical salvation through conscious aesthetic illusion. Beauty becomes not just an artistic principle but a last defense against complete spiritual collapse — even if, as the final image of desperate intoxication suggests, this solution contains its own form of decadence.

8 Pierre Loti (1850–1923), born Julien Viaud, was an officer in the French Navy turned novelist who drew his exotic tales from his military travels. Elected to the Académie Française in 1891, he helped establish a tradition of naval officers writing literary works. His novels like *Madame Chrysanthème* (1887, set in Japan) became international bestsellers, influencing how European readers viewed the "exotic" East. Like Farrère after him, Loti wrote under a pseudonym while serving on active duty.

Farrère's and Loti's naval careers intersected symbolically through their service on the same ships. First, Farrère served on the *Couronne*, where Loti had earlier fallen in love with the Circassian woman who inspired his novel *Aziyadé*. Then, Farrère was posted as a midshipman to the *Bayard* in Ha Long Bay, drawing inspiration from this exotic setting for *The Civilized*. Twelve years earlier, this same *Bayard* had carried Loti during the Tonkin campaign under the flag of Vice-Admiral Courbet.

9 The Académie Française, founded in 1635, is France's preeminent learned body on matters of the French language. It is composed of forty members, known as "the Immortals," and election to it is the highest honor in French letters. While the institution was founded to create and maintain a definitive French dictionary, by the late nineteenth century membership had become primarily a form of recognition of those who best exemplified French literary achievement and cultural influence through their writing.

sea, wild coastlines, storms, typhoons, and smiling bays amid the verdure. Then there are the human spectacles — knowledge of diverse races with such different customs, romances that leave behind the perfume of exotic flowers, dramas before which one must remain a silent spectator; perhaps no one is better suited to know the world, nature, peoples, the human soul and heart than the naval officer.

Driven by long reveries, how many sailors have written beautiful verses in the secrecy of their cabins, verses that never saw the light of day! How many have yielded to the demon of the inkwell, writing novels that blend professional knowledge with a love of the palette whose style makes colors shine...

I mentioned earlier the name of Pierre Loti, whose real name is Commander Viaud, captain of the frigate commanding our station in the Bosporus. Is there a more prestigious painter? Is there a more incomparable stylist among living writers? With what an enchanting and emotionally delicate pen he has painted Japan, China, Africa, India, and the strange Basque country, with a tribe of Huns remaining at the foot of the Pyrenees.[10] Claude Farrère has another style, very personal. In his book *The Civilized* he has written a masterful page in which he makes us witness the moving struggle of a torpedo boat against a battleship that ultimately succumbs.

Other literary sailors have dedicated themselves to giving us accounts of lived experiences, such as Frigate Captain René Diaveluy, who, in a book entitled *La Lutte pour l'Empire des Mers*, has told us of the terrifying Battle of Tsushima.[11]

One could cite a hundred others who, following Dumont-d'Urville,

---

10 This peculiar characterization of the Basques as "a tribe of Huns" reflects a nineteenth-century fascination with the mysterious origins of the Basque people. The Basques, with their unique pre-Indo-European language and distinct cultural traditions, were the subject of much anthropological speculation. The reference to Huns suggests an Eastern origin, a common theory of the time, though refuted by modern scholarship. Loti, himself from the Basque region (born in Rochefort), wrote extensively about Basque culture, particularly in his novel *Ramuntcho* (1897), though he portrayed it more romantically than the exotic Hun theory suggested here. The comparison with Huns seems to be the reviewer's attempt to place the Basque country among Loti's other "exotic" settings, like Japan and China.

11 René Diaveluy (1860–1934) wrote about the decisive Battle of Tsushima (May 27–28, 1905), where the Japanese navy destroyed the Russian fleet in the Strait of Tsushima. This battle would later serve as the centerpiece for Farrère's *La Bataille* (1909), his fifth novel, which explored Japanese nationalism and military prowess through the lens of this historic naval engagement. That this review mentions Diaveluy's account of Tsushima is particularly interesting, as Farrère would incorporate this same battle into his fiction just a few years later, though he had only spent three days in Nagasaki during his naval service.

Bougainville, and Fleuriot de Langle, have written their maritime memoirs or books of powerful technical interest, like Admiral Paris, who was a member of the Institute.[12]

None, however, has equaled Admiral Julien de la Gravière, who was rightly elected to the Académie Française. His *Guerres maritimes* is not merely a classic work. Need we recall his description of the Battle of Trafalgar, which constitutes an unforgettable piece, so clear, so precise, yet so engaging that one cannot forget it.[13]

Nor has anyone forgotten Admiral Gourdon's *L'Incomprise*,[14] or the book by Lieutenant Darcy, who so valiantly defended the French legation in Peking during the Boxer Rebellion,[15] nor the charming book by a very

---

12   The reviewer cites several key figures in French naval exploration and literature. Jules Dumont d'Urville (1790–1842) led important scientific expeditions to the Pacific and claimed parts of Antarctica for France. Louis Antoine de Bougainville (1729–1811), best known for his voyage of circumnavigation (1766–69), wrote popular accounts that influenced Enlightenment views of "natural man."

Paul Antoine Fleuriot de Langle (1744–87) served as second-in-command to Jean-François de La Pérouse on an ambitious French scientific expedition (1785–88) meant to rival the voyages of Captain James Cook. The expedition's two ships — the *Astrolabe* and the *Boussole* — disappeared without trace after leaving Botany Bay, Australia. Fleuriot de Langle, commanding the *Astrolabe*, was killed along with eleven of his crew in a clash with natives in Samoa in December 1787. La Pérouse and the *Boussole* vanished completely. One of naval history's great mysteries went unsolved until 1826, when the wreckage was discovered on the reefs of Vanikoro in the Solomon Islands.

Admiral François-Edmond Pâris (1806–93), elected to the Académie des Sciences in 1863, was a prolific writer on naval technology and maritime ethnography. Together, these figures established a strong tradition in which French naval officers would contribute both scientific knowledge and compelling literature about exploration — a tradition that Farrère would continue in his own way.

13   Vice Admiral Jean-Pierre-Edmond Jurien de la Gravière (1812–92) represents another significant intersection between naval service and literary achievement. He was elected to the Académie Française in 1888, and his *Guerres maritimes* offered what was considered the definitive French analysis of naval warfare. It included an acclaimed account of the Battle of Trafalgar (1805). The reviewer's emphasis on La Gravière's "rightly" earned election and his praise of the Trafalgar description are noteworthy. Trafalgar was both Britain's greatest naval victory and France's most devastating defeat. That a French admiral could write about this battle with such objectivity and style made his work particularly remarkable. The reviewer's citation of La Gravière serves to reinforce the tradition of naval officers who could write with both technical precision and literary merit.

14   Admiral Palma Firmin Christian Gourdon (1843–1913) was a distinguished French naval officer who saw action in Tunisia (1881) and Tonkin (1883–85). In the Combat of Shipu (1885), he led a daring torpedo attack that sank two Chinese warships while he was second-in-command of the battleship *Bayard;* the same ship that Loti and Farrère served on. As an author, he is known for his 1881 book, *La Frégate 'L'Incomprise' voyage autour du monde*, an illustrated account of his ship's journey around the world.

15   Lieutenant Eugène Darcy (1868–1928) gained fame for his bravery defending the French Legation in Peking during the Boxer Rebellion (1899–1901). Darcy wrote a vivid account of his experiences, which earned him the prestigious Montyon Prize from the Académie Française in 1903.

young newcomer, M. de Blois, a mere midshipman, who described his shipboard impressions during his first year at sea.[16]

Officers are forbidden to publish anything without their superiors' authorization, but this authorization is quickly granted for serious works, and eyes are closed to literary works published under pseudonyms. Certain works, however, hostile and scandalous, require preliminary resignation; we will not needlessly recall the titles of these works.

Among the literary sailors, some dying gloriously in service to France, others of natural causes, we should cite among the first Commander Rivière, whose heroic end in Tonkin no one has forgotten. We owe him several works of literature and memoirs that demonstrate great delicacy of heart and mind. Notable among these are *Edmée*, *La Jeunesse d'un Désespéré*, *Le Combat de la Vie*, and a charming one-act play that was performed at the Comédie-Française. [17]

The mention of Tonkin brings to mind Francis Garnier, who produced two fine books: *Paris au Thibet* and *L'Exploration du Mékong*. The Prince de Joinville, who was Admiral of France, also wrote several memoirs, and there is a famous page of him describing a Mediterranean storm that can be counted among the purest masterpieces of our literature.[18]

Some have left the navy to become journalists, like M. Maurice Loir,[19] who has done much to popularize naval matters and who published a very fine volume entitled "The French Navy." Another curious character: that of an excellent officer who, after the war, left the navy for the press. At the beginning

---

16   Your editor has been unable to identify this author or his book.

17   Henri Laurent Rivière (1827–83) was a French naval officer and prolific writer who played a key role in France's expansion into Indochina. He is best known for his actions in Tonkin (northern Vietnam), where he captured Hanoi in 1882, sparking conflict with both the Vietnamese and China. Rivière's legacy is complex. While his military actions initially advanced French interests, they also led to increased tensions and ultimately the Sino-French War (1884–85). He was killed in action on May 19, 1883, during the Battle of Paper Bridge, near Hanoi, further fueling the conflict.

18   François d'Orléans, Prince de Joinville (1818–1900), was a French admiral and writer. He was the third son of King Louis-Philippe and had a distinguished naval career, having among his commands the fleet that brought Napoleon's remains back to France from Saint Helena in 1840. He also served in the American Civil War as a Union staff officer.

19   Maurice Loir (1852–1924) was a French naval officer, journalist, and historian who wrote extensively about the French Navy. Loir, who also used the pen name Marc Landry, graduated from the École Navale and served in the navy, reaching the rank of lieutenant before retiring in 1896. He continued to contribute to naval affairs as a journalist for *Le Figaro*, often writing under his pseudonym. Loir authored numerous books on French naval history, including works on Admiral Courbet's squadron, naval battles, and the navy's role in Madagascar and the Sudan. He was connected to the famed scientist Louis Pasteur through his mother's family. Loir's diverse career and prolific writing cemented his place as a chronicler of French maritime history.

of the 1870 war, he commanded an aviso on the African coast where we were warring against a native tribe.

He had forbidden his officers to speak to him outside of official business, which led to the following rather amusing incident, whose outcome, though consistent with discipline, will seem rather stern to us today.

"Word came, however, that on September 4th, the Empire had fallen. The ship's officers gathered and wondered whether they should tell the commander, whom they knew to be deeply devoted to the Empire.

"'Well, too bad,' said one of them. 'I'll tell him; it will make him furious.'

"And he presented himself before the commander:

"'What is it?' asked the latter.

"'Commander, the Empire has fallen, the Republic has been proclaimed in Paris.'

"The commander, perfectly composed, remained impassive:

"'Very well, sir, you will serve four days' confinement.'"

True or false, this anecdote, which has been told before, was worth recounting.

:+€

The Bad

First, it is important to reiterate is that a "bad" review is not necessarily bad; it just presents a different opinion about the value of the book at hand.

We start with a mirror image of the previous "good" review above, in which M. De Pène lauded M. Farrère and other naval writers perpetuating the noble military literary tradition. Five days later, Louis Roubaud, who honestly notes that he didn't even read the book(!), responded with a diatribe criticizing military and "non-professional writers, and novels in general.

"It is true that novels have enjoyed a vogue in the final years of the nineteenth century; one that continues and grows in these early days of the twentieth.

"Unfortunately, while poetry, like music, elevates the soul, novels all too often poison it. It is difficult to make beautiful verses serve an evil cause, but how many talented prose writers have been the deplorable apostles of a detestable religion!"

Next, however, M. Paul Reuss delivers the pinnacle of "bad" reviews with his absolutely savage (though thinly-veiled) rant. His style of attack is almost a modern celebrity roast of Farrère, the Academy, and colonists in general, but always with velvet gloves on. I confess, this is one of my favorite reviews, and he accomplishes his task without any spoilers. Bravo!

"I do not wish to examine here the utility of literary competitions, those supposed encouragements given to young (?) writers. Suffice it to note that only very rarely are prizes awarded intelligently. Almost always, they go either to a well-connected imbecile or to a writer who cares very little about these few coins falling, by chance, into his purse.

"I do not mean to suggest that Mr. Claude Farrère is an imbecile. Far be it from me to have such a thought; I simply wish to point out that awarding the Goncourt Prize to his work is preposterous; it is nothing short of an egregious error..."

Ha, ha. And Paul is only warming up in those lines!

ᘔ✦ᘒ

Source: *Le Journal du Midi* (1905 December 18)
Reviewer: Louis Roubaud
Title: *Parisian Chronicle*

It is true that novels have enjoyed a vogue in the final years of the nineteenth century; one that continues and grows in these early days of the twentieth.

Unfortunately, while poetry, like music, elevates the soul, novels all too often poison it. It is difficult to make beautiful verses serve an evil cause, but how many talented prose writers have been the deplorable apostles of a detestable religion!

I have not read *The Civilized* by M. Farrère, which has just won the Prix Goncourt, which dispenses me from classifying it in any category. I have merely noted that the Académie Goncourt has not crowned, this year, a professional man of letters, and this fact, which at first appears inconsequential, reveals a very alarming state of affairs.

Indeed, not only does the crowd of writers leading miserable existences continue to grow, but now in every profession we find minds awakening, tormented by the disease of writing.

It is in the navy that one finds the most writers. M. Farrère, whose real name is Bargone, is a lieutenant; he has before him numerous illustrious precedents of various degrees.

Besides Commander Viaud (Pierre Loti), how many names could one cite? The *Guerres Maritimes* by Admiral Julien de la Gravière, who was a member of the Académie Française, remains famous; Admiral Gourdon wrote *La Frégate 'l'Incomprise*; Commander Rivière is the author of numerous novels and a play performed at the Comédie-Française; *La Lutte pour l'Empire des mers* by Frigate Captain Diaveluy is a work of merit. But the list is too long of romantic books whose authors are all members of our navy.[20]

If all other careers contain similar literary seeds, the professional writer, already so miserable, will tomorrow be nothing but a pariah whose reason for being will be questioned. He will still have, no doubt, the resource of becoming a journalist, but that is indeed a dark prospect.[21]

Louis Roubaud (1884–1941) was a significant French journalist and author who specialized in investigative journalism and colonial affairs. Born in Marseille and educated at the prestigious Lycée Thiers, where he later taught, Roubaud went on to write for such major publications as *Le Quotidien*, *L'Intransigeant*, *Le Petit Parisien*, and *Paris Soir*.

His work frequently engaged with colonial themes, as evidenced by books like *Viet-Nam, la tragédie indochinoise* (1931) and *Images et Réalités Coloniales* (1931). He also wrote *Christiane de Saïgon* (1932), making his early criticism of Farrère's portrayal of Saigon particularly interesting. We can get some idea of Roubaud's standing in French journalism by observing that he was part of the first jury for the prestigious Prix Albert-Londres.

His admission that he did not read *Les Civilisés* before reviewing it reflects both the hasty nature of daily journalism and, perhaps, the competitive tensions between writers covering colonial subjects. His eventual extensive writing about Indochina suggests he may have later developed a more nuanced view of Farrère's work. Indeed, Roubaud's harsh early criticism of Farrère's portrayal of Saigon takes on new significance later, when he stakes his own literary claim to representing French Indochina. This professional

---

20 Somewhat ironically, this passage catalogs notable French naval officers who became writers. Admiral Jean-Pierre-Edmond Jurien de la Gravière (1812-1892) was both a distinguished naval commander and prolific author whose works on naval history earned him election to the Académie française in 1866. Admiral Adolphe Gourdon (1834-1901) wrote fiction drawing on his naval experiences, including *La Frégate l'Incomprise* (*The Frigate Misunderstood*). Henri Laurent Rivière (1827-1883) was a naval officer and man of letters who wrote plays and novels; he later died in combat in Tonkin. Captain Charles Diaveluy published extensively on naval strategy and history.

21 Roubaud's closing paragraph reveals an anxiety that professional writers are being displaced by military men turning to literature, a particularly pointed concern given that Farrère (Charles Bargone) was himself a naval officer. The reference to becoming "nothing but a pariah" and having to resort to journalism drips with self-deprecating irony, as Roubaud himself was a journalist reviewing a naval officer's novel.

territory — the literary representation of colonial life — was fiercely contested by French writers of the period, with each author asserting his own authority to portray these distant territories for metropolitan readers.

ଔ✦ଓ

Source: Salon des poètes méridionaux, *Arts et lettres : revue mensuelle méridionale* (1905 November 1)
Editorial committee: Robert Hugues, Charles Phalippou, Paul Reuss
Reviewer: Paul Reuss
Title: II. — Prose. *Les Civilisés*, by Claude Farrère

For the third time since its founding, the Académie Goncourt has just awarded its annual prize, to Mr. Claude Farrère for his novel *The Civilized*. I do not wish to examine here the utility of literary competitions, those supposed encouragements given to young (?) writers. Suffice it to note that only very rarely are prizes awarded intelligently. Almost always, they go either to a well-connected imbecile or to a writer who cares very little about these few coins falling, by chance, into his purse.

I do not mean to suggest that Mr. Claude Farrère is an imbecile. Far be it from me to have such a thought; I simply wish to point out that awarding the Goncourt Prize to his work is preposterous; it is nothing short of an egregious error...

And I am greatly astonished by the decision of this Academy, which counts among its members perhaps the finest in our contemporary literature. As for me, I do not hesitate to declare that *The Civilized* is a very bad book and that awarding this prize to Mr. Claude Farrère is an insult to the true talent of J.-A. Nau or Léon Frapié.[22]

---

22   The reviewer references the first two winners of the Prix Goncourt, contrasting their "serious" social themes with Farrère's colonial subject matter.

John-Antoine Nau (1860–1918), the inaugural winner in 1903 for *Force ennemie*, wrote about psychological themes and altered states of consciousness. Like Farrère's novel, *Force ennemie* was controversial, but for its groundbreaking portrayal of mental illness from the perspective of an asylum inmate possessed by a South American spirit. The novel's innovative narrative technique and serious treatment of psychological themes established a high literary standard for the new prize.

Léon Frapié (1863–1949) continued this focus on social issues, winning in 1904 for *La Maternelle*, which examined class inequality through the story of a well-educated woman forced by circumstances to work as an assistant at a working-class kindergarten in Paris. The novel was praised for its unflinching portrayal of urban poverty and its effects on children.

By citing these predecessors, the reviewer implies that the Prix Goncourt should reward social realism and psychological depth rather than what he sees as Farrère's mix of colonial exoticism and sentimentality. This speaks to a larger debate about what constituted "serious" literature worthy of recognition in early twentieth-century France.

Reading this work reminded me of that category of people whom I shall call — lacking a more precise term — the friends one has in the colonies.[23] Each of our readers certainly counts, among his friends, a colonial. And if he is at all psychologically observant, he will have quickly noticed that the latter always tries to "impress his audience" by recounting adventures of all kinds, each one, in the teller's estimation, more extraordinary than the last. This man, moreover, who claims to be jaded — disgusted by the too-monotonous life of the metropole — will spend his money in the most foolish way possible on inept, archaic pleasures so outdated that even the least of schoolboys wouldn't want them.

Oh, the cruel irony of these worldly matters![24]

Mr. Farrère, too, first seeks to astonish and unsettle us with his vivid descriptions of questionable morality and his crudely realistic narratives. He lingers at length over the debaucheries of his heroes Torral and Méril. One would think he takes pleasure in exposing all the sordid underbelly of life in Saigon. And he does this so clumsily that one is led to believe that Mr. Claude Farrère is either terribly naive or, worse still, that he has never read History. Does he not go so far as to claim that the behaviors he presents to us belong exclusively to our colonies? As if there wasn't more vice in Paris than in Saigon!

Furthermore, all this is not even literature. Such subjects should be left to those mere scribblers, those designated purveyors of pornographic collections, who at least have the self-awareness of shaming themselves by wallowing in such matters. The author of *The Civilized* fails even to interest us in that way; reading his work is simply tiresome. But most curious of all is that Mr. Farrère then attempts to move us, to make us shed tears over the sad idyll of a Fierce and a Sélysette.

Here is Mr. Claude Farrère transformed into an author of the saccharine Bibliothèque Rose: his sentimentalism is completely ridiculous. The

---

23 The reviewer's mocking description reveals complex attitudes towards colonial administrators and military personnel serving in French Indochina during this period. While colonial service offered opportunities for advancement, particularly for young naval officers like Farrère, those who returned often faced metropolitan skepticism about their experiences.

24 Here, the reviewer highlights the contradiction between the sophisticated pretensions of colonials when they return to Paris, and their actual unsophisticated behavior. It is quite a specific kind of metropolitan French snobbery about colonial returnees trying and failing to fit back into Parisian society. This tension was particularly acute in the early 1900s, when colonial service was seen as both an opportunity for advancement and a kind of exile from "civilized" Parisian society. The reviewer's mock-philosophical tone — affecting world-weary sophistication while criticizing the same pose in others — exemplifies the complex social dynamics between metropolitan elites and those who served in France's colonial empire.

state of mind of his Fierce is that of a ten-year-old child.[25]

His thesis is also ridiculous, and quite stale. Everyone knows, and we needn't wait for Mr. Claude Farrère to point out, that the colonies are a refuge for all adventurers, all of life's losers, and that they are an excellent springboard for a good many politicians. To say otherwise would, I believe, be madness, and there was really no need to remind us of this in such a boring book.

With its clumsy realism and weak psychology, Mr. Claude Farrère's work has almost no value from a stylistic point of view: utterly unoriginal, it rings hollow. At most, one must grant it correctness of form. And I consider it a serious mistake to have dedicated such a book to that dazzling stylist Pierre Louÿs. The comparison is far too disadvantageous.[26]

CଓƏ♦ଟ୬

---

25 The Bibliothèque Rose was a famous imprint of Hachette Publishing, created in 1852 by Louis Hachette himself. It became one of the first and most successful book series specifically aimed at children and young readers in France.

 The collection was known for moral stories with educational value, and sentimental, wholesome content suitable for young people. It often featured young protagonists learning life lessons, and included both original French works and translations of foreign children's classics. The series got its name from the distinctive pink/rose-colored covers.

 When the reviewer's mocking comparison of Farrère's romantic subplot to the Bibliothèque Rose is particularly biting because it comes right after the criticism of Farrère's "crude realism" in other parts of the novel. The reviewer is saying Farrère swings between inappropriate debauchery and childish sentimentality.

 The further reference to Fierce's having "the state of mind of a ten-year-old child" reinforces this criticism.

 French readers of the time would have immediately understood the reference to the Bibliothèque Rose, whose literature was the exact opposite of what a serious adult novel should be.

26 This closing criticism proved particularly misguided. Pierre Louÿs (1870–1925) was indeed a dazzling stylist. Louÿs was known for works like *Aphrodite* (1896), which masterfully evoked ancient Greek culture and sensuality. The impact of this novel on Farrère was profound — he discovered it by chance on his last night in France before departing for Asia, and spent the night captivated by its revolutionary style and frank sensuality. However, far from being offended by the dedication, Louÿs became a key player in revealing Farrère's talent. In 1902, serving as a judge for a literary competition in *Le Journal*, Louÿs was struck by the quality of a tale titled "Fumée d'opium," submitted under the pen name Pierre Toulven. He wrote to its author, praising its originality and predicting a bright literary future. This began a deep friendship between Louÿs and Farrère that would last until Louÿs's death, in 1925. The reviewer's attempt to use Farrère's dedication to criticize the author inadvertently highlighted one of the most important literary relationships of his career.

The Ugly

Well, here we have, in my personal opinion, the worst of the worst type
of review; which is especially sad because these reviews include excellent
commentary. But, in that ugly style of the era, their spoilers reveal the biggest
surprises and denouements in the plot.

We open with a positive review in *Mercure* by Farrère's friend Rachide,
and one that the author credits with getting his book sales off to a roaring start.
She was influential and made a powerful case for the quality of his writing, but
her spoilers are hard to ignore.

Rachilde champions Farrère's contemporary relevance, saying, "His
studies of exotic mores are thoroughly fascinating, meticulously researched,
boldly executed, and arrive at precisely the moment when the public, with
its appetite for spicy tales, dreams of curious details about the Gaud-Toqué
affairs [a political scandal in French Indochina] and all the refined vices that
reign in native lands."

Next, though unsigned, the detailed review in *Le National* is among
the best for its literary depth, and it is remarkably sagacious in identifying
weaknesses and strengths:

"M. Claude Farrère's novel aims to observe real, contemporary life. A
few men, having retained only one religion — 'the harsh religion of shameless
truth' — flaunt their debauchery in Saigon, disdainful of all European
prejudices — in other words, of all barbarity."

The reviewer shows particular insight in recognizing how the
book improves when it moves from artificial "literary" effects to more
straightforward depictions of colonial life and warfare, drawing on Farrère's
actual experiences as a naval officer. But, alas, the spoilers nearly eliminate the
need to read the book…the whole plot is there!

Next, Louis Vauxcelles, writing for *Gil Blas*, does the same. At 3,300
words, his review is the most substantive, with excellent analysis…at the
beginning. Then in a few paragraphs he reveals the worst spoilers possible. But
he still appreciated Farrère's craft:

"This novel, I want to say straight away, is one of the most
magnificently daring books that contemporary literature has produced. Since
Louis Bertrand, who was revealed to us some four or five years ago, I do not
believe one could find a more powerful colorist or more acerbic thinker."

Next, in *Patria*, we have a 600-word review by Charles Ponsonailhe,
a respected writer and art critic of the era, saying, "In some respects, Mr.

Farrère's work is worthy of the highest praise. It is written with mastery by an artist, a colorful raconteur, a poet, a sensitive soul."

He does a decent (but short) job of assessing the book's importance, but then spoils the most dramatic (and unexpected) scenes at the end of the book.

To conclude, we have Gabriel Trarieux, writing for *Gironde*. He doesn't make it a secret that he's highly critical of Farrère, *and* of the Academy for making what is, in his view, a horrible choice. His exaggerated critical approach would be rather fun to read if he hadn't included so many spoilers. He concludes saying, "I regret that such a document of our colonial rot is signaled as a masterpiece by ten good French writers."

Well, you can't please everyone!

೮♦ಐ

Source: *Mercure de France, série moderne* (1905 November 15)
Director: Alfred Vallette
Reviewer: Rachilde
Title: The Novels – *Les Civilisés*, by Claude Farrère

The author, whom I might fondly call "the gentleman who has read *Aphrodite*" — much as one might say "the Woman who knew the Emperor" of our dearly missed Hugues Rebell[27] — is a newcomer to literature, yet one not lacking in experience or talent. Although he occasionally advocates for laws, religion, and certain established barbaric customs, his studies of exotic mores are thoroughly fascinating, meticulously researched, boldly executed, and arrive at precisely the moment when the public, with its appetite for spicy tales, dreams of curious details about the Gaud-Toqué affairs and all the refined vices that reign in native lands.[28]

---

27 "The Woman who knew the Emperor" (*La Femme qui a connu l'empereur*) is the title of a 1904 novel by French decadent writer Hugues Rebell (1867–1905). The reference creates a literary parallel between Farrère's relationship to Pierre Louÿs's *Aphrodite* (1896) and Rebell's protagonist's relationship to Napoleon. Just as Rebell's character is defined by her connection to the Emperor, the reviewer suggests Farrère's early writing is notably influenced by Louÿs's erotic novel, set in ancient Alexandria. Rebell, who had recently died when this review was published (hence "dearly missed"), was known for his libertine historical fiction, which often mixed eroticism with political themes. The comparison is particularly apt as both Louÿs and Rebell were associated with the French Decadent movement, and their works often explored themes of sexuality, exoticism, and moral transgression that also appear in Farrère's *Les Civilisés*.

28 "The Gaud-Toqué affairs" refers to a colonial scandal that erupted in French Indochina in 1904–05, involving Lieutenant Gaud and Sergeant Toqué. The two French military officers were convicted of extreme brutality and murder in Tonkin (northern Vietnam). Their crimes included torturing and executing Vietnamese villagers, most notoriously by tying victims

The story concerns a cruise to Saigon. Count de Fierce, a most civilized Frenchman, exports the art nouveau tastes of the New France. He is somewhat jaded, somewhat neurotic, somewhat taciturn, and possesses no great measure of moral sense. In contact with certain friends, far more intoxicated than he by the drugs and customs of pleasure cities — sirens waiting to roll shipwrecked souls of all nations in their peculiarly perfumed mire — the poor young officer grows increasingly jaded and neurotic.

Mévil, the ladies' doctor, and Torral, the seeker of abstractions, teach him respectively to renounce sentimental love and to forget the old military faith. Yet he grows disgusted with debauchery, all too easily found in these hot lands, and the smile of Sélysette, a hero's daughter, fortunately shines upon him like the beam of a protective star. For a moment, he regains his energy, takes possession of himself once more, and strives to believe in things that once made him shrug his shoulders. There is also a fine admiral whose condescension in finding him an honest fellow sets his heart right.

However, an hour of forgetfulness ruins him. Having drunk from the sirens' cup, he will drink again, and returning from a wild night out, he encounters his lucky star, which is sadly obliged to shine upon a most unedifying tableau: the fiancé embraced by the arms of a scantily clad person in the back of a hired carriage. Sélysette fades away, a cloud darkens the horizon. Fierce feels himself drifting. He seeks revenge on civilized life by sinking a large English warship — a barbaric way of finally being right.

On this subject, there is a magnificent passage about the death throes of the vessel struck in its hull by the small torpedo boat that fires only at point-blank range. The scenes of exotic *civilizations* are admirably painted with a style both light and brutal, with a certain cold worldliness, very elegant, telling all, and risking technical terms without any trace of vulgarity. Despite some more than risky adventures, it is never crude because it is not hypocritical. I do not care for the principle that one cannot live, in the colonies or elsewhere, without God, without master, and without laws, but questions of principle are simply opportunities to reveal one's personal visions of humanity. The author

---

together and throwing them into rivers to drown — a practice they called "making rafts" ("*faire des radeaux*"). The case caused a sensation in France, coming at a time of growing debate about colonial violence and "civilizing missions." The reviewer's reference to these affairs is pointed, as Farrère's novel *Les Civilisés* appeared just as this scandal was making headlines, and similarly questioned the moral degradation of Europeans in colonial settings. The timing added particular resonance to the novel's critique of so-called "civilized" behavior in the colonies. The case became emblematic of colonial abuse and hypocrisy, much like the themes explored in Farrère's work.

of *The Civilized*, the gentleman who has read *Aphrodite*, has quite personal visions despite his Aphrodisiac influences.

Marguerite Vallette-Eymery (1860–1953), who wrote under the pen name **Rachilde**, was a major figure in French Decadent and Symbolist literature. As co-founder and literary critic of the influential *Mercure de France* with her husband, Alfred Vallette, she wielded considerable influence in fin de siècle Paris literary circles.

Known for controversial novels, like *Monsieur Vénus* (1884), that challenged norms between the sexes and conventional morality, Rachilde hosted famous Tuesday salons attended by Oscar Wilde, Paul Verlaine, and many other artistic and literary luminaries. Her support of Farrère was significant. In 1948, he wrote to her, "It was even you who gave it to me," regarding the Goncourt Prize.

Although her extensive discussion of the plot of *Les Civilisés* reveals her enthusiasm, it also reflects her broader role in championing new writers who challenged social conventions. As a critic, Rachilde was particularly drawn to works that questioned bourgeois morality, making her an ideal early supporter of Farrère's critique of colonial "civilization." Her own gender-bending persona (she often dressed as a man and carried calling cards identifying herself as "Rachilde, *homme de lettres*") and her exploration of controversial themes in her writing made her naturally sympathetic to Farrère's provocative debut novel.

ଓ♦ଛ

Source: *Le National* (1906 January 1)
Publisher: Maujan, Adolphe (1853–1914)
Reviewer: Unknown (but to judge by the style and depth of literary analysis, it appears to be written by a serious literary critic rather than a general journalist)
Title: A Book – *Les Civilisés*, a novel by Claude Farrère (Paul Ollendorff, publishers)

"Let me tell you why your *Aphrodite* drew me in so fast, why it took me whole," writes M. Claude Farrère to M. Pierre Louÿs. "It was quite simply of my religion, the religion of lovely lines harmonious and still, the religion of pure, naked Beauty."

Even before leafing through the book, one expects some curious and elegant flight of imagination toward a less petty world. Will M. Claude Farrère, in imitation of his dear master (between Racine, La Bruyère, and M.

Pierre Louÿs, the author of *The Civilized* finds only "the tumultuous, the agape, and the excessive as so many categories of impotent character"), reconstruct a refined civilization where sensuality will be the only accepted principle, and create on earth some paradise of voluptuousness?[29]

No: M. Claude Farrère's novel aims to observe real, contemporary life. A few men, having preserved only one religion — "the harsh religion of shameless truth" — flaunt their debauchery in Saigon, disdainful of all European prejudices — in other words, of all barbarity. Are they happy? More or less. But then one of them, Naval Ensign de Fierce, falls in love, innocently in love with the adorable and ingenuous Sélysette. Despite his civilized theories, he becomes engaged. Barely separated from his fiancée, his vice seizes him again; one fine morning, Sélysette encounters him flanked by two half-naked women. The marriage is broken off. But at the same moment, war is declared, and Ensign de Fierce, rediscovering in himself the noble barbarity of his ancestors, charges at the enemy — what am I saying? — at that "quintessence of civilization shut within their walls, a quintessence of civilization fit for dynamite"; and this desperate man, finally converted, dies a hero, while his two usual companions collapse, one in a pitiful death, the other in abjection.

And thus, M. Claude Farrère abandons the path of his master, who was so harsh on modern writers who, "using a laborious stratagem whose hypocrisy displeases," say "I have painted voluptuousness as it is in order to exalt virtue." Decidedly, there is little in common between M. Claude Farrère and M. Pierre Louÿs.[30]

---

29   The reviewer is drawing a literary contrast between classical French stylists and more contemporary authors. Jean Racine (1639–99) and Jean de La Bruyère (1645–96) represent the height of seventeenth-century French classicism, known for their elegant restraint and precise psychological observations. Pierre Louÿs (1870–1925), in contrast, was a contemporary aesthete and symbolist writer whose works, particularly *Aphrodite* (1896), revived classical themes and presented them through an explicitly sensual lens. The reviewer notes that Farrère claims to prefer Louÿs's refined eroticism to what he sees as the uncontrolled excesses ("the tumultuous, the agape") of other writers. However, the reviewer suggests some irony here, as Farrère's actual writing in *The Civilized* proves to be quite different from Louÿs's polished sensuality, more aligned with naturalistic observation despite his stated aesthetic preferences. This tension between classical restraint, aesthetic refinement, and raw realism would remain a critical focus in discussions of Farrère's early work.

30   This passage reveals a key tension in French literary attitudes toward sensual themes. Pierre Louÿs was known for his disdain of writers who claimed moral purposes for erotic content — a common practice where authors would justify depicting vice by claiming it served to promote virtue. The reviewer suggests some irony in Farrère's relationship with his 'master' Louÿs: while Farrère claims to follow Louÿs's aesthetic of unashamed sensuality, his novel ultimately punishes its hedonistic characters and ends with a conventional moral lesson. This places Farrère, despite his protestations, squarely in the tradition of moralistic literature that

This is not to say that the young writer's work is without merit. It has precisely the kind of qualities and the kind of flaws in which the Goncourts delighted, which can be summed up in one word: literature — yes, literature that distorts reality, that interests itself only in the novel, that aims for effect, but which charms nevertheless and which must be encouraged — even with prizes and crowns.

I have just read *The Civilized*, and I still find myself wondering what the author means by a "civilized person." A libertine? The thing is as banal as the word is outdated. A skeptic? Skeptics, I mean true ones, are extremely rare, and the type is already old. Let us then take the definitions that M. Claude Farrère offers here and there. Here, according to him, is what Jacques de Fierce should confess to Sélysette:

"There is nothing in my heart or mind that you could love or comprehend. My innards, were you to glimpse them, would horrify you. I am a jaded man, a skeptic, an infidel. I believe in neither good nor evil, neither God nor the Devil. I have been all over, and have thus returned from all things. Swayed by the grace of my uniform, you have heaped on me a full lot of archaic virtues that are not my own and that I despise. The only cult I keep, the bitter cult of impudent truth, would strike you with horror as a blasphemy."

When I said there was much literature at the bottom of all this! Here's another portrait of a civilized man:

"Mévil was one of the Civilized: that is, a hothouse plant, modified, deformed, atrophied by fussy cultivation, and now become monstrous, with dwarf leaves, overly big flowers, and petals instead of stamens — with speculation instead of instinct, and a brain at once admirable and deformed. This brain had at first ensconced itself in a comfortable egotism, leaving the senses at liberty, and taking no part in their games; but the gangrene of the nerves had one day reached it a last. Come to the end of his truncated youth, to the end of his dulled sensations, Mévil had wholly and in one go broken down and gone soft."

Is this type of elegant and despicable egotistical pleasure-seeker new? No, certainly not, and contemporary novels offer far too many of them. But what hadn't been done until now was to place him in the environment where he can best be studied: the colonial milieu. Outside France, there exists a certain freedom, an absence of prejudices that affects even the least corrupted

---

Louÿs despised. The archival materials show that Louÿs acted as Farrère's literary patron and helped secure him the Goncourt Prize, making this divergence particularly noteworthy.

French people. And thus, the true interest of the novel perhaps lies not in the character of the ensign but in the portrayal of Saigon itself.

Here again, I believe the author has yielded to the very literary desire to shock us, to scandalize us, only to edify us later when virtue is rewarded and vice punished. — I know from experience, as everyone knows today, that colonial "society" differs from Parisian society through a sort of unconscious cynicism. But I doubt that Saigon, with its constantly renewing population, is the den of dinner-jacketed pirates that the author shows us. And even if it were, what advantage does the writer find in dwelling on such exaggerated and repugnant details? If at least this became for him the occasion for one of those marvelous pages he admires in *Aphrodite*! But no! He only reveals himself as a writer toward the end of the volume, in the relatively chaste portion: he understands nothing about obscenity, which in his hands is neither refined nor grandly ignoble, but banal and clumsy. Read rather this description of a pleasure house in the seedy quarters of Saigon:

"Opening to the left and right were doghouses, with slatted doors to shut them off. These were in fact bedrooms for lovemaking — because one made love in this sty. One would make love with drunken women who sprawled on the ground and whom one could not at first make out, by the smoky light of the single oil lamp, always on the verge of being snuffed, but whom one would soon verify were indeed women, some young and some old, the latter more hideous, though not by much, and more experienced…"

I leave aside the details that follow, and I sincerely ask: are these the incisive phrases that Edmond de Goncourt loved, or the picturesque ones like Daudet's, or refined like those of M. Pierre Louÿs, or even ample and rich like sometimes those of Zola? [31]

Truly, the first hundred pages of this novel, deliberately outrageous, wallowing in the cynicism so poorly handled a bit further on, too often devoid of genuine writing, have nothing very captivating about them. I would add

---

31   The reviewer skillfully notes four different literary approaches to erotic content to highlight Farrère's shortcomings. Edmond de Goncourt (1822-1896) was known for his precise, cutting observations of social decadence, captured in sharp, clinical prose. Alphonse Daudet (1840-1897) brought a more picturesque, almost impressionistic style to similar subjects. Pierre Louÿs (1870-1925) crafted highly aestheticized eroticism draped in classical references and refined imagery. Émile Zola (1840-1902), while direct in his treatment of sexuality, elevated such scenes through rich, naturalistic detail and broader social commentary. By suggesting Farrère achieves none of these established approaches — neither Goncourt's precision, Daudet's pictorial quality, Louÿs's refinement, nor Zola's expansive naturalism — the reviewer effectively dismisses Farrère's attempt at writing erotic content as amateurish. This critique is particularly pointed given that the Goncourt Prize was named for Edmond de Goncourt, implying that the winner failed to live up to the award's namesake.

that the dialogue is rather painful, rather flat, that it sometimes turns into lecture (successive lectures on colonization, on travel, on the education of girls), and that the author seems to admire his heroes whom he will later condemn; for they are, after all, the only honest people in Saigon!

And yet, *The Civilized* has its merits.

First, the author, while exaggerating, gives a personal impression of things he has observed; at a time when light is being shed on certain crimes in the Congo and elsewhere, we well know that there is a special mentality in the colonies, and we catch glimpses of this mentality in the wheeler-dealer Malais, in the feared journalist Rochet, in Lieutenant-Governor Abel, vaguely honest but needy, in the cynical Torral, flaunting his vices out of disgust for hypocrisy and contempt for his contemporaries. We discover life over there in its superficial aspect rather than in its real depths; but even that is interesting. And if M. Claude Farrère is more of a tourist than a colonial, he is a very well-informed tourist, who doesn't always stop at the easy effects of local color. [32]

He knows the country and describes it, but less in its outward appearance than in its inner essence, to use his favorite expression; I mean to say that he hardly evokes landscapes in the manner of M. Pierre Loti, but rather constantly recovers and communicates to us the sensations he experienced, allowing us to perceive without too much difficulty the environment in which the novel's action unfolds. We do not see Indo-China; but we are immersed in it, and that is no small praise for a writer.

Has he been involved, in his capacity as a naval officer, in the suppression of native revolts? One would think so, given how clearly and precisely he describes colonial warfare. Here, there seems to be none of the "literary" exaggeration of the beginning, but truth, the all-powerful truth that

---

32   The "crimes in the Congo" refer to one of the most notorious colonial scandals of the era. King Leopold II of Belgium's personal rule of the Congo Free State (1885–1908) was marked by mutilations, murder, and forced labor. These atrocities were exposed by journalists and activists, most notably Edmund Morel and Roger Casement, whose 1904 report was horrific.

The phrase "and elsewhere" likely refers to similar colonial abuses in French Indochina and other territories. The "special mentality" was the moral flexibility that European colonials often developed, with its racial theories and claims of a "civilizing mission," to justify exploitation and cruelty.

The reviewer suggests that Farrère's characters — the corrupt businessman Malais, the compromised journalist Rochet, the morally ambiguous Lieutenant-Governor Abel, and the cynical Torral — accurately reflect this colonial psychology of moral degradation, even if the portrayal remains somewhat superficial. This aspect of the novel proved particularly controversial, with some critics praising its unflinching portrayal of colonial corruption while others, like Ernest Rabut, condemned it as defamation of French Indochina.

alone holds the reader, that alone makes the author a writer. In the manner of Flaubert,[33] of the naturalists, of the impressionists, he seeks and finds the characteristic detail, not the one that surprises, but the one we expect, because it follows the logic of the narrative, the logic of things.

Would you like an example of this excellent technique? Here is night on the river, where Jacques de Fierce's gunboat pursues the fight against rebels hidden along the banks:

"Night would fall, however, and in the black thickets tardy rifle-fire would break out; the bullets would whistle all the way to the river, and set the metal ringing on the gunboats; the cannons would enter the fray; there would at last be a real battle, lasting till dawn. But at dawn the shots would suddenly cease, because things would become clear: there would be no enemy. Gone astray or betrayed, the French would have fired on themselves, massacred themselves by mistake. There would be ten or twenty dead men on the ground. The living would bury them — and move on to other errors. They would kill and die without glory, weary and bored."

In good faith, wouldn't the book have benefited from maintaining this tone, this simplicity that is far more skillful than artifice and exaggeration, throughout? Emotion here arises from documentation, and along with emotion comes style.

One could generalize and say that the second part of the work is superior in all respects to the first, because it is more true, because the author gradually abandons exceptional states of mind that seem false in favor of feelings more human, more accessible, more real. I am not saying that his psychology is always very tight, that the characters don't sometimes have rather obvious premonitions, but, carried away by his subject, the author tries to account for everything he imagines and replaces literary fantasy with reasonable simplicity, such as he no doubt once admired in the seventeenth-century writers for whom he professes his preference.

೫✦೮

---

33 This reference points to Gustave Flaubert's (1821–80) revolutionary approach to realist description. Unlike the romantics, who sought exotic or shocking details, Flaubert sought the "*mot juste*" (the right word), the one that would seem inevitable rather than surprising. His method involved careful observation and selection of details that revealed essential truths about characters and situations. When the reviewer links this to "the naturalists" and "the impressionists," he suggests that Farrère's best writing, particularly in his war scenes, achieves a similar effect — selecting details that feel authentic rather than sensational. This marks a significant shift from the novel's early sections, where Farrère strains for exotic effect. The approach exemplifies what Flaubert called "objective writing," where the author disappears behind precise, carefully chosen details that speak for themselves.

Source: *Gil Blas* (1905 November 29)

Director: A. Dumont

Reviewer: Louis Vauxcelles

Title: *Les Civilisés*

I would not wish — at a time when Jules Bois, in this very journal, is precluding studies of substantial literary criticism — to trespass without competence upon my neighbor's hunting grounds.[34]

I am making an exception, with apologies, in venturing to speak of letters. But *The Civilized* deserves a second look.

I am aware that this book is bold to the point of being startling, and I am inclined to think that the author would have benefited by erasing half a dozen unnecessary passages. But, having stated this reservation, I shall not dwell on it further.

It appears that the word "civilized," whose meaning is quite precise on the banks of the Seine, possesses a mysterious, esoteric, disturbing meaning in the colonies. In Indo-China, particularly, this word takes on an abominable intensity. The "civilized" are those people who, spurned by Europe, go to Saigon, for example, to practice the Epicurean method that can be summed up in two words: maximum pleasure, minimum effort.[35]

Saigon is a city of luxury, voluptuousness, indulgence, and shamelessness. It is the Far Eastern Abbey of Thélème.[36] An Asian perfume, mingling the

---

34 Jules Bois (1868–1943) was a complex figure in French literary circles — a novelist, playwright, essayist, and art critic who wrote for *Gil Blas*, among other publications. In the 1890s, he was deeply involved in Paris's occult scene, even engaging in a celebrated dispute over supposed magical assassination that nearly led to a duel with occultist Stanislas de Guaita. His 1895 book *Le Satanisme et la magie* became a bestseller, demonstrating the period's fascination with esoteric themes. Yet by 1905, when Vauxcelles references him, Bois had established himself as one of *Gil Blas*'s leading literary critics, known for combining cultural criticism with both esoteric interests and feminist causes. Vauxcelles's deferential opening reference to Bois's "substantial literary criticism" shows professional courtesy while positioning his own review as an exception to his usual art criticism — a domain where he would soon become famous for naming both the Fauve and the Cubist movements.

35 Vauxcelles's reference to the Epicurean method deliberately misrepresents the philosophical school founded by Epicurus (341–270 BCE). While Epicureanism did advocate the pursuit of pleasure, it defined this as the absence of pain and anxiety through moderation, self-control, and the cultivation of friendship — not hedonistic excess. By reducing it to "maximum pleasure, minimum effort," Vauxcelles creates an ironic contrast between classical philosophy and colonial decadence. This distortion of Epicureanism was common in French literature of the period, where *epicurean* had become shorthand for sensual indulgence rather than the measured approach to life that Epicurus actually taught. The term serves here to emphasize how the "civilized" corrupt even classical wisdom in their pursuit of pleasure.

36 The Abbey of Thélème is a fictinal anti-monastery in François Rabelais's satirical fantasy in *Gargantua* (1534). Its sole rule is "Do what thou wilt." Vauxcelles's allusion links colonial license to both classical and esoteric traditions, and suggests that in Saigon conventional morality is inverted — as the original Abbey of Thélème inverts monastic rules. However,

composite aromas of magnolias, wild beasts, pepper, rotting incense, and women, that intoxicates the senses and anesthetizes the conscience. Along the "Inspection" — the Acacia trees of Saigon — Victorias drawn by Annamite horses, as big as donkeys but lively as squirrels, amble about, carrying couples who all indulge in a thousand sorts of liberties that the night hardly veils.

What do you expect to become of a European transplanted into this colonial dunghill?

Such is the question posed by M. Claude Farrère in his novel, published just yesterday. This novel, I want to say straight away, is one of the most magnificently daring books that contemporary literature has produced. Since Louis Bertrand, who was revealed to us some four or five years ago, I do not believe one could find a more powerful colorist or more acerbic thinker. Such a book elevates us a thousand feet above all the insipid volumes of worldly adultery, whether vapid or spiced, signed by our usual suppliers. The entire book is captivating, at times irritating, but of the first order; and the final fifty pages are a masterpiece.

In an age when the least qualified present themselves to the French Academy, the appearance of such a rare book as *The Civilized* warrants our attention. Moreover, a study of the colonial mentality proves to be of the most burning relevance; MM. Gentil, Rouanet, Gaud, Liégeois, Challaye, and Tocqué will not contradict me,[37] nor will the shadow of the late Brazza, that generous and candid Don Quixote of the Congo.[38]

---

while Rabelais's abbey was populated by educated nobles pursuing enlightened pleasure, Vauxcelles implies that Saigon's "Thélèmites" are merely debauched colonials pursuing base gratification.

This reference would have been particularly resonant for readers familiar with *fin de siècle* occult circles, where Rabelais's phrase had gained new currency. Indeed, the concept would later inspire Aleister Crowley to establish his own Abbey of Thelema in Sicily (1920) as a temple and spiritual center. While this occurred after Vauxcelles's review, it demonstrates how the idea of Thélème as a place of unrestricted behavior continued to capture imaginations, whether in satirical criticism of colonial excess or in actual attempts to create spaces outside conventional morality.

37 Vauxcelles references a group of figures then dominating French colonial discourse, particularly with regard to African territories. Émile Gentil (1866–1914), explorer and colonial administrator, established French control in Chad and Congo. Gustave Rouanet (1855–1927), a Socialist deputy, gained prominence for his vocal criticism of colonial abuses. The mention of Fernand Gaud carries particular weight as he had just been tried and convicted in 1905 for atrocious crimes against indigenous people in Congo, including having a man blown up with dynamite for entertainment. Félicien Challaye (1875–1967), a journalist and philosopher, had recently published damning reports about conditions in French Congo. Georges Liégeois and Tocqué were colonial administrators implicated in the Congo scandals. By invoking both critics and perpetrators of colonial abuse, Vauxcelles suggests how examination of "colonial mentality" had become an urgent matter in French society.

38 Pierre Savorgnan de Brazza (1852–1905), whom Vauxcelles calls "that generous and

When ordinary "colonials" disembark in Saigon, they are more often than not blemished men, suspect, often even tainted and corrupt; the dual influence of the abnormal environment and the depressing climate completes and finishes them. Quickly, they disregard all principles. Here I let my author speak; one of his heroes expounds the thesis thus:

"It is perhaps best that over these colonial lands, freshly plowed and tilled beneath the stomping of the many races that mix here, some human manure be spread, so that from the purulent rot of old ideas and old morals the lands might yield future civilizations."

Among this contemptible colonial rabble live a few superior individuals. For these, the environment and climate have proven beneficial, and they have become like forerunners of tomorrow's civilizations. They live on the margins of our conventional life; they have abjured all its fanaticisms and all its religions; and if they agree to observe our penal code, I believe it is merely in a spirit of conciliation. The emergence of such men was possible only in this Indochina that is at once very old and very new; it required the ambiance of Aryan, Chinese, and Malay philosophies slowly worn down against one another; it required the corruption of a society in which European morality has gone bankrupt; it required the burning humidity of Saigon, where everything melts and dissolves in the sun — energies, beliefs, and the sense of good and evil! These men, ahead of our time, are the civilized ones. We are the barbarians.[39]

---

candid Don Quixote of the Congo," had died just two months before this review appeared, lending poignancy to the reference to his "shadow." Born in Italy but naturalized French, Brazza founded French Congo and established Brazzaville through largely peaceful means, in contrast with the brutal methods used in Belgian King Leopold II's neighboring territory. His death in September 1905 followed his return from French Congo, where he had led an investigation into colonial abuses and documented numerous atrocities. His final report was so damaging to colonial interests that it was suppressed until 2014. Vauxcelles's characterization of him as Don Quixote suggests both admiration for his idealistic approach to colonization and recognition of how his humane methods were defeated by brutal reality.

39   This pivotal paragraph captures several of Farrère's most provocative themes. Vauxcelles emphasizes how the novel inverts traditional colonial discourse: the truly "civilized" are those who have been transformed by Indochina's philosophical crucible, where different traditions collide and erode each other. The "Aryan" philosophies refer both to ancient Indian influences in Southeast Asia (particularly Buddhism) and to European thought, which claimed "Aryan" heritage. Chinese philosophical traditions — especially Confucianism and Taoism — had shaped Vietnamese culture through centuries of interaction, while the Malay reference encompasses broader Southeast Asian spiritual and cultural practices.

By describing these philosophies as "slowly worn down against one another," Vauxcelles highlights Farrère's vision of colonial Indochina as a place where all certainties dissolve. His mention of "bankrupt" European morality is particularly telling — suggesting that Western ethical systems, rather than elevating colonial spaces, become corrupted by contact with them. The metaphor of Saigon's "burning humidity" dissolving everything

Three distinguished civilized ones: Doctor Raymond Mévil, the engineer Torral, and the naval officer Jacques de Fierce.

Raymond Mévil is a young and seductive physician, with velvety eyes and an ebony beard, whom the beautiful Saigonese ladies adore; he drugs them with cocaine, caresses them, unhinges them. Mévil devotes part of his afternoons and nights to various persons, including a venal socialite, a singer, an Annamite *congai*[40] in his pay, and a Japanese adolescent.

Torral, an engineer infused with logic and exactitude, of a wounding intellectual superiority, balances his pleasures according to Epicurean arithmetic; he prides himself on extracting from life all the happiness contained therein; he smokes opium pipes, delights in analytics, despises women, and...

The Count de Fierce, an orphan, very wealthy, who, after a stormy adolescence, roams the world — he is a naval ensign — weary of everything, having tasted everything, disgusted with everything.

"Fierce roams the world, ferrying from one climate to the next his disdain for all laws, his irony for all religions, his hatred for all lies, and his hunger and thirst for all the novel and miraculous nourishment that life promises and never delivers."

In Saigon, these three friends lead a kind of existence where cocktails, pure spirits, dry champagne and the fumes of opium, hashish, ether, morphine and poker, pubescent Chinese girls and a thousand other devilishly incorrect things blend together harmoniously. One could not be more civilized.

The social milieu in which they move is worthy of them: here is Monsieur Malais, an "enormous brute, square all over," with "wolf's teeth and the fearsome hands," a "farmer of rice, tea, and opium," with "forty million in the coin of the realm, all of it ill gotten"; the cunning and devious Ariette, enriched by his wife's caprices; the publicist Claude Rochet, a wreck

---

— "energies, beliefs, and the sense of good and evil" — reinforces this idea of colonial space as a moral solvent. The paragraph's conclusion ironically labels metropolitan French as "barbarians," inverting the usual colonial hierarchy. These "civilized" men, by rejecting European "fanaticisms" while maintaining only a pragmatic relationship with its laws, represent for Vauxcelles both the promise and the threat of Farrère's colonial vision.

40   *Congaï* (from Vietnamese *con gái*, meaning "young woman" or "daughter") was a French colonial term for local women who had relationships with European men, often in concubinage arrangements. The word's casual use in reviews like this reflects how such relationships were openly acknowledged in colonial society, though the term itself carries condescending and racist overtones. In *The Civilized*, the reference to a "*congaï* annamite" (Annamite being the period term for Vietnamese) in a list of Doctor Mévil's sexual conquests emphasizes both the character's exploitation of colonial power dynamics and the novel's frank treatment of interracial relationships.

of blackmail, ataxia, and senility. There are a few good people nevertheless, notably the Duke d'Orvilliers, rear admiral commanding a division of the China Squadron, who paternally loves his aide-de-camp Jacques de Fierce, believing him spotless and irreproachable; d'Orvilliers is a kind of outdated hero, somewhat caricatural, somewhat old guard, very noble and very pious; the Sylva family, a charming blind lady and her daughter Sélysette, a lily; and others besides.

The question posed is this: which will prevail, modern corrupting civilization or the sentiments of yesteryear — love, patriotism? It is in Fierce's soul that this conflict erupts.[41] Fierce, one fine day, falls in love with Sélysette Sylva, and the virginal purity of this child regenerates him and will save him from himself.

She loves him. Alas! Scarcely is Fierce engaged to her when orders come for the cruiser *Bayard* to sail for Hong Kong. And temptations assail both soul and body of the young convalescent; far from Sélysette, Fierce, deprived of his dear talisman, is stalked by debauchery. He manages to save himself from it in Hong Kong, that prodigious howling, teeming city; but unwholesome reminiscences, resembling nostalgia, traverse his brain and flesh. A party aboard the British battleship *King-Edward* gathers all the cosmopolitans of Hong Kong, Shanghai, Nagasaki, Hanoi, and Saigon; they dance, they sup, they flirt. Fierce nearly succumbs to the teasing of an Australian demi-virgin; he pulls himself back at the supreme moment.

But Sélysette is not there to protect her fiancé; a relapse is imminent. A few weeks later, Fierce spends a feverish night yielding to murderous poker. Fate separates the ensign from his beloved. Here he is promoted to commander of the *Avalanche*, a small gunboat that must fight a few bands of rebellious native Annamites; a treacherous and cowardly war of fierce ambushes and raids in the tropical forest. One night, deep in the jungle, Fierce, maddened by the bloodthirsty contagion, rushes, sword drawn, into a hut. A terrified Asian girl, half-naked, offers herself as ransom for her life. He stumbles, rushes in, and falls upon his prey.

Finally, he returns to Saigon, finds his friends, Torral and Mévil, who win him back: he participates in a frightful nocturnal orgy; in the morning, Sélysette encounters him, sobered but flanked by two girls. Nothing remains for him but to die.

---

41 If only M. Vauxcelles had ended his brilliant review with this question. But unfortunately, he now proceeds to reveal, and spoil, the entire book for potential readers in the next 650 words.

Fortunately, a quick and clean exit presents itself. War has just been declared on England. Thus, he can get himself killed without scandal. "Civilization" has not abolished all human sentiment in his sick soul. Raymond Mévil, who for his part has spent two months obsessively pursuing two women — one married, one marriageable — who want nothing to do with him, sinks into madness and ataxic suicide. Torral, a reserve officer, deserts his battery! Fierce, for his part, will proudly die on the quarterdeck of his torpedo boat.

M. Claude Farrère has dedicated the final two tragic chapters of his novel to the dead of Tsu-Shima.[42] The battle of torpedo boat 412 against the British battleships. Ah! I swear to you that one cannot read this naval combat narrative without shuddering; this is neither Jules Verne nor Driant.[43] These pages rank among the finest I have ever read. Fierce is killed; but the torpedo has struck the battleship amidships at its boiler rooms, below the armor, and the sea enters into the heart of the monster about to sink; the twenty-six men in the boiler room kill each other, blinded by steam and boiling water; they die like dogs, stones around their necks; this scene is unspeakable in its horror.

* * *

I do not know if all this is quite logical, and if only "barbarians" can be brave in war. This need to deal death to "the enemy" is perhaps the summit of civilization, if one accepts that word in the sense given to it in *The Civilized*. And what the author calls an "awakening" is perhaps only a result.

Nothing proves that the love of alcohol and women — long live wine, love and tobacco! — cannot marvelously reconcile itself with martial frenzy. Fierce, who dies for his country, is very gallant, agreed. I would prefer that he had lived a useful life for his country. You will tell me he was not given the choice. Nevertheless, I am inclined to think that one need not have come back from all vices to be patriotic: the "zephyrs" and the "Bat' d'Af'" are excellent

---

42   The Battle of Tsushima (May 27–28, 1905) was a decisive naval engagement of the Russo-Japanese War, where the Japanese fleet destroyed the Russian Baltic Fleet in the Strait of Tsushima. This stunning victory established Japan as a major naval power and marked the first defeat of a European power by an Asian nation in modern times. The battle occurred just months before this review, and would later serve as the centerpiece for Farrère's 1909 novel *La Bataille*, soon to be released in English in a deluxe illustrated edition.

43   Vauxcelles distinguishes Farrère's naval combat scenes from the popular maritime adventure fiction of Jules Verne (1828–1905) and Émile Driant (1855–1916). Verne was famous for scientific romances like *Twenty Thousand Leagues Under the Sea*, while Driant (writing as Capitaine Danrit) specialized in military fiction. The comparison suggests Farrère's battle scenes achieve a more serious literary, and graphic, realism.

soldiers and Hamilcar's mercenaries, the condottieri of the Renaissance, knew how to die.[44]

But let us not quibble with M. Claude Farrère about the doctrine underpinning his novel. This book, which is not by a professional — I believe M. Farrère is a naval officer — is written in a style alert, precise, eloquently and painfully simple: without padding or phraseology. Amateurs of this caliber are worth twenty times the professional men of letters. Indeed Saint-Evremond, and La Rochefoucauld, and Vauvenargues, and Benjamin Constant — and also Pierre Loti — were amateurs.[45]

Louis Vauxcelles (born Louis Meyer, 1870–1943) was one of France's most influential art critics, remembered for inadvertently naming two major artistic movements: Fauvism (1905) and Cubism (1908). Though primarily an art critic for *Gil Blas*, he occasionally reviewed literature, as shown in this piece. His critical style combined sharp cultural observation with both wit and irony, and he had a particular talent for recognizing revolutionary approaches in art and literature, even when he maintained critical distance from them.

This review of *Les Civilisés* appeared in the same year he coined the term *Fauvism*, when he was at the height of his influence. His praise for the novel as "one of the most magnificently bold books that contemporary literature has produced" demonstrates his eye for innovative work, while his characterization of it as "fascinating, sometimes irritating, but first-rate" exemplifies his balanced critical approach.

ঙ✦ঞ

Source: *Patria : revue illustrée de l'officier et de sa famille* (1905 August 1)
Reviewer: Charles Ponsonailhe
Title: Arts & Livres, *Les Civilisés* (p. 23)

---

44 The reviewer references various types of soldiers to argue that vice and valor can coexist: "*zéphyrs*" were members of disciplinary infantry units in Africa, while "Bat' d'Af'" (Bataillons d'Afrique) were military units composed of convicts and disciplinary cases. Hamilcar's mercenaries fought for Carthage in the third century BC, while the condottieri were Renaissance Italian mercenary leaders. These examples support his critique of Farrère's implication that only moral reformation enables heroic action.

45 Vauxcelles closes by placing Farrère in a tradition of "amateur" writers who achieve literary distinction while pursuing other careers. Charles de Saint-Evremond (1614–1703), François de La Rochefoucauld (1613–80), and Luc de Clapiers, marquis de Vauvenargues (1715–47) were aristocratic moralists; Benjamin Constant (1767–1830) was a political theorist and novelist. Pierre Loti (1850–1923), born Julien Viaud, was like Farrère a naval officer whose exotic novels drew from his travels. Their success as "amateurs" validates Farrère's literary achievement despite his naval career.

Below, the reader will find a review of an important collection of superb books to serve as New Years' gifts.[46] For lack of space, I must devote these final lines to a single work, but a very sensational one, *Les Civilisés* by Mr. Claude Farrère, the pseudonym of an officer, Mr. Charles Bargone, twenty-nine years old, naval ensign aboard the *Saint-Louis* in Toulon. Through him, the Navy has achieved a brilliant literary success, as Mr. Farrère's volume was chosen by the Académie des Goncourt for its annual prize of five thousand francs.

In some respects, Mr. Farrère's work is worthy of the highest praise. It is written with mastery by an artist, a colorful raconteur, a poet, a sensitive soul. *The Civilized*, who are essentially the dregs of modern civilization — like Romans in their decadent decline — who seek out distant colonies to indulge appetites that would be forbidden by the civil and criminal laws back home. They are portrayed with vigor and remarkable artistic flair though, unfortunately, their spectacle is far from being edifying or flattering to the White Race.

In his work, one reads a vibrant combat scene, the duel between a French torpedo boat and an English vessel, the *King-Edward*. It is splendid in its colorful and poetic vision. But why does the author spoil it with the horrific spectacle of the flagship's boiler room, where sailors, invaded by water and condemned to inevitable death, turn into human brutes that expire while stabbing each other?

It is "a monstrous fistfight: all these human beasts, returned as if by magic wand to ancient ferocity, bludgeon and tear at each other with their teeth, etc., etc."

Is Mr. Farrère quite certain that in the armies and navies of European nations, the fear of death produces such sudden demoralization in soldiers or sailors? History is full of indisputable proven facts that contradict this school of thought, the pessimistic philosophy of Tolstoy. I recommend Mr. Farrère visit the Picpus Ossuary[47] and meditate on the forty magistrates of Parliament

---

46 Ponsonailhe writes *"livres d'Étrennes,"* the term for special editions traditionally published as New Year's gifts (étrennes). These typically appear in November and December, with luxurious features like gilt edges and decorative bindings. However, this review was published in August 1905, well before the gift-book season, and *The Civilized* was issued as a standard edition by Ollendorff. Its only distinction was winning the Prix Goncourt. The reviewer's characterization suggests either confusion about the book's format or an attempt to classify it among more prestigious holiday publications, though it was neither marketed nor produced as such.

47 Created at the height of the French Revolution, Picpus Cemetery is the only private necropolis in Paris still in operation. It consists of an enclosed sanctuary closed to the public

who walked to the guillotine according to the court's order of precedence, at ceremonial pace, calm and indifferent.

It is as false to say that the sight of death turns man into a brute as it is to maintain that poverty makes a man a scoundrel. There are, thank God, still thousands of heroes and irreducible honest people in our civilization.

Charles Ponsonailhe (1855–1915) was a French art critic, journalist, and nationalist intellectual whose review of *Les Civilisés* reflects his conservative cultural and political views. After briefly practicing law in Paris, he devoted himself to art criticism, writing for numerous prestigious publications, such as *L'Artiste* and *La Grande Revue*. He founded the military journal *Patria* (where this review appeared) around 1904, aiming it at officers and their families. Hence his special attention to Farrère's naval background and his criticism of the novel's depiction of military behavior.

Ponsonailhe's royalist politics and Catholic faith influenced his literary judgments. His book *L'Année française : un héros par jour* (1893) and his membership in the nationalist Ligue de la Patrie Française suggest why he was particularly troubled by Farrère's portrayal of "civilized" Europeans behaving badly in the colonies. His objection to the boilerroom scene, with its suggestion that fear reduces soldiers to barbarism, contradicted his belief in French heroic virtue, exemplified by his counter-example of the dignified aristocrats facing the guillotine.

⋙✦⋘

Source: *La Petite Gironde : journal républicain quotidien* (1906 January 6)
Reviewer: Gabriel Trarieux
Title: *Les Civilisés*: A volume from Ollendorff'

The awarding of the Prix Goncourt does not go unnoticed. Public opinion concerns itself with it. It's a singular windfall for a young writer, unknown yesterday, to place this banner on his book. And public opinion is not wrong. Clearly, to be preferred by writers like the Rosnys, the Marguerittes,[48]

---

and a small adjoining cemetery. The enclosure contains two mass graves, where the bodies of 1,306 people guillotined at Place de la Nation from June 14 to July 27, 1794, were piled. The cemetery is reserved for members of the victims' families, who purchased the property by subscription in June 1802.

48   The reviewer's use of plurals reflects the period's complex literary partnerships. "The Rosnys" refers to two brothers who shared a seat in the Académie Goncourt: J.-H. Rosny aîné (Joseph Henri Honoré Boex, 1856–1940) and Rosny jeune (Séraphin Justin François Boex, 1859–1948). The brothers had previously collaborated on novels before dividing their literary careers. "The Marguerittes" refers to brothers Paul Margueritte (1860–1918) and Victor

Mirbeau, Descaves, Hennique, Geffroy, Huysmans, Léon Daudet, and Élémir Bourges is rather flattering, all the same. These people are alive. They produce, they are loved, they are admired, they are hated. Yes, their vote is precious, much more so than that of, for example, the rare marshals of letters and solemn unknowns who compose the other Academy. We must hope, therefore, that it does not go astray, that it serves us, you and me, the ignorant who do not read all books. Already, it has drawn out of obscurity two unequal but strong works, altogether rather remarkable: *Force ennemie*, by John-Antoine Nau; *La Maternelle*, by Léon Frapié. This time, it has designated *Les Civilisés*, by Claude Farrère. What are these *Civilized* people worth?

The story is simple and banal. A naval officer sails in the Far East. He makes port in Saigon, city of delights, orgies, and vile drunkenness. He exhausts this type of sport with conscience and method, in the company of two comrades, an engineer and a doctor, for whom this is ordinary pastime. One fine day, he meets a young woman, Mlle Sélysette Sylva (whose father, a colonel, in the style of Maeterlinck,[49] evidently, before getting himself killed in Africa).

This young woman pleases him. She has gray-blue eyes and a French soul. She is ingenuous and believing. The young exotic Rolla[50] feels stirrings of candor within himself. He was Catholic, formerly; he is the son of an ancient and noble race — the Marquis de Fierce, if you please. He asks for the young woman's hand in marriage. She accepts, sees in him a hero. Unfortunately, engaged just yesterday, he must depart for Hong Kong. Separation. Love letters. Impure hauntings. Sin. When he returns to Saigon, young de Fierce is seized again by primal degradation. He brazenly displays himself with girls. Drunk, embraced by two actresses, he encounters, one afternoon, Mlle Sylva and her mother. It's over. His beautiful dream is finished. He has nothing

---

Margueritte (1866–1942), though only Paul held a seat in the Académie. This plural usage reflects how these literary brothers were often viewed as creative units, even when only one served officially.

49   This sardonic reference to Maurice Maeterlinck (1862–1949) warrants unpacking. The name Sélysette appears in Maeterlinck's play *Aglavaine et Sélysette* (1896), a symbolist work featuring an innocent young woman who ultimately commits suicide. The reviewer suggests Farrère's choice of name is deliberately literary and precious, implying artificiality in the character's construction. The parenthetical mention of the father's death in Africa adds to the suggestion of melodramatic convention.

50   Alfred de Musset's poem "Rolla" (1833) tells the story of a young nobleman who methodically spends his inheritance on debauchery before committing suicide. Like Fierce, Rolla experiences a moment of possible redemption through pure love, but cannot overcome his moral degradation. The reviewer uses this parallel to suggest Farrère's novel merely recycles romantic clichés about corruption and redemption rather than offering fresh insights.

left but to get himself killed, in the least unseemly way possible. He boards a torpedo boat, he expires while dealing death, having had the supreme joy of seeing an English battleship, the *King-Edwards* [*sic*], sink before him.[51] Meanwhile Mlle Sylva, before her Madonna, is in prayer.

You see, the story is commonplace. Stripped of its exoticism, it's a familiar adventure. The author, truth be told, doesn't elevate it with any new psychology. Nothing is more old-fashioned, more conventional, or more artificial than his hero. A young Rolla, as I said. Yes, that's it, more or less. It's even exactly that, minus the eloquence and lyricism. The theory, for it is a theory, which inspires the book's title, is of pure romantic essence.

The Civilized, who are they? They are those whom a century without faith has refined and corrupted; those who no longer want to have children, because the human task is done; those whose motto is: enjoy, with the minimum of effort. It's Fierce, the desperate one; it's Raymond Mévil, the ladies' man (who ends up committing suicide); it's Torral, the hideous homosexual.[52] What has ruined them? Reason, excess, an implacable logic. They carouse because they are atheists. Is the author mocking us?

No. He says this without laughing. And he seems to see refuge only in some kind of deranged sensualist mysticism. Isn't this thoroughly the thesis of Rolla: "Sleep you content, Voltaire, with your hideous smile?…"

Now there's a resurrection, isn't it? Rather unexpected. It's true that in his preface M. Claude Farrère assures us that he is exactly the opposite of his hero. He detests sentiment, the agape, the lyrical. He loves "our pure French classics." His two literary deities are Sophocles and Pierre Louÿs. He puts them on the same pedestal. (Sophocles looks a bit uncomfortable.) How does he manage to reconcile these contradictory tendencies? In truth, I have no idea. Let him sort it out!

What I know well is that this reading leaves me infinitely perplexed. What? That's the Prix Goncourt? *Why*, my God? Abyss! Abyss![53] Neither novelty

---

51   The reviewer's error regarding *HMS King Edward VII* (launched 1903) — which he incorrectly calls *King-Edwards* — somewhat undermines his critique. The presence of this modern British pre-dreadnought battleship in the novel actually demonstrates Farrère's attention to contemporary naval details, drawing on his experience as a naval officer. The ship's inclusion adds historical authenticity to the novel's colonial setting rather than mere exoticism.

52   The original French word, *inverti*, is often associated with far more derogatory terms.

53   This is the literal translation, but here the expression means that awarding this prize has brought the contest to a damaging new low.

in the narrative, nor singularity in the thesis, nor original psychology, nor … nor anything at all. So, what is it? Certainly, I can see, I see well that Claude Farrère knows how to write. He has grace and force, a certain pure sobriety. He shows rather well what he has seen: Saigon, the landscapes, the women. The episode of the battleship doesn't lack a certain grandeur. But these qualities are common. More than one rejected competitor possessed them, and some others. There were: Jules Huret, André Chevrillon, Romain Rolland. No, the more I rack my brain, the less I understand what, in this book, could have seduced Mirbeau, Descaves, Hennique, Rosny, Geffroy, Margueritte, to speak only of those. Are they already playing politics? Are they accessible to reasons that reason doesn't know? I flatly refuse to believe it. I will therefore remain in my dejection. For I cannot help, while reading this insistent pornography, remembering, by contrast, the rough and chaste heroes drawn by Rudyard Kipling. And I regret that such a document of our colonial rot is signaled as a masterpiece by ten good French writers.

Gabriel TRARIEUX (1870–1940) presents a fascinating case of how background influences literary criticism. Born into France's intellectual elite as the son of Ludovic Trarieux (senator, Minister of Justice, and founder of the League of Human Rights), Trarieux's critique of *Les Civilisés* reflects both his sophisticated literary education and his idealistic social views.

Educated at the prestigious Lycée Condorcet and established as a poet and playwright by age 20, Trarieux had strong opinions about what constituted serious literature. His own work favored elevated themes — notably his trilogy *Les Vaincus*, dealing with historical and religious subjects. His experience directing literary reviews (*L'Art et la vie* and *Revue d'art dramatique*) and his deep engagement with symbolist theater (particularly Maeterlinck, whom he references in the review) shaped his aesthetic standards.

His dismissal of Farrère's novel reveals several key biases:

His disdain for what he sees as recycled romantic tropes (the repeated Rolla references)

His skepticism of Farrère's attempt to combine classical influences (Sophocles) with modern decadence (Pierre Louÿs)

His preference for "pure" literature over commercial success

Interestingly, Trarieux would later turn from theater to occultism and astrology, in a spiritual quest that might explain his hostile reaction to what he saw as Farrère's "deranged sensualist mysticism." The review's emphasis on faith and moral decay reflects Trarieux's own preoccupation with spiritual questions, even as he mocks Farrère's treatment of them.

The invocation of Kipling's "rough and chaste heroes" versus Farrère's decadent colonials suggests that, like many French intellectuals of his era, Trarieux preferred an idealized vision of empire to Farrère's dark portrait of colonial reality.

END

Selected French Language Reviews (1905–06)
Oldest to newest by date

Date	Paper	Words	Author
1905/08/01	*Patria*	600	Charles PONSONAILHE
1905/10/27	*Figaro*	340	Ph.-Emmanuel GLASER
1905/11/01	*Salon*	1,500	Paul REUSS
1905/11/15	*Mercure*	850	RACHILDE
1905/11/29	*Gil Blas*	3.3	Louis VAUXCELLES
1905/12/13	*Gazette*	2,200	Henry DE PÈNE
1905/12/18	*Midi*	700	Louis ROUBAUD
1906/01/01	*National*	2,600	Unknown
1906/01/06	*Gironde*	950	Gabriel TRARIEUX.
1906/03/13	*L'Idée*	2,100	Yves NILS

Source: *Patria : revue illustrée de l'officier et de sa famille* (1905 August 1)
Reviewer: Charles Ponsonailhe
Title: Arts & Livres, *Les Civilisés*

Le lecteur trouvera plus loin le compte rendu d'un lot important de superbes livres d'Étrennes. Je dois, faute d'espace, consacrer ces dernières lignes à un seul ouvrage, mais très sensationnel, "Les Civilisés", de M. Charles Bargone, pseudonyme d'un officier, M. Claude Farrère, âgé de vingt-neuf ans, enseigne de vaisseau à bord du Saint-Louis à Toulon. En sa personne, la Marine vient d'obtenir un éclatant succès littéraire, le volume de M. Farrère a été choisi par l'Académie des Goncourt pour son prix annuel de cinq mille francs.

Sous certains angles, l'œuvre de M. Farrère est digne des plus absolus éloges. Elle est écrite de main de maître par un artiste, un coloriste, un poète, un sensitif. Les Civilisés, qui sont en somme le déchet de la civilisation moderne — des Romains de la décadence — allant chercher dans des colonies lointaines la satisfaction d'appétits que contrarierait le Code civil et pénal, sont peints avec vigueur, avec un esprit de touche remarquable. Malheureusement leur spectacle est loin d'être moralisant ou flatteur pour la Race blanche.

On lit dans son ouvrage une vibrante page de combat, le duel d'un torpilleur français contre un vaisseau anglais le King-Edward. Elle est splendide de vision colorée et poétique. Pourquoi l'auteur la gâte-t-il par l'immonde spectacle de la chaufferie du vaisseau amiral, où les matelots envahis par l'eau, condamnés à une inévitable mort, tournent à la brute humaine et expirent en se lardant de coups de couteau?

C'est "un pugilat monstrueux: toutes ces bêtes humaines, rendues comme d'un coup de baguette à la férocité ancienne, s'assomment et se déchirent des dents, etc., etc."

M. Farrère est-il bien sûr que dans les armées et les marines des nations européennes, la peur de la mort produise chez le soldat ou le matelot cette subite démoralisation? L'histoire est pleine de faits avérés indiscutables qui donnent un démenti à cette école, à l'école de philosophie pessimiste de Tolstoï. Je recommande à M. Farrère de visiter l'Ossuaire de Picpus et de méditer sur les quarante magistrats du Parlement qui marchèrent au couperet d'après l'ordre des préséances des cours, au pas de cérémonie, calmes et indifférents.

Il est aussi faux de dire que la vue de la mort fait de l'homme une brute que de soutenir que la pauvreté fait de l'homme une canaille. Il y a, Dieu merci, encore dans notre civilisation des milliers de héros et d'honnêtes gens irréductibles.

ෆ✦ඐ

Source: *Figaro : Non politique* (1905 October 27)
Reviewer: Ph.-Emmanuel GLASER
Title: "Petite Chronique des Lettres"

L'an dernier, je signalais à cette place un livre, "Fumée d'opium", dont l'auteur, M. Claude Farrère, tout à fait inconnu dans le monde des lettres, se présentait au public sous l'égide de Pierre Louÿs, qui avait « découvert » son livre et le présentait en une préface débordante d'enthousiasme inspiré. Le livre tenait d'ailleurs toutes les promesses de la préface, et toutes les menaces du titre : inquiétant, douloureux, maladif, il vous emportait, en des pages souvent admirables, dans un tourbillon échevelé de fantômes et de rêves qui ravissait et empoignait tout en faisant mal.

M. Claude Farrère, qui n'est rien moins qu'un écrivain de métier, ne pouvait s'en tenir là ; quand on a écrit un pareil livre, quand on a à tel point

« reçu du ciel l'influence secrète », on persévère, et entre deux voyages au long cours ou deux expéditions - car je soupçonne fort M. Farrère d'être un marin - on ne résiste pas au désir impérieux de revivre et de faire revivre en descriptions lumineuses, en phrases harmonieuses et sonores les émotions qu'on a ressenties.

Et c'est ainsi que M. Claude Farrère publie cette semaine chez Ollendorff les "Civilisés", un roman qu'il a écrit « pour Pierre Louÿs ». Tout différent de son précédent volume de rêves et de fantômes, celui-ci est un pur roman qui nous fait voir de brûlantes et vivantes réalités. C'est dans cet Extrême-Orient qu'il connaît si bien que M. Claude Farrère nous montre « les civilisés » dans la plénitude et le débordement de leur civilisation en antagonisme avec celle des vieilles races auxquelles nous nous imposons. Et c'est, dans ces paysages de Saïgon qu'il nous décrit avec une rare splendeur d'images et de mots, un extraordinaire tableau de mœurs, un drame d'amour et de destruction, de sensualité, de folie, de meurtre, de civilisation pour tout dire.

♦€

Source: *Salon des poètes méridionaux, Arts et lettres : revue mensuelle méridionale* (1905 November 1)
Editorial committee: Robert Hugues, Charles Phalippou, Paul Reuss
Reviewer: Paul Reuss
Title: II. — Prose. *Les Civilisés*, de M. Claude Farrère

Pour la troisième fois depuis sa fondation, l'Académie Goncourt vient d'attribuer son prix annuel à M. Claude Farrère pour son roman «Les Civilisés». Il ne me convient pas d'examiner ici l'utilité des concours littéraires, des prétendus encouragements donnés aux jeunes (?) écrivains. Il me suffira de constater que ce n'est que fort rarement que les prix sont donnés d'une manière intelligente. Presque toujours, ils reviennent à un imbécile fortement pistonné ou à un écrivain qui se soucie fort peu de ces quelques gros sous tombant, par hasard, dans sa bourse.

Je ne veux point dire par là que M. Claude Farrère soit un imbécile. Loin de moi cette pensée, je veux faire simplement remarquer que l'attribution du prix Goncourt à son ouvrage est chose exagérée ; c'est presque un grossier contresens...

Et je m'étonne fort de la décision de cette Académie, qui compte pourtant parmi ses membres ce qu'il y a peut-être de meilleur dans notre littérature contemporaine. Quant à moi, je n'hésite pas à déclarer que «Les

Civilisés» est un bien mauvais livre et qu'octroyer ce prix à M. Claude Farrère c'est faire injure au vrai talent d'un J.-A. Nau ou d'un Léon Frapié.

La lecture de cet ouvrage m'a fait songer à cette catégorie de personnes que j'appellerai — ne pouvant les qualifier par un terme précis — les amis que l'on a aux colonies. Chacun de nos lecteurs compte certainement, parmi ses amis, un colonial. Et s'il est un tant soit peu psychologue, il se sera aperçu bien vite que ce dernier cherche toujours à « épater son monde », en racontant des aventures de tout genre et selon lui plus extraordinaires les unes que les autres. Cet homme d'ailleurs, qui se dit blasé, dégoûté de la vie par trop monotone de la métropole, dépensera son argent le plus sottement possible à des plaisirs ineptes, archaïques et si démodés que le dernier des potaches n'en voudrait même pas.

Cruelle ironie des choses d'ici-bas !

M. Farrère lui aussi cherche tout d'abord à nous étonner, à nous dérouter par ses peintures de mœurs douteuses, par des histoires d'un réalisme grossier. Il s'attarde longuement à nous conter les débauches de ses héros Torral et Méril. L'on dirait qu'il prend plaisir à découvrir tous les dessous malpropres de la vie de Saïgon. Et cela, il le fait si maladroitement que l'on est porté à croire que M. Claude Farrère est un gros naïf ou, chose plus grave, qu'il n'a jamais lu l'Histoire. Ne va-t-il pas jusqu'à prétendre que les mœurs qu'il nous présente appartiennent d'une manière exclusive à nos colonies ? Comme s'il n'y avait pas plus de vicieux à Paris qu'à Saïgon !

Et puis, tout cela n'est pas de la littérature. Il faut laisser à tous ces vagues plumitifs, fournisseurs attitrés de certaines collections pornographiques, la honte de s'appesantir sur de pareils sujets. L'auteur des «Civilisés» ne parvient même pas à nous intéresser et la lecture de son ouvrage est fatigante. Mais le plus curieux, c'est que M. Farrère cherche ensuite à nous émouvoir, à nous faire verser des larmes sur la triste idylle d'un Fierce et d'une Sélysette.

Voilà M. Claude Farrère transformé en auteur de la doucereuse Bibliothèque Rose : son sentimentalisme est tout à fait ridicule. L'état d'âme de son Fierce est celui d'un enfant de dix ans.

Ridicule aussi et bien vieille nous apparaît sa thèse. Tout le monde sait, et on n'a pas attendu M. Claude Farrère pour en faire la remarque, que les colonies servent de refuge à tous les aventuriers, à tous les ratés de la vie, qu'elles sont un excellent tremplin pour bon nombre de politiciens. Dire le contraire serait, je crois, de la folie et vraiment il n'était pas besoin de nous le rappeler dans un livre si ennuyeux.

D'un réalisme bien maladroit, d'une psychologie bien faible, l'ouvrage de M. Claude Farrère n'a presque pas de valeur au point de vue du style : sans originalité aucune, il sonne creux ; c'est tout au plus s'il faut lui reconnaître de la correction. Et je tiens pour une grosse maladresse le fait d'avoir dédié un tel livre au styliste éblouissant qu'est Pierre Louÿs. La comparaison est par trop désavantageuse.

☙❧

Source: *Mercure de France*, Série moderne (1905 November 15)
Director: Alfred Vallette
Reviewer: Rachilde
Title: Les Romans – *Les Civilisés*, par Claude Farrère

L'auteur, que j'appellerais volontiers le monsieur qui a lu « Aphrodite », comme on dirait la Femme qui a connu l'empereur de notre bien regretté Hugues Rebell, est un nouveau venu dans les lettres, mais point sans expérience ni talent. À part qu'il prône de temps à autre les lois, la religion et quelques barbares usages établis, ses études de mœurs exotiques sont fort intéressantes, très fouillées, très poussées, osées même, arrivant juste au moment où le public, amateur de piments rouges, rêve de détails curieux sur les affaires Gaud-Toqué et toutes les gentillesses des vices qui sont rois dans les pays de nègres.

Il s'agit d'une croisière à Saïgon. Le comte de Fierce, un Français des plus civilisés, exporte les goûts art-nouveau de la France nouvelle. Il est un peu blasé, un peu névrosé, un peu taciturne et ne possède pas une dose énorme de sens moral. Au contact de quelques amis, beaucoup plus intoxiqués que lui par les drogues et les mœurs des cités de plaisirs, sirènes attendant le naufragé de toutes les patries pour le rouler dans une fange singulièrement haute en parfums, le pauvre jeune officier se blase et se névrose de plus en plus.

Mévil, le médecin pour dames, Torral, le chercheur d'abstractions, lui apprennent l'un à renier l'amour sentimental, l'autre à oublier la vieille foi militaire, mais il se dégoûte de la débauche, vraiment trop facile dans ces contrées chaudes, et le sourire de Sélysette, la fille d'un héros, vient heureusement luire sur lui comme le rayon de l'étoile protectrice. Un instant il retrouve son énergie, reprend possession de lui-même et s'efforce de croire à des choses qui jadis lui faisaient hausser les épaules. Il y a aussi un bon type d'amiral dont la condescendance à le découvrir honnête garçon lui remet le cœur en place.

Cependant, une heure d'oubli le perd. Il a bu à la coupe des sirènes, il y boira encore et revenant d'une folle partie nocturne il rencontre sa bonne étoile qui est tristement obligée de luire sur un tableau des moins édifiants : le fiancé enlacé par les bras d'une personne court vêtue au fond d'une voiture également de louage. Sélysette s'efface, un nuage obscurcit l'horizon. Fierce se sent aller à la dérive. Il cherche à se venger de la vie des civilisés en coulant bas un grand navire de guerre anglais. Manière barbare d'avoir enfin raison.

À ce sujet une très belle page sur l'agonie du vaisseau frappé en pleine coque par le petit torpilleur qui ne tire qu'à bout portant. Les scènes de *civilisations* exotiques sont admirablement peintes à l'aide d'un style léger et brutal, d'une certaine mondanité froide, très élégante, disant tout, et risquant le mot technique sans un embarras de mauvaise compagnie. Malgré quelques aventures plus que risquées, ce n'est jamais vulgaire parce que ce n'est pas hypocrite. Je n'aime pas la question de principe qui serait qu'on ne peut pas vivre, aux colonies ou ailleurs, sans Dieu, sans maître et sans lois, mais les questions de principes sont simplement des occasions de sortir ses personnelles visions d'humanité. L'auteur des Civilisés, le monsieur qui a lu *Aphrodite*, a de bien personnelles visions en dépit des influences Aphrodisiaques.

ඏ♦ඈ

Source: *Gil Blas* **/ dir. A. Dumont** (1905 November 29)
Reviewer: Louis Vauxcelles.
Title: *Les Civilisés*

Je ne voudrais pas — au moment où Jules Bois prélude en ce journal même à des études de substantielle critique littéraire — empiéter sans compétence sur les chasses du voisin.

C'est à titre exceptionnel, et je m'en excuse, que je m'aventure à parler lettres. Mais les Civilisés valent qu'on y revienne à deux fois.

Je n'ignore pas que ce livre est hardi au point d'effaroucher, et j'incline à penser que l'auteur eût gagné à raturer une demi-douzaine de passages inutiles. Mais, cette réserve formulée, je ne m'attarde point davantage.

Il paraît que le vocable « civilisé », dont le sens est fort précis sur les rives de la Seine, possède aux colonies une signification mystérieuse, ésotérique, troublante. En Indo-Chine, notamment, ce mot acquiert une intensité abominable. Les « civilisés », ce sont les gens qui, vomis par l'Europe, vont pratiquer à Saïgon, par exemple, la méthode épicurienne qui tient en deux mots : maximum de jouissance, minimum d'effort.

Saigon est une ville de luxe, de volupté, de complaisance, d'impudeur. C'est l'abbaye de Thélème extrême-orientale. Un parfum asiatique, où se mêle l'arôme composite des magnolias, des fauves, du poivre, de l'encens pourri, des femmes, grise les sens et anesthésie les consciences. Le long de l'« Inspection

» — les Acacias de Saïgon — les Victorias attelées de chevaux annamites, gros comme des ânes, vifs comme des écureuils, déambulent, emportant des couples qui, tous, prennent mille sortes de libertés que la nuit ne voile guère.

Que voulez-vous que devienne un Européen transplanté en ce fumier colonial ? Tel est le problème que pose M. Claude Farrère en son roman, paru d'hier. Ce roman, je tiens à le dire tout de suite, est un des livres les plus magnifiquement hardis que la littérature contemporaine ait produits. Depuis Louis Bertrand, qui nous fut révélé voici quatre ou cinq ans, je ne crois pas qu'on puisse trouver coloriste plus fort, et penseur plus acerbe. Un tel livre nous élève à mille pieds au-dessus de tous les fades bouquins d'adultères mondains, niais ou pimentés, que signent nos fournisseurs usuels. Tout le livre est passionnant, irritant parfois, mais de premier ordre ; et les cinquante dernières pages sont un chef-d'œuvre. En un temps où les moins qualifiés se présentent à l'Académie française, l'apparition d'un livre rare tel que les Civilisés vaut qu'on s'y arrête. Et, d'autre part, une étude sur la mentalité coloniale s'affirme de la plus brûlante actualité ; MM. Gentil, Rouanet, Gaud, Liégeois, Challaye, Tocqué ne me démentiront point, non plus que l'ombre de feu Brazza, le généreux et candide 'Don Quichotte congolais'...

Les « coloniaux » ordinaires, lorsqu'ils débarquent à Saïgon, sont le plus souvent des gens marqués, suspects, souvent même tarés et viciés ; la double influence du milieu anormal et du climat déprimant les complète et les achève. Promptement, ils font litière de tous principes. Je laisse ici la parole à mon auteur ; un de ses héros expose la thèse ainsi qu'il suit :

« Sur ces terres coloniales fraîchement retournées et labourées par le piétinement de toutes les races qui s'y heurtent, il vaut peut-être mieux qu'un fumier humain soit jeté, pour que de la décomposition purulente des vieilles idées et des vieilles morales naisse la moisson des civilisations futures...

« Parmi cette plèbe coloniale et méprisable vivent quelques individus supérieurs. À ceux-ci le milieu et le climat ont profité, et ils sont devenus comme les avant-coureurs de ces civilisations de demain. Ils vivent en marge de notre vie conventionnelle ; ils en ont abjuré tous les fanatismes et toutes les religions ; et, s'ils acceptent d'observer notre code pénal, je crois bien que c'est par esprit de conciliation. L'éclosion de pareils hommes n'était possible que dans cette Indo-Chine à la fois très vieille et très neuve ; il y fallait l'ambiance des philosophies aryenne, chinoise et malaise lentement usées les unes contre les autres ; il y fallait la corruption d'une société en qui la morale d'Europe a fait faillite ; il y fallait l'humidité brûlante de Saïgon, où tout fond au soleil et se dissout — les énergies, les croyances et le sens du bien et du mal ! Ces hommes en avance sur notre siècle sont des civilisés. Nous des barbares. »

Trois civilisés de marque, le docteur Raymond Mévil, l'ingénieur Torral, l'officier de marine Jacques de Fierce.

Raymond Mévil est un jeune et séduisant médecin, aux yeux veloutés, à la barbe d'ébène, dont raffolent les belles madames saïgonnaises ; il les drogue à la cocaïne, les caresse, les détraque. Mévil consacre une partie de ses après-midi et de ses nuits à diverses personnes, dont une mondaine vénale, une chanteuse, une congaï annamite à ses gages et une adolescente japonaise.

Torral, ingénieur saturé de logique et d'exactitude, d'une supériorité intellectuelle blessante, équilibre ses plaisirs selon l'arithmétique épicurienne ; il se vante d'exprimer de la vie tout le bonheur y contenu ; il fume des pipes d'opium, se délecte d'analytique, méprise les femmes, et...

Le comte de Fierce, orphelin, très fortuné, après une adolescence orageuse, court le monde — il est enseigne de vaisseau — las de tout, ayant goûté à tout, dégoûté de tout. « Fierce promène de climat en climat son dédain de toutes les lois, son ironie pour toutes les religions, sa haine contre tous les mensonges, et sa faim et sa soif de toutes les nourritures inédites et miraculeuses que la vie promet et qu'elle ne donne pas. »

Ces trois amis mènent à Saïgon une sorte d'existence où les cocktails, les alcools purs, le champagne sec et les fumées d'opium, de haschich, d'éther, la morphine et le poker, les Chinoises impubères et mille autres choses diablement incorrectes se dosent harmonieusement. On n'est pas plus civilisé.

Le milieu social où ils évoluent est digne d'eux : voici le sieur Malais, « énorme brute, carrée de partout, avec des dents de loup et des mains qui font peur ; fermier du riz, du thé et de l'alcool, quarante millions trébuchant au soleil, tous mal acquis » ; le chicanous retors Ariette, enrichi par les caprices de son épouse ; le publiciste Claude Rochet, épave du chantage, de l'ataxie, du gâtisme. Quelques braves gens toutefois, notamment le duc d'Orvilliers, contre-amiral commandant une division de l'escadre de Chine, qui aime paternellement son aide de camp Jacques de Fierce, le croit sans tache et irréprochable ; d'Orvilliers est une manière de héros suranné, un peu caricatural, un peu baderne, très noble et très pieux ; la famille Sylva, une dame aveugle et charmante, sa fille Sélysette, un lys ; d'autres encore.

La question posée est celle-ci : qui l'emportera, de la civilisation moderne, corruptrice, ou des sentiments d'autrefois, l'amour, le patriotisme ? C'est en l'âme de Fierce qu'éclate le conflit. Fierce, un beau jour, s'éprend de Sélysette Sylva, et la virginale pureté de cette enfant le régénère et va le sauver de lui-même.

Elle l'aime. Hélas ! à peine Fierce est-il fiancé, que l'ordre vient au croiseur le Bayard d'appareiller pour Hong-Kong. Et les tentations assaillent l'âme et le corps du jeune convalescent ; loin de Sélysette, Fierce, privé de son cher talisman, est guetté par l'orgie. Il parvient à s'en sauver, à Hong-Kong, prodigieuse ville hurlante et grouillante ; mais les réminiscences malsaines, qui ressemblent à des nostalgies, traversent son cerveau et sa chair. Une fête donnée à bord du cuirassé anglais King-Edward réunit tous les cosmopolites de Hong-Kong, de Changhaï, de Nagasaki, de Hanoï et de Saïgon ; on danse, on soupe, on flirte, Fierce va succomber aux agaceries d'une demi-vierge australienne ; il se reprend, à l'instant suprême.

Mais Sélysette n'est pas là pour protéger son fiancé ; la rechute est proche ; quelques semaines plus tard, Fierce passe une nuit fiévreuse à céder au poker meurtrier. La fatalité écarte l'enseigne de vaisseau de son amie. Le voici promu commandant de l'Avalanche, une petite canonnière qui doit combattre quelques bandes d'Annamites indigènes révoltés ; la guerre perfide et lâchement féroce, d'embuscades, de randonnées s'organise dans la forêt tropicale. Une nuit, au fin fond des bois, Fierce, affolé par la contagion sanglante, se rue, sabre au clair, dans une cahute. Une fillette asiatique, terrifiée, à demi-nue, s'offre en rançon de sa vie. Il trébuche, se rue, tombe sur la proie.

Il revient enfin à Saïgon, retrouve ses amis, Torral et Mévil, qui le reconquièrent : il participe à une effroyable orgie nocturne ; Sélysette le rencontre au matin, dégrisé mais flanqué de deux filles. Il ne lui reste plus qu'à mourir.

Par bonheur, une sortie prompte et propre s'offre à lui. La guerre vient d'être déclarée à l'Angleterre. Il pourra donc se faire tuer, sans scandale. La « civilisation » n'a pas aboli en son âme malade tout sentiment humain. Raymond Mévil qui, lui, s'est acharné depuis deux mois à la capture de deux femmes, une mariée, l'autre à marier, qui ne veulent point de lui, sombre dans la folie et le suicide ataxique. Torral, officier de réserve, déserte sa batterie ! Fierce, lui, va fièrement mourir sur le banc de quart de son torpilleur.

M. Claude Farrère a dédié aux morts de Tsu-Shima les deux derniers chapitres, tragiques, de son roman. La lutte du torpilleur 412 contre les cuirassés britanniques. Ah ! je vous jure qu'on ne peut lire ce récit de combat naval sans frissonner ; ce n'est ni du Jules Verne ni du Driant. Ces pages comptent parmi les plus belles que j'aie jamais lues. Fierce est tué ; mais la torpille a frappé le cuirassé par le travers de ses chaufferies milieu, au-dessous du blindage, et la mer entre, au cœur du monstre qui va sombrer ; les vingt-six hommes de la chaufferie s'entre-tuent, aveuglés par la vapeur et l'eau bouillante ; ils crèvent comme des chiens, la pierre au cou ; cette scène est indicible d'horreur.

***

Je ne sais si tout cela est bien logique et s'il n'est de braves à la guerre que les « barbares ». Ce besoin de donner la mort à « l'ennemi » est peut-être le summum de la civilisation, si l'on accepte ce mot au sens qui lui est donné dans les Civilisés. Et ce que l'auteur appelle un « réveil » n'est peut-être qu'une résultante.

Rien ne prouve que l'amour des alcools et des femmes — vivent le vin, l'amour et le tabac ! — ne se concilie pas à merveille avec la frénésie guerrière. Fierce, qui meurt pour la patrie, est très crâne, d'accord. J'aimerais mieux qu'il eût vécu utilement, pour sa patrie. Vous me direz qu'on ne lui en donne pas le choix. Toutefois j'incline à penser que point n'est besoin de revenir de tous les vices pour être patriote : les « zéphirs » et les « bat' d'Af' » sont d'excellents soldats et les mercenaires d'Hamilcar, les condottieri de la Renaissance savaient mourir.

Mais ne chicanons point M. Claude Farrère sur la doctrine qui étaie son roman. Ce livre-là, qui n'est pas d'un professionnel — je crois que M. Farrère est officier de marine — est écrit d'un style alerte, précis, éloquemment et douloureusement simple : ni chevilles, ni phraséologie. Les amateurs de ce calibre-là valent vingt fois les hommes de lettres de métier. Aussi bien Saint-Evremond, et La Rochefoucauld, et Vauvenargues, et Benjamin Constant, — et aussi Pierre Loti — étaient-ils des amateurs.

ॐ✦ॐ

Source: *Ancienne Gazette des étrangers*, Paris (1905 December 13)
Reviewer: Henry de Pène, rédacteur en chef [et directeur-gérant]
Title: Marins de Lettres

C'est à un marin de Lettres que l'Académie Goncourt vient de décerner son prix de prose annuel.

La marine française, qui s'enorgueillit avec raison d'avoir l'un de ses représentants, et non des moins distingués, M. Pierre Loti à l'Académie Française, a produit nombre d'écrivains de talent. Ils sont en effet très nombreux les officiers de marine qui ont écrit, soit en activité de service, sous un pseudonyme, soit à l'âge de la retraite.

M. Bargone, qui a signé Claude Farrère un livre mordant, "Les Civilisés" que l'Académie Goncourt a distingué entre tous, est donc loin de constituer une exception.

Faut-il en conclure que les longues heures de solitude en face de l'Océan et des étoiles sont vraiment faites pour faire naître les pensées, jaillir les conceptions et incruster dans le cerveau les observations recueillies. Sans doute.

Certes, la vie de l'officier de marine n'est pas oisive, mais quatre heures de quart sur la dunette laissent de la marge aux émotions que procurent les beaux spectacles de la nature, les couchers de soleil, les nuits étoilées des tropiques, les îles qui émergent de la mer, les côtes sauvages, les orages, les typhons, les baies souriantes parmi la verdure. Puis ce sont les spectacles humains, la connaissance des races si diverses, de mœurs si différentes, des idylles qui laissent un parfum de fleur exotique, des drames dont il faut rester le spectateur muet ; personne peut-être n'est mieux fait pour connaître le monde, la nature, les peuples, l'âme et le cœur humain que l'officier de marine.

Combien, poussés par les longues rêveries ont écrit dans le secret de la cabine, de beaux vers qui n'ont jamais vu le jour! Combien ont cédé au démon de l'encrier en écrivant des romans où se mêlait la connaissance du métier, où l'amour de la palette dont le style fait briller les couleurs...

J'évoquais tout à l'heure le nom de Pierre Loti, de son vrai nom le commandant Viaud, capitaine de frégate commandant notre stationnaire dans le Bosphore. Est-il un peintre plus prestigieux? Est-il un styliste plus incomparable parmi les écrivains vivants? Avec quelle plume enchanteresse et si délicatement émue nous a-t-il peint et le Japon, et la Chine, et l'Afrique, et l'Inde, et l'étrange pays basque, tribu des Huns restée au pied des Pyrénées. Claude Farrère a un autre genre, très personnel. Dans son livre "Les Civilisés" il a écrit une magistrale page dans laquelle il nous fait assister à l'émouvante lutte d'un torpilleur contre un cuirassé qui finit par succomber.

D'autres marins de lettres se sont attachés à nous donner des récits de faits vécus, tel ce capitaine de frégate René Diaveluy qui, dans un livre intitulé "La lutte pour l'Empire des Mers", nous a raconté la terrifiante bataille de Tsu-Shima.

On en pourrait citer cent autres, qui après Dumont-d'Urville, Bougainville et Fleuriot de Langle, ont écrit leurs souvenirs maritimes ou des livres d'un puissant intérêt technique comme l'amiral Paris qui fut membre de l'Institut.

Aucun cependant n'a égalé l'amiral Julien de la Gravière qui fut justement élu membre de l'Académie française. Ses "Guerres maritimes" ne sont pas seulement un livre classique. Faut-il rappeler sa description de la bataille de Trafalgar, qui constitue un morceau inoubliable, si clair si précis, si attrayant en même temps, qu'on ne peut l'oublier.

On n'a pas oublié non plus la frégate "L'Incomprise" de l'amiral Gourdon, ou le livre du lieutenant Darcy qui défendit si vaillamment la légation de France à Pékin pendant l'insurrection des Boxers, ni le livre charmant d'un tout jeune débutant M. de Blois, simple aspirant, qui a décrit ses impressions de bord pendant sa première année de navigation.

Il est interdit aux officiers de publier quoi que ce soit sans l'autorisation de leurs chefs, mais cette autorisation est vite accordée pour les ouvrages sérieux, et l'on ferme les yeux sur les œuvres littéraires signées d'un pseudonyme. Certains ouvrages cependant, hostiles et scandaleux, exigent une démission préalable; nous ne rappellerons pas inutilement le titre de ces ouvrages.

Parmi les marins de lettres, morts les uns glorieusement au service de la France, les autres de leur mort naturelle, il convient de citer parmi les premiers le commandant Rivière, dont personne n'a oublié l'héroïque fin au Tonkin. On lui doit plusieurs ouvrages de littérature et de souvenirs qui témoignent d'une grande délicatesse de cœur et d'esprit. Citons notamment "Edmée", "La Jeunesse d'un Désespéré", "Le Combat de la Vie" et une charmante pièce en un acte qui fut jouée à la Comédie-Française.

L'évocation du Tonkin me fait songer à Francis Garnier, qui a eu deux beaux livres: "Paris au Thibet" et "L'Exploration du Mékong". Le prince de Joinville, qui fut amiral de France, a écrit lui aussi, quelques ouvrages de souvenirs et l'on cite de lui une page qui est la description d'une tempête en Méditerranée et qu'on peut compter parmi les plus purs chefs-d'œuvre de notre littérature.

Quelques-uns ont quitté la marine et sont devenus journalistes comme M. Maurice Loir, qui a beaucoup fait pour la vulgarisation des choses de la marine et qui a publié un fort beau volume intitulé: "La Marine française". Autre physionomie curieuse: celle d'un excellent officier qui, après la guerre, quitta la marine pour la presse. Au début de la guerre de 1870, il commandait un aviso sur la côte africaine où nous guerroyions contre une peuplade noire.

Or il avait interdit à ses officiers de lui parler en dehors des affaires de service, ce qui a donné lieu à la très jolie infraction suivante, dont le dénouement, quoique conforme à la discipline nous paraîtra aujourd'hui d'un tempérament assombri.

"On apprend cependant que le 4 septembre, l'Empire a été renversé.

Les officiers du bord se réunissent et se demandent s'ils doivent l'annoncer au commandant qu'ils savent très dévoué à l'Empire.

— Ma foi, tant pis, dit l'un d'eux: je vais le lui dire; cela le fera enrager.

Et il se présente devant le commandant:

— Qu'y a-t-il? demanda celui-ci.

— Commandant, l'Empire est renversé, la République est proclamée à Paris.

Le commandant, très maître de lui, resta impassible:

— C'est bien, monsieur, vous me ferez quatre jours d'arrêts."

Vraie ou fausse, l'anecdote, qui a déjà été racontée, valait la peine d'être rappelée.

ಜ♦ಜ

Source: *Le Journal du Midi* (1905 December 18)
Reviewer: Louis Roubaud
Title: Chronique Parisienne

Il est vrai que, par contre, le roman a eu dans les dernières années du XIXe siècle, une vogue qui se continue et s'accroît dans les premiers jours du XXe.

Malheureusement si la poésie comme la musique élève l'âme, le roman l'empoisonne bien souvent. Il est difficile de faire servir de beaux vers à une mauvaise cause, mais combien de prosateurs de talent ont été les déplorables apôtres d'une détestable religion!

Je n'ai pas lu "Les Civilisés" de M. Farrère qui vient d'obtenir le prix Goncourt, ce qui me dispense de le classer en aucune catégorie. J'ai seulement remarqué que l'Académie des Goncourt n'avait pas couronné, cette année, un professionnel de la littérature, et ce fait qui paraît tout d'abord sans conséquence exprime un état de choses très alarmant.

En effet, non seulement la foule va toujours grossissant des littérateurs menant une existence misérable, mais voici que dans tous les métiers des esprits s'éveillent tourmentés du mal d'écrire.

C'est dans la marine que l'on trouve le plus d'écrivains. M. Farrère, de son véritable nom Bargone, est lieutenant de vaisseau ; il a devant loi un grand nombre de précédents illustres à divers degrés.

En outre du commandant Viaud (Pierre Loti), que de noms ne pourrait-on citer? Les "Guerres Maritimes" de l'amiral Julien de la Gravière, qui fut membre de l'Académie française, sont restées célèbres; l'amiral Gourdon a écrit "La Frégate 'l'Incomprise'"; le commandant Rivière est l'auteur de nombreux romans et d'une pièce jouée à la Comédie-Française; "La Lutte pour l'Empire des mers", du capitaine de frégate Diaveluy, est une œuvre de valeur. Mais la liste est trop longue des livres romanesques qui ont tous pour auteur des membres de notre marine.

Si toutes les autres carrières contiennent de pareils germes littéraires, le professionnel déjà si misérable ne sera plus demain qu'un paria dont on se demandera la raison d'être. Il lui restera, sans doute, la ressource de se faire journaliste, mais c'est là une perspective bien sombre.

Louis Roubaud

ങ⋆ഌ

Source: *Le National* (1906 January 1)
Publisher: Maujan, Adolphe (1853–1914)
Reviewer: Unknown
Title: Un livre – *Les Civilisés*, un roman de Claude Farrère (éditions Paul Ollendorff)

« Votre Aphrodite s'empara de moi et me posséda entier, écrit M. Claude Farrère à M. Pierre Louÿs, parce qu'elle était de ma religion — la religion des belles lignes harmonieuses et immobiles, la religion de la Beauté toute nue et toute pure. »

Et avant même de feuilleter le livre, on s'attend à quelque curieux et élégant effort d'imagination vers un monde moins mesquin. M. Claude Farrère, à l'imitation de son cher maître (entre Racine, La Bruyère et M. Pierre Louÿs, l'auteur des Civilisés ne trouve que « des tumultueux, des bouches rondes, des excessifs, des impuissants ») va-t-il reconstituer une civilisation raffinée, où la sensualité sera le seul principe admis, et réalisera sur terre je ne sais quel paradis de volupté ?

Non : le roman de M. Claude Farrère vise à l'observation de la vie réelle et contemporaine. Quelques hommes, n'ayant gardé qu'un seul culte, « le culte âpre de la vérité impudique », étalent à Saigon leur débauche dédaigneuse de tous préjugés européens, autrement dit, de toute barbarie. Sont-ils heureux ? À peu près. Mais voilà que l'un d'eux, l'enseigne de vaisseau de Fierce, devient amoureux, innocemment amoureux de l'adorable et ingénue Sélysette. Malgré ses théories de civilisé, il se fiance. À peine éloigné de sa fiancée, son vice le ressaisit ; Sélysette, un beau matin, le rencontre flanqué de deux femmes demi-nues. Le mariage est rompu. Mais au même moment, la guerre est déclarée, et l'enseigne de Fierce, retrouvant en lui la noble barbarie de ses aïeux, court sus à l'ennemi, que dis-je ? «

à cette quintessence de civilisation que les cuirassés concentrent derrière leurs murailles, quintessence de civilisation bonne pour la dynamite » ; et ce désespéré, enfin converti, meurt en héros, pendant que ses deux compagnons ordinaires s'effondrent l'un dans une mort lamentable, l'autre dans l'abjection.

Et ainsi, M. Claude Farrère abandonne les traces de son maître, très dur pour les écrivains modernes qui, « usant d'un stratagème laborieux dont l'hypocrisie déplaît », disent « j'ai peint la volupté telle qu'elle est afin d'exalter la vertu. » Décidément, il n'y a pas grand'chose de commun entre M. Claude Farrère et M. Pierre Louÿs.

Ceci ne signifie pas que l'œuvre du jeune écrivain soit sans mérites. Elle a précisément le genre de qualités et le genre de défauts dans lesquels se complaisaient les Goncourt et qui peuvent se résumer d'un mot : la littérature, oui, la littérature, qui déforme la réalité, qui ne s'intéresse qu'à l'inédit, qui vise à l'effet, mais qui charme malgré tout et qu'il faut encourager — même par des prix et des couronnes.

Je viens de lire Les Civilisés, et j'en suis encore à me demander ce que l'auteur entend par un « civilisé ». Un libertin ? La chose est banale autant que le mot est démodé. Un sceptique ? Les sceptiques, j'entends les vrais, sont extrêmement rares, et le type en est déjà vieux. Prenons donc les définitions que nous offre çà et là M. Claude Farrère. Voici, selon lui, ce que Jacques de Fierce devrait avouer à Sélysette :

« Je n'ai rien dans le cœur ni dans la tête que vous puissiez aimer ni comprendre. Et si vous entrevoyiez mon par-dedans, je vous ferais horreur. Je suis blasé, sceptique et mécréant : je ne crois ni au bien, ni au mal, ni à Dieu ni à Diable. À force d'être allé partout, je suis revenu de tout. Vous entassez en moi, de par la grâce de mon uniforme, tout un lot de vertus archaïques qui ne sont pas miennes et que je méprise. Et le seul culte que je garde, le culte âpre de la vérité impudique, vous épouvanterait comme un blasphème. »

Quand je disais qu'il y a au fond de tout cela beaucoup de littérature ! Autre portrait civilisé :

« Mévil était un Civilisé, c'est-à-dire une plante de serre, modifiée, déformée, atrophiée par une culture maniaque, et devenue monstrueuse avec des feuilles naines, des fleurs trop grosses et des pétales en guise d'étamines, avec de la spéculation en place d'instinct et un cerveau tout ensemble admirable et difforme. Ce cerveau-là, d'abord, s'était enfermé dans un égoïsme confortable, laissant aux siens leur liberté et ne se mêlant pas à leurs jeux ; mais la gangrène des nerfs l'avait un jour gagné. Mévil, parvenu au bout de sa jeunesse écourtée, s'était tout entier, et d'un seul coup, détraqué et amolli. »

Ce type de jouisseur égoïste, élégant et méprisable est-il nouveau ? Non, sans doute, et le roman contemporain en offre beaucoup trop. Mais ce qu'on n'avait pas fait jusqu'ici, c'était de le placer dans le milieu où il se laisse le mieux étudier, dans le milieu colonial. Il y a, en dehors de la France, une liberté d'ailleurs, une absence de préjugés que subissent les Français les moins corrompus. Et ainsi, le véritable intérêt du roman ne réside pas peut-être dans le personnage de l'enseigne, mais dans la peinture même de Saigon.

Ici encore, je crois bien que l'auteur a cédé au désir très littéraire de nous étonner, de nous scandaliser, quitte à nous édifier plus tard, quand la vertu sera récompensée et le vice puni. — Je sais par expérience, chacun sait aujourd'hui que « le monde » colonial diffère du monde parisien par une sorte de cynisme inconscient. Mais je doute que Saigon, avec sa population sans cesse renouvelée, soit le repaire de forbans en smoking que nous montre l'auteur. Et même si cela était, quel avantage trouve l'écrivain à insister sur tel ou tel détail exagéré et répugnant ? Si du moins cela devenait pour lui l'occasion d'une de ces pages merveilleuses qu'il admire dans l'Aphrodite ! Mais non ! Il ne se révèle écrivain que vers la fin du volume, dans la partie relativement chaste : il n'entend rien à l'obscénité qui n'est chez lui ni raffinée, ni largement ignoble, mais banale et maladroite. Lisez plutôt cette description d'une maison de plaisir dans les quartiers louches de Saïgon :

« À droite et à gauche, des niches à chiens s'ouvraient, closes d'une claire-voie ; c'étaient les chambres d'amour — car on aimait dans cette porcherie. On aimait les femelles saoules qui se vautraient à terre, et que tout d'abord on ne distinguait pas, à cause de la lueur trop fumeuse du quinquet unique, toujours prêt de s'éteindre, mais qu'on vérifiait bientôt être des femmes, les unes jaunes et les autres vieilles, celles-ci plus hideuses, mais pas de beaucoup, et plus expérimentées... »

Je laisse de côté les détails qui suivent, et je demande sincèrement : sont-ce là des phrases incisives, comme les aimait Edmond de Goncourt, ou pittoresques, comme chez Daudet, ou raffinées comme celles de M. Pierre Louÿs, ou même amples et riches comme parfois celles de Zola ?

Vraiment, les cent premières pages de ce roman, délibérément outrancières, se complaisant dans le cynisme si maltraité un peu plus loin, trop souvent dénuées d'écriture, n'ont rien de bien captivant. J'ajoute que le dialogue y est assez pénible, assez plat, qu'il tourne parfois à la conférence (conférences successives sur la colonisation, sur les voyages, sur l'éducation des filles), et que l'auteur y semble admirer ses héros qu'il désignera plus tard ; car ce sont, après tout, les seuls honnêtes gens de Saïgon !

Et cependant, Les Civilisés ont leurs mérites.

D'abord l'auteur, tout en exagérant, donne une impression personnelle des choses qu'il a observées ; au moment où la lumière se fait jour sur tels crimes du Congo ou d'ailleurs, nous savons bien qu'il y a une mentalité spéciale aux colonies, et cette mentalité, nous la surprenons chez le brasseur d'affaires qu'est Malais, chez le journaliste redouté qu'est Rochet, chez le lieutenant-gouverneur Abel, vaguement honnête, mais besogneux, chez le cynique Torral, affichant ses vices par dégoût de l'hypocrisie et par mépris de ses contemporains. Nous découvrons la vie de là-bas dans son aspect superficiel plutôt que dans ses profondeurs réelles ; mais cela même est intéressant. Et si M. Claude Farrère est un touriste bien plus qu'un colonial, c'est un touriste très averti, qui ne s'arrête pas toujours aux effets faciles de couleur locale.

Il connaît le pays et le décrit, mais moins dans son par-dehors que dans son par-dedans, selon l'expression qui lui est chère ; je veux dire qu'il n'évoque guère les paysages à la façon de M. Pierre Loti, mais qu'il retrouve sans cesse les sensations subies, qu'il nous communique et que nous percevons ainsi sans trop de peine le milieu où se déroule l'action du roman. Nous ne voyons pas l'Indo-Chine ; mais nous y plongeons, et ce n'est pas un mince éloge pour l'écrivain.

A-t-il été mêlé, en sa qualité d'officier de marine, à la répression de révoltes indigènes ? On le croirait, tant il décrit avec clarté, avec précision, la guerre coloniale. Là, plus rien, semble-t-il, de l'exagération « littéraire » du début, mais la vérité, la toute puissante vérité qui seule retient le lecteur, qui seule fait de l'auteur un écrivain. À la façon de Flaubert, des naturalistes, des impressionnistes, il cherche et trouve le détail caractéristique, non pas celui qui étonne, mais celui qu'on attend, parce qu'il est dans la logique du récit, dans la logique des choses.

Veut-on un exemple de cette manière excellente ? Voici la nuit sur le fleuve, où la canonnière de Jacques de Fierce poursuit la lutte contre les rebelles cachés le long des rives :

« La nuit tombait, et dans les fourrés noirs une fusillade tardive éclatait : des balles sifflaient jusqu'au fleuve, et les tôles des canonnières sonnaient sous les coups ; le canon s'en mêlait ; c'était enfin une vraie bataille qui durait jusqu'à l'aube. Le feu cessait soudain, car on s'était trompé : il n'y avait point d'ennemi. Égaré ou trahi, on s'était fusillé entre soi, on s'était massacré par mégarde. Dix, vingt morts jonchaient le sol. On les enterrait — et l'on recommençait d'autres erreurs. On tuait et on mourait sans gloire, avec lassitude et ennui. »

De bonne foi, le livre n'eût-il pas gagné à conserver d'un bout à l'autre cette tenue, cette simplicité bien plus habile que la recherche et l'exagération ? L'émotion naît ici de la documentation et en même temps que l'émotion, le style.

On pourrait généraliser et dire que la seconde partie de l'ouvrage est supérieure à tous égards à la première, parce qu'elle est plus vraie, parce que l'auteur abandonne pas à pas les états d'âme exceptionnels et qui semblent faux pour des sentiments plus humains, plus accessibles, plus réels. Je ne dis pas que sa psychologie soit toujours très serrée, que les personnages n'aient pas quelquefois des pressentiments un peu gros, mais, entraîné par son sujet, l'auteur cherche à se rendre compte de tout ce qu'il imagine et remplace la fantaisie littéraire par la simplicité raisonnable, telle sans doute qu'il l'admirait jadis chez les écrivains du dix-septième siècle pour lesquels il avoue ses préférences.

⊗✦⊗

Source: *La Petite Gironde : journal républicain quotidien* (1906 January 6)
Reviewer: Gabriel Trarieux
Title: *Les Civilisés* : Un volume chez Ollendorff

L'attribution du Prix Goncourt ne passe point inaperçue. L'opinion s'en préoccupe. C'est une singulière aubaine pour un jeune écrivain hier inconnu de mettre cette enseigne à son livre. Et l'opinion n'a pas tort. Il est clair qu'être préféré par des écrivains comme les Rosny, les Margueritte, Mirbeau, Descaves, Henniquc, Geffroy, Huysmans, Léon Daudet, Elémir Bourges, c'est assez flatteur, tout de même. Ces gens-là sont vivants. Ils produisent, on les aime, on les admire, on les hait. Oui, leur suffrage est précieux, beaucoup plus que celui, par exemple, des rares maréchaux de lettres et des solennels inconnus qui composent l'autre Académie. Nous devons souhaiter, par suite, qu'il ne s'égare pas, qu'il nous serve, à vous, à moi, les ignorants qui ne lisons pas tous les livres. Déjà, il tira hors de pair deux œuvres inégales, mais fortes, somme toute assez remarquables: Force ennemie, de John-Antoine Nau ; la Maternelle, de Léon Frapié. Il vient, cette fois, de désigner les Civilisês, de Claude Farrère. Que valent ces Civilisés ?

***

L'histoire en est simple et banale. Un officier de marine navigue en Extrême Orient. Il fait escale à Saigon, ville de délices, d'orgies et de soûleries crapuleuses. Il épuise ce genre de sport avec conscience et méthode, en compagnie de deux camarades, un ingénieur et un médecin, dont c'est le passe-temps ordinaire. Un beau jour, il rencontre une jeune fille, Mlle Sélysette Sylva (de qui le père, un colonel, à la Maeterlinck, évidemment, avant de se faire tuer en Afrique).

Cette jeune fille lui plaît. Elle a des yeux pers et une âme française. Elle est ingénue et croyante. Le jeune Rolla exotique sent frémir en lui des candeurs. Il fut catholique, naguère ; il est fils de race noble et ancienne, — marquis de Fierce, s'il vous plaît. Il demande la jeune fille en mariage. Elle accepte, voit en lui un héros. Par malheur, fiancé de la veilla, il lui faut repartir pour Hong-Kong. Séparation. Lettres d'amour. Impures hantises. Péché. Quand il revient à Saigon, le jeune de Fierce est repris par le vomissement primitif. Il s'affiche brutalement avec des filles. Ivre, enlacé par deux actrices, il rencontre, une après-midi, Mlle Sylva et sa mère. C'est fini. Son beau rêve est fini. Il n'a plus qu'à se faire tuer, le moins malproprement possible. Il monte à bord d'un torpilleur, il expire eu donnant la mort, ayant eu cette joie suprême de voir un cuirassé anglais, le King-Edwards, couler avant lui. Cependant que Mlle Sylva, devant sa madone, est en prières.

***

Vous voyez, le récit est quelconque. Débarrassé de l'exotisme, c'est une aventure connue. L'auteur, à vrai dire, ne la relève d'aucune psychologie nouvelle. Rien de plus vieux-jeu, de plus conventionnel, de plus factice que son héros. Un jeune Rolla, ni je dit. Oui, c'est bien cela, à peu près. C'est même cela tout à fart, moins l'éloquence et le lyrisme. La théorie, car c'en est une, dont s'inspire le titre du livre, est de pure essence romantique. Les Civilisés, qu'est-ce donc ? Ce sont ceux qu'un siècle sans foi a raffinés et corrompus ; ceux qui ne veulent plus avoir d'enfants, car la besogne humaine est faite ; veux qui ont pour devise : jouir, avec le minimum d'effort. C'est Fierce, le désespéré ; c'est Raymond Mévil, l'homme à femmes (qui sombre aussi dans le suicide); c'est Torral, le hideux inverti. Qui les a perdus ? la raison, l'excès, d'une logique implacable. Ils font la noce, parce qu'ils sont athées. L'auteur se moque-t-il de nous ?

Non. Il dit cela sans rire. Et il semble ne voir de refuge que dans je ne sais quel mysticisme sensualiste et détraqué. Est-ce assez la thèse de Rolla:

Dors tu content, Voltaire, et ton hideux sourire ?...

Voilà une résurrection, n'est-ce pas ? Assez imprévue. Il est vrai que dans sa préface M. Claude Farrère nous affirme qu'il est juste l'inverse de son héros. Il déteste le sentiment, les bouches ou rond, les lyriques. Il aime « nos purs classiques français ». Ses deux déités littéraires, c'est Sophocle et Pierre Louÿs. Il les met sur le même piédestal. (Sophocle a l'air un peu gêné.)

Comment fait-il pour concilier ces tendances contradictoires ? Ma foi, je n'en sais rien. Qu'il s'arrange !

***

Ce que je sais bien, c'est que cette lecture me laisse infiniment perplexe. Quoi ! C'est cela, le Prix Goncourt ? Pourquoi, mon Dieu ? Abîme ! Abîme ! Ni nouveauté dans le récit, ni singularité de thèse, ni psychologie inédite, ni... ni rien du tout. Alors, quoi ? Sans doute, je vois, je vois bien que Claude Farrère sait écrire. Il a de la grâce et de la force, une certaine sobriété pure. Il montre assez bien ce qu'il a vu : Saigon, les paysages, les femmes. L'épisode du cuirassé ne manque pas de quelque grandeur. Mais ces qualités sont courantes. Plus d'un concurrent évincé les possédait, et quelques autres. Il y avait là : Jules Huret, André Chevrillon, Romain Rolland. Non, plus je me creuse la tête, moins je comprends ce qui, dans ce livre, a pu séduire Mirbeau, Decaves, Hennique, Rosny, Geffroy, Margueritte, pour ne parler que de ceux-là. Feraient-ils — déjà !— de la politique ? Seraient-ils accessibles à des raisons que la raison ne connaît pas ? Je me refuse net à le croire. Je demeurerai donc dans le marasme. Car je ne puis me tenir, en lisant cette pornographie insistante, de nie rappeler, par contraste, les rudes et chastes héros dessinés par Rudyard Kipling. Et je regrette qu'un tel document de nos pourritures coloniales soit signalé comme un chef-d'œuvre par dix bons écrivains français.

⋆

Source: *L'Idée : revue littéraire* (1906 March 13)
Director: Georges Fagot
Reviewer: Yves Nils

Les Civilisés! Quel beau titre, profond jusqu'à l'abime, intéressant jusqu'à l'exclusivisme. Claude Farrère en a écrit un volume ; il ne serait pas trop d'y consacre une œuvre…

Mais ce volume, avant-coureur peut-être d'un mouvement sauveur (oui, si quelqu'un de ces événements qui remuent les éléments d'une race venait à nous redonner, pour un temps, la sensation de l'équilibre) ce volume est merveilleusement net et précis. On le voit avec épouvante s'étendre sur tout l'organisme d'une société, sur toute la littérature d'un siècle, et il n'est pas superflu de dite qu'écrivains, artistes, psychologues et philosophes contemporains, Loti avec sa tristesse, Bazin avec sa pitié, et Barrès, chef d'école, lancé en plein combat, et Daudet, et Serao — nous nous y résumons tous.

Parbleu ! la lutte n'est pas nouvelle, et voilà bien des années que Musset, dans L'Enfant du Siècle, lançait l'anathème précurseur à la froide déesse Raison. Voilà bien longtemps que parle Desgenais et que sa voix impitoyable a lentement pénétré les jeunes cœurs. Voilà bien longtemps que le vase est vide, dont pariait Renan, mais le parfum dont nous vivions encore, le parfum divin va mourir... Ce que nous serons quand il sera mort, le livre de Farrère nous l'apprend.

Trop brutalement sans doute, dans l'exagération inutile et cynique d'un climat qui développe les vices jusqu'à la frénésie, avec des insistances blessantes qui ressemblent à des complicités, — mais avec aussi une hardiesse et une clairvoyance que nul ne niera et à l'aide d'une composition si forte et si savante que bien peu de romanciers, peut-être l'ont dépassée.

Quelques critiques, que je m'explique mal, ont voulu voir dans cette œuvre des réminiscences, ou tout au moins l'influence de Loti. Il n'y en a pas. Loti écrit des œuvres d'art. Ceci est une œuvre de pensée. Pensée si puissante et si apte même qu'elle nous emporte, comme dans Stendhal, bien au-dessus du style. Le style, on le sent exact et net, ingénieux dans les descriptions, et tel passage, comme la lettre de Fierce à Sélysette, montre qu'il pourrait, s'il voulait, s'attendrir jusqu'à la plus exquise poésie... Mais ce n'est pas de poésie qu'il s'agit. C'est là un document hâtif et angoissé pris sur les entrailles même de l'empoisonné, un diagnostic brutal jeté parmi l'inquiétude de tant d'œuvres irrésolues et c'est aussi — d'ailleurs, il eût été faux dans cela, faux el hideux autant que Bel Ami — un cri de gare avant le précipice.

Vous nous aurez donné un titre. Farrère, qui pourrait tailler comme un étendard les combattants de l'Ancienne Histoire, ceux qui portent encore un cœur de barbare et que préoccupe d'ailleurs la seule culture des sentiments. Ce titre élastique et cinglant nomme l'ennemi que l'on cherchait, que Musset subissait sans le voir et favorise la guerre en l'illuminant.

La Civilisation ! Oui, l'individualisme, le scepticisme, l'athéisme, l'auto-psychologie qui dévore et glace les intellectuels, le socialisme qui corrompt la bonne conscience du peuple, ce mot contient tout cela. Cependant, il est des coûtants dont la source mystérieuse, à jamais indécouverte, roule des ondes à lasser tous les courages. Et qui donc aura assez de force, d'amour et de gloire pour détourner celui-là? Quand viendra le Messie nouveau capable de nous refaire un équilibre ? Hélas ! comme disait Musset pleurant sut les même deuils :

> Où donc vibre dans l'air une voix plut qu'humaine,
>
> Qui de nous, qui de nous, va devenir un Dieu ?

Oui, c'est un Dieu qu'il nous faudrait. De même que par l'amour seul eût pu de sauvée Fierce, énervé par treize ans de débauche et près d'un siècle de décadence, de même c'est sur les pas d'un héros adoré que la race fléchissant retrouverait sa voie. Que ce soit le prophète ou le soldat, Jésus ou Napoléon, il importe surtot ; que le cœur national sente ses vérités et qu'il n'y ait pas pour lui de jouissances plus hautes que celles contenues dans cette formule : ta foi jusqu'au dévouement, l'amour jusqu'au sacrifice.

Parmi ceux qui suivaient Jésus sur les chemins de Galilée et qui l'écoutaient pour la douceur ignorée de sa voix, combien peu l'ont entendu ! Mais tous l'ont aimé ; et cet amour a suscité tous les cœurs une floraison de sentiments si pure et si intense que c'est elle encore peut-être qui nous défend du tombeau.

Mais aujourd'hui quel temple élire, quelle idole relever ? Au nom de quel idéal réveiller l'âme barbare qui dort sous la corruption des civilisés ? Quelle nouvelle muse lui présenter, après tant de fières mortes qui suscitèrent ses activités ? Il en reste une encore et Farrère la nomme dans sa préface à Pierre Loti : la Beauté.

La Beauté ! Oui, ce serait très français, très élégant et très hautain que nous, les sceptiques et les matérialistes, nous qui ne croyons plus à la revanche des au-delà, nous les sans-foi, les sans-patrie, tes sans-scrupules, nous nous arrêtions au bord des vestiges mauvais uniquement parce que laideur de la chute blesse noire délicatesse esthétique. Il serait beau que nous restions des héros pas dilettantisme et qu'ayant su que nous adorions des chimères, nous leur restions fidèles pour la gloire de ce culte amer et dédaigneux. Petit groupe au regard partout désenchanté, rassemblons-nous sous les colonnes d'Athènes et cultivons en nous les enthousiasmes qui soulèvent les cœurs, qui satisfont les énergies et qui immortalisent les nobles gestes... Trouvons leurs propres ressources et constituons-leur un champ d'exercice assez vaste pour se développer complètement, sans nous sourcier d'un but qui se refuse sans cesse... Et que le ciel soit vide vers qui s'en vont toutes les roses mories, que nous importera, si nous avons su capter le parfum et nous en griser éperdument ?

END

Prix Goncourt Origins
and the 1905 Farrère Judges

By Kent Davis

The Académie Goncourt emerged from a singular vision of literary patronage. When Edmond de Goncourt (b. 1822) died, in 1896, his will specified the creation of a literary society unlike any other — not a traditional academy but an intimate group of ten working writers who would meet monthly and award an annual prize of 5,000 francs. This substantial sum (equivalent to roughly a year's middle-class salary) was to be given to "the best volume of imagination in prose" published that year. Edmond's brother Jules (b. 1830) predeceased him in 1870. Of note is that the source of this award was the sale of the Goncourt brothers' art collection, in consolidation of their commitment to supporting future artists through their own artistic legacy.

The implementation proved complex. Legal challenges from Goncourt's natural heirs delayed the Academy's official establishment until 1903, when the Conseil d'État finally declared it to be in the public interest. Edmond had personally selected the first members, though three positions needed to be filled after his death. This carefully chosen group represented various literary movements and philosophies, from naturalism to symbolism, conservative to radical views.

By 1905, when *Les Civilisés* was selected, the prize was still finding its feet. Only two previous awards had been given: to John-Antoine Nau's *Force ennemie*, in 1903, and Léon Frapié's *La Maternelle,* in 1904. The selection of Claude Farrère's novel proved particularly contentious, and exposed the various aesthetic and ideological divisions between the ten judges profiled below.

The voting took place at the Café de Paris, on Avenue de l'Opéra, where nine of the ten members gathered for dinner under

Edmond Louis Antoine Huot de Goncourt

26 May 1822 – 16 July 1896

French writer, literary critic, art critic, book publisher, and founder of the
Académie Goncourt.

the chairmanship of Gustave Geffroy. Joris-Karl Huysmans, unwell, voted by correspondence. After several preliminary rounds in which the vote split between multiple candidates, with strong support for Marius-Ary Leblond's *Sortilèges*,[1] the final ballot came down to a five-five split. Huysmans's vote as president counted double, breaking the tie in Farrère's favor. The result was then formally announced as unanimous, following Academy custom, awarding the 1905 Prix Goncourt to Claude Farrère for *Les Civilisés*.[2]

The Profiles

JORIS-KARL HUYSMANS (1848–1907), President of the Académie Goncourt, embodied the spiritual journey of many French intellectuals in the late nineteenth century. Born Charles-Marie-Georges Huysmans to a Dutch father and French mother, he began his career as a naturalist writer in Zola's

J.-K. Huysmans.

circle. His novel *À rebours* (1884) marked a dramatic shift toward decadence, featuring an aristocrat who retreats from modern civilization into artificial pleasures. However, Huysmans's most profound transformation came with his conversion to Catholicism, chronicled in *En Route* (1895) and *La Cathédrale* (1898).

His decisive double vote for *Les Civilisés* may have been influenced by the novel's treatment of Catholic faith as a potential remedy for colonial moral decay. Despite Farrère's explicit eroticism (which the younger Huysmans might have appreciated), the novel's underlying theme of spiritual crisis in a materialistic age must have resonated with Huysmans's own preoccupations.

LUCIEN DESCAVES (1861–1949) emerged as the key champion of Farrère's novel among the Académie members. A controversial naturalist writer and anarchist sympathizer, Descaves gained notoriety with his anti-

---

1 This is actually the pen name of two historians, writers, art critics and journalists, George Athénas and Aimé Merlo, who were cousins from the island of Réunion, an overseas department and region of France. In 1909, their novel, *En France*, was awarded the Prix Goncourt, vindicating their strong showing in 1905.

2 Key details about the voting process and judges are drawn from Alain Quella-Villéger's 1989 biography. *Le Cas Farrère : Du Goncourt à La Disgrâce* (Paris: Presses de la Renaissance), the most authoritative work available about the author's life.

Lucien Descaves.

military novel *Sous-Offs* (1889), which led to his prosecution for insulting the army. As the influential literary critic for *Le Journal*, he wielded considerable power in Parisian literary circles.

Descaves not only voted for the novel but campaigned for it among his fellow academicians. He may have seen in Farrère's critique of colonial society echoes of his own attacks on military and social hierarchies. His role as the Académie's "grand elector" was particularly evident in this case; Pierre Louÿs credited him specifically for securing the prize, writing to Farrère: "It's to him that you owe the prize." In his *Journal littéraire* (October 1906), Paul Léautaud recounts meeting Descaves and eliciting his agreement that the Prix Goncourt should have "a certain subversive, revolutionary character." Descaves replies that, had the book been ready in time, Léautaud's *In Memoriam* would have received the prize for 1905. "Unable to do any better," the committee had given it to Farrère, whose book was "nothing out of the ordinary."

LÉON DAUDET (1867–1942) represented a fascinating convergence of literary heritage and political activism in the Académie. Son of the celebrated novelist Alphonse Daudet, he occupied the seat originally intended for his father. Daudet had abandoned medicine for journalism and literature, becoming a leading voice for French monarchism and anti-republicanism as co-founder of the nationalist newspaper *L'Action française*.

His support for Farrère's novel likely stemmed from multiple factors: his friendship with Pierre Loti (who had influenced Farrère), his own interest in novels of social criticism, and perhaps the book's implicit questioning of republican colonial values. Though a fierce political polemicist, Daudet maintained surprisingly cordial relationships with writers of opposing views within the Académie. His literary criticism, while often politically charged, showed genuine appreciation for stylistic talent regardless of the author's politics. This ability to separate aesthetic judgment from ideological differences may have contributed to his support of Farrère's controversial debut.

Léon Daudet.

GUSTAVE GEFFROY (1855–1926) embodied the ideal of the politically engaged art critic and literary intellectual. A champion of Impressionism who wrote definitive studies of Monet and other painters, he brought this same sensitivity to literary criticism. As one of the original

Gustave Geffroy.

members chosen by Edmond de Goncourt himself, Geffroy represented the naturalist tradition, but also embraced newer artistic movements. His own novels, particularly *L'Apprentie* (1904), demonstrated his commitment to social realism and working-class subjects. Despite his socialist leanings, he maintained an aesthetic independence that allowed him to appreciate works on their artistic merits.

His support of *Les Civilisés* likely stemmed from his appreciation of Farrère's vivid descriptive passages and social observation, qualities that aligned with his own interests in both visual and literary arts. Geffroy's background in art criticism may have made him particularly receptive to the novel's rich portrayal of colonial Saigon's physical and moral landscape.

LÉON HENNIQUE (1851–1935), a founding member of the Académie Goncourt, brought both literary prestige and personal connection to the Goncourt legacy. He was a founding member also of the Médan group,

Léon Hennique.

alongside Zola, and had co-authored *L'Attaque du Moulin* with the younger Goncourt brother, Jules. His own work evolved from naturalism toward a more refined psychological style, as seen in his successful plays and novels, like *La Mort du duc d'Enghien* (1886).

Hennique was one of the ten original members chosen by Edmond de Goncourt, and his vote for Farrère carried particular weight given his close association with the Goncourt

brothers' literary ideals. His support suggests he saw in *Les Civilisés*, despite its more decadent elements, echoes of the psychological precision and social observation that characterized his own later work.

OCTAVE MIRBEAU (1848–1917) was perhaps the most ferocious literary voice of his generation. A master of vitriolic criticism and satirical fiction, he was known for works, like *Le Journal d'une femme de chambre* (1900), that mercilessly exposed social hypocrisy.

His opposition to *Les Civilisés* is particularly interesting given his own reputation for shocking content — but Mirbeau had a deep-seated aversion to anyone in military uniform, which may explain his resistance to a novel by a naval officer. Despite his reputation for savage criticism, Mirbeau was also known for championing artists he admired, from Van Gogh to Rodin. His vote against Farrère likely stemmed not just from the author's military background but from what Mirbeau might have seen as artificial decadence rather than

Octave Mirbeau.

genuine social critique. As J.-H. Rosny aîné later recalled, Mirbeau found the book "very mediocre" and believed the prize should go to a more deserving but "handicapped" work.

PAUL MARGUERITTE (1860–1918) brought a uniquely theatrical sensibility to the Académie Goncourt. Born in French Algeria to a military hero father (killed at Sedan), he began his artistic career not as a writer but as a mime, creating notable pantomimes including *Pierrot assassin de sa femme*. This theatrical background perhaps informed his opposition to Farrère's novel — he may have found its colonial decadence too melodramatic. As a novelist, Margueritte frequently collaborated with his brother Victor, but he was also known for challenging literary conventions, as seen in his lesbian novel *Tous Quatre*.

Despite opposing Farrère's novel, he wrote him a "very cordial letter" explaining that he "couldn't" vote for him but was nonetheless pleased with the outcome. His own complex relationship with colonialism, evident in his memoir *Le Jardin du passé*, about his Algerian childhood, adds weight to his judgment of Farrère's portrayal of colonial life. Interestingly, Margueritte had earlier joined with fellow Goncourt judge Lucien Descaves (who supported

Paul Margueritte.

Farrère) in signing "The Manifesto of the Five," an attack on Zola's naturalism. Literary alliances, it seems, could shift on aesthetic rather than personal grounds.

J.-H. ROSNY AÎNÉ (1856–1940), born Joseph Henri Honoré Boex, was among the most versatile and forward-thinking writers of his era. While best known for pioneering prehistoric fiction and scientific romance, his work under the pseudonym Enacryos reveals his interest in exploring different literary modes — and suggests a writer unbound by genre conventions. As he later explained about the 1905 prize: "The dispute was bitter the evening *Les Civilisés* by Farrère was crowned. Convinced that Farrère would succeed with the public without the help of our prize, I thought it better to choose a book of equal value but 'handicapped.'" This pragmatic reasoning suggests Rosny aîné was less concerned with the novel's literary merits than with the Académie's role in supporting struggling authors.

J.-H. ROSNY JEUNE (1859–1948), born Séraphin Justin François Boex, joined the Académie alongside his elder brother. The brothers had previously collaborated on novels before dividing their literary careers and adopting their respective "aîné" and "jeune" designations. Known for often voting contrary to his brother's position, Rosny jeune represented a younger generation's perspective within the Académie, though records do not indicate his position on Farrère's novel.

ÉLÉMIR BOURGES (1852–1925) was perhaps the most aesthetically uncompromising member of the Académie, known for his refined style and philosophical ambitions. His book *Le Crépuscule des dieux* (1884) tells the story of the decadent decline of a German princely family, clearly inspired by Wagner's operatic cycle and the real-life tragedy of Ludwig II of Bavaria. The novel follows Charles d'Este, who squanders his fortune on artistic obsessions while his dynasty crumbles — a theme that resonated with *fin de siècle* anxieties about cultural decay. *La Nef* (1904), his masterwork, is even more ambitious: a vast philosophical allegory in dialogue form that extends from ancient times to the modern era, examining humanity's eternal quest for meaning

Élemir Bourges.

through conversations between historical and mythological figures. Its dense, ornate style and intellectual complexity represented everything Bourges valued in literature and, by extension, everything he likely found lacking in Farrère's more direct colonial narrative.

A perfectionist who published relatively little, Bourges represented a stark contrast to the younger generation's more commercial approach to literature. His own works dealt with themes of decadence and spiritual crisis but in a far more elevated style than Farrère's direct colonial critique. Bourges's negative vote likely reflected both his exacting literary standards and his resistance to newer, more accessible forms of writing.

ଔ♦ଚ

The 1905 Goncourt decision reflected the complex literary and ideological currents of the era. The judges represented a remarkable spectrum: from Huysmans's Catholic mysticism to Mirbeau's anarchist sympathies, from Daudet's monarchism to Geffroy's socialism, from Hennique's naturalism to Bourges' philosophical idealism. That such a diverse group ultimately reached consensus on Farrère's novel suggests both the text's broad appeal and the Académie's ability to transcend personal politics in service of its mission to recognize new literary talents.

The controversy surrounding the choice — particularly regarding the novel's treatment of colonial decadence — presaged ongoing debates about the relationship between literature and empire that would persist throughout the twentieth century. More immediately, the decision validated Edmond de Goncourt's vision of an academy that could identify and promote innovative voices in French letters, even when those voices challenged conventional literary and social values.

ଔ) ✺ (ଚ

List of Characters
(by chapter)

I – The Medicine Man

- **Dr. Raymond Mévil**, a handsome young doctor who courts many women, and wives, around the city.
- **M. Ariette**, a courtroom lawyer, and his attractive wife.
- **Cap'taine Malais**, a financier, and his attractive wife.

II – A Sailor Out of Atavism

- **Cap'taine Torral**, an engineer and best friend of Dr. Mévil.

111 – Common Nourishment

- **Fierce**, a young naval officer and aid-de-camp to Admiral d'Orvilliers, formally known as Jacques-Raoul-Gaston de Civadière, Count of Fierce.

V – Mlle Liseron's Debut

- **Admiral d'Orvilliers**, duke and peer, rear admiral in command of a division of the China squadron, and Fierce's commanding officer.
- **Miss Jeanne Nguyen-Hoc**, only daughter to the new Phou of Cholon, Nguyen-Hoc.
- **Lieutenant Governor Abel**, his 1st (pretty) daughter, Marthe, and his 2nd (ugly) wife.
- **Hélène Liseron**, a singer, newly arrived in Saigon.
- **What's-his-name**, Fierce's former shipmate, shot in Constantinople, and former lover of Mlle Liseron.

VII – The Civilized

- **Otake-San, Miss Bamboo**, a thirteen-year-old Japanese prostitute.
- **Claude Rochet**, journalist, pamphleteer, muckraker, and multi-millionaire.

VIII – Jacques-Raoul-Gaston de Civadière

- **Count Fred-Raoul de Civadière de Fierce**, Fierce's late father.

- **Simone de Marroy**, Fierce's late mother.
- Troarn, Fierce's schoolmate from Belgium.
- **Mme d'Harteval**, Fierce's first liaison.

X – "Good town, Saigon…"

- **Mlle Sélysette**, known as **Sylva**, a 20-year-old pupil of the Duke d'Orvilliers, whose mother, a blind widow, never attended society functions.
- **Marthe Abel**, we now learn that this is the name of Lt. Governor Abel's 1st (pretty) daughter, who has a cool, sphinx-like demeanor.
- **M. Portalière**, residential chancellor at Tonkin.
- **M. Dubois**, the former minister who appointed M. Portalière.
- **Madame Dupont**, wife of the former minister of justice.

XII – Unknown Joys

- **Fernande** – An attractive Jewess who runs a fashionable jewelry shop.

XXIII – The Uncured

- **Maud Ivory** — A blonde, single, American woman from New Orleans traveling the world with her friend Alix for the last three years.
- **Alix Routh** — Maud's American traveling companion, who is engaged to be married when they arrive in Bombay.

XXXI – A Discreet Vehicle

- **The Marneffes** – A wealthy Saigonese family with civil servant father, mother, and 16-year-old daughter who fell into Dr. Mévil's circle.

ଗ) 0 (ଞ

OUVRAGE AYANT OBTENU LE PRIX GONCOURT
EN 1905

CLAUDE FARRÈRE

Les Civilisés

ROMAN

QUATRE-VINGT-QUINZIÈME ÉDITION

PARIS

Société d'Éditions Littéraires et Artistiques

LIBRAIRIE PAUL OLLENDORFF

50, CHAUSSÉE D'ANTIN, 50

LES
CIVILISÉS

roman par

CLAUDE FARRÈRE

EAUX-FORTES ORIGINALES EN NOIR
ET EN COULEURS
DE
HENRI LE RICHE

LIBRAIRIE DE LA COLLECTION DES DIX
V^{VE} ROMAGNOL - A. CIAVARRI, DIR.
85, RUE DE SEINE, PARIS
MCMXXVI

Books by George Groslier − the Khmerophile

A romance of colnial Cambodia.
ISBN: 978-1-934431-16-0

A romance of colonial Cambodia.
ISBN: 978-1-934431-94-8

First Study of Cambodian Dance.
ISBN: 978-1-934431-12-2

1912 exploration in Cambodia.
ISBN: 978-1-934431-90-0

A Travel Journal of the Cambodian Mekong — 1929

Edited by Groslier biographer Kent Davis, foreword by Henri Copin, and literary translation by Pedro Rodríguez. This full color edition features 70 hand-tinted vintage illustrations, including Groslier's original photos; appendix articles by Paul Boudet, Dr. Paul Cravath and Solang Uk; and the complete original French text.

ISBN: 978-1-934431-87-0